Library of
Davidson College

FRANZ SCHUBERT'S MUSIC IN PERFORMANCE

Compositional Ideals, Notational Intent, Historical Realities, Pedagogical Foundations

David Montgomery

FRANZ SCHUBERT'S MUSIC IN PERFORMANCE

Compositional Ideals, Notational Intent, Historical Realities, Pedagogical Foundations

MONOGRAPHS IN MUSICOLOGY No. 11

PENDRAGON PRESS
HILLSDALE, NY

for Jean Dane

and in memory of two wonderful teachers

René Leibowitz (1913–1972)
Rudolf Kolisch (1896–1978)

Library of Congress Cataloguing-in-Publication Data

Montgomery, David, 1944 July 28-
    Franz Schubert's music in performance: compositional ideals, notational intent, historical realities, pedagogical foundations / David Montgomery.
    p.cm. — (Monographs in Musicology; no. 11)
  Includes bibliographical references and index.
  ISBN 1-57647-025-3
  1. Schubert, Franz, 1797-1828--Criticism and interpretation. I. Title. II. Series.

ML410.S3 M66 2003
780'.92--dc21

2002035895

© D. Montgomery, 2003

Table of Contents

Foreword by Ernst Hilmar   *vii*
Author's Preface   *viii*
Abbreviations   *xi*
Introduction   *xiii*

I. The Sonic Imagination   1
The "sound" of the instrumental works. The "sound" of Schubert's lieder. Voice types and techniques. Dramatic vs. narrative. Accompanimental transcriptions. Keys and transpositions. Temperaments and tuning. Translations.

II. The Thematic, Structural and Temporal Imagination   36
Repeats. Harmonic direction, repetition, and length. Metaphors of time. A note on introductions and postludes.

III. Reading Schubert's Music   65
Assessing editions and choosing scores. Schubert's notation. Lingering myths about Schubert's notation. Literal vs. contextual values in Schubert: the historical background. The flexible dot. Overdotting. Underdotting. The Viennese sources. Dotted figures against sextuplets. The alignment theory. Assimilation as a contextual choice. Fermatas. Notational shorthand: implied vs. explicit.

IV. Expression and Expressive Devices   117
Rubato. Schubert and "Viennese" rhythm. Trillo, Bebung, tremolo, vibrato, ondeggiando, etc. Dynamics: ranges, levels, and layering. Accentuation. Hairpin accents vs. decrescendos. The tenuto-agogic-hairpin. The pure tenuto. Articulation: dots, strokes, slurs, tenutos, bowing vs. phrasing marks, pizzicatos. Bowing, slurring, and breathing. Pedalling.

V. Essential and Voluntary Ornamentation 173
Essential ornamentation. Trills. Appoggiaturas. The long appoggiatura. Short appoggiatura. Voluntary ornamentation and improvisation. Improvisation and ornamentation in the opera. Ornamentation in the lieder. The "Vogl" controversy, once again. The Abschriften (copies). Ornamentation and embellishment in the instrumental music. Musical structure and the argument for embellishment.

VI. Tempo, Time, and Character 210
Relative tempos. Tempo, meter, and character. The duple meters. The triple meters. The quadruple meters. Thinking down, thinking up. Tempo fluctuation. Absolute tempo.

In Conclusion 269

Appendices

IA: *Tempo Rubato:* A short overview 270

IB: Ludwig van Beethoven: *So oder so* 275

IIA: The Pedagogical Sources: Methods and Tutors 277

IIB: Selected Period and Modern Literature 307

IIC: Recordings Mentioned in this Book 315

Index 317

Foreword

One of the central goals of Schubert research today must be to solve a number of problems concerning the performance of his music. Beginning with Leopold von Sonnleithner's report of 1860 on the manner in which Schubert's music should be played, some half a hundred articles have been written (mostly after 1960) wherein specific questions on that subject have been raised – answered mostly, however, in cursory or provisional ways. Only in 1981 were the results of an international gathering of musicologists and musicians published on the subject of Schubert in performance. Unfortunately, this collection failed to address and answer most of the truly pressing questions. The Old Complete Edition (Gesamtausgabe) and the New Edition of Schubert's Works (Neue Schubert-Ausgabe) both were created to help clarify a number of performance matters, but in reality each in its own way has given rise to even more uncertainty.

Because insights won from hard research once were (and still are) few and far between, many Schubert performers have come to believe that intuition suffices as a mainstay for interpreting his music. On that basis, however, musicians can offer their listeners nothing more than performances marked by highly subjective mannerisms. Schubert interpretation over the generations has been hindered further in that players, singers, and conductors have had only limited access to the important original materials for study and comparison. Without a solid theoretical understanding – the exact knowledge of texts (i.e. the ability to decipher Schubert's true intentions in reading his scores) – the results of those ubiquitous Lied and interpretation courses, for example, remain questionable at best. Specific awareness, then, of the manifold questions concerning these texts and their transformation into sound is an essential prerequisite, especially for those who teach others.

The present book should have been written many decades ago. First, it is an extensive study based on a scholar's view of the pertinent sources coupled with an experienced performer's practical knowledge. It deals with the entire gamut of important performance issues, and in detail. Also it offers an aesthetic and acoustic context for Schubert's music and introduces a range of topics from tunings to musical structure, tempo, meter, rhythm, articulation, notation and much more. Concerning the major aspects of Franz Schubert's music in performance, then, this book will prove to be an essential guide, not only for present and future interpretation, but also for further research and the production of new editions.

Dr. Ernst Hilmar
International Franz Schubert Institute, Vienna

Preface

This book is the first comprehensive publication dedicated to the performance of Franz Schubert's music. It presents an information-base designed to allow performers to reach as close an understanding of Franz Schubert's music as the coordination of talent, thought, and research permits.

The last published volume on the subject of Schubert and performance was in reality a group of articles and reports from various authors, compiled and edited by the late Vera Schwarz and released in 1981 as *Zur Aufführungspraxis der Werke Franz Schuberts*. It remains a partially useful secondary tool but is no longer adequate for the challenges that face devoted Schubertians. In the *Schubert Handbuch* readers also will find a chapter on performance by Walther Dürr, general editor emeritus of the *Neue Schubert-Ausgabe* (hereafter *NSA*). It reflects the reasoning behind many of the decisions that have guided the *NSA*. Unfortunately, it is not only too general for in-depth Schubert study but is deeply flawed in its conclusions. The three best general works on performing music in this period have been only partially helpful to Schubertians: the Laaber *Handbook*, the Norton volumes, and Clive Brown's recent book on classical and romantic practices (for full citations see Appendix IIB). In terms of Schubert all of the writings mentioned above tend to repeat the same clichés that we find expressed in articles, books, and editorial commentary reaching back well over a hundred years. Sadly but predictably, we also encounter these clichés as they are put into practice by many performers today, backed by an astonishing variety of feelings and intuitions—and almost never by careful research or even logic.

For those readers who care to review the secondary literature on Schubert, a simple examination of most footnotes reveals, particularly in terms of biographical details, that the majority of discussion is still based on the extensive but often improvised work of Otto Erich Deutsch. Where performance practice is concerned, scholars sometimes cite the pedagogical sources as well—a good sign in itself — but to date, only a few of these citations have been geographically and temporally appropriate to Schubert and his Vienna. In Vol. XXV/1 of *Early Music* (February 1997) I offered a selected list of some 80 pedagogical sources (methods, tutors, etc.) pertinent to the study of Franz Schubert's music in performance, hoping to stimulate new research. In Appendix IIA readers will find an augmented version of that list, from which the current book draws a portion of its conclusions. In relying on such sources I follow the path of many predecessors in a tradition stretching from Arnold Dolmetsch to the late Frederick Neumann. But

Preface

while pedagogical sources remain the single most important body of evidence concerning performance styles of the past, they are neither infallible nor complete in their information. They must be supplemented by other data, measured against established fact and analyzed within reasonable historical contexts. Here the work of Deutsch and his successors is indeed useful as a supplement to the internal evidence to be found in Schubert's scores and manuscripts.

The only judgments I have tried to avoid in this book are those known familiarly as "musical," believed to make "musical sense." Scholarship that seeks to authenticate itself through arguments based on such concepts must fail, stopped in its tracks by the first reader whose "musical sense" does not agree with that of the author. The reader must not interpret this last caveat, however, as a denial of those instincts and impulses which come under the heading of good musicianship. Without a doubt these phenomena exist, have always existed, and continue to prove essential to performance. That they have always been of concern to musicians and teachers is confirmed in every tutor and method, historical or modern, whose author has urged his readers to perform "in good taste." Mimetic in nature, they constitute an arsenal of learned devices, the combination and adjustment of which is slightly different in each emerging musician. Where such ineffabilities arise regarding Schubert, I have tried to discuss them in ways that might prove useful rather than merely personal.

This book is the result of about ten years of research. Perhaps I shall never be able to repay the generosity of the colleagues who have helped me with it during this long gestation, but certainly I thank them: Jean Dane, Dr. Susan Kagan, and Dr. David Goldberger for untold information, insight, reading, criticism, and encouragement; Jean Dane, Joseph Gottesmann, John Moran, and Marius Sima for technical advice on string playing; my four-hand partner Camelia Sima for helping to realize a number of hitherto untried ideas in the duo works; Dennis Heath for technical advice concerning voices; Dr. Alden Ashforth for listening graciously to many formative ideas, most of which probably had occurred to him long ago.

For the Caspar David Friedrich plates I thank the Stiftung Preussische Schlösser- und-Gärten Berlin-Brandenburg, the Museumstiftung Oskar Reinhart in Winterthur, and the Kunstmuseum Düsseldorf. I owe special thanks to the staffs of the library system of the University of California (particularly Martin Silver, UCSB), Tulane University (Robert Curtis), the Library of Congress Music Division and the New York Public Library Research Collection (too many helpful colleagues to single out), where my work began; the Musikwissenschaftliches Institut (Frau Adler) and the Staatsbibliothek (Frau Heim) connected with the Carl von Ossietzky Universität Hamburg, the Musikwissenschaftliches Seminar at the University of Göttingen, the Deutsche Staatsbibliothek in Berlin, the Bayerische Staatsbibliothek in Munich, the Universitets Bibliotek in Lund, Sweden (Eric Nicander); and in Vienna the Wiener Stadt- und Landesbibliothek, the Österreichische Nationalbibliothek, and the Library of the Gesellschaft der Musikfreunde. I thank J. Rigbie Turner of the Pierpont Morgan Library in New York, whose patience and humor undoubtedly allowed him to survive my numerous long-distance questions about the autographs of *Winterreise* and the String Quartet *Death and the Maiden*. Dr. Michael Lorenz (Vienna) generously offered research findings from Viennese libraries, and Arthur Intelmann (Munich) guided me more than once through the remoter paths of the German language. The three principal readers of the main text were Jean Dane (New York Chamber Symphony, NYC), Alan Newcombe (Deutsche Grammophon, Hamburg) and Dr. Ernst Hilmar (Internationales Franz Schubert Institut, Vienna). Jean Dane has brought a lifetime of analysis and playing experience to bear on this work, and Alan Newcombe has commented from the standpoint of an extraordinary knowledge of musical literature and the writing process. Ernst Hilmar has put at my disposal more knowledge of Schubert's life and legacy than I might have expected from any living scholar.

David Montgomery
San Francisco, 2001

Abbreviations for Libraries, Catalogues, Editions, Journals and Modern Dictionaries

AM	= *Acta Musicologica.*
AMW	= *Archiv für Musikwissenschaft.*
AmZ	= *[Leipziger] Allgemeine musikalische Zeitung,* founding ed. Friedrich Rochlitz, from 1798ff.
BA	= *Berliner Abendblätter.*
BamZ	= *Berliner allgemeine musikalische Zeitung.*
Cä	= *Cäcilia.*
Die Brille	= *Schubert durch die Brille, Journal of the Internationales Franz Schubert Institut,* ed. Ernst Hilmar.
EM	= *Early Music.*
GA	= *Schubert Gesamtausgabe.*
GMF	= *Gesellschaft der Musikfreunde, Vienna.*
HP	= *Historical Performance.*
JAMS	= *Journal of the American Musicological Society.*
JMus	= *Journal of Musicology.*
LST	= *London Sunday Times.*
LT	= *London Times.*
MF	= *Die Musikforschung.*
MGG	= *Die Musik in Geschichte und Gegenwart,* eds 1949ff (ed. Friedrich Blume) / 1994ff (ed. Ludwig Finscher).
ML	= *Music & Letters.*
MMR	= *Monthly Musical Record.*
MQ	= *Musical Quarterly.*
MT	= *Musical Times.*
MR	= *The Music Review.*
Mu	= *Musica.*
NG	= *The New Grove Dictionary of Music and Musicians,* Stanley Sadie, editor (1980 / 2001).
NI	= *19th Century Music.*
NL	= *Newberry Library, Chicago.*
NSA	= *Neue Schubert-Ausgabe.*
NYT	= *New York Times.*

NZM	= *Neue Zeitschrift für Musik.*
PPM	= *Pierpont Morgan Library.*
PPR	= *Performance Practice Review.*
RC	= *Catalogue of the Archduke Rudolph's private music library, ms in GMF.*
Sml	= *[Der] Sammler.*
SBB	= *Staatsbibliothek Berlin.*
SL	= *Schubert Lexikon,* comp. Ernst Hilmar and Margret Jestremski.
UeM	= *Üben & Musizieren.*
WamZ	= *Wiener allgemeine musikalische Zeitung,* ed. I. von Schönholz: 1813.
WamZ	= *Allgemeine musikalische Zeitung, mit besonderer Rücksicht auf den österreichischen Kaiserstaat,* ed. Franz von Mosel, 1817–1824. 1824ff: *Wiener allgemeine musikalische Zeitung.*
WaThZ	= *Wiener allgemeine Theaterzeitung.* 1807–1811: *Zeitung für Theater, Musik und Poesie.* 1811–1817: *Theaterzeitung.* 1817–1823: *Wiener allgemeine Theaterzeitung.* 1823–1831: *Allgemeine Theaterzeitung und Unterhaltungsblatt.* 1831–1845: *Allgemeine Theaterzeitung und Originalblatt.*
WSV	= *Wiener Stadtbibliothek.*
WVB	= *Wiener Vaterländische Blätter.*
WZK	= *Wiener Zeitschrift für Kunst.*
WZ	= *Wiener Zeitung.*
ZeW	= *Zeitung für die elegante Welt.*
ZMT	= *Zeitschrift für Musiktheorie.*
ZMW	= *Zeitschrift für Musikwissenschaft.*

Pitch indications: The names of pitches in this book have been made in capital letters and refer to pitch class only, i.e. without specified octaves.

Introduction

Considering that the effective scope of Franz Schubert's career was less than fifteen years in duration, that his musical impact in life was limited primarily to one city, that most of his work was unpublished at his death in 1828, and, finally, that his music was ignored by almost every pedagogical author in the nineteenth century, it may seem a bit akin to the proverbial search for the needle in the haystack to devote an entire book to the historically-informed performance of his music. It would be easier to expand things a bit, to discuss the performance of Viennese music in general from the beginning of the nineteenth century (for which there exists ample documentation), concentrating, perhaps, on Beethoven, Schubert, and others of importance.

Franz Schubert's Vienna, however, although often viewed historically in the same sweep with, say, Ludwig van Beethoven's Vienna, was not the same place. The cultural and commercial atmosphere had changed significantly as a result of the financial ravages of the Napoleonic wars and the monarchy's heavy-handed control. As Schubert's career began (about the same time as the opening of the Vienna Congress in 1815), Beethoven and others already had seen the final years of noble patronage. Schubert was able to cultivate only limited contact with the great houses; his most influential friends were of the so-called "ennobled working class" who occupied minor government positions. His two short periods of direct employment under the nobility were not as a composer, but as a piano teacher to the Esterházy children.

Popular music history has always held that it was not in Schubert's character to master Vienna in the same aggressive way as had Beethoven and other temporarily fashionable composers (indeed even Beethoven in his distempered way became fashionable for a while). Some scholars now maintain that at the time of Schubert's death he was on the verge of a career breakthrough, and not just as a composer of lieder. In the most recent major biography of the composer, Brian Newbould speculates that Schubert "would surely have fused Classical and Romantic elements in the symphony even more powerfully than he had in the 'Unfinished' and 'Great,' looking ahead to the synthesis achieved by Brahms a generation later..."[1] Although composers do not consciously "look ahead" in time—even those who, like Beethoven, created works that severely taxed the existing

---

[1] *Schubert: The Music and the Man* (University of California Press: 1997): 388. The image of Franz Schubert as a progressive composer also has been explored and strengthened by studies such as those offered by the International Franz Schubert Institute: *Franz Schubert – Der Fortschrittliche?: Analysen–*

norms and capacities—one cannot help but think that Schubert had the capacity to develop with which Newbould credits him. Whether Vienna herself still had the capacity or the interest to allow him such a development is another matter.

Alice Hanson notes that in post-Napoleonic Vienna concert life had taken two distinct directions: the one in which "serious" works (of Germanic composers) began to be preserved somewhat like precious museum pieces by private societies, as opposed to the other more faddish direction taken by the still lucrative public concerts (which had no use for serious German music). Concerning the public concerts, she offers a delightful example:

> The arrival of the first giraffe to the city's zoo [1828] inspired giraffe fashions, theatrical parodies, and giraffe waltzes. Likewise Paganini's concerts led to the creation of new foods, new figures of speech, more theatrical parodies, and many transcriptions of his works.
>
> In such a culture both Beethoven and Schubert could be considered to be failures, according to the standards of their contemporaries.[2]

Also in "such a culture," the level of performance competence that Beethoven and Schubert received seems to have dropped even lower than before, to judge by Beethoven's fate in his public concert of 1824 and the rejection of Schubert's "Great" C-major Symphony.

The goals of this book are to explore the performance practices and ideals of Schubert's Vienna, taking all that we have said above into consideration. Actualities in performance practices of that time were usually different than ideals, just as they are in concert halls and recordings today. Those of us who enjoy researching the period often labor diligently to discover and discuss the actualities of those times, but sometimes fail, perhaps, to distinguish between them and the real hopes that a composer might have had for his music in performance. A good example concerns the assimilation of dotted figures to triplets in piano playing, which we know must have occurred in some performances of those days. On the basis of this awareness, a few modern players have not only adopted the practice but have proposed it as a musical ideal on the part of the composer. Examination of the pedagogical evidence of the time, however, has shown this practice to have originated (mostly among students and amateurs) out of technical necessity, not musical vision. For modern professionals to recreate the technical inadequacies of the past simply because they existed would be a disservice to audiences and students who depend on those professionals to sort through history for them.

Perspektiven–Fakten (series vol. IV), ed. Erich Wolfgang Partsch. Gen. ed. Ernst Hilmar. Numerous other analyses of Schubert's harmonic and rhythmic language have been published in the last decade, and gradually it would seem that the musical community is forming a more weighty opinion of his music. Beyond studies of this nature, however, scholarship has not yet brought this changing assessment of Schubert's importance in the development of Western music to bear upon the actual performance of his works.

[2]*Musical Life in Biedermeier Vienna* (London: Cambridge, 1985): 183. A newer version of this book appeared in German as *Die zensurierte Muse: Musikleben im Wiener Biedermeier* (Vienna: Böhlau, 1987).

Introduction

The pedagogical sources document the changes in the performance styles in Vienna from Wolfgang Mozart's last years until the years after Schubert's death, but they do not always explain them. Some reasons for change are clear: According to Czerny, Beethoven once observed, for example, that Mozart's keyboard playing style was derived from and more suited to the harpsichord than to the pianoforte.[3] In this case, then, we can infer that a transition in some aspects of piano touch had almost been forced by the invention and continual evolution of the pianoforte itself. Mozart's pupil Johann Nepomuk Hummel had begun as a pianist, and probably learned Mozart's staccato touch at first – developing his own elegant *legato* style along with the new pianos in the last decade of the eighteenth century. And yet we cannot explain so easily why this same pupil of Mozart would have developed so early a flowery figuration almost unknown in the 18th century except in the Italian opera.

Schubert's piano-playing, which from all we know was non-virtuosic but competent, lyrical, and expressive, was distinguished again from either the Hummel school or Beethoven's highly personal delivery. Beethoven's pupils Ries and Czerny appear to have maintained another style for most of their lives; it seems to have been akin to Hummel's playing, but less flowery. We might attribute the differences in these phenomena to the musical imagination and innate creativity of each protagonist (intimately bound up with their own compositional limitations and strengths), but that explanation carries certain value judgments that ultimately must fail.

Before reverting to the general "it was in the air" theory that accompanies most of the history of artistic change, we might investigate some specific conditions that brought such change about. A close look at the education of any musician usually reveals some plausible explanations for his later preferences and reputation. In the case of Franz Schubert, for example, the family setting of his earliest performance training may explain somewhat his later attraction to the "salon" as an important forum for his own music-making. His training as a composer, however, went well beyond the private setting of these early performance experiences. Throughout Europe in the early nineteenth century the training of young composers and performers shifted from the private to the public sphere. In the 1750s and 60s Wolfgang Mozart had been given an exclusive private musical education by his father. A generation later the young Johann Nepomuk Hummel was guided by one or two older musicians, including Mozart. Beethoven had been trained on a private basis, but Franz Schubert (b. 1797)—in addition to fundamental studies in violin with his father—learned his trade in a school, the Stadtkonvikt (City Seminary). To be sure, he had the opportunity to study privately with Antonio Salieri,

---

[3] "Beethoven told me that he had heard Mozart play on several occasions and that, since at that time the fortepiano was still in its infancy, Mozart, more accustomed to the then still prevalent *Flügel,* used a technique entirely unsuited for the fortepiano. I, too, subsequently made the acquaintance of several persons who had studied with Mozart, and found that Beethoven's observation was confirmed by their manner of playing." in "Erinnerungen aus meinem Leben", MS, Gesellschaft der Musikfreunde (hereafter *GMF*), trans. Ernest Sanders as *Recollections From My Life,* in *Musical Quarterly* 42 (1956):307. Readers will find a scholarly edition of the *Erinnerungen,* ed. Walter Kolneder in *Collection d'études musicologiques,* vol. 46 (Strasbourg/Baden-Baden: Heitz, 1968).

but in other ways his instruction depended on his coexistence with other students. He tried out his first pieces with a school orchestra, an ensemble in which he had played the violin and which he had learned to conduct (with no apparent formal training) as well. Exactly how he learned as much about piano playing as he seems to have known also cannot be explained by the idea of a single private teacher, although neither can we point to a strong generalized keyboard program at the Seminary. Ferdinand Schubert's account of Franz's private instruction in singing, violin and piano from Michael Holzer recalls Holzer's supposed assertion that "...whenever I wanted to teach him something new, [I discovered] that he knew it already.".[4]

Schubert's institutional training was not unusual for the time: a general course of intellectual studies akin to what students must have taken at schools such as the famous "Graue Kloster" Gymnasium in Berlin. Schubert's report card for September 1813 included the following categories and subjects: morals, endeavor, religious studies, Latin, Greek, geography, natural history, natural studies [philosophy?], and mathematics. The Seminary was also home to the Court Singing-Boys (*Hofsängerknaben*), to which Schubert belonged before his voice broke. In this regard the school followed vaguely in the tradition of the older Italian conservatories, for example, the celebrated ones in Naples, which focussed primarily upon the training of singers. (Instrumental training in Venetian schools such as the Pietà of Vivaldi's day, had been exceptions.) Schubert's musical training at the school was providential, however, for, as his fellow-pupil Anton Holzapfel recalled, the entire orchestral program was an extra-curricular labor of love encouraged and financed by the director, the Reverend Innocenz Lang. Lang must have been a progressive and insightful educator, for when Schubert's father petitioned him to allow Franz to concentrate entirely on music (including lessons with Salieri), Lang consented. Nevertheless, Schubert probably continued to learn as much about music directly by experimentation in the seminary setting as he did in his new private lessons.

"Familial," then, is the right description of a major portion of Schubert's training. He might have known of the existence of such internationally-respected pedagogical classics of the recent past – CPE Bach's *Die Wahre Art das Klavier zu spielen,* Daniel Gottlob Türk's *Clavierschule,* Leopold Mozart's *Violinschule,* Johann Adam Hiller's *Anweisung zum...Gesange,* etc., but he probably did not learn directly from them.[5] Salieri would not have pushed these works particularly (he had produced two pedagogical works of his own), and Schubert's essentially non-professional teachers at the Seminary might never have read them. If Otto Erich Deutsch is correct, the only pedagogical source which we know that Schubert used in his youth was Joseph Drechsler's *Harmonie- und Generalbasslehre* (Vienna: Steiner).[6] In light of this supposition, two questions arise: 1)

---

[4] O.E. Deutsch, ed., *Schubert: Die Erinnerungen seiner Freunde* (1957):29.
[5] C.P.E. Bach, *Versuch über die Wahre Art das Klavier zu spielen* (Pt. I: Berlin, 1753; Pt. II, 1762); Daniel Gottlob Türk, *Clavierschule, oder Anweisung zum Clavierspiel für Lehrer und Lernende* (Halle, 1789); Leopold Mozart, *Versuch einer gründlichen Violinschule* (Augsburg: Lotter, 1756); Johann Adam Hiller, *Anweisung zum musikalisch-richtigen Gesange* (Leipzig: Johann Friedrich Junius, 1774).
[6] Schubert: *Die Dokumente seines Lebens*, ed. O.E. Deutsch (Kassel: Bärenreiter, 1964): 20. Deutsch is unclear. First he states that Schubert used Drechsler's text, but then that Drechsler had written it in 1816

how might Schubert and his generation have been influenced by the existing pedagogical sources; and 2) to what extent do the sources of his time as an adult (and some years after, in that his was an early death) reflect proper performance practices either for his music or for Viennese music in general? Having posed these queries, we need to forge slightly ahead in the history of things in order to set the stage.

Somewhat too late for Schubert's education, Vienna eventually established a true conservatory of music with a complete program of studies (instrumental, vocal, theoretical), which grew out of the choral society of the Gesellschaft der Musikfreunde (founded in 1812). By 1817 the Wiener Konservatorium (not the current conservatory, but the forerunner of the present university-based Hochschule für Musik und Darstellende Kunst) had developed along the lines of the Conservatoire National de Musique et de Déclamation in Paris, the first major institution of its kind (founded 1795).

The Paris Conservatoire had lost no time in ossifying its instructional principles. Concepts such as Fux's squeaky-clean formulation of the "rules" of ancient counterpoint (based on Palestrina) represented the instructional front, and academic powermongers such as Luigi Cherubini worked out or supervised other pedagogical methods designed to standardize the teaching of everything from ear-training to cello playing.[7] With somewhat less rigor the Vienna Conservatory, too, encouraged pedagogical methods by its professors (among the surviving tutors are those by J.N. Breitschädel, Joseph Fischhof, Josef Sellner, and August Swoboda). In this endeavor they were aided by the government, which discouraged foreign publications (not for the sake of competition, but in fear of progressive ideas). Laurenz Weiss's *Theoretisch-praktische Gesangschule für das Conservatorium der Musik in Wien* (Vienna: Spina, 1840: 2nd ed. a.1855) – which actually mentions the Conservatory in its title – is one of the last of such works that still might shed light on the pedagogical methodology of Schubert's time.

The earliest sources on the list in the Appendix were written about the middle of Mozart's career. Celebrated treatises tended to remain in use for years, and one cannot assume that the latest works were adopted immediately for teaching. Pedagogues, both good and bad, fell back on the way in which they themselves were trained. Then as now, only extraordinary teachers took the trouble to sift through their experience and introduce new principles as a result. The latest instructional works – where they departed from older principles, and where they were not written by the progressive composers themselves – were often forced into newer stances not by voluntary pedagogical insight

---

for the Normal-Hauptschule, which Schubert had attended in 1813/14. We know of a Drechsler text from 1816, but it is the *Fortschreitende Generalbassübungen, nebst Anleitung u. Beispielen z. präludieren auf d. Orgel* (Vienna: Diabelli).

[7] Later in the century, conservatories began to apply already stultified taxonomical thinking to such subjects as "form" (one remembers the old doggerel: "of all the academic wretches, the very worst is Percy Goetschius!"), analysis, and history. But in terms of sheer neatness, nothing short of the twentieth century's frightened acceptance of Schenker's reductionist method for analyzing tonal music and the Princetonians' systematically abstracted applications of set theory (said to elucidate the creative thinking of the composers of chromatically atonal music) has so captured the imagination of pedagogues apparently unable to confront music in its natural and untidy splendor.

but by general changes in compositional styles. Furthermore, the approval time required by the Austrian censors was often a matter of years (even for such apparently non-subversive works as instructional methods for musical instruments), which means that many tutors were written long before they were published. We are indebted to Hanson for a specific example, J.N. Hummel's *Ausführliche theoretisch-praktische Anweisung zum Pianofortespiel* (Haslinger), now dated at 1828. Actually, it was completed by 1826, when Hummel applied for permission to publish it.

Along with an appropriate time frame, factors concerning availability and local impact have played a role in assembling the list of tutors considered in this book. For example, although the piano virtuosi Franz (François) Hünten, Henrich (Henri) Herz, and Daniel Steibelt had some ties to Vienna, their treatises were brought out in Mainz, Berlin, and Paris. Although it is possible – perhaps even probable – that these works were distributed in Vienna, we can find no general evidence of their impact there during the early nineteenth century. On the other hand, Leopold Mozart's *Violinschule*, first published in Augsburg, eventually came out directly in a Viennese edition in 1785 and again in 1804. By then it had become a celebrated tutor, and we can regard it as a pertinent source. The same judgment might be made of authors from much further away – such as Devienne, Baillot, or Pleyel (Paris), Clementi and Cramer (London), although their real impact on Vienna cannot be assessed with accuracy. Apparently the Leipzig publishers Breitkopf & Härtel maintained a representative in Vienna (Traeg, see Appendix I), but which of the many Breitkopf-published tutors Traeg was able to sell in Vienna is also unknown.

We should look first to competitive Viennese treatises to give us a picture of styles in that city and culture. In this regard, however, we might remember that Vienna's population was exotically international in the first place. Hanson (p. 10) offers a sample list of 64 prominent foreign-born musicians performing and teaching in Vienna beteween 1815–30. Many of these names appear again in the list of historical sources below. It was rare, apparently, to find a native-born *Wiener* among the ranks of the finest musicians – with major exceptions such as Schubert and Strauß. The phenomenon that we call "Viennese" style may not be looked upon as a pure strain. In discussing music and pedagogy in early nineteenth-century Vienna, we must identify not one major style but several—perhaps even six or eight—important compositional and pedagogical currents.[8]

---

[8]In terms of piano playing alone we can identify at least four approaches that existed simultaneously – the older classical style (Wölfl and others), Beethoven's *sui generis* style, Hummel's "new school" pianism, and Schubert's simpler, lyrical style. We know of two major trends in operatic presentations: Italian and "German," and several distinctive ways of delivering lieder. If we tally up various schools of composition, we find that many composers cannot be classed together in a single group to form a "Viennese" style. Beethoven provides the most obvious example, but others—such as the Czech school (Czapak, Dussek, Vořišek, Tomášek *et al*)—form an almost independent branch of music-making.

In recent writings concerning performance of the music of Schubert and Beethoven, research has relied heavily on Türk's *Clavierschule* and CPE Bach's *Die Wahre Art*—almost as if these two tutors from the galant years in northern Germany provide standard wisdom for the interpretation of music written decades after their time in Vienna. (To be sure, Türk published his book when Beethoven was a

Introduction   xix

A point to remember in the debate about the continuing usefulness of a treatise: not all of its aspects went out of date at the same time. Comments on "good taste" in CPE Bach and Leopold Mozart, for example, do not sound much different than parallel passages three-quarters of a century later in Carl Czerny and Louis Spohr. In the period from about 1750–1850 what changed most fundamentally was the approach to ornamentation, as composers began to exert more expressive control in the composition process itself. Also, anything pertinent to the changing nature of instruments themselves (touch, range, fingering, etc.) soon went out of date. Singing, of course, was not affected in this regard, and thus may have been slower to develop.

In addition to ascertaining the appropriate applications of the pedagogical sources according to a certain amount of historical common sense, we can evaluate each one in more specific ways: the author's reputation, its impact (reputation of the publisher, circulation, longevity through reprints, translations, etc.),[9] its critical reception in the journals,

---

nineteen-year-old in Bonn—Beethoven left for Vienna in 1792— but 1) Türk's treatise was published in Halle and Leipzig, and represented a typically northern galant musical style as evidenced in virtually all of Türk's examples; 2) it was a summation of an antecedent period; and 3) Beethoven's compositional imagination and demands upon the performer had far outstripped Türk's musical thinking by the first years of the new century.)

Carl Czerny (*Recollections*: 307) asserts that Beethoven used CPE Bach's tutor in instructing him at the keyboard, and that he had requested that Czerny use it to instruct Karl Beethoven in the rudiments of playing. The keywords here are "instruct" and "rudiments." Both Beethoven and Czerny believed in priming students, as indeed we do today, in the "classics," which for them were the two great Bachs as well as Haydn and Mozart. For modern performance practices, however, this request—if it indeed occurred—does not mean that we should seek to apply CPE Bach's eighteenth-century ornamentation to the progressive nineteenth-century music of Beethoven and Schubert. In arranging for Karl's lessons, Beethoven was concerned first with elementary procedures: reading music, assuming proper hand positons, etc. When Karl was far enough along at the piano, of course, he must have learned to apply ornamentation to the eighteenth-century pieces he played.

We cannot prove (even if we suspect) that Beethoven himself was taught Bach's principles at the keyboard. We know only that Neefe used primers of CPE Bach and Marpurg to instruct the young Beethoven in composition. In teaching composition (mostly general bass) to the Archduke Rudolph, Beethoven also used theoretical excerpts from CPE Bach, Türk, Kirnberger, Fux, and Albrechtsberger. But to find in these venerable writers a performance practice for the fast-developing styles of a later age—and different place—is probably unrealistic. The strongest argument against these eighteenth-century texts in relation to Franz Schubert, however, is that they were written with entirely different instruments in mind: clavichord and harpsichord. Schubert's works are written for the hammerflügel, which—as Czerny points out (fn3)—had developed well beyond the instruments of the eighteenth century.

[9] Obviously if an author was forced to publish his own work, it would never have the backing afforded by a commercial company. Even if it were brought out by a recognized publisher, the size of the run played a role. Johann Nepomuk Breitschädel's *Versuch einer theoretisch-praktischen Klavierschule,* for example, was brought out by Mechetti in 1818 (printed by A. Strauss), but appears to have had an unusually limited run; we have not been able to find a single copy of it in Vienna or anywhere else. The fact that the major German and Austrian libraries lost so much material as a result of transferring their holdings to safe quarters during World War II may have some bearing on this problem, but this does not explain why no copies whatsoever can be discovered. Other cases, such as Max Joseph Leidesdorf's *Wiener Clavierschule* (advertised in two languages for 1824 but possibly never published) are equally intriguing.

its competence as a source, its comprehensiveness, its specific relationship to Vienna and matters Viennese, its originality[10] and its exclusivity.[11]

We can ignore the question of a tutor's specific relevance to Schubert, for no tutor of his day mentions his name. To my current knowledge, Czerny was the first pedagogue to recognize him. In Pt. IV of his comprehensive piano method Czerny lists Schubert as one of the leading young composers of songs and four-hand music, but does not talk about his music. Pedagogical neglect of Schubert continued throughout the century, even among those who championed his music. The Hamburg maestro Julius Stockhausen, for example, who sang (often accompanied by Clara Schumann) and conducted Schubert's works with enthusiasm, failed even to mention the composer in his otherwise historically-rich *Gesangmethode*.[12] As this text goes to press, I have learned of the possibility that a later edition (1830) of an Ignace Pleyel *Klavierschule* may contain a reference to Franz Schubert, but I have not seen the source.

A certain amount of hypothesis will be required, then, to find the best principles for performing Schubert among the pedagogical sources. We possess enough material, however, to render this procedure admissible.

David Montgomery

---

[10] What is the tutor's relationship to earlier tutors? Does it quote mechanically, or do we find new thinking? We must examine such methods for their influences, both local and international. In Johann Wenzel's *Pedal- und Hackenharfen-Schule nach Lang, Krumpholz, Bierfreund and Backoven* of 1818 (Vienna: Cappi), for example, the author reveals his international influences in the title. Other works must be analyzed internally for such lines of thought and inheritance. We can still trace the outlines of Leopold Mozart's *Versuch einer gründlichen Violinschule* (Augsburg: Lotter, 1756), for example, in Louis Spohr's 1832 *Violinschule* (Vienna: Haslinger / Paris: Richault / London: Wessel). However, in some areas Spohr updated his information, not only according to changes in bows and violins, but in modern musical style and expressive devices as well. Thus we know that his treatise is not a mere pedagogical copy, and we can take parts of it quite seriously for its time.

[11] Glancing down the list of sources, we see that Viennese tutors for singing, pianoforte, guitar, flute, and czakan, for example, were plentiful and therefore competititve. Vincent Schuster's tutor for the arpeggione (App. I, 1825), however, appears to have been the only one of its kind; therefore it remains authoritative. On the other hand, we find no Viennese tutors for brass instruments or bassoon; trumpet players, for example, would have looked to a major treatise in the German language, such as Altenburg's *Anleitung zur heroisch-musikalischen Trompeter-und Paukerkunst* (Halle, 1795). Bassoon players might have looked to the classic Parisian treatises of Abraham (*Méthode de basson*, Paris: Frère, 1780) and Etienne Ozi (*Méthode nouvelle et raisonée pour le basson*, Paris: Boyer/LeMenu, 1787/1803) or—as the instrument evolved—to the German treatises by Carl Almenraeder (*Abhandlung über die Verbesserung des Fagotts*, Mainz: 1820, and *Die Kunst des Fagottsblasens*, 1843).

[12] Leipzig: Peters, 1884.

Chapter 1

The Sonic Imagination

Wenn auf dem höchsten Fels ich steh',
In's tiefe Tal hernieder seh',
Und singe.
Fern aus dem tiefen dunkeln Tal
Schwingt sich empor der Widerhall
Der Klüfte.
Je weiter meine Stimme dringt,
Je heller sie mir wieder klingt
Von unten.

Wilhelm Müller, from *Der Berghirt*[1]

It is fair to say that Franz Schubert was one of the first modern composers whose response to poetry and other literature was central to his creativity, and that in this sense he set a precedent for composers of the later nineteenth century (one thinks immediately of Mendelssohn, Schumann, Liszt and Brahms). Of course, if we remember John Dowland, in the time of Elizabeth I, we find a man who may have been as great a poet as he was a composer. Dowland's Italian contemporary Claudio Monteverdi was hardly less affected by words and their images, to judge from his madrigals alone. Considering the instrumental works of Vivaldi and Tartini, so often bound up and presented with poetic effusions, we discover a most sensitive and intimate side of these two eighteenth-century virtuosi. Such examples are plentiful. But when we think of Viennese classical composers and their relationship to the written word (apart from opera libretti), neither Haydn nor Mozart appears to have enjoyed so essentially such extra-musical inspiration. Even Beethoven with his profound idealism was not so dependent upon the written word as was Franz Schubert, the culminating musical figure of the lineage.

---

[1] As I stand upon the highest rock, gazing down into the deep valley and singing, up from within that deep, dark ravine sounds the echo. The further my voice carries, the brighter it resounds from below.

The basic proof of this supposition exists in Schubert's enormous output of lieder, unmatched by any other major composer, not merely for its scope, but for its innovation as well.[2] Even more important is that his creative imagination as a song composer extended well beyond this genre, pervading the very structures of his instrumental music as well. Analysts ranging from Felix Salzer[3] and Hans Költzsch[4] in the early part of this century to Thrasybulos Georgiades,[5] Erdmute Schwarmath,[6] Arthur Godel,[7] Hans-Joachim Hinrichsen[8] and others in more recent years have devoted significant attention to the subject of Schubert and musical structure. But whereas scholarship to date has concentrated admirably on Schubert's innovations in this area, few modern writers have devoted much attention to his basic sonic innovations, his departures from the typical sound envelope of classicism (the sum, so to speak, of orchestration, instrumentation, spacing, voicing, tessitura, dynamics and dynamic layering, etc.) in favor of an enhanced and personalized tonal language. Here the inspiration of literature and aesthetics appears to have had an even more profound and demonstrable effect upon his music. Therefore it is puzzling to read so little about it. Perhaps the subject of Schubert's sound is considered so self-evident, so unresearchable or even so personal that it is left to performers to sort out on their own. If so, however, it belongs even more within the confines of the present book.

Before going any further, we must remind ourselves that most performances of Schubert's music today take place on modern instruments and with modern vocal techniques. To ignore this fact, even in an historical study such as this one, would be unrealistic. Having said this, we encourage all players and singers to become conversant with the older instruments and vocal techniques, reflecting such knowledge in the intelligent use of modern concert means. For example, for violinists, more effective than the use of gut strings and reconverted instruments is the proper use of the bow (much can be achieved by avoiding strong pressure at the frog and seeking a lighter stroke in general). Pianists need not thunder away in the outer registers of the present-day Steinway, and can learn easily to use pedal as a means to local effect and special ambience rather than basic *legato*. And contrary to modern pedagogical opinion, singers can learn to adapt to period expression without damaging their general techniques. Such changes take place in the mind, not in the throat. Here we are concerned with musical ideas that transcend these issues.

The "sound" of the instrumental works

Without a doubt, the general sonic characteristics of Schubert's early music were suggested to him early on by the best and most interesting music of his recent predecessors and col-

---

[2] Among a significant number of major and minor literary figures, the only great turn-of-the-century German poet whose lines Schubert did not set, indeed, may not have known, appears to have been Friedrich Hölderlin (1770–1843).
[3] *Die Sonatenform bei Schubert* (Dissertation, University of Vienna, 1926).
[4] *Franz Schubert in seinen Klaviersonaten* (Leipzig, 1927).
[5] *Schubert: Musik und Lyrik* (Göttingen: Vandenhoeck & Ruprecht, 1967).
[6] *Musikalischer Bau und Sprachvertonung in Schuberts Liedern* (Tutzing, 1969).
[7] *Schuberts letzte drei Klaviersonaten* (Baden-Baden: Koerner, 1985).
[8] *Sonatenform in der Instrumentalmusik Franz Schuberts* (Tutzing: Schneider, 1994).

leagues: Haydn,[9] Mozart,[10] Beethoven[11] and perhaps even Rossini, not to mention the Czech school active in Vienna.[12] We could not discuss his formative style apart from the context established by these and many lesser composers of the late eighteenth and early nineteenth centuries. In addition, his sonic ideas clearly developed in response to the characteristics of the instruments and performing forces which he knew most intimately: the 5 1/2 to 6-octave pianoforte with its fuller middle register and weaker outer registers, the period violin, the viola, the small string ensemble, the choir and, eventually, the large orchestra.

One of the rites of passage that distinguishes composers of originality from their predecessors and contemporaries appears to commence at the moment in which their sonic and structural formulations begin to be freed somewhat from the models of earlier works and / or sounds with which they are familiar, and are dictated instead by a more abstract creativity. But even abstract creativity must be prompted in some way. In Schubert's case it appears to have been set in sympathetic motion by the new spiritual flow around him, by the larger ideation of romanticism itself. He must have come in contact with it principally through a censored literature (poetry perhaps not so closely guarded as philosophy), for the politically-constricted Vienna of his formative years as a professional musician (ca. 1810–1815) was preoccupied mostly with its own survival, and not with the flourishing of a new cultural age. The watchdogs of Vienna discouraged any kind of radical intellectual freedom, particularly if it involved groups of young people such as we associate with Jena, Heidelberg, Weimar, Berlin and other German-speaking cultural centers of the late eighteenth and early nineteenth centuries. Romanticism obviously reached Schubert, however, for his works reveal his important part in it.

Even for the best historians the tenets of early German romanticism remain difficult to define. Romantic theory was fleeting and chaotic, often taking the form of art itself. Its early proponents, particularly the Jena group, were cabalistic, secretive and overly-sensitive about their thoughts. Still in all, they wrote and published, their painters painted and

---

[9] In *Musik und Lyrik*:158, Thrasybulos Georgiades offers a comparison between the slow introduction to Haydn's London Symphony in C major, No. 97 and the opening of the C-major Quintet D956, noting both the harmonic movement and the similar shape of their upper lines (the difference in tempos is compensated for by the slow harmonic motion in the Quintet: see Ch. VI). Long before, Kathleen Dale had pointed out a number of other specific examples ("Schubert's Indebtedness to Haydn" in *Music & Letters* (hereafter *ML*) 21 (1940): 23–30. In more general terms, however, it must have been Haydn's music that suggested to Schubert the unusual but rich juxtaposition of harmonies regarded as distant to each other, particularly that which produced the celebrated mediant relationships that mark Schubert's mature music.
[10] Schubert's love of Mozart's music is documentable and well-known. Georgiades finds specific traces of Mozart's 40th Symphony in Schubert's 5th Symphony, and, as in the case with Haydn, we find many general stylistic similarities as well.
[11] A list of specific examples of Beethoven-inspired works by Schubert as proposed by the musicological community would be too long to include or illustrate here. We believe the most profound influence to lie in certain large-scale harmonic sequencing and deceptively-static scaffolding (see Ch. II), characteristic of a particular side of Beethoven's musical thinking and demonstrable in works such as the Sixth Symphony or the Waldstein Sonata, op. 53. We find these characteristics present in Rossini's structures as well, and some specific melodic influences to be found in Schubert's Sixth Symphony and the Italian Overtures. For a short overview of Czech influences, see Paul Nettl, "Schubert's Czech Predecessors" in *ML* 23 (1942): 61–68.
[12] See Agnes Ziffer, *Kleinmeister zur Zeit der Wiener Klassik* (Tutzing: Schneider, 1984).

their bards sang. Through all of it we can identify a central and consistent artistic thread, a transcendental principle which we might describe as "the Ideal implied in the Actual". Friedrich von Hardenberg (Novalis) stated it most succinctly:

> When I give the common a higher meaning, the ordinary a secret aspect, the known the dignity of the unknown, the finite the appearance of the infinite, I romanticize.[13]

The idea of making something larger-than-life out of something merely life-size or "life-limited" had been one of the central dreams of the literary generation in the late years of the eighteenth century and early years of the nineteenth. It was expressed in Goethe's reworkings of the Faust legend, whose chief character sought to transcend his earthly limitations; and in the mystical landscapes of Caspar David Friedrich and Phillip Otto Runge, which were designed to direct the viewer's imagination far beyond the confines of canvas, frame, and immediate subject. The idea reflected a desire to find the entrance to a secret, mystical world invisible to the eye, undetectable to the ear, incomprehensible to the brain. In a critical moment Friedrich once touched upon this point:

> When an area is enveloped in fog it seems larger, more sublime, and the power of impression seems charged. Like a veiled maiden, it stretches the expectation.[14]

In an age no longer delighted particularly by rationalism and light, art sought to show mankind how to see behind the veil, into the darkness and beyond mortality, and perhaps even to master time itself.

For musicians, these transcendental aspirations were expressed through specific techniques. Sonically, for example, composers began to experiment with ways of simulating a larger acoustical space than that in which a given composition was actually experienced. The newest instruments contributed decisively to this endeavor. For example, the modern pianoforte offered a novelty that we can regard as a direct result of this new aesthetic thinking, namely, the sustaining mechanism (by which general term we include all means of raising the dampers: pedal, knee-levers, etc.). It was developed, among other things, to enhance the ambience of slow movements, which became, sometimes, the most progressive arenas for new musical ideas. With interest we read J.B. Cramer's 1812 description of extras on the newest pianofortes:

> Die neusten Pianoforte's [sic] haben fünf Züge: 1) Den Fagott, 2) Den Dämpfer, 3) Das grosse Pedal, 4) Das jeu de buffles, 5) [Die Verschiebung]: Ein Zug, durch welchen man die Klaviature verschieben kann.

Concerning the five pedal stops, we can take Cramer's rather conservative information or leave it (not forgetting that treatises often reflected realities and practices from as much as 5 to 10 years prior to publication). These stops still existed on some pianos (and other Viennese pianos never had them), but in the course of the early nineteenth century the more

---

[13] "Wenn ich dem Gemeinen einen hohen Sinn, dem Gewöhnlichen ein geheinmisvolles Ansehen, dem Bekannten die Würde des Unbekannten, dem Endlichen einen unendlichen Schein gebe, so romantisiere ich es." *Novalis:Werke, Tagebücher, und Briefe*, ed. Hans-Joachim Mähl and Richard Samuel (Munich: Hanser, 1978):II:335.
[14] Cited in *Caspar David Friedrich in Briefen und Bekenntnissen,* ed. Sigrid Hinz (Berlin: Henschelverlag, 1968): 129.

important Viennese makers ceased trying to imitate harpsichords (cf. nos. 1 and 4 above) and settled upon two principal mechanisms: the *Verschiebung* and the *Grosse Pedal* (what we now call the *sostenuto* pedal). Cramer's description of the effect of the latter is very interesting:

> [with it] one imitates the tones of the harmonica [...]. Only in soft, gracious places, where the harmony allows ... should it be used, so that each tone beats continually.[15]

A comparison with the harmonica is technically inaccurate, of course, but still apt. The celesting harmonica imparts an impression of phase differential brought about in its individual pitches by activating simultaneously two metal reeds of slightly different length, something like the *voix celeste* on the organ. The simulated phase differential invokes, especially when played softly, a sense of distance, which is the quality prized in the harmonica. The pianoforte's pedal imitates this quality linearly by allowing the player to mix successive harmonies.[16]

The function of the *una corda* or *Verschiebung* pedals on fortepianos (some instruments had more than one, the second one used for extreme effects) was twofold: first, to help the player achieve a quieter sound, and second, to lend that quiet sound a special quality. On many instruments the *una corda* pedal could shift the mechanism so that the hammer struck two strings, but not so far that it struck only one string, as the term might appear to mean. The fact that the hammer strikes two strings instead of one is interesting, for no matter how perfectly tuned, two independent bodies sounding simultaneously on the same pitch tend to produce something of the phase differential described above. That a special quality was intended (i.e. that the instruction was not meant only in dynamic terms, but sonority as well) can be inferred from the fact that *mit Verschiebung* or *una corda* instructions are often to be found where the dynamic is only ***pp***, not ***ppp***, as Schubert was well capable of writing.[17]

---

[15] Johann Baptist Cramer, *Instructions*: 1812. For complete citations of all Viennese pedagogical works pertinent to the period see App. IIA.

[16] Beethoven used the sustaining pedal often to invoke ideas of transcendence, as, for example, in the opening of the slow movement of the C-minor Piano Concerto. Here he called for the soloist to sustain the pedal over a series of harmonic changes. His pupil Czerny wrote that through the manipulation of both pedals, this theme must sound "distant, holy and supraterrestrial." Czerny also explained how to achieve this effect on later instruments with stronger basic sonorities by changing the pedal with each harmony, but in such a way that no sonic gaps occur. Although, as noted above, such effects lent themselves particularly to slow movements, where the pedals were often used for special purposes beyond *legato* or general ambience, we find also a special use of the mechanism in Beethoven: for example, in the first movement of the *Sonata quasi una fantasia,* op. 27/2 or the opening of the last movement of the *Waldstein* Sonata, Op. 53. Again, in both of these works the combination of the sostenuto pedal and a dynamic of ***pp*** (for which the una corda pedal is appropriate) creates the impression of distance. See App. IIA, 1839: Pianoforte Schule: IV: "Die Kunst des Vortrags" III:109/10. In conversation Ernst Hilmar has pointed out an orchestrated version of such blurring in Beethoven's music, at the point shortly before the recapitulation in the first movement of the Eroica Symphony, where as from afar the horn signals the main theme in the tonic against a V^7 backdrop.

[17] The special quality achieved by the *Verschiebung* pedal extends no further than the domain of sound: the instruction does not carry implications for tempo, rhythm or other areas. We are indebted to Michael Lorenz for pointing out the absurdities in a recent article by Richard Kurth, who seeks to interpret "mit Verschiebung" at the beginning of Suleika D720 as a license for certain vague rhythmic liberties. Kurth writes, "Although the prelude is notated unambiguously in 3/4, the marking 'mit Verschiebung' suggests that the 3/4

Schubert himself never owned a modern Viennese piano (a Graf, a Streicher or a Schantz, to name some of the best), and he must have played on many instruments that did not even possess pedals. But clearly he was aware of the celestial power of the pedal. In Mayrhofer's *Nachtstück* D672 he used it to symbolize a magical animation. Without doubt the text was inspired by Goethe's *Wandrers Nachtlied,* "Über allen Gipfeln:" As darkness descends and fog and clouds obscure his sight, an old man takes his harp and sings to Night, seeking his final peace; the forest comes alive and whispers back to him. Schubert first calls for the pedal ("mit gehobener Dämpfung") at the moment in which the old man begins to play his harp, invoking a hidden universe with the words "Du heil'ge Nacht." The pedal helps to imitate the shimmering tones of the harp, and to reveal to the listener a secret world where inanimate objects come alive and wishes are granted (See Example 1.1).In performance, this wonderful effect works only if the dynamic at m. 11 (***pp***) is maintained into the harp music, and if pianists are willing to forego the pedal from the beginning of the song until Schubert's instruction. As we mentioned above, the pedal in Schubert's music cannot be seen merely as a useful substitute for true finger *legato*, but often must be reserved for special ambience.

We can cite myriad examples of such pianistic effects in the lieder, whose texts are so richly suggestive, but the transcendental idea, the simulation of a higher condition, appears to have permeated Schubert's approach to the piano even in abstract works. Here instead of the simulation of distance, the ideal concerns a higher and / or more complex medium. The romantic characterization of a "song without words" provides an example, and here Felix Mendelssohn (whose original English title for his *Songs Without Words* was *Songs for the Pianoforte*) actually may have been preempted by Franz Schubert. The Archduke Rudolph's private music catalogue (hereafter *RC,* representing his collection in the *Gesellschaft der Musikfreunde*, hereafter *GMF*) contains a fascinating card entry (ca. 1823), a "Lied für das Pianoforte" by Franz Schubert. Unfortunately, the item itself cannot be located, and we are left with only the tantalizing thought of a new Schubert discovery.[18]

---

metric sensation [?] could be slightly obscured in performance." Kurth's footnote reads, "Although 'mit Verschiebung' is difficult to translate and interpret, it implies shifting, displacement, rearrangement, postponement, etc. In this instance, Schubert's marking seems to indicate a slightly agitated *quasi ad libitum* that blurs the relative values of beats and their subdivision of the measure. [sic!] ("On the Subject of Schubert's 'Unfinished' Symphony: Was bedeutet die Bewegung?" in *19th Century Music* XXIII/1:4).

Nothing could be further from the truth. The instruction 'mit Verschiebung' is not at all difficult to translate: its technical meaning for pianists was and is, simply, "with the action shifted" (i.e. with the use of the *una corda* pedal): nothing less and nothing more. Such wishful and precious reinterpretation of basic technical language represents an appalling trend towards fanciful theory in search of hard facts. Such soft musicology is encouraged, apparently, by the editorship of a growing number of musicological journals. We would discourage this particular notion quickly, before it makes its way into a performing community already hungry for novelty at any cost.

Kurth, incidentally, is not alone in his unfamiliarity with the mechanism of the piano. Even the well-known Schubert expert John Reed has mistranslated *Verschiebung* as "the sustaining pedal" instead of the *una corda* pedal (see *The Schubert Song Companion*, p. 434 on "Wer sich der Einsamkeit Ergibt" D478).

[18] See Otto Biba, "Franz Schubert und seine Zeit": Ausstellung im Archiv der Gesellschaft der Musikfreunde 1978: Katalog (Vienna, 1978):54, and Susan Kagan, "Schuberts Lieder für das Pianoforte" in *Schubert Durch die Brille* 15: 103–106, Journal of the Internationales Franz Schubert Institut, Vienna (hereafter *Die*

The Sonic Imagination

EXAMPLE 1.1

The characterization of an implied medium, song in the guise of piano music, is perfectly in line with the transcendental aspiration. Turning to concrete examples, we might consider the slow movement of the B♭ Piano Sonata, D960 (Example 1.2a), whose secret higher medium is an entire string ensemble. Vertically, the movement is divided into two main interior, *legato* voices (three in the trio) complemented by and contrasted with *pizzicato* outer voices, not unlike the voicing in the *Adagio* of the C-major Quintet (Example 1.2b). At the outset the single concession to the piano are the words *col pedale,* which have led

EXAMPLE 1.2a

EXAMPLE 1.2b

Brille). Transcendental aesthetics eventually entered even the popular consciousness of the mid-nineteeth century, revealing itself in exotic titles attached to pieces for commercial reasons: for example, Josef Strauß's *Sphären-Klänge* (Music of the Spheres), op. 235 (1868) or Josef Lanner's *Geheime Anziehungs-kräfte* ("Dynamiden" or Secret Magnetic Forces), op. 173 (1865). But even Mendelssohn and Schumann were attracted to such concepts, as we see in titles such as *Lieder ohne Worte* or performance instructions such as "Wie aus der Ferne" from the *Davidsbündlertänze* of 1837. See Berthold Hoeckner, "Schumann and Romantic Distance" in the *Journal of the American Musicological Society* (hereafter *JAMS*) 50/1 (Spring 1997):55–132. In order to achieve an ethereal effect in the latter piece Schumann called for a sensitive manipulation of both pedals. Mendelssohn clearly had a transcendental sound in mind for some of his orchestral works: the celestial beauty of the opening of the Nocturne from *Midsummer Night's Dream* (1842), for example, is no accident. Mendelssohn created it through the mixture of a single horn and two bassoons many modern pianists to inundate the movement with a general ambience. However, an overuse of the sustaining pedal here (and we speak particularly of modern concert instruments) defeats Schubert's purpose. *Col pedale* is best taken to apply not to the whole sound envelope, but only to the inner lines. Thus the pianist does not lose the contrast between middle and outer voices, and with it the implication of an idealized ensemble.[19]

The slow movements of the other two sonatas which Schubert composed in this last period also reveal his subconscious string-quartet idealization in their four-part writing. The sketches for the second movement of the A-major Piano Sonata D959 reveal a particularly fascinating example. In m. 5 we see a pianistic impossibility in the form of a *crescendo* on a single note. Comparing the sketches to the finished version, Arthur Godel has traced two occurrences of this gesture in the first section of the movement (m. 5: sketch / m. 5 fair copy / m. 23 sketch / m. 23 fair copy), and from this comparison we can divine Schubert's thinking in the course of rewriting. In the fair copy Schubert reveals his conscious recognition that the original markings, notated in the heat of first fantasy, could not be executed upon a piano.[20] In both cases he modifies the idea to a pianistically realizable formation, the second occurrence typically more ornate than the first:

EXAMPLE 1.3

(where another composer, say Carl Maria von Weber, might have used horns only, as in the famous theme near the beginning of the Overture to *Der Freischütz*, 1821). Mendelssohn was thinking, perhaps, with his organist's mind, imagining the soft cathedral effect obtained by certain stops and combinations.

[19] We do not have to look far to find Beethovenian models for the idea of an idealized string ensemble in the guise of piano music. Orchestrationally, Schubert's *Andante sostenuto* has strong similarities with the opening of the *Largo appassionata* from Beethoven's Piano Sonata in A major, Op. 2/2 (1795). In its actual form as string music, the constellation of *pizzicato* motion under a four-part *legato* ensemble in slow harmonic motion also has a famous precedent in the opening of the first-act Quartet from *Fidelio*, featuring a middle-voice sound which Beethoven achieves through divided viola and cello lines.

[20] *Schuberts letzte drei Klaviersonaten*: 95.

Followed throughout the movement in their final versions, these two formations offer an interesting compositional lesson which demonstrates different ways of converting an expressive string gesture into functional analogues for the piano.

To treat this line as one would a long, vocal *cantilena*, as we sometimes hear in performance, is contrary to Schubert's idealization, for it is not a vocal work. The famous recitative-like, interruptive passage in later measures of this movement has often led analysts to characterize it as operatic in nature, and indeed it is strikingly dramatic. Nevertheless, it cannot have been meant to simulate an operatic scene, for the style is wrong. This kind of writing may have belonged to the opera of the late nineteenth century or perhaps even the twentieth century, but not to that of Schubert's day and style. (We find a related passage in Schubert's G-major String Quartet D887, and here the effect is even more startling—almost schizophrenic in its sudden juxtaposition of contrasting elements—but decidedly not derived from the opera.)

EXAMPLE 1.4
Sonata D959, *Andante un poco mosso, mm. 120–146*

Had Schubert lived to realize such gripping gestures and conflicts in a large orchestral work, his posthumous reputation in relationship to Beethoven's might have been entirely different.

Looking through Schubert's earliest works, we find that from the beginning he must have heard his own prospective music ambivalently, as if he were sometimes undecided whether a musical idea was best cast for keyboard, string ensemble or even orchestra. Perhaps we can confirm this supposition by comparing the lied *Hagars Klage* D5, with its keyboard introduction, to its reappearance in separated parts as the opening of the Overture in C-minor D8 for string quintet (as well as in altered forms in several other early works):[21]

EXAMPLE 1.5a/b
a. *Hagars Klage*

b. Overture in C minor for String Quintet

All of the slow movements (and many other movements as well) in Schubert's piano sonatas appear to be string-ensemble inspired. Without exception, all of them can be played by a string quartet (barring certain extended ranges and two or three passages of figuration), in many cases literally and for long stretches. Except in portions of the *Wanderer* Fantasy D760 Schubert's solo keyboard thinking remained faithful to this voicing principle throughout his life.[22] In his string and orchestral music Schubert appears rarely to have written slurs that were longer than a string player could manage on a single bow. Longer slurs also are rare in his piano music. The same can be said of all Viennese music until certain late works of Beethoven and Schubert, and, with some striking exceptions, can be seen as representing the classicist side of their compositional thinking. Later, Johannes Brahms also limited most of his slurs to the length of a bow, a characteristic that contributes to his own reputa-

---

[21] See Martin Chusid, "Schubert's Overture for String Quintet and Cherubini's Overture to Faniska" in *JAMS* XV (1962):78–84, and Chusid's Foreword to Vol. VI/2 of the *NSA*.
[22] Returning briefly to Beethoven's extraordinary idea in the spacing of Op. 111/2, we might find some truth in the supposition that his idealized medium for this work was the string ensemble or even the orchestra (cf. the wide spacing in the opening of the Sixth Symphony). This thought could hold true for the first movement of Op. 111 as well. One need merely replay this work mentally as a string quartet in order to appreciate the idea. Can it be that we too often hold Beethoven's deafness or his decreasing sympathy for performers responsible for the abstractions and difficulties in his late works, without recognizing the possible interplay between real and ideal media in his creative subconscious?

tion as a romantic-classicist. (Meanwhile, Schumann, Chopin and Liszt indeed had developed such independent phrasing slurs in their piano music.) Nevertheless, without the effect of these classical bowing slurs, the romantic simulations would be weakened. Successful Schubert pianists take his string-thinking seriously; they have trained mind and fingers not only to voice the horizontally-oriented formations through independently-gauged pressure, but to treat his slurs as if they were using a bow.

Having emphasized Schubert's string-thinking in his piano writing, we might mention the odd possibility of an opposite effect, whereby the characteristic middle-register richness of his string writing may have been reinforced by the nature of the early nineteenth-century fortepiano itself. We refer to the natural dynamic discrepancy between registers of the Schubert-period piano, which, even on the best instruments, favored the middle. Thus, everything being equal, the figuration in the right hand often had the effect of floating away into the ether, a fact which Schubert may have taken into consideration in passages such as the following, from the A-minor Sonata D784:

EXAMPLE 1.6
Andante, mm. 29–34

The effect is even more pronounced in a four-hand passage such as this one in the *Lebensstürme* Allegro D947 (see Example 1.7 on facing page). Performers on modern instruments, of course, must recreate such balances artificially.

The piano methods of Schubert's day do not have much to say about dynamic individuation, but we have proof that the violinist Louis Spohr was well aware of the need for it in string-quartet playing. Spohr made a distinction between "genuine" quartets, under which rubric we can include Schubert's works, and "solo" quartets ("Quatuors brillans" [sic]), wherein the lower three instruments are largely accompanimental:

> A new species of Quartett [sic] has latterly been invented, in which the first Violin performs the solo-part, and the other three instruments merely an accompaniment. In order to distinguish compositions of this kind from genuine Quartetts, they are termed Solo-quartetts (Quatuors brillans). They are designed to give the Solo-player an opportunity of displaying his talent in small musical assemblies, and they therefore belong, in so far as regards their performance, to the category of Concerto-pieces; hence, all that has been said of the performance of Concertos in the foregoing sections, is applicable not only to these, but to all similar Solo-compositions with a three or four part accompaniment (as Variations, Pot-pourris, &c.).

EXAMPLE 1.7

The genuine Quartett demands quite a different style of performance [than the solo quartet]. In such, it is not intended that any single instrument should predominate, but that all should alike enter into the idea of the composer and render the same intelligible. The first Violinist, therefore, should not aim at distinguishing himself above the others, either by peculiar strength of tone, or by his style of delivery; he ought rather to unite cordially with them, nay, even to be subordinate, in passages where he has not the principal melody.[23]

In accordance with this last sentence, a Spohr performance of a Schubert quartet passage marked across the board with a single dynamic, such as in the excerpt from the variations in D810 below, might still have been characterized by carefully differentiated volume relationships. As obvious as such a necessity may appear to modern performers, it apparently was not clear to everyone in Spohr's time, else he would not have had to make the point.

EXAMPLE 1.8

[23] From the London edition of his *Violin-Schule*: 232-33. App. IIA, 1832.

Schubert built such sonic spatial techniques into his orchestral works as well. One of his most striking effects is the use of two horns in the soft opening of the Great C-major Symphony, where the dynamic level would require only one. He not only risked the out-of-phase effect of the two instruments playing together, but encouraged it, specifically to achieve the impression of distance. Not even the wonders of modern stereo separation can match this simple but brilliant inspiration. The idea requires no particular performance technique beyond following Schubert's demand for two horns (shown by double stems in the autograph). It works in all tempos, from Wilhelm Furtwängler's to Roger Norrington's, so long as it remains soft.[24] In the final two measures Schubert increases the sense of distance by halving the volume (the traditional echo analogue) and, in an imaginative stroke, by doubling the time values as well.

EXAMPLE 1.9a/b
a. autograph (*GMF*)

b. modern edition (Eulenberg)

A sure key to finding the proper general sound for Schubert's orchestral music lies not only in taking the instrumentation and dynamics seriously, but recreating more of the balance between winds and strings that existed in his day. Modern performances generally are made with the over-large string sections of our day, whereby much of the softer figuration and instrumental effects of the winds are obscured. The nature of modern winds, developed to penetrate, only exacerbates the problem. Wind players, then, must trust themselves to abide by the entire gamut (especially on the soft end) of Schubert's dynamics. For all instruments, Schubert's accentuation must be put into proper context (often as metrical stress patterning rather than insistent accentuation in the modern sense. (Cf. Ch. IV).

We cannot explain fully Schubert's overall romantic sound through such isolated examples; we have chosen them merely to emphasize that his extraordinary "mind's ear" was attuned to a larger world. It is a sonic world, to be sure, but it is not activated particularly by the use of period instruments, nor particularly by modern ones. It certainly cannot be reached through the abstract search for a "beautiful" sound, an unfocussed notion which dominates, sadly, not only in modern concert halls, criticism and recordings, but in teaching studios as well. We believe Schubert's sonic imagination to be accessible through a renewed attention to his apparent aesthetic intuition (with the caveat that we do not confuse his intuition with our own), as well as the thinking and writing of his generation. His own intuition we find expressed in a notation which is both exacting and, contrary to popular opinion, exact.

---

[24] Furtwängler's original recording has been reprocessed and reissued by Deutsche Grammophon on CD447 439-2. Norrington's was issued by EMI (567-749 949-2).

The "sound" of Schubert's lieder

Finding the right sound for Schubert's lieder with piano is not a matter of finding the right voice or the right venue. Nor has it to do with period instruments and vocal techniques, although it is truly helpful to be familiar with them, particularly for concepts of articulation, dynamics and pedalling. A surprising number of modern musicians have had no experience playing period instruments, but most of them have heard Schubert's music in historically-conscious performances and can recognize the timbre of Viennese instruments of the day. Indeed, since the collaboration of Elly Ameling and Jörg Demus (playing on a period instrument) in the 1970s, recording companies sporadically have issued a number of Schubert lieder in similar veins.[25] Recent releases have featured teams such as Pregardien / Staier (see App. IIC), and we can only be grateful for the chance to hear and compare such efforts.

We must remember that the very act of recording negates one of the most important aspects of historical reality: each musical performance of Schubert's day was a unique experience. Furthermore, recordings, which cater to the modern conditioning for artificial ambience, give us no feel whatsoever for the diverse Schubertian lied venues; these ranged from small private homes to larger salons such as Ignaz Sonnleithner's and even to the out of doors. In Schubert's day the only true criterion for a venue was that the acoustics permitted the song to be understood in all of its dimensions. The *Sammler* (28 June 1827, hereafter *Sml*) reported that Schubert and Tietze's performance of *Im Freien* D880 (which begins *pp* with a pedal effect) got a bit swamped in the acoustics of the Large Hall of the University (Grosser Universitätssaal). The reviewer stated that "for a song, wherein the finest nuances should not be lost, this space is too large. It would sound much better in a drawing room [Zimmer]."[26] Here, not even more volume from the performers would have helped; it probably would have made things worse.

The *Sammler* reviewer's mention of the "finest nuances" is the key to finding a good Schubert sound. In terms of dynamics we seem to have no problem producing extreme loudness, only extreme softness, and Schubert's dynamics require subtle shadings extending down to *ppp* and beyond. Schubert's rich articulation, part of his classical inheritance, is equally important. It often goes lost in the interests of singing in long lines, which, generally speaking, is more appropriate to music of a later age. Pianists tend to sacrifice his articulation to a modern ideal of concert-hall ambience (achieved via pedal) that is only sometimes required in Schubert's songs. Our example of *Nachtstück* D672 is a case in point. Lastly, in all pedalling matters, no amount of stylistic intuition could substitute for an hour spent playing on a good Graf copy.

For singers, the main bone of contention between those who train their voices for the dynamic demands of the modern opera stage and those who specialize in earlier styles has been "what to do about *vibrato*." As we will find later in this book, the issue has been avoidable all along. *Vibrato* always has been a natural part of singing, the more natural, of

---

[25] EMI 1c 065-99 630.
[26] Dokumente: 430.

course, in the voices of gifted singers. In terms of Schubert singing, it is time to move on to more important questions, such as the interaction and dynamic balance between singer and pianist, or the detailed matters of articulation, phrasing, enunciation and logical breathing.

Voice types and techniques

Although in retrospect Schubert made something special and wonderful out of a simple lied tradition, he neither turned it towards the esoteric nor did he write his songs to be sung by only certain kinds of voices. Of course he composed for specific occasions and people, and on commission, but when those occasions were past and the songs offered to the public they assumed a kind of artistic independence. Because Schubert was a professional composer he needed famous singers to represent him; nevertheless, in reading through the documents of his life we get the sense that his songs were there for anyone who could sing them. In this regard, what Heinrich Christoph Koch had articulated for the earlier tradition applies to Schubert's songs as well:

> Lied : Generally, any lyric poem of several stanzas designed to be sung and fitted with a melody repeated in each stanza, and which also has the characteristic of being singable by anyone with sound vocal organs ... regardless of their artistic training.
>
> *Musikalisches Lexikon* (1802)[27]

Koch's simplistic description already was outdated by the time he published it, for the through-composed song and other variants were well-known by the turn of the century. What interests us here is the new spirit of *égalité* which has crept into his definition. In terms of voices, the later nineteenth century gradually reverted back to professionalism, and for that reason what is preserved are, for the most part, the known opera singers on the early recordings made at the end of the century. Some singers became known as lieder specialists, but in fact their basic singing techniques were no different from those of the great opera stars.

The main issues in Schubert lieder singing concern dynamics, articulation, pronunciation and vocal control. If a modern singer can and would be willing to manage the seven levels between ***ppp*** and ***fff***, and to respect Schubert's notation, then he or she can sing Schubert's songs. Furthermore, if the narrative principle holds, then any singer could have sung or still can sing any song, regardless of sex or sexual orientation. As we shall see, Schubert himself was not negatively sensitive to transpositions, and no other problems stand in the way.[28] Preparation for modern operatic careers (still the dominant preoccupation among young singers), with its great emphasis on role-playing, not to mention its confining reliance upon the *Fach* (voice-type) concept, has done enormous damage in this regard.

---

[27] *Musikalisches Lexikon, welches die theoretische und praktische Tonkunst, encyclopädisch bearbeitet, alle alten und neuen Kunstwörter erklärt, und die alten und neuen Instrumente beschieben, enthält* (Frankfurt a. M., 1802): 902.

[28] In terms of Schumann, Lotte Lehman's ground-breaking recording of the *Dichterliebe* with Bruno Walter (Sony MPK 44840), while not her best singing, made this point years ago. She also recorded *Die schöne Müllerin* (LYS 821 66 07 with Paul Ulanowsky) and *Winterreise* (VA 821 12 20, also with Ulanowsky). In recent years, Brigitte Fassbaender recorded *Winterreise* (EMI 574 99 46), as well as a mixed group including *Erlkönig, Ganymed* and other "male" songs (SONY SK 53104 with Cord Garben). On the other hand, it is sad that the DG box of Schubert lieder (Fischer-Dieskau, FOOG 29097/118 in 22 CDs) omits the "female" songs.

The Sonic Imagination

The long list of Schubert singers active during his lifetime, many of whom he accompanied personally, shows us that almost any reasonable voice can be a Schubert voice: from amateur to professional, from light to operatic, and from basso to high soprano.

Herr Adolph
Josef Barth (tenor at the Hofkapelle; teacher and instrumentalist as well)
Franz Borschitzky (singer at the Hofoper)
Decani (probably a bass)
Franz Xaver Dunst (baritone)
Josef Eichelberger (tenor)
Johann Karl, Graf von Esterházy (bass; twice Schubert's employer)
Rosine, Gräfin von Esterházy (wife of the above)
Marie Esterházy (soprano and pianist; older daughter of the Esterházys)
Caroline Esterházy (alto and pianist; second daughter of the Esterházys)
Louise Fabiani (sang in the 23rd Psalm)
Josefine Fleischmann (sang in the 23rd Psalm)
Franz Anton Forti (tenor or high baritone; sang Pizarro in *Fidelio*)
Maria Anna [Nanette] Fröhlich (soprano; premiered the piano part of *Erlkönig*; taught voice and piano; close professional contact with Schubert)
Barbara [Betty, Babette] Fröhlich [later Bogner] (soprano and teacher; sister of the above)
Josefina [Josefa] Fröhlich (soprano, composer; made her debut at the Hofkapelle at eighteen; sister of the other Fröhlichs)
Katharina ["Katty"] Fröhlich (amateur singer; Grillparzer's "ewige Braut," sister of the three Fröhlich's above)
Karoline Frontini
Josef Frühwald (tenor; sang the first Jacquino in *Fidelio*)
Aloys Fuchs (amateur bass; also played cello and collected manuscripts)
Josef Götz (bass and composer; sang at the Hofkapelle and Kärntnertortheater; died in early1822)
Vincenz Franz Gottfried (tenor)
Karl Greisinger
Therese Grob (soprano; premiered soprano part in the F-minor Mass D105; Schubert may have written *Grechen am Spinnrade* for her)
Karl Maria Groß (also played violin)
August von Gymnich (tenor; premiered *Erlkönig* 1 Dec. 1820 and *Der Wanderer* 19 Jan. 1821 at the GMD; died in Oct. 1821)
Anton Haizinger, Sr. (tenor; pupil of Mozatti; sang Florestan in *Fidelio*; sang in premiere of Beethoven's Ninth Symphony)
Anton Haizinger, Jr. (bass)
Anna von Hartmann
Fritz von Hartmann
Emerenzia Heinrich [later Riechel] (soprano)
Adelbert Herz
Johann Hoffmann (bass)
Fanny von Hügel
Josef Hüttenbrenner (probably a tenor; primarily a pianist)
Franz Jäger (the first person to sing a Schubert song in public)
Theresia Josephi
Franz Sales Kandler (singer; pianist)
Raphael Georg Kiesewetter von Wiesenbrunn (bass)
Franz Kirchlehner (bass; also a violinist)
Herr [Wenzel?] Kral (professional singer)
Georg Krebner (tenor)
Wilhelm Krebs (bass)
Johann Leschetizky [Leschetizki]
Sophie Linhard [Linhart; later Schuller]
Peter Lugano (tenor)
Johanna Lutz [later Kupelwieser]
Herr Marschall
Edler von Mayer
Anna Milder (protégé of Vogl; premiered Leonore in *Fidelio*)
Joseph Mozatti (tenor)
Sophie Müller
[Johann] Wenzel Nejebse (bass)
Johann Nestroy (bass; sang Don Fernando in *Fidelio*)
Anton Obermüller
Marie Pachler
Bertha von Pratobevera [later married Kreißle von Hellborn]
Franziska von Pratobevera [later Tremier]
Louise von Pratobevera
Maria von Pratobevera [later Bergmann]
Josef Preisinger (bass; played piano)
Julius Radicchi (tenor; sang Florestan in *Fidelio*)

Benedikt Randhartinger
Jakob Wilhelm Rauscher (tenor; sang Jacquino in *Fidelio*)
Karl Gottlieb Reißiger (bass)
Adalbert Rotter (bass)
Franz Rueß (tenor)
Martin Ruprecht
Julie Schauff [later Schmiedel] (soprano and pianist)
Karoline Schindler
Kolumban Schindler
Johann Schmiedel (bass)
Johann Karl Schoberlechner (bass)
Karl von Schönstein (protégé of Vogl; dedicatee of the *Müllerlieder*)
Wilhelmine Schröder [after 1823 Schröder-Devrient] (sang Leonore in *Fidelio*)
Franz Schubert (tenor)
Herr Schütze
Moritz von Schwind
Joseph Seipelt (bass; premiered the bass part of Beethoven's Ninth Symphony)
Ignaz Sonnleithner (bass; uncle of Franz Grillparzer)
Leopold Sonnleithner
Henriette Sontag (sang in premiere of Beethoven's Ninth Symphony)
Joseph von Spaun
Josef Spitzeder (buffo bass)
Eleanore Staudinger (soprano)
Herr Stefan (tenor; brother of baritone Franz Xaver Dunst)
Amalie Tewils (soprano; sang in the 23rd Psalm)
Ludwig Tietze (tenor)
Josef [Kalasanz?] Tobiaschek
Johann Karl Umlauff [later Ritter von Frankwell] (pupil of Vogl)
Karoline Unger [later Sabatier](alto; sang in the premiere of Beethoven's Ninth Symphony)
Betty Vio (married to Spitzeder)
Johann Michael Vogl (high baritone)
Johann Michael Wächter (bass)
Ferdinand Walcher
Herr Weber
Johann Michael Weinkopf (bass; sang the first Don Fernando in *Fidelio*)
Marie Pauline Weis[s] [later Rokitansky] (soprano)
Louise Weis[s] (sister of the above)
Marie Mathilde Weiß [not to be confused with Marie Weis] (alto and pianist)

We have named only those who were known to have sung Schubert's lieder.[29] Further, we might name Louis LaBlache, Josephine Fodor-Mainvielle (from 1823 at the Hofoper), possibly Karl Devrient, and Heinrich Panofka. In performances outside of Austria we can cite Karl Bader in Berlin (with Felix Mendelssohn at the piano) and Henriette Grabow in Leipzig. The cast lists of Schubert's stage productions yield other names as well.[30] Many, but not all of these singers were professionals. In the light of the variety of this list, we can hardly look upon Vogl, or any other artist, as the "representative" Schubert singer. Of the Fröhlich sisters, for example, the [Wiener] *Allgemeine Musikzeitung* (1841, hereafter *WamZ*) later wrote

---

[29] The list of pianists is slimmer: Karl Haas, Anselm Hüttenbrenner, Josef Hüttenbrenner, Albert Schellmann, Karoline Esterházy, Marie Esterházy, Josef von Gahy, Joseph Groß, Anna Fröhlich, Louis Hartmann, Betty Wanderer, Herr Winkler, Maria Blahetka, Franz Schubert, Carl Maria von Bocklet, Carl Czerny, J.N. Hummel (who at least once improvised on Schubert's music), possibly Hiller, Moritz von Schwind, Johann Baptist Jenger, Louise Weiss, Marie Wagner, Therese Kunz, Babette Kunz.

[30] *Das Zauberglöckchen*: Franz Siebert, Josef Gottdank, Franz Rosner. *Rosamunde*: Moritz Rott (Rosenberg), Mlle. Eichenhoff, Georg Palmer, Herr Klein, Katharina Vogel, Mlle. Neumann, Friedrich Demmer, Herr Hahn, Herr Posinger, Adolf Vollkommen, Julius La Roche, Franz Mayerhofer, Herr Wille, Herr Sandner, Herr Urban, Herr Renner, Herr Willax, Herr Tomaselli.

that they had "done more for singing than many of Europe's most famous 'Amazon-throats'...".[31]

Dramatic vs. Narrative

The sheer variety of singers and voice types listed above gives rise to a question which scholarship has yet to answer satisfactorily. Does the lieder singer seek to interpret a song dramatically, externalizing his or her emotions to a more-or-less passively receptive audience as in the opera, or lyrically, taking a neutral position as a narrator and effectively inviting the audience to develop its own active fantasy in relation to events and thoughts in the song? Of the members of Schubert's circle, Leopold Sonnleithner left the clearest, most decisive opinion on this subject that we possess.

> The lied singer ... himself does not represent the person whose feelings he portrays; [thus] poet, composer and singer must conceive the song as lyrical, not dramatic.[32]

Sonnleithner elaborated further in a series of writings on singing, from which the following excerpt is taken:

Sonnleithner's "Manifesto" (1860)

> I hope I may be allowed to add a few words in particular about Franz Schubert, who has the right, wherever lieder are discussed, to be thought of with utmost deference. I had the privilege of belonging to the small circle wherein Schubert's great gifts were first recognized, and whose members made an effort to promote his works and bring him into the larger musical world. I often heard him sing his own songs, with his weak but pleasing ["sympathische"] voice, wherewith he often had to employ falsetto when he could not reach the higher tones. I heard him even more often accompanying at the pianoforte, rehearsing his works with the finest artists and musical amateurs of his time. It is all the more painful, then, to hear the magnificent songs of my long-deceased friend as they are generally performed today, in a way which opposes the intentions of their creator.
>
> One main characteristic of Schubert's songs consists of completely noble, beautiful and expressive melody; this always remains the central consideration. As interesting as his accompaniments usually are, they are there only as support, and they often portray just the background, the general mood or a characteristic movement: for example, the galloping horse, the spinning wheel, the boat oar, the mill wheel, the lapping of waves upon the shore, etc. The beauty of his melodies is also (with few exceptions) of an independent, purely musical kind; this means that such beauty in no way depends on the text, even if in every way it complements and often even ennobles the words and thoughts of the poet. As with Mozart's music, one can play Schubert's melodies on the stick-flute or on the hurdy-gurdy and they would remain attractive; their musical beauty calls in no way for a declamatory interpretation. For this reason Schubert insisted above all that his songs should not be declaimed, but far more flowingly sung so that each note might avoid the unmusical tone of actual speech, and so that the purely musical thought might thrive.
>
> The accomplishment of this goal depends upon the strictest observance of the tempo. Schubert has marked everywhere the places in which he wanted pulling-back or speeding-up,

---

[31] *Dokumente:* 112.
[32] *Erinnerungen:* Sonnleithner's *Anhang:* 98 (1857).

or the places in which he wanted or allowed a free interpretation. Where he did not mark such places, he did not countenance the least deviance in tempo. If this fact were not corroborated among all still-living witnesses to his music-making, it also could be ascertained without a doubt by every competent musician from studying Schubert's accompaniments. A trotting or galloping horse cannot be diverted from his pace [*ERLKÖNIG* D328] ; a spinning wheel in motion can come to a stop if the person using it forgets – diverted by some passionate feeling – to keep it going, but it cannot turn slowly in one moment and fast in the next, changing from measure to measure [*GRETCHEN AM SPINNRADE* D118]. Except in the case of an attack [Blutschlagflusse], a fast-beating heart cannot suddenly cease to beat so that on the words "Dein ist mein Herz und wird [soll] es ewig bleiben" the singer can hold out his high A in order to vent excessive feeling [*UNGEDULD* D795/7]. When the crusaders' march sounds in the distance and the monk adds his observations to these sounds, he must sing forth in the strictest tempo – the march does not orient itself to his dawdling paroxyms [*DER KREUZZUG* D932]. We can offer these wretchednesses, which unfortunately we hear all too often, only as isolated examples, for this senseless approach has become the general rule. The perpetrators of these crimes against music would hope to take no small advantage of the deeper feelings of this immortal master [Schubert], who, if he were still living, would be compelled to stop up his ears or else run miles away from them because his human kindness would not allow him to take a stick to these criminals, as would be their rightful punishment.

By no means should it be said that Schubert wanted his songs to be sung mechanically. A true and purely musical performance never shuns feeling and sensitivity, but the singer should not seek to let himself be taken for a more poetic and spiritual being than the composer himself, who – through his notation – has indicated exactly what he wanted to hear sung, and whose works are injured and ruined by every voluntary deviation [Willkürlichkeit, see Voluntary Ornamentation, Ch. V]. For a composer such as Schubert, whose music is best suited to the simplest and most natural way of singing (for example, that of the well-known singer Tietze, a "naturalist" with a nice voice), even the subtlest [raffiniertesten] declamation should be avoided completely. We wish to leave such things to those who always look behind the musical ideas (which they cannot grasp *per se,* and therefore reject) for other, poetic or philosophical ideas. [...] Let singers heed and take these words to heart! Their reward will be the recognition of those who are truly informed.[33]

Sonnleithner's purist position here has been taken as a criticism of the kind of singing once practised by Johann Michael Vogl, but this is not the case. Sonnleithner was writing after the mid-nineteenth century and was lamenting the excesses of that later period, when theater and concert traditions had reached a grand low point in Austria. After 1828 Vienna had been left with no major composer (major talents, yes, in the Strauß family, but only for the entertainment industry). Great figures passed through, Liszt, Mendelssohn, Chopin, the Schumanns, etc., but not until the arrival of Brahms and Bruckner was Vienna to regain a semblance of its former creative musical life. By that time, it had become a city

---

[33] From "Über den Vortrag des Liedes, mit besonderer Beziehung auf Franz Schubert", from "Bemerkungen zur Gesangskunst" IV (7 November 1860) in *Wiener Zeitschrift* (hereafter *WZ*): "Rezensionen und Mitteilungen über Theater und Musik." Selected by O.E. Deutsch in *Erinnerungen* 291–3. Elsewhere Sonnleithner writes: "More than a hundred times I heard him [Schubert] rehearse and accompany his own songs. Above all, he kept strict time, except in those few instances where he had specifically marked a *ritardando, morendo, accelerando,* etc. Furthermore, he permitted no excessive expression." *Erinnerungen:* 98.

of cultural memories instead of realities. Schubert's songs must have suffered enormously in the hands of sentimentally-minded personalities determined to recapture past times.[34]

It may be unwise to rely too heavily on any single one of the long-time survivors of Schubert's circle. As we can see, for example, Sonnleithner's distinction between lyrical and dramatic singing is at best a simplistic one. Anyway, one suspects that on all sides the posthumous reportage about Schubert grew less reliable with the years, and thus more susceptible to polemics. This is a natural state of affairs, of course, and we should not be surprised that each of the *Erinnerungen* about Schubert might have gained something in color and presumed importance the further removed that it was from the period in question (although Sonnleithner may have relied upon earlier notes).[35] The fact that Schubert's biographers, supposedly impartial reporters, soon made out of him that happy-go-lucky genius with the "little mushroom" image is evidence enough that both memory and "historical information" are slippery things indeed. In general, it would not seem safe to base our concept of a good Schubert singer on the reportage of any single person, and certainly not on the model of any one singer.

In other writings Sonnleithner criticized Vogl directly, objecting to the theatrical approach that the singer had taken to Schubert's lieder, and contrasting it with the lyrical approach which Sonnleithner valued so highly in other performers such as Baron von Schönstein and Ludwig Tietze. In the Appendix to his *Erinnerungen* (1857, based on notes and other documents) Sonnleithner described Vogl's transpositions to exotic keys, his falsetto and whispered delivery, sudden outcries, etc.[36] Sonnleithner's remarks are corroborated by several other of the surviving Schubert circle. Indeed, Vogl seems not only to have indulged in such histrionics, but to have grown worse in this regard as he grew older (he sang Schubert's works after the composer's death as well).

Many musicologists submit that Schubert revealed his own tacit approval of such musical behavior in a remark made in a letter of 1825 to his brother Ferdinand. Concerning

---

[34] Sonnleithner mentions Julius Stockhausen as the leading Schubert singer of the mid-century, praising him even though Stockhausen appears not to have been able to eschew all of the current trends so odious to Sonnleithner.

[35] Even within a short time after his death Schubert's legacy had been exploited from all sides: for example, Adolf Müller's scoring of *Erlkönig* for the stage, or Diabelli's irresponsible "second" edition of *Die schöne Müllerin*. Some of Schubert's most intimate friends and family also realized what they could from their inheritances: Ferdinand Schubert, who had been willing to trade on his brother's talent even while Franz lived, now sought to gain the maximum financial mileage from the scores he had inherited. The Hüttenbrenners acted quite strangely over possession of the manuscript of the *Unfinished* Symphony. As with the *Müllerlieder,* Diabelli and others brought out almost everything that they imagined might sell. (The only prohibitive criteria in this regard appears to have been technical and or conceptual difficulty; thus a few of Schubert's greatest works remained unpublished for a while.) Performing artists who had been most intimately associated with Schubert now found many opportunities to perform his music. Vogl appears to have sung Schubert's songs with increasingly personal input and interpretation until long after he should have hung up his frock coat. Moritz von Schwind reports that Schönstein, whom Schwind called the "Wandering Millerlad" (Müllerbursch) was still singing his single greatest artistic treasure (hopefully in the Sauer & Leidesdorf version) well into the middle of the century. Karl Maria von Bocklet premiered the *Wanderer* Fantasy to the public in 1832, although why he had not done this while Schubert lived and was struggling for recognition is a mystery.

[36] *Erinnerungen:* 94. Also see discussion in Liess: 135/36.

his own performing rapport with Vogl, Schubert wrote: "The manner and means with which Vogl sings and I accompany him, the way we seem to be a single unit in these moments, is for these people something really new and novel." [etwas ganz Neues, unerhörtes].[37] Eric Van Tassel speculates that this remark "is most easily understood if the Vogl-Schubert partnership did indeed exhibit all the distortions described by Sonnleithner." Van Tassel continues: "For if Schubert meant to say merely that he and Vogl were applauded for performances that were 'purely musical', it is hard to see how their collaboration could have been 'utterly new, unheard-of' [Van Tassel's translation] – unless we imagine that audiences in upper Austria had never heard a singer and pianist perform together in a musically competent fashion."[38]

We have no idea what Van Tassel means by "purely musical", but having attended concerts in upper Austria in the twentieth century we can well imagine the lack of precision in ensemble performing that must have reigned in Schubert's day. Indeed we can believe that such a competent and sensitive accompanist as Franz Schubert had never been heard before in the provinces, the more credit due him the harder he had to concentrate in order to cover for any excesses by Vogl. Professional accompanists with long experience of theatrically "expressive" singers will appreciate this surmise. Also, in addition to the performance level itself, we must not forget that the very nature of Schubert's songs was quite new and interesting for these people.[39]

In Sonnleithner's view the singer always must remain a kind of musical reporter, involved to some degree, but also able to pass on with relatively unruffled demeanor the most wonderful as well as the most horrifying words, feelings and experiences of the characters whom the composer and his poets might construct. Simplicity of delivery was one of the keys to this style, and one of the singers whom Sonnleithner admired particularly for this trait was Karl, Baron von Schönstein, the dedicatee of *Die schöne Müllerin*. Sonnleithner does not actually specify Schönstein by name, but his admiration of and deference to Schönstein[40] seems unequivocal:

> There still lives a contemporary of Schubert's, a noble friend of the arts, who sang entirely in Schubert's spirit. In order not to tread too closely upon his modesty, we do not name him here.[41]

Sonnleithner's assessment of several other Schubert singers appears to support the idea of

---

[37] Dated 12 September 1825. *Dokumente:*314. In modern German the word "unerhörtes" has negative implications, bordering on the insulting, but in the context of Schubert's remark it is obviously a positive term.

[38] "'Something utterly new': listening to Schubert lieder" in *EM* XXV/4 (November 1997): 707.

[39] It might help to form a context for this issue if we had one or two lieder methods, but almost all singing tutors through the middle of the nineteenth century (except those which dealt with religious music, general school curricula, or the bare basics of singing) concentrated upon operatic and oratorio singing. Theory usually follows practice at a safe distance, but in this case we possess not a single period tutor that can assist us, Austrian, German or other. The occasional song (but, astonishingly, never by Schubert) pops up here and there as an exercise in other singing tutors, but the lied as an independent art form was neglected by even the greatest pedagogues.

[40] Sonnleithner and his father Ignaz had been ennobled together on 14 June 1828 as "Edler von". Schönstein's rank was higher and his lineage already established.

[41] *Erinnerungen:* 292. Walter Dahms wrote also that Schönstein sang the *Müllerlieder* in a direct and uncom-

direct and uncomplicated interpretation as an ideal:

> Singers with merely a good voice and a natural singing style have had great success with these songs [Müllerlieder]: for example, [Ludwig] Tietze and [Johanna] Lutz, neither of whom could claim a true knowledge of singing or higher aesthetics.[42]

"Merely a good voice and a natural singing style" seems to have served even for the more dramatic works of Schubert. The *WamZ* (1 April 1824) wrote about Tietze's performance of *Erlkönig* (accompanied by one of the Hüttenbrenners): "Herr Tietze delighted us once again with his [ingratiating and heart-rending voice]." One always should be wary of newspaper reviews, but if this one can be believed, then simplicity as an ideal for lieder singing acquires further support.

The Schubert singer of greatest historical interest, Franz Schubert himself, probably had a clear, uncomplicated voice. Like Tietze and Lutz, he must also have sung in a straightforward manner. Deutsch's unflattering remark that Schubert's "voix de compositeur" was not suited to performance was merely an ill-considered commentary on a letter from Anton Freiherr von Doblhoff to Franz von Schober of 2 April 1824, in which Doblhoff was reporting the current lamentable state of affairs. It reads: "Schubert himself cannot sing", which meant only that Schubert was not feeling well, that he had a cold, or, more likely, that he was still recovering from a bad phase of syphilis.[43] In any case, Anton Ottenwalt writes on 27 November 1825 that Schubert sang "quite beautifully" at Schober's; and Franz von Hartmann writes on 17 December 1826 that "Schubert sang magnificently, particularly *Der Einsame* and *Dürre* [Trockne] *Blumen.*"

Schubert's piano playing appears to have conformed to his uncomplicated singing style. Albert Stadler (Schubert's senior by three years) wrote:

> [Schubert had] a beautiful touch, a quiet hand; his was nice, clear playing, full of soul and expression. He belonged to the old school of good pianists, where the fingers did not attack the poor keys like birds of prey.[44]

Stadler's report is supported by Schubert, writing from on tour in a letter to his parents:

> In Upper Austria I come occasionally across my own works, particularly in the [St.] Florian and Kremsmünster abbeys, where with the aid of a good pianist I presented my variations and marches with a nice success. The variations from my new 2-hand sonata were especially well-

---

plicated manner: "... his voice, more youthful than Vogl's, showed its magic in intimate and lyrical ["getragene"] singing. His performance style was plain, unadorned ["schmucklos", probably meaning without the use of ornaments] and without 'nuancen,' as it had to be for singing Schubert. For this reason the *Müllerlieder* were particularly suited to him." Unfortunately, Dahms, writing in 1912, did not specify the source of this information about Schönstein. He himself could not have heard Schönstein, at least not in the latter's prime, for Schönstein was born in the same year as Schubert and died in 1876. Dahms probably got his impression from Leopold von Sonnleithner's *Erinnerungen*.

[42] Ibid.

[43] Just eight days later (10 April) Schwind reported that "Schubert is almost well", and then (14 April) that "Schubert is not entirely well"! Can Deutsch really have overlooked Schubert's own famous, heart-wrenching letter of two days previous to Doblhoff's, in which he poured out his misery over his health to Kupelwieser, ending so pitifully with "Lebe wohl! recht wohl!" ? *Dokumente* : 237.

[44] *Erinnerungen:* 124.

received; I played them myself, and apparently not without an angel over my shoulder, because a few people assured me that under my hands the keys became like voices. If this is true I am really pleased, because I can't stand this damnable chopping that even quite advanced pianists indulge in. It pleases neither the ear nor the spirit.[45]

Not much of specific value can be learned from this report, but at least we know, as if we didn't know already, that Schubert stood on the side of lyricism in performance. We can have no reason to believe that Schubert's style as a lieder accompanist would have differed.

All this talk of lyricism and narration is interesting, of course, but rather vague. We know many Schubert lied accompaniments that simply cannot be described as lyrical, or thus rendered: from early in his career (*Rastlose Liebe* D138) to later (*Der Atlas* D957/8). Just so, we know of several songs whose vocal parts border on the theatrical, also from the early period (*Erlkönig, Gretchen am Spinnrade*) to middle years (*Der Tod und das Mädchen* D 531) and later (*Der Leiermann* D911/24). As to avoiding the sounds of speech, we have only to mention *Abschied* ("Leb' wohl, du schöne Erde" D829, 1826, on a monologue from *Der Falke*) written specifically to be performed as declamation over music. In this regard, if we return now to the Vogl case we encounter specific historical problems, the first of which is provided by Sonnleithner's own description of Vogl's lieder delivery.

Sonnleithner maintained that Vogl's singing style was more dramatic than lyrical, and that Vogl transposed certain songs into difficult and unusual keys and registers in order to create or force extraordinary effects through pitchless and whispered delivery, falsetto, or sudden outcries: i.e. that Vogl approached Schubert's songs with high theater in mind, rather than musical narration.[46] Whether Vogl devised these tricks to cover for an aging voice, or whether he was simply an actor at heart is difficult to ascertain. The answer to this question would be important, for Schubert appears not only to have tolerated Vogl's singing, but to have welcomed the famous singer's attention. In any case, Sonnleithner's opinion of this aspect of Vogl's delivery was rather deprecatory. We have period confirmation of Vogl's style in such reports as Eduard von Bauernfeld's diary entry of 17 December 1826:

> Day before yesterday a social evening at Josef Spaun's. Vogl sang Schubert's songs masterfully, but not without foppishness [Geckerei].[47]

In fairness to Vogl we must point out that his first operatic performances in Vienna had taken place in the mid-1790s, before Schubert was born, and that by the time he began to make Schubert's songs famous nearly a quarter of a century had passed. He had retired before many of Schubert's best songs were written. Anselm Hüttenbrenner, who performed *Erlkönig* with Vogl on 7 March 1821, recalled that even at that time the singer had begged Schubert to add a few measures to the piano part so that he could catch his breath.[48] Furthermore, Sonnleithner speaks only of "certain" songs, not all songs. Writing much later

---

[45] Dated 25 July 1825. Dokumente: 299.
[46] See Andreas Liess, *Johann Michael Vogl: Hofoperist und Schubertsänger* (Graz / Köln, 1954): 135-6.
[47] *Dokumente:* 389. "Vorgestern Gesellschaft bei Josef Spaun. Vogl sang Schubertsche Lieder meisterlich, aber nicht ohne Geckerei."
[48] *Dokumente:* 117.

than the Schubert period, Sonnleithner easily could have been talking about Vogl only in the latter's final singing years, including perhaps even the years after Schubert's death. Sonnleithner notes that "Vogl certainly overstepped the written boundaries the more his voice deserted him, but he always sang strictly in tempo."[49] This statement admits of two important possibilities: first, that Vogl had not always sung Schubert's songs with such theatrical effects and, second, that at least one of Vogl's good habits, which was not dependent on the state of his voice and diaphragm, had remained with him as he grew older.

For a comparison with Vogl, it would be fascinating to know more about the singing style of the opera singer Franz Rueß. When on 10 October 1822 the *WamZ* reported on Rueß's performance of *Erlkönig* (repeating the terminology in a review in Graz of 21 September), it spoke encouragingly about his declamatory delivery:

> In the last piece [*Erlkönig*], masterfully accompanied at the piano by Herrn Anselm Hüttenbrenner, Herr Rueß proved himself as a declamatory singer.[50]

Rueß, who sang Schubert's works a number of times in public, must have had a reasonably big voice, and must have been quite effective in his musical contrasts. Younger than Vogl, he tried to rival him in his theatricality. On the other hand, the word "deklamatorisch" might simply have referred to the power of his voice in *ff*, to a wide dynamic range, or perhaps to an effective enunciation. That the words of song texts were important to the public can be shown in a remark made by a critic in the *Wiener Zeitschrift für Kunst* (1 October 1822, hereafter *WZK*) about a performance of the vocal quartet *Geist der Liebe* D233 (1815, text by Kosegarten) by Haizinger, Rauscher, Ruprecht and Seipelt, "die auch das Lob einer deutlichen Artikulation verdienen" [who also earned praise through their clear articulation (of the text)].[51]

---

[49] Liess: 132.

[50] *Dokumente:* 164: "Herr Rueß bewährte sich in lezterem Gesangstücke, welches Herr Anselm Hüttenbrenner auf dem Pianoforte meisterlich begleitete, als deklamatorischer Sänger." We might remember, however, that even positive reviews can be written by less than brilliant reviewers.

[51] In general, this declamatory style in Germany and Austria, which in theaters was tangential to purely lyrical singing, needs far more musicological research. J.C. Wöltzel's *Grundriß einer pragmatischen Geschichte der Declamation und Musik, nach Schoeher's Ideen* (Outline of a Pragmatic History of Declamation and Music, according to Schoeher's Ideas) points to a long tradition. Also see: Ernst Christoph Dressler, *Theaterschule für die Deutschen, den ernsthafte Singe-Schauspiel betreffend* (Hannover / Kassel: J.W. Schmidt 1777) and J.C.F. Rellstab, *Versuch über die Vereinigung der musikalischen und oratorischen Declamation, hauptsächlich für Musiker und Componisten mit erläuternden Beyspielen* (Berlin, 1786). Anselm Bayly (Tosi's English translator-rewriter) wrote a text that mentions various national declamatory styles: *The Alliance of Music, Poetry and Oratory* (London: printed for Stockdale, 1788 / Hildesheim, Olms reprint, 1989). For further insight, one also might consult Edward Kravitt, "The Influence of Theatrical Declamation on Composers of the Late Romantic Lied" in *Acta Musicologica* 34 (1962, hereafter *AM*):18–28, although the article is not directed at Franz Schubert.

Heinrich Anschütz (b. 1785) came to Vienna mid 1820s and was engaged at the Burgtheater. Schubert evidently regarded him as the best declamatory speaker in Vienna. It was he who actually delivered Grillparzer's funeral oration for Beethoven at the gate of the cemetery. One of the polite reasons Schubert gave for evading Rochlitz's "guided commission" for a melodramatic piece [*Dokumente:* 464] was that "a Declamator such as Anschütz was not always to be had."

Perhaps we should not forget that all of the stage personalities of that day (not just Vogl and Rueß, but Anna Milder, Johann Nestroy and the other professional opera singers listed earlier in this chapter) would often have been called upon to sing and speak within the same works, particularly in the German *Singspiel* repertoire. Schubert himself wrote "melodramas" for the opera, and in one case, as we have mentioned, as a solo lied setting – *Abschied von der Erde* D829 – to be declaimed with piano accompaniment. Schubert's great contemporary, Carl Loewe, even called for singing and spoken effects within a single song, as one can hear in the last of his *Frauenliebe* (on the Chamisso text). Nevertheless, we must make a clear distinction between performance practices and composition itself. Schubert obviously knew the difference, and where he does not indicate declamation his lieder are meant to be sung throughout.

Note that Sonnleithner's distinction between lyrical and dramatic singing is not based on the emotional depth and effect with which one sang, but on the persona taken by the singer proper. When Sonnleithner wrote, "The lied singer ... himself does not represent the person whose feelings he portrays", he did not discourage vocal intensity, highly effective enunciations of the text, or the general demeanor that marks all good singing. He simply discourages any acting out of the roles portrayed through the song and any extraordinary vocalizations. Sonnleithner was reacting particularly to the decadence of mid-century lied singing, which appears to have taken on a number of theatrical qualities: 1) physical demonstration on the part of the singer characteristic of the dramatic monologue of those days: pacing the stage, casting the eyes to heaven, gesturing, etc.; 2) replacement of notated pitches and rhythms with speech; and 3) actualization of roles in a given song through extreme vocal tricks. Although in this regard he does not mention the role of the accompaniment, we can assume that he was no friend of actualization through orchestrations (whereby the piano's figures can be realized more specifically).[52]

Beyond good singing and playing, Schubert needs no particular help from the performers, for he himself defines and controls both the dramatic and the narrational aspects of his songs. In *Erlkönig* he already has underscored the drama in Goethe's story line by differentiating the roles motivically and modally, and by imparting to them separate and widely-ranging dynamics and tessiture. The motivic / modal features consist of the father's characteristically rising interval of a perfect fourth, the boy's sequence (noted above) and the Erlking's major modality within a minor-key work (which he abandons only at the end

---

[52] If indeed Vogl made great vocal distinctions between Father, Erlking and Child (and reasonably we can assume that he did), then Schubert himself may innocently have given him his blessing in this regard. Albert Stadler recalled an "Erlkönig evening" in Steyr (midsummer 1819), where the roles in this work were divided among separate voices (*Erinnerungen:* 130). Deutsch summarizes:

> "Der Eisenhändler Josef v. Koller, geboren 1780 in Steyr, wohnte am Hauptplatz [...] mit Frau und Tochter. Fräulein Josefine[...] spielte Klavier und sang. Mit Stadler im Bunde führten die vier dort einmal den 'Erlkönig' mit verteilten Stimmen auf: Schubert sang den Vater, Josefine das Kind, Vogl den Erlkönig, und Stadler saß am Klavier." [Dokumente: 83]

Arguably, Schubert must have regarded this performance as a diversion, amusing in itself but not suitable for the public or even the semi-public. We have no record, at least, of a single such performance at the Schubertiades or at the Gesellschaft, even though opportunities to do so presented themselves constantly.

as he reveals his truly threatening self to the boy). Of the three characters, one might expect the lines of the boy to be the highest and most susceptible to falsetto or head-tone delivery (representing a less-developed masculinity). They are not so, however, for Schubert's dramaticism is not merely a matter of character "imitation." The boy's outbursts must be sung full out, and the first two of these three outbursts (which constitute a kind of rising sequence) reach only to a high F—whereas the Erlking himself has the most difficult ***ppp*** lines up to G (inviting the falsetto, head- or pharyngial-voice, *voix-mixte*). Only when singing the Erlking's lines might the singer take advantage of a soft, alluring falsetto over the course of a complete section, although enormous control in the form of changing "compression" is required to reach the low notes successfully (did Vogl alter these notes upwards in order to stay better in falsetto for the role of the Erlking?). The peculiar vocal manipulation known in Italian tutors as the *voce di strega* (witch's voice) and other similar contortions have been applied to the Erlking's lines, but Viennese and German tutors support no such tradition. Considering the straightforwardness of Schubert's own singing and the lieder style in general, it would seem that his overall dynamic for the Erlking (ranging mostly from ***pp*** to ***ppp***!) would be effective enough, especially considering that ***ppp*** is a full six notches lower (counting ***mp*** and ***mf***) than ***ff***, the loudest marking in the song. The father's part remains steadfastly in the lowest register, admitting of no particular manipulation.

Balanced against these dramatic aspects are 1) the context of a narrating persona, the "fourth voice" (which, ironically, has the most dramatic music of all); and 2) a second contextual element, characteristic of narrational ballads, in the single insistent tempo (apart from the *accelerando* at the end) enforced by the pianist. The function of the pianist, or of the piano part, is an interesting one. As Edward Cone has pointed out, the accompaniment itself can be looked upon as an "analogue of a narrative voice."[53] Cone constructs an analogy in the form of a mathematical formula, wherein the accompaniment is to the vocal persona (the totality of characters, including the narrator) what the narrator is to a given poetic character. Thus, the piano part (we cannot call it an "accompaniment") provides an even larger narrative context than that provided by the singer and the totality of his text.

Concerning the difficulties of this piano part, one must express true admiration for pianists who can manage *Erlkönig* successfully. Even in Schubert's day, when pianists reckoned with far less key resistance and could bring more control to the lower registers than later was possible on the modern piano, the *WamZ* complained that:

> The triplet accompaniment sustains the life of this song throughout and at the same time imparts more unity. One might wish only that Herr Schubert had transferred the triplets a few times to the left hand, thus making the accompaniment easier to play. Repeated striking of the same tone throughout whole measures [passages] tires the hand if one takes the piece in the fast tempo demanded by Herr Schubert.[54]

---

[53] *The Composer's Voice* (Berkeley: UC Press, 1974): "Some thoughts on 'Erlkönig' ", p. 16.
[54] Dated 16 May 1821. *Dokumente:* 127: "Das Triolen-Akkompagnement erhält das Leben durch das Ganze und gibt ihn gleichsam mehr Einheit; allein es wäre zu wünschen, daß Herr Schubert es ein paarmal in die linke Hand gelegt und dadurch den Vortrag erleichtert hätte; denn der immerwährende Anschlag eines und desselben Tones durch ganze Takte in Triolen ermüdet die Hand, wenn man das Tonstück in dem schnellen Tempo nehmen will, als Herr Schubert fordert."

We know, then, that quarter = 152 (plus *accelerando* at the end) struck them the same way that it strikes us – muscle binding. But the reviewer also makes it clear that Schubert's marking was at least attempted. That fact alone puts modern Schubert thinking far ahead of modern Beethoven thinking, which, with no such period evidence as an incentive, continually gravitates towards more comfortable tempos than that master indicated – searching for its rationale from among aesthetics of the Wagnerian age. (On the other hand, some modern pianists attempt this work at a tempo faster than quarter = 152, but nothing is gained by the extra speed. In fact, some pianos of Schubert's day might well have hampered a successful repetition at speeds much in excess of 152.)

In *Gretchen am Spinnrade* the piano part as abstract narration, suggested by Cone, provides a time-line apart from the singer's message. The entire piano part represents an inexorable temporal consciousness as a backdrop for Gretchen's relatively small personal drama. We are exposed to a momentary section of this consciousness in order to contemplate Gretchen's condition, but the totality implied by Schubert can only be grasped by the gods. On Parnassus the whole story can be told, but the insistent figuration of the right hand piano part accompanied by the rocking, ballad-like left hand part actualizes a tiny section, at least, of this eternal story in a form that we know and can understand. Just so, the inexorable sextuplets of *Erlkönig* are a revealed section of narrative line, against which a local drama plays out, complete with its own local reporter. The total effect is made by the simultaneity of two contrasting elements: a crushing forward motion on the one hand, and the frail plasticity of the human events on the other. This contrast holds true in slower-moving pieces as well: *Am Meer* D957/12, *Nacht und Träume* D827, and many others. ("Forward motion" is our perceived direction of the time line, of course, but the gods can make time go backwards as well. The artistic expression of this last supposition is contained in the flashback, and it is no accident that Schubert used the technique so often and so successfully.)

In addition to expressing the abstractions we have just suggested above, however, the piano parts of Schubert songs also have a less fanciful, less abstract function in providing the mental *Bühnenbild* (the "set") for these little scenes. Schubert was the composer who most effectively turned abstract eighteenth-century figuration into nineteenth-century mill wheels, trout streams, spinning wheels and galloping horses: narrative abstractions masquerading as musical pictorialism for the entertainment of his drawing room and concert hall audiences. Of the two functions we have described here, however, this one is relatively superficial. Unfortunately, it is the one that receives the most interpretational attention from pianists in the form of tempo changes, agogics, pedalling, dynamics, etc., and lately with renewed attention to the wide palette of effects possible on old instruments. But just as Schubert's text settings are less concerned with word-painting than those of other composers and eras, the pictorialism in his piano figuration—no matter how attractive — remains a fortuitous side effect.[55]

---

[55] One of the more amusing examples of the latter occurs in a recent recording, where on the last note of *Der Musensohn* D764 one of the performers, presumably the pianist via pedal, activates a little bell that sounds suspiciously as if it had issued from a toaster oven. The recording in question is "Schubert: Lieder nach Gedichten von Johann Wolfgang von Goethe," with Christoph Prégardien, tenor, and Andreas Staier, fortepiano: Deutsche Harmonia Mundi 05472 77342 2.

The Sonic Imagination

The piano parts of Schubert's lieder are not merely accompanimental, but contextual. In an abstract sense, we might be able to play through many of them without the voice parts in order to acquire a feel for the larger narrative line involved. Liszt's enthusiasm for Schubert's songs in solo piano versions and Mendelssohn's taste for "songs without words" are not so far removed from the spirit of the piano parts of Schubert's lieder. If we factor in the simultaneous rise of the piano *étude,* which became so popular in this period and which had a noticeable influence on the motivic continuity of Schubert's impromptus, we arrive at a possible approach (at least in terms of tempo and tempo change) to Schubert's independent piano pieces as well. In theory we would not have to go to such lengths to find a reasonable approach to Schubert's piano writing, for there he has also indicated what is necessary to the performance.[56] Nevertheless, comparative reinforcement never hurts, and in the face of today's rather diversified approaches to performance it might be useful for performers to know that Schubert's music, at the very least, can be read almost directly from the page.

Accompanimental transcriptions

Schubert's song accompaniments have been transcribed in two principal ways: for voice and orchestra, and for voice and guitar. We read about such transcriptions (a practice that, after all, had had a rich tradition among great composers of the past) and speculate on how Schubert would have reacted to them. The first documented orchestral transcription of a Schubert song is Adolf Müller's version of *Erlkönig* (see his singing method in the source list, App. IIA, 1844), made after Schubert's death. By the twentieth century the Third Viennese School still had not given up the practice. Such experiments in realization, even in the hands of the finest composers – in this case, Berlioz, Brahms, Reger, Webern, etc. – can be looked upon only through philosophical eyes. One must be aware, as well, of the fact that the accompaniment cannot be delivered in such a setting without altering the demands upon the voice.

Guitar accompaniments are another case indeed. Here the voice part can remain intact in its intimacy and shading. Publishers advertised guitar settings as alternatives to piano accompaniments, simply to attract a wider buying public. Furthermore, a tradition of lieder with guitar accompaniment was already in place by Schubert's day; even the young Carl Maria von Weber occasionlly had sung and accompanied his own songs on the guitar, for example, where no piano was available. As the reader can see from the list of sources in Appendix IIA, the classical guitar in early nineteenth-century Vienna was a popular instrument whose masters and pedagogues included (among others) Franz Bathioli, Bartolomeo Bortolazzi, Mauro Giuliani, Anton Gräffer, Simon Molitor and Andreas Traeg – not to mention one of Schubert's own publishers, Anton Diabelli.

---

[56] Although in general this is a statement to be reckoned with, it has exceptions. One which comes to mind readily is the reprise section in *Grechen am Spinnrade,* where no *a tempo* is indicated, even though one is clearly meant. A number of similar examples occur in Schubert's scores, and, coincidentally, in the scores of his great admirer Robert Schumann.

For all of this strong representation, however, the guitar had, and has, a limited capacity to recreate the figuration and dynamics of piano music. We can imagine a successful *Heidenröslein* with guitar accompaniment, but not the Heine songs D957/8–13 from *Schwanengesang*. On the other hand, we were once pleasantly surprised at a concert by the late Hermann Prey at the Frick Gallery in New York in the early 1990s, where he sang the entire *Müllerlieder* accompanied by not one guitar (as Sauer & Leidesdorf also offered it) but by two. One player provided the underpinnings of the piano part and the other was free to recreate the figuration. Still in all, such experiments appear to be undertaken largely for the sake of novelty instead of necessity (the Frick Gallery, we believe, must own a beautiful concert piano).

Keys and transpositions

Schubert's lieder groups do not function completely as cycles in the way that Schumann's do, united by musical motives and larger tonal plans as well as by narrative sequence. At the most one might say that Schubert organized things harmonically to achieve continuing interest during the course of a cycle. Certain smaller groups of songs within the cycles, however, are carefully united by tonal patterns. Thus, individual transpositions within a big group such as the *Müllerlieder* or *Winterreise,* then, are reasonable except where they break up those smaller harmonic patterns. An example of the latter is the group comprising nos. 16–18 of the *Müllerlieder* (*Die liebe Farbe* in B minor, *Die böse Farbe* in B major, leading to *Trockne Blumen* in E minor). Likewise, the C-major of No. 3, *Halt!*, leads quite naturally to the G-major of No. 4, *Danksagung an den Bach,* particularly in that the last text line of the former ("War es also gemeint") is also the first line of the latter. It is therefore needless to say that these smaller, unified groups are best performed in a way that maintains and reflects their original harmonic relationships.

A particularly interesting case of Schubert's own transposition is provided by three other songs from the *Müllerlieder*. He transposed them at Zselitz in 1824: *Ungeduld,* from A major to F major; *Morgengruß,* from C major to A major; and *Des Müllers Blumen,* from A major to G major. Deutsch states that these three transpositions were for Baron Schönstein, to whom the composer had dedicated the cycle, but this supposition makes little sense. Why would Schönstein, at the age of 27, have required the lower transposition of only three songs from a 20-song cycle in which many songs remained in a high tessitura with equally high notes (with the single exception of the A in *Ungeduld*), only recently written for him and which he continued to sing for decades? Ernst Hilmar's theory that the transpositions were for Caroline Esterházy, who had an alto voice, (and we should add the possibility of their having been made for her father, a bass) is quite plausible, on evidence provided by Schubert himself.[57] At the end of *Des Müllers Blumen* Schubert writes "Die Begleitung dieses Liede kann füglich um eine Octave höher gespielt werden" [the accompaniment of this song can be played an octave higher if necessary] (See Example 1.10 on facing page). Schubert transposed at least one other song, *Rastlose Liebe* D138 (down one whole step in

---

[57] See "Ein 'geheimes Programm' in den drei wiederentdeckten Mss. zum Zyklus 'Die Schöne Müllerin'?" in *Die Brille* 11 (June 1993).

The Sonic Imagination   *31*

EXAMPLE 1.10

the 2nd autograph), and, if Sonnleithner is accurate, Schubert allowed Vogl to sing his songs in transposition. Schönstein must have sung the *Müllerlieder* as a complete, unified group during his career, but we have no proof for this supposition. Julius Stockhausen, contemporary of Johannes Brahms (and often accompanied by Clara Schumann), was the first singer officially to perform Schubert's three large lied groups as cycles. Here Schubert may not have meant to indicate the entire piano part but merely the right-hand figure, which for this song he has conceived to lie a third below the voice (at least in the first measure), no matter whether sung by a male or a female. The left hand continues to provide harmonic support as usual. Incidentally, in terms of sound and style, Schubert's concern with the right hand part here may give us a significant hint about balance, specifically that the voice should not dominate, but that (unlike the way we usually hear this Lied sung) the two lines should have equal weight.

On a technical note: Schubert's choice of B minor for *Die liebe Farbe* and B major for *Die böse Farbe* may not have been based solely on his sense of irony, i.e. with the stock harmonic imagery of major for "positive" (happy) and minor for "negative" (unhappy) reversed. He could have chosen these keys according to the relative strength of their beating patterns on a piano tuned in one of the well-temperaments still in fashion, whereby certain keys beat faster than others. On a piano tuned in one of the well temperaments designed for everyday use, B minor, directly related to the common key of D major, would beat far less obtrusively than B major, a more unusual key. The effect of faster beating is unpleasant, and thus B major would be more suitable to *Die böse Farbe,* despite the conventions of tonal imagery. Evidence against the well-temperament theory, however, is provided by Streicher (see p. 32), who describes the process for tuning in equal temperament as if it were quite normal for the time. Hummel (1828, written 1826) confirms that equal temperament had superseded the others, but still mentions Kirnberger's well-tempered tuning (see below) as having once set a standard. At what keyboard Schubert might have composed *Die schöne Müllerin* cannot yet be determined, if indeed he composed it at the keyboard at all. The instruments which he knew ranged from extremely old-fashioned (without pedals and some still possibly with single actions) to the latest models that he tried out in the shops.

Temperaments and tuning

For players who prefer Schubert on historical instruments or modern copies thereof, the choice of a proper temperament still should present no problems. By the turn of the nineteenth century, equal temperament (at least for pianos) was accepted and widely described. See, for example, Johann Andreas Streicher, *Kurze Bemerkungen über das Spielen, Stimmen und Erhalten des Forte-Piano* (Vienna, 1801/2). Streicher's booklet concentrates more on the maintenance of the instrument rather than on musical and technical issues, and thus it is not a piano method *per se*. Classic piano methods, however, often included sections on tunings (cf. Starke, 1819–21; Junghanns, before 1824; or Hummel, 1826/28), describing some form of equal temperament. We say "some form" of equal temperament, because from the rudimentary instructions contained in such treatises no one could learn to tune the sophisticated equal temperaments that we use today. Indeed, piano tuning as a profession was just beginning to emerge. Thus, considering Austria's traditional lag in technical thinking, we cannot say for sure how much a typical Viennese tuner might have known about the intricacies of counting beats and setting temperaments, even by Schubert's time.[58]

Undoubtably, the older well-temperaments continued to be used by many players who tuned their own instruments, and possibly even by some few professional tuners. Hummel's pianoforte treatise contains a statement to the effect that Kirnberger's most famous tuning (now known as "Kirnberger II") was still theoretically in use, although Hummel makes it clear that equal temperament had taken precedence. We must remember that only the harmonically simpler music of an older language would still have withstood the well-temperaments. Hummel's own music demanded an equal temperament, and certainly Schubert's music, with its beautiful enharmonic modulations and full range of key areas, could not have been presented successfully in anything but equal temperament.

The news, however, is not all good. One of the most astonishing problems connected with the now 200-year old tradition of performing chamber and orchestral music with pianos tuned in equal temperament (today virtually 99% of cases) is the almost complete and consistent refusal by other musicians to tune their instruments accordingly. We refer principally to string players, of course, and the number and importance of affected works (for Schubert, as well as for all others) are legion. As an example of the problem, when an A=440 is taken by a violinist as the referential pitch for tuning, the G-string will

---

[58] Certainly such modern tuning habits as octave-stretching in the extremities of the modern keyboard (bass notes downwards and high treble notes upwards) must have come into use after Schubert's day, increasing with developments in keyboard range, structural strength and string tension.

The Sonic Imagination

turn out to be about one-half of a cycle flat in relationship to the same G on the piano: in practical terms, about one cancellation beat in every two seconds. Nevertheless, almost all string players religiously tune their instruments in perfect non-beating fifths, as if the world were still hearing music in the old eighteenth-century well-temperaments (which indeed had featured some non-beating fifths). This blithe non-acceptance of a newer reality has given rise to innumerable problems *vis-à-vis* the piano, and in the long run it has caused millions of listeners to readjust their ears to what is truly an unnecessary technical mediocrity. Thus, we have moved an entire mountain, as the saying goes, to suit a rather misinformed and quite stubborn little band of prophets dressed in tails. Concert- and recital goers who are inclined to disbelieve this statement are invited to keep track of the number of times that string players or whole string sections take anything but an A directly from the piano: i.e. no E, D, G or C.

Translations

The appropriateness of singing any composer's songs in translation centers around the musical word painting: whether or not it is local and specific, or whether it exists at all. Franz Schubert makes most of his connections between the text and the music at a general, atmospheric level; but occasionally we find localized word-painting, some of it quite effective. As an example, the word "Hammerschlag" in *Das Geheimnis* D250 (m. 36):

EXAMPLE 1.11

We can think of no more wonderfully effective word-painting than the treatment of Death's last tones in *Der Tod und das Mädchen* (predominantly in D minor). Here, on the word "schlafen," Death seeks to pacify the girl with his peaceful drop from the dominant to the tonic, and Schubert, with stunning foresight and impact, makes it the major tonic. Where such moments exist it would be difficult to support the idea of singing a Schubert song in translation, unless in such places, of course, the translator managed to find either a cognate or some word with the same meaning and color as the original one.

EXAMPLE 1.12
(last 7 mm)

Of course, in songs where the musical imagery contributes principally to a general atmosphere, and where no specific words are underscored in the manner shown above, translation must be a plus. *Der Leiermann* is a good example, and it is no accident that the early twentieth-century singer Harry Plunket-Greene could have had such success with this song in English as he did.[59] Schubert creates the major effect here through the abstract litany of the *Drehleier* itself, and the narrator's words function independently – holding, of course, to the bleak mood conjured up by the piano part.

Schubert composed the *Drei Gesänge für Luigi Lablache* (D902) to Italian words[60] and then himself supplied German texts as well. If we take seriously the *WamZ's* remark (above) about clear enunciation, then we must assume that the actual sense of the words was as important to composers and listeners as the music itself. It would have suited Schubert better, apparently, that a tale was understood than to worry over the musical imagery imparted to single words as in the late-Renaissance Italian madrigal. For this reason, it appears most reasonable that novice lieder singers with limited command of German learn the songs first in their native language, if for no other reason than to master the narrator's art. We cannot help but remark, on the basis of long experience, that many singers and listeners outside of central Europe find German lieder more beautiful in the original language not because they know that language, particularly, but for exactly the opposite reason, because they do not know that language. This preference has less to do with some odd form of reverse cultural snobbery, however, than with the mistaken idea that Schubert's music alone could impart the proper mood of a lyrical poem or give a true

---

[59] His recording has been re-released on LP by EMI (Schubert Lieder on Record, RLS 766).
[60] *L'incanto degli occhi* and *Il traditor deluso* (Metastasio) and *Il modo di predern moglie* (poet unknown).

feel for the emotions evoked by the events related in a ballad. We submit that no serious lied singer, and without question no historically-minded singer, will want to remain unfamiliar with the subtleties of the German language. We have seen above that close attention to the words to *Gretchen am Spinnrade,* for example, helps not only to understand the song in general, but to define its emotional structure and suggest performance choices as well.

CHAPTER II

The Thematic, Structural, and Temporal Imagination

We can have no doubt that Schubert's early conception of structure, at least in instrumental music, was deeply rooted in tradition. We find many three- and four-movement sonata-form works from this period, wherein the tonic-dominant axes determine structure in the way they had done for decades before. Nevertheless, beginning with Schubert's earliest output we also find this inherited formal-harmonic language existing side-by-side with a personal musical vision which challenged profoundly the normative aspects of that language as we now understand it. For example, amongst a number of youthful instrumental works with cyclical tonal schemes (beginning and ending in the same key), we suddenly find the String Quartet D18 (1811), which progresses in its first movement from the initial c-minor tonality of the slow introduction to a g-minor main section, then to a menuetto in F major and an andante and finale in B♭ major. We cannot chalk up this abnormality to immaturity, for we find the same avoidance of tonal closure in a lovely work from 1817, the Sonata in A♭-E♭ D557, ignored since its first publication in 1888.

Nowhere, however, is Schubert's romantic-progressive thinking more evident than in the themes and corresponding tonal structures of the important works of the 1820s, such as the *Wanderer* Fantasy, the later sonatas, the mature chamber works and the last two symphonies. By that time he appears to have developed an approach to internal form characterized by the repetition and gradual variation of small motivic and thematic modules in order to achieve the great lengths of his movements. It was in such contexts that the harmonic innovations mentioned above were most effective, for the repetitive modules insured intelligibility even within remote harmonic regions: familiarity within unfamiliar contexts. Nothing could make more sense, and yet no other important composer in history has been criticized more freely for his sense of structure. Disagreements concerning the proper performance approach to such "problems" have been many and varied.

Perhaps we might approach this difficult topic by mentioning some points of modern agreement about structure and performance in Schubert, no matter how elementary they may appear. For example, no longer would we interrupt a major work in order to accommodate a virtuoso instrumentalist or singer in the performance of a completely unrelated work, as often was done in concerts of Schubert's day in Vienna. Nor have serious modern concert societies yet reacquired the nineteenth-century habit of presenting only certain movements of larger works (although this is indeed a growing practice among classical radio disc jockeys and repertoire planners who plead a shortened attention span on the part of modern listeners). Here the reader may protest that these two points are so absurdly self-evident that we hardly need mention them, and yet they may represent the only patch of terra firma known to us along this difficult path.

Repeats

As we approach other fundamental questions, such as whether to take Schubert's repeats, we discover less and less agreement about performance in light of structure. For example, although one might presume that we have learned to respect Schubert's repeat signs, it was only a few short years ago that Edward Cone could still lament a common failing in this regard. Having noted that one must take the repeat in the first movement in Mendelssohn's *Italian* Symphony because of singular material that does not reappear until the coda, Cone pointed to an apparently widespread lack of structural compulsion concerning a similar situation in Schubert's music:

> The first ending of the opening Moderato of Schubert's B♭ Sonata contains material heard nowhere else in the movement, and the contrast of its harmonic directness is needed to justify the striking modulation that constitutes the second ending. Yet who would be bold enough to repeat this exposition in a public recital? [1]

Cone's observations were made in 1968, but they still apply to some conservatory thinking, teaching and practices today. Teachers still pass on to unsuspecting pupils the misinformation that many of Schubert's repeat signs are optional instructions. If resultant practices are meant to make things easier for the listener, however, we can only state that they achieve just the opposite. Listeners who are not given the second chance to sort out one of Schubert's great harmonic journeys, for example, through an exposition repeat, have not only been misguided by the player, but actually deprived of a major roadsign.

We cannot say exactly when or why the practice of ignoring repeat signs arose. Presumably it happened in the course of the mid-to-late nineteenth century, but certainly by the early recording age, when the impetus for doing so became entwined with considerations of limited roll or disc space. It may well have arisen during the formative age of German musicology (the 1880s), which coincided with the age of through-composed sonata forms, including even some of Brahms's works. The state of sonata forms in that day may easily have influenced the vision of performance practices in an earlier day, in which case we must exercise great caution in abiding unwittingly by rules for which the explanations have been lost. In the absence of hard evidence to the contrary, our first instincts must be to take Schubert's sonata-form notations at face value, including the repeat signs. This statement applies as well to those movements

---

[1] *Musical Form and Musical Performance* (NY: Norton):52–54. According to the evidence of recordings, at least, serious interpreters of Schubert's music indeed were respecting that repeat at the time Cone wrote; but perhaps they represented a minority.

with repeated second halves (cf. D537/1, D664/1 or D557/3), where performers may resist presenting developmental and concluding material again, having reached "the end." Modern performers argue for a linear approach to sonata form, wherein a movement is generally considered to have only one beginning (despite the fact that they may have already taken an exposition repeat!), leading logically to only one end (despite the fact that immediately following this "end" one is confronted with a pesky repeat sign written by the composer himself, when he was presumably in some state of sobriety).

It may appear inconsistent for Schubert to have combined what we might regard as an old-fashioned practice (repeats in sign) with harmonic structures on the cutting edge of musical art. But we must remember that 1) Schubert's time was not yet the age of through-composed sonata forms; 2) that even during and after that age some composers continued to write repeat signs in sonata structures; and 3) most importantly, that the very presence of unusual harmonies must have demanded a commensurate reaffirmation of "navigational" intelligibility over the course of the form.

In the matter of scherzos and menuets as sonata forms we find an almost universal agreement among modern performers that reprise repeats may and should be dropped, although the reasons given for doing so are far less convincing than that for deleting second half repeats (above). Here it is maintained that the reprise repeats are vestigial and that to take them would devote too much time to such a diminutive form as a minuet or scherzo. Thus we have (1) an historical argument, and (2) a "musical" argument, which latter we shall ignore for reasons stated in the preface to this study. But is even the historical argument valid? These same performers drop reprise repeats in minuets as far back as Mozart, Haydn and even J.S. Bach: composers who wrote in the heyday of the courtly minuet. How far back must we reach, then, before such repeats can be considered functional: Kusser, Muffat, Lully? We see immediately, of course, that the historical argument hinges upon a single consideration: whether or not the minuet is played within or apart from the context of a larger work, such as a sonata or a suite of dances. The same minuet played apart from a larger work, for example, at a ball, wedding, or party, is presumed to require the reprise repeats as if those added 30 seconds made all the difference! None of this makes sense: Lully's menuets were played in the context of ballets within operas. Dance pieces for general participation (in Schubert's day menuets, *ländler*, waltzes, *deutscher*, etc.) were played, often improvised, in chains – which means that they, too, were part of larger contexts. A single musical piece was not strung out through repeats over the whole length of a dance; nothing might have been more boring. What we possess in the way of single written-out dances – for example, from the *Anna Magdalena Notebook*, or, in a faster tempo, Schubert's two Scherzi D593 – are merely prime examples of the form, nothing more. The commonly advanced argument that dance forms within sonatas and suites gradually developed a different character – having acquired, perhaps, a slower or faster tempo (which of these is correct?), or perhaps more or less room for ornamentation (which of these is correct?) – makes even less sense. The validity of this argument cannot be demonstrated in the least until the advent of the scherzo (Beethoven), in which case a demonstrably increased tempo would appear to render repeats even more acceptable.

Here, although we must be cautious in comparing Beethoven to Schubert, we sometimes find hints in Beethoven's music which at least may raise some of the right issues for Schubert. In most of Beethoven's piano sonatas beginning with Op. 10/2 (where he writes out a varied scherzo reprise in the *Allegretto*) and 10/3 (where he specifies *Men.D.C.,ma senza replica*) we usually (but not always) find clear indications of his wishes. As often as he called for *senza replica,* however, we cannot assume that he gradually intended a performance practice of that nature for the scherzo form in general. In the scherzo of the late Sonata Op. 110, for example, Beethoven writes out a literal reprise, including the original repeat signs. These repeat signs are clearly not vestigial; he had no reason to write them out a second time if he did not wish them to be followed. Schubert's scores do not provide us with many such hints. Nor can we arrive at the answer contextually, i.e. what was generally practised among performing musicians, for not much of Schubert's instrumental music was played in public or by musicians outside of his circle. He supervised those performances, and we can presume that he had specific ideas on the matter of repeats. The only contextual evidence we might wish to consider is Beethoven's continued reliance on repeat signs, which would indicate that dropping repeats in reprises was by no means the universal performance understanding in Vienna, as we have been led to believe by our recent musical ancestors. Thus, in the absence of evidence to the contrary, it would appear most logical (if we truly wish to come to know Schubert's music) to take all marked repeats.

Whereas concerning repeats we have developed historical arguments – right or wrong – to back our practices, in other cases we fly entirely blind (or at least instinctually). As an illustration we might cite the problem of joins between sections, for example between the end of the scherzo B section and the beginning of the trio in the *Grand Duo* Sonata D812, where almost all performers come to a complete stop, most likely with the intention of preparing the listener for a contrasting affect. This practice, acquired perhaps, through unintentional emulation, interrupts the continuity of the movement; and although not a scrap of historical evidence exists to support it, the habit is now so ingrained, in this work, at least, that to perform the movement without the accustomed *caesura* now sounds unnatural ("unmusical" is the argument) to many modern players.[2] And yet in other Schubert scherzos or menuets, many of these same players would proceed directly to the trio, for not to do so in these cases would seem equally "unmusical". In the Preface we have explained the problem of "musical" judgments concerning performance practices, and we can only reiterate here that in the absence of written instructions to the contrary, trios remain a consistent part of the metrical flow initiated with their corresponding main sections. Related to this last issue is that of voluntary *ritards* into trios, separate tempos for trios, and *ritards* before returning to the A section. Here Schubert may have provided some interpretable indications, which we will consider in Ch. VI under "Tempo Fluctuation." Further mapping considerations *vis-à-vis* tempo concern the planning of proportion itself: for example between slow introductions and main sections, which we also will discuss in Ch. VI.

Harmonic Direction, Repetition and Length

Structural issues in the context of performance become even more thorny as we consider Schubert's historical-theoretical position. Musicologists began to grapple with

---

[2] A performance of this passage without the *caesura* can be heard on the author's own recording of this work (Klavier KCD 11094) with Camelia Sima, made in 1997.

this subject in the early years of this century, noting Schubert's "problematic" departure from traditional Viennese sonata-form thinking. This position rested upon two main assumptions: first, that Viennese structural thinking through Beethoven could be defined as a unified phenomenon; and second, that it found its highest development in Beethoven's music. In this paradigmatic view Schubert's structural procedures were found wanting, and even his motivation found lacking. We have already listed the problems at the beginning of this section, but perhaps we can be more specific about them here. The accusations against Schubert include: 1) a propensity for unvaried recapitulations and internal section repeats; 2) a reliance upon harmonically coloristic and additive-repetitive structural scaffolding in the place of true thematic disassembly and linear development; and 3) the sheer length of certain movements, incorporating some or all of the above characteristics. Although each of these characteristics can be found in Beethoven's music as well (perhaps in lesser abundance), there they were viewed as marks of originality; in Schubert's music they were viewed as a source of conceptual difficulty. Historically speaking, the best thing to be made out of these characteristics was to identify them corporately as a procedural watershed; composers from Robert Schumann to Gustav Mahler would follow along Schubertian lines of structural thinking. Johannes Brahms's position in this scheme would begin to present some difficulties, but only with Arnold Schoenberg would composition turn truly once again to the linear, thematic development so highly prized in the works of Beethoven. Here we cannot take the space to review the individual contributions to this general theory, of which we have presented the merest outline. An excellent starting place for the interested reader to pursue the topic is Joachim Hinrichsen's *Sonatenform ...* (see App. IIB), which also contains a useful bibliography for further study.

Critics in Schubert's own day did not discuss structural problems in the same ways that we do today. Concepts such as musical "form" had not yet been codified, at least not with any systematic pedagogical or aesthetical intent. We cannot help but think that the slow acceptance of Schubert's instrumental works was not accidental or merely a sign of the times, but was a reaction to his formal and developmental procedures in the context of length. Clearly this was the case, for example, in the rejection of the *Great* C-major Symphony D944 during his lifetime by the orchestra of the *GMF*. Technical difficulty alone could not have constituted the entire problem concerning this work, as we have so often been led to believe. This symphony presents no more technical difficulties than does Beethoven's Seventh, and yet not a critical growl was heard concerning the first performance of the latter. It would appear most credible that Schubert's large-scale instrumental works were simply misunderstood. Even the positive, supportive reviewer of the A-minor Sonata D845 in the *AmZ* (1 March 1826) shook his head at Schubert's harmonic procedures. Having praised the sonata for its elements of fantasy, originality, and harmonic inventiveness, the author continued:

> That these [melodic and harmonic] inventions are often wonderful and even more wonderfully set up ... that seems easy enough to grasp; by the same token ... with certain of the importunate and partially odd harmonies ... the present writer hardly knew where things were leading and, moreover, had to shake his head a bit.[3]

---

[3] *Dokumente:* 349. "Daß diese Erfindungen nicht selten etwas wunderlich und noch wunderlicher aufgestellt sind (besonders im ersten Satze; wo z.B. das an sich fast trockene Hauptthema nicht nur

In 1829 Joseph von Spaun wrote: "Despite all my admiration for this dear man, I am still of the opinion that in instrumental and sacred compositions we will never be able to see in him a Mozart or a Haydn, whereas in song writing he remains unsurpassed." Nothing could have been more unfair. Even Beethoven had been criticized for perceived unintelligibility. Beethoven, however, had established himself previously as a great and successful virtuoso artist and thus could remain relatively impervious to such reactions. Schubert did not live to the point at which he could afford the negative criticism.[4]

Many performers have tried to compensate for what they perceived as Schubert's formal problems. We know, for example, that in early performances of the *Great* C-major Symphony, Mendelssohn and other conductors took cuts as a remedy for length and stasis. Julius Stockhausen and others restored the deleted material in their own performances later in the century, but the notion that Schubert's scores might need such corrective applications has lingered on. In modern times a common performance reaction to the perceived laxity of Schubert's structures has taken the form of generous application of non-notated *ritards* and *accelerandos*. One masterpiece which has suffered particularly in this regard is the F-minor Fantasy D940. Professional four-hand teams and amateur enthusiasts alike have responded to the hauntingly beautiful lines of this work with an array of gestures and devices that might astonish a musician who had never heard the piece and was merely following a performance with the score. One might believe oneself listening to a performance from later in the nineteenth century, with all the freedom that one might apply to the music of Liszt or Franck. The rich tempo-flux applied to this work (not to be confused with the melodic *tenuto-rubato* appropriate to this period and style), have become so ingrained, in fact, that one almost cannot read through it with another Schubert enthusiast without engaging somewhat religiously in certain "known" *ritards* thought to enhance the searching, romantic atmosphere of the piece. A comparison of recordings available today reveals the average metronomic swing in the first section alone at a minimum of 20 points, and in odd cases a much greater maximum. A similarly problematic tradition concerns the first move-

---

auch absichtlich trocken hingesagt, sondern dann oft, und offenbar wieder absichtlich, ebenso wiederholt wird), das findet man leicht; desgleichen, daß der Verfasser mit den sich ihm zudrängen, zum Teil seltsamen Harmonien öfters (sogar was die grammatisch richtige Schreibart anbelangt) kaum gewußt hat, wohin? und was dergleichen mehr ist, wobei man nicht unterlassen kann, den Kopf ein wenig zu schütteln [...]".

[4] Georgiades points to Schubert's developmental procedures in the instrumental music as a direct outgrowth of his thematic and structural imagination as a song writer (See *Musik und Lyrik,* pp. 154ff and 177ff). Specific relationships between subject and structure are indisputable, of course, only in the case of variation movements. Nor can we point to thematic paradigms, either for variation movements or sonata forms: Schubert's opening material ranges in nature from the distinctly lyrical (*Unfinished* Symphony, both movements) to the unmistakably instrumental (*Great* C-major symphony, all movements). In length they range from the generating dactylic cell of the *Wanderer* Fantasy to full-blown periods, as in the A-minor String Quartet. In all cases his developmental techniques remain constant, and so we cannot make a general argument for cause and effect. Even if we view his procedures merely as characteristic for a lied composer our argument does not withstand logic. For one thing, we cannot prove that lieder must develop additionally, regardless of the structure of poetry; for another, Schubert began his compositional life as a creator of instrumental works and must not be pigeonholed as a lied composer merely because his recognition as a master of instrumental music was delayed. His developmental procedures must be explained in other ways and criticized, if at all, on other grounds.

ment of the *Grand Duo* Sonata D812, where, for example, in the first ending of the exposition piano teams often slow down to a crawl (and in one recording to what is, effectively, a complete stop),[5] where no tempo change whatsoever is indicated by Schubert. The flexibility problem arises in some cases from misguided basic tempo choices, which themselves arise from misconceptions about meter. In the *Grand Duo* Sonata, for example, almost all teams read the *Allegro moderato* as if it applied to the quarter. But as marked unequivocally by Schubert, it applies instead to the half.

In recent years a new approach to structural "problems" in Schubert's music has arisen, this one decidedly corrective in spirit. Arthur Godel identifies the basic thesis:

> The strongest criticism brought against Schubert's sonatas concerns the repetition of larger sections unchanged. What is meant here are the recapitulations, the prescribed exposition repeats which occur up to and in the last sonatas, and the larger sequences in development sections.[6]

The performance reaction of which we speak consists of adding ornaments in the style of the eighteenth century to Schubert's literally-repeated sections. Champions of this practice explain that the literal repetition of internal sections of movements is static and thus unacceptable. In general, performers who embrace this point of view appear to regard Schubert's scores as notationally inadequate documents in need of supplemental interpretation.[7] Such procedures have included not only free ornamentation, but harmonically altered and even newly-composed material. Sadly, of all the reactions to Schubert's structures that we have described thus far, ornamentation and newly-composed material lead us most distinctly backwards in time, characteristic, as they are, of the performance styles of a previous century. In earlier times composers indeed allowed for such additions and changes (at least they allowed for ornamentation, but could not have been thrilled by supplementary composition). By Schubert's day, however, the responsibility for ornamentation, except in opera and instrumental showpieces in the brilliant style (cf. Spohr above), already had been taken over by composers themselves. Now they either provided signs for the player to interpret or else wove their ornamentation directly into the fabric of the music itself. Oddly enough, the anti-historical practice of free ornamentation in Schubert's instrumental music, inappropriate and self-serving as it is in this context, has been introduced of late by well-known adherents of the very historical performance movement that instead should be protecting him from such anachronisms and abuses.[8]

Responses to Schubert's structural characteristics, then, have taken us in two historical directions at once: the one (great tempo swings and non-metrical *rubato*) towards a later mid-romantic period and the other (ornamentation and embellishment)

---

[5] Yaara Tal and Andreas Groethuysen, Sony Classical CD 68 240, graced with a newly unearthed but spurious cover portrait, supposedly of Schubert as a thin, darkly elegant young man.
[6] Godel: 243.
[7] See David Montgomery, "Franz Schubert's Scores: Meticulous Documents or Informal Springboards for Improvisation?" in *Die Brille* 23: 75–102.
[8] Cf. Schubert Sonatas D537 and D850 (Vivarte SK 53364), played by Robert Levin and supervised by Wolf Erichson.

Thematic, Structural, and Temporal Imagination

straight back to the eighteenth century. Neither of them pinpoints Schubert's own period or his highly personal style.

On the subject of unvaried repeats, Arthur Godel, having made the statement cited several paragraphs earlier, continues:

> Concerning exposition repeats and unchanged recapitulations, if Schubert constantly employs such conventional [structural] means, then for him, the quick-change artist, they must have compositional significance.[9]

Godel goes on to explain that the very act of repetition is an act of variation, a thought which Karl Michael Komma had formulated in more philosophical terms:

> Even in the most normal "construction of the Gesamtwerk" [citing Theodor Adorno], we cannot speak of "invariance," because from the harmonic plan alone a decisive "variance" arises. Out of harmonic striving a harmonious balance is born. Furthermore, following the events of a development section, one does not hear "sameness" in a recapitulation. "We enter the same river, and yet not the same river:"in this regard nothing has changed since Heraclitus.[10]

The length of a work, seen in this light, was not a defect or an accident of the compositional process, but a conscious objective: a kind of extended journey along which the audience could not only examine but reexamine certain specific interludes and experiences while moving constantly ahead in time.

The Heracletian viewpoint may be insightful as far as it goes, but it still may leave many readers unsatisfied as to the actual function of a literal repeat. Perhaps before attempting further exploration, we might take a wider artistic look at things, noting that the criticism of progressive structural attributes in this period was not limited to music. For example, the conservative Saxon Chancellor-cum-critic F.W.B. Ramdohr, in reviewing Caspar David Friedrich's *Tetschner Altar* (1807/8), complained of a misuse of light and shade, a lack of atmospheric perspective, the infusion of religious allegory into landscape painting, not to mention Friedrich's basic sense of composition.[11] Somehow, these complaints are not unlike those levelled at Franz Schubert. If paintings had to be "performed," and if Friedrich had died before establishing himself, his posthumous reputation might have suffered a fate similar to Schubert's.[12] Happily, he lived and was sufficiently verbal to comment upon his own radical procedures:

> The business of the artist is not the accurate representation of air, water, rocks and trees, but the representation of his soul, which his perception should reflect [in these things].[13]

Friedrich declared, then, that the admitted departures from tradition in his canvasses were not accidental, but highly purposeful. Art historians demonstrate this point by

---

[9] Godel, 243.
[10] "Franz Schuberts Klaviersonate a-moll op. posth. 64 (D537)" in *Zeitschrift für Musiktheorie* 3:II:4 (1972, hereafter *ZMT*), citing Theodor Adorno, *Einleitung in die Musiksoziologie* (Frankfurt, 1968). Heraclitus (ca. 544-484), greatest of the pre-Socratic philosophers, used the river metaphor to characterize a world in constant flux, incessant change.
[11] *Zeitung für die elegante Welt* (hereafter *ZeW*), cited in Hinz:134–151.
[12] Perhaps this was the very fate of Friedrich's young colleague, Philip Otto Runge.
[13] "Äusserung bei Betrachtung einer Sammlung von Gemälden von größtenteils noch lebenden und unlängst verstorbenen Künstlern" in Hinz:101.

showing us a specific tree that appears in several Friedrich landscapes.[14] The explanation may be that instead of painting landscapes on location, as did so many of his colleagues, Friedrich gathered some images during field trips and saved them for his studio, where he "assembled" his works. This practice reflected his apparent conception of the painterly process not in terms of a passive and linearly true representation of reality, but as an active representation (if not real, at least equally acceptable in terms of linear perspective) of the effect which that very reality had upon him. Thus it is that we see crosses and other man-made religious images where they did not really exist in the midst of such natural scenes as Friedrich's predecessors had painted simply for the sake of beauty. He was just as capable of creating the artifice of symmetry or at least of loosely symmetrical frames through the manipulation (quasi-mirroring) of picture parts which could not have had real life models in such abundance or perfection. *Das Kreuz im Gebirge* (Cross in the Fir Wood, ca. 1811) is typical:[15]

PLATE I

Caspar David Friedrich: *Das Kreuz im Gebirge*

[14] See, for example, William Vaughan, *German Romantic Painting* (New Haven: Yale University Press, 1980): 68/9, plates 41–43.
[15] Original in the Kunstmuseum Düsseldorf.

Thematic, Structural, and Temporal Imagination 45

Thus, the modular treatment of a tree or even of half a picture was part of one and the same expression of Friedrich's painterly vision. This creative manipulation also went hand in hand with a radical sense of perspective in the composition of his pictures (see further discussion of frames, below, and in Ch. VI).

Just as Friedrich might move his images around, place them in disturbing contexts, set them up symmetrically or even use them again in other contexts, Schubert may have looked upon musical structure in similar ways. Hans Költsch and Thrasybulos Georgiades described Schubert's sonata-form construct as a *Gefäß* (container) into which the composer poured a new kind of music, a concept which they shared with many scholars before and after their own times. By the time of Georgiades's publication in 1979, Michael Komma already had taken exception to the *Gefäß* or *Gehäuse* (housing) concept of musical structure, which indeed, upon first reading, would appear to engender a misleading contrast between form and content. But Georgiades probably did not subscribe to such a simplistic notion. Apart from his general theory that Schubert's instrumental music took its thematic and developmental cues from his songs, a popular concept with which we cannot entirely agree, Georgiades recognized a structural scaffolding wherein the planking consisted of similar but harmonically-changing segments progressing in size from motives to sequences, phrases and periods of sequences, to entire formal sections. Any part or combination of this planking could be deleted, replaced, fragmented, moved around or repeated at will in reaching various formal junctures and goals. The word "modular" is perhaps unattractive in a musical context, but it may help to elucidate Schubert's compositional thinking.[16]

Let us examine first an unsuccessful Schubert module, in this case an early sequence of the sort that justly has given rise to negative criticism. Then let us compare it with a great sequence, from which all composers can learn. In the following example from the A-minor Sonata D537 Schubert does not avoid a certain repetitiveness, even though the sequence comprises only three steps.

EXAMPLE 2.1
Allegro, ma non troppo: mm. 73–84

[16] For citations and a history of these issues and arguments, see Hinrichsen: 17–31.

Schubert might have sensed the weakness here and other places in this work, for although he gave the sonata a tentative number in his private log he did not publish it. Perhaps he kept it back intentionally, a surmise strengthened by the fact that he mined its second movement for thematic use in the big A-major Sonata D959.

Now we might consider a section of the Presto in the *Wanderer* Fantasy. After having spent most of the movement in A♭—D♭, and started his reprise in A♭, Schubert suddenly directs us once again towards C major for the fugue. In this way he fragments the normative scherzo form as he had done previously with the first movement in order to achieve the fantasy aspect and to connect the movements. He does not modulate linearly (by motivic-harmonic transformation), but arrives at his goal through a sequence of four-measure sections cloned rhythmically from the opening of the scherzo (*Presto*). With the sure instinct of a now fully-matured composer, Schubert overcomes the danger of stasis in this remarkable four-step sequence (one step further than in D537, described above!), and actually increases the tension by dropping measures one and four from the pattern at the last two levels.

EXAMPLE 2.2

Many analysts and teachers believe that Schubert's sequential thinking influenced nineteenth century instrumental music through Bruckner and Mahler, a difficult supposition to prove in that many of his greatest works remained unknown for such a long time after his death.[17] Other authors have mentioned Wagner's indebtedness to Schubert, but one is struck by the absence of Schubert's name in Wagner's writings. Nevertheless, whether or not Schubert's music was the direct touchstone for new structural pro-

---

[17] See, for example, Franz Grasberger, "Schubert und Bruckner" in the report of the *Schubert-Kongress Wien 1978* (Graz: Akademische Druck- u. Verlagsanstalt, 1979): 215–228. Previously, William Newman also had posited a Schubertian influence upon Bruckner, although not specifically in terms of structure. See "Freedom of Tempo in Schubert's Instrumental Music" in *Musical Quarterly* (hereafter, *MQ*): 61 (1975): 544. Recently, a comparative biographical study of the two composers has been made by Ernst Hilmar in *Die Brille* 27 (2001).

cedures in composers other than the two who knew his music best, Schumann and Mendelssohn, the fact is that music and aesthetics did change, and from historical hindsight the new era starts with Schubert.

It is only a small conceptual step from small modules to large ones, from the motive or even the small sequence to, say, an entire structural section such as an exposition or a recapitulation. As did Friedrich, Schubert must have viewed his larger forms, if only subconsciously, in useful segments. Komma notes, for example, the rather significant number of manuscripts in which Schubert breaks off at the point of recapitulation, as if to say, "the rest we already know." Clearly in such cases Schubert placed his interest in the essential sectional balance provided by a return (which he would copy out later), but not particularly in the Beethovenian thirst for continuing variation or through-composed repeats. For this reason, any artificial imitation of the Beethovenian stance through the practice of voluntary embellishment in Schubert's music is simply not consistent with Schubert's own compositional instincts. This statement holds for his building blocks at all levels.[18]

Rather than attempting to compensate for Schubert's accretive lengths through artifically-introduced deletions in form, changes in tempo, or additions to a score, our task is to embrace and enhance these lengths. Care must be taken not to treat Schubert as a companion to Bruckner and Mahler, in whose works the accretive scaffolding (especially in terms of large sequences) grew ever more weighty – in fact, dangerously so, according to Arnold Schoenberg.[19] These two late nineteenth-century composers built many prescribed moments of *ritard* and resumption into their large forms, but we cannot make such devices retroactive for Schubert – despite the fact that his music may have served in some ways as a model for those later works. In Schubert's long accretive passages the key to success lies in propelling the music forward by understanding and controlling the performing forces, the dynamics and accentuation (see Ch. III–V). In reality the small units do not remain static for long periods of time as in modern minimalism. They change quite rapidly, evolving motivically, transpositionally and spatially throughout his passagework.

Metaphors of time

When Charles Rosen writes that Schubert represents Goethe's poetry in *Gretchen am Spinnrade* D118 not only mimetically but phenomenologically, he confirms Schubert's early orientation as a song writer towards the transcendental creativity described above:

---

[18] This kind of musical construction appears to have worked profoundly upon the young Robert Schumann, who literally pieced his early works together from fragments. We see this technique in *Papillons,* Op. 2, where the Introduction was made from a previous compositional fragment and merely tacked on to the piece just before publication. All the movements of this work were designed as fragments of a larger single whole, an idea which Schumann eventually emphasized by introducing cyclical elements (tonal and motivic) to bind all of his fragments together. Although Schubert worked in longer forms, we can see forerunners of Schumann's additive structures in such movements as the *Andante* of the A-minor Sonata D537. Schumann, too, eventually came to compose in larger structures, but the modular spirit never left him. Where Beethoven might have altered the linear shape of his constellations in order to reach a desired key through direct modulation, Schumann often achieves the same goal by means of sequential steps, particularly in his larger works.

[19] See, for example, "Criteria for the Evaluation of Music" (1946), and / or "Brahms the Progressive" (1947) in *Style and Idea,* ed. L. Stein, trans. L. Black (Berkeley: University of California Press, 1975).

This is the first song in which Schubert was able to represent a double time-scale, a relationship so crucial to Romantic poetry, both the sense of the immediate present and the power of past memory and how they interact with each other.[20]

As in the mature examples above, this early lied seeks to express something beyond itself: not a greater acoustic envelope or a higher medium, but a longer time-line: a metaphoric preexistence, a simultaneous present existence and, by implication, a future existence. Rosen points out the technique by which Schubert achieves the necessary fluidity for his time-line, namely the avoidance, throughout the lied, of hard cadences with their sense of local closures. In this sense, the most perfect of Schubert's time-line works is *Der Leiermann* D911/24, with no hard cadences until the last measure (and even this is part of the repetitive fragment which represents the *Drehleier*):

EXAMPLE 2.3

In *Gretchen am Spinnrade* Schubert actually reveals two kinds of time-lines. The first is represented by a unified affect in the piano's figuration which he appears to have taken over and modified from two sources: classical motor figurations (Alberti basses, driving repeated notes and preluding patterns), as well as a newer phenomenon, the purposefully repetitive piano étude that was evolving in the early nineteenth century. The idea was to set up an image of continuance and immutability, over and against which was contrasted the second kind of time-line in the guise of a scene from life itself, narrated by the singer, ephemeral and local in its impact. The contrast between accompaniment and vocal line was merely a spin on the contrast of godliness with the mortal human condition or, more abstractly formulated, the conflict of eternal time vs. perceived time that had been played out in art at least since the days of Sophocles.

In light of this contrast let us examine two problematic places in the piano part of *Gretchen am Spinnrade*. Pianists who concentrate on the surface pictorialism of the piano part may find themselves recovering the forward motion after the *fermata* in m. 68 quite slowly, as if a distracted Gretchen had let the wheel come to a stop and now was coaxing it once again into motion (Schubert's fragmented line reinforces this picture). Later on, over the course of m. 85 to m.112, Schubert has introduced a *crescendo-accelerando* ("*poco a poco crescendo ed accelerando*"). He waits until mm. 112/113 to write "*decrescendo e ritard*," and from this point on the pictorially-minded pianist is easily tempted to bring the spinning wheel to a stop with a *ritard* that takes the music well below the opening tempo before reaching the last note. These are understandable temptations, reinforced in almost every singing studio and master class, and yet the abstract narrative function (the time-line metaphor), combined with a closer look at the text, may suggest an even more effective and interesting approach.

---

[20] "Schubert's inflections of Classical form" in *The Cambridge Companion to Schubert,* ed. Christopher Gibbs (Cambridge: Cambridge University Press, 1997): 73/77.

To begin with, most performers interpret the *fermata* in m. 68 as a long, "annunciatory" pause instead of what it really is, a brief, "inline" *fermata* (for further definition of these terms, see Ch. III). If we understand the hold as an inline *fermata*, we make no break afterwards but continue on our way merely as if having been detained momentarily by some local consideration. Indeed, that consideration can be found in the text: "sein Händedruck, und ach, sein Kuss!". Here, for the first time Gretchen, in the course of "recreating" Faust, suddenly remembers not just the way he had looked, but the actual physical contact she had had with him as well. She continues, not with this new thought (in which case an annunciatory *fermata* might have been appropriate), but in a state of denial. She shuns the erotic memory by reverting quickly to "Meine Ruh' ist hin", and the litany continues. In order to reinforce this impression, the narratively-inclined pianist begins his or her recovery in m. 69 directly upon the heels of the short *fermata*, with no break, and strictly in tempo. In the absence of other instructions, this is the most logical interpretation. Gretchen's denial does not last long; within a few measures the yearning breaks out again, and Schubert underscores it again with his *cresc. / accel.* marking. In mm. 91 and 93 he shows us the dynamic levels to be reached, and we remain *ff* from m. 93 until m. 112. Since Schubert has combined his change of dynamic mark with his change of tempo mark, presumably we reach the maximum tempo in m. 93 as well, remaining there until m. 112. Again the text guides us, for Gretchen turns her memory of the kiss into an active wish to repeat and augment the moment, this time openly embracing the erotic thought: "... ach dürft' ich fassen und halten ihn, und küssen ihn, so wie ich wollt' ...." Nevertheless, her fantasy is not long-lived; she is brought back to the inexorable line of time (for her, the present) in m. 112, and the narrative resumes. Correspondingly, the pianist resumes at exactly the opening tempo and never ritards, for the story itself has no end.

Gretchen am Spinnrade displays what we might call "layered" time lines, because they are presented simultaneously. In this kind of lied, of which Schubert wrote many, the universal line usually is established several measures before the contrasting local line enters, and continues after the latter has ended. To find instrumental models for this technique we need not search too long among the works of Schubert's Viennese predecessors: the first movement of Beethoven's C♯-minor Sonata, op. 27/2, for example. But the most obvious (and perhaps ground-breaking) instrumental forerunner is the opening motor of Mozart's Symphony No. 40, a work which Schubert may have admired more than any other instrumental masterpiece of the eighteenth century. That a symphony of the late eighteenth-century might open directly with the *allegro* section was nothing new, but that it might open with such a vague and independent accompanimental motor instead of directly with the main subject was most unusual:[21] (See Example 2.4 on p. 50.)

Although layered time lines may have been suggested to Schubert not only by other lieder but by the beginnings of certain instrumental movements, the idea could not really function throughout the complexity of an extended sonata form. The lack of hard cadences, as in *Gretchen am Spinnrade,* was possible only in shorter works (for

---

[21] That such an exposed passage was entrusted to the violas was unheard-of, and that the violas themselves were divided into two parts was a self-written invitation to symphonic disaster. To have been a fly on the wall at the first reading of that work would be worth many Schillings.

EXAMPLE 2.4

example, Beethoven's "preluding" in the first movement of the *Moonlight* Sonata). A decade later Robert Schumann indeed tried to make the idea work in the first movement of a longer work, the C-major Fantasy, and it is no accident that hard cadences to the tonic do not occur in that movement until near the end. Furthermore, Schumann required the diversion of the *Im Legendenton* section to fill out the movement, which otherwise could not have sustained such a constant time-line unbroken.

Gretchen am Spinnrade was Schubert's first attempt at such a dichotomy. He had not yet begun to think of the affect abstractly, but was still fascinated by the pictorial aspect (also relatively new for the times). Thus, while the affect of the accompaniment in this lied remains constant, the tempo fluctuates according to Schubert's instructions (two written *accelerandos* and the final *ritardando*). His tempo fluctuations, of course, do not constitute an invitation to further pianistic fluctuation, such as the traditional "undertempo-to-tempo-primo" *accelerando* in m. 69, which would present the lied as a miniature operatic scene (as many singing teachers describe it to their students). As we pointed out concerning the A-major Sonata and the G-major Quartet, above, this "scene" is not related to the opera of Schubert's day, but belongs to the pure imagination (to the phenomenological imagination, in Rosen's terms). Opera itself was a public entertainment and functioned in far more prosaic ways: even such magical moments as the Wolf's-Glen Scene or "Und ob die Wolken" in Weber's *Der Freischütz* functioned on single time lines.

Later, Schubert's time-line affects became less openly mimetic, as in, say, the piano figuration of *Liebesbotschaft* D957/1.

EXAMPLE 2.5

In vocal master classes one hears much talk of a "rauschendes Bächlein" and Schubert's "water imagery" here, but what is there, really, to support this notion? He could just as well have used this figuration to portray Gretchen's spinning wheel or any other image of ongoing motion.

Thematic, Structural, and Temporal Imagination

In some works the continuance affect, while mimetic in origin, is reduced to an *ostinato*, as in *Der Leiermann,* where the piano plays a single fragment over and over. It can also become a kind of *passacaglia*, as in *Der Doppelgänger.* Correspondingly, in terms of performance, the most important implication of the contrast between time lines, as Schubert eventually developed it, is that the continuance or "universal" line be portrayed rather strictly, in contrast to the plasticity of the local line. Because Schubert's continuance lines may have been suggested partially by instrumental models, we should not be surprised that he developed them also in his own strictly instrumental works. One of the earliest examples may be the opening of the D-major String Quartet D74, where the local line (1st violin) is intriguingly fragmentary in its first statement:

EXAMPLE 2.6

In the A-minor Quartet D804, we find an example of a highly expressive, full-blown theme in two periods floating above the motor, or strict time-line:

EXAMPLE 2.7

Many string quartets execute slight *ritards* in all voices at the end of phrases and periods, and between the major joins of this work. Such gestures, especially in the accompanimental motor, seriously weaken Schubert's contrast between strict and fluid time; they divert us from the power of the transcendental idea into the domain of the merely comfortable and pleasing, from the true intellectualism of the romantic to the safe sentimentalism of the *Biedermeier*. What we have said here about strict vs. fluid touches partly upon the concept of *tempo rubato*, which we will discuss in Ch. IV.

The layered time line is represented in a kind of "open" context: theoretically, the continuance line could have begun several measures, several pages, or several centuries before the local line enters; and it might continue afterwards with the same impression. A second type, the "closed" or "framed" time line, allows us a limited glimpse of continuance whereby the two lines appear not simultaneously, but in juxtaposition. Here a short frame of several measures occurs at the beginning and often at the end as well, surrounding a central section that represents a contrasting time line. Usually, what stands outside of the central section represents the attitude of continuance, as in *Am Meer* D957/12. Here the inexorable opening and closing chords "lock in" the plastic, mortal action:

EXAMPLE 2.8

Again, we can identify forerunners, as in Beethoven's *Bagatelle,* op. 126/6, where the powerful and frenetic opening and closing bars (identical passages, like bookends) frame a fragmented but highly expressive main section:

Thematic, Structural, and Temporal Imagination

EXAMPLE 2.9

Related to the frame in Schubert's lieder, which is often provided by the piano's introduction and postlude, is the instrumental curtain.[22] Simply defined, it is a small musical statement at the opening of a movement, often seemingly unrelated to the rest, which serves to "draw open the curtain" onto the musical scene.[23] Beethoven used the device often, as in the slow movements of the Ninth Symphony, the Piano Sonata, Op. 106/3 (a single measure), and several of the string quartets. Schubert used the device occasionally, as in the opening of the slow movement of the G-major Quartet:

EXAMPLE 2.10

He also used a modified version of the curtain in the *Unfinished* Symphony and the Fourth Symphony. In these examples the curtain returns, marking off major events. In the Fourth Symphony, it signals the recapitulation of the finale:

---

[22] A concept traceable to Hugo Riemann in *System der musikalischen Rhythmik und Metrik* (Leipzig, 1903): § 22m "Vorhänge:" 230-241.

[23] Exactly this definition can be applied to more vigorous "head motifs" as well, represented, for example, by the opening chords of Beethoven's Third Symphony.

EXAMPLE 2.11a/c

a.

b.

In the *Unfinished* Symphony Schubert reintroduces the curtain within the movement itself to separate musical statements, not unlike J.S. Bach in his "explosion" chorales.[24]

[24] In demonstrating Schubert's "break" with the *Wiener Klassik,* Georgiades (169) and others maintain that successive generations tend to fall back on principles not developed by their immediate predecessors but that they skip a generation (or unified style period) instead. How much Schubert may have known of the early glalant and the late Baroque, however, is difficult to assess.

Thematic, Structural, and Temporal Imagination 55

c.

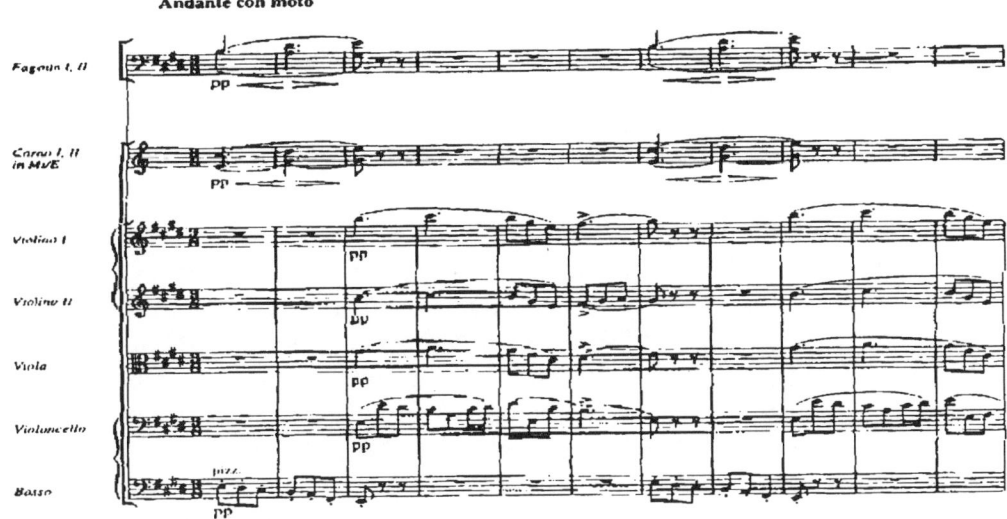

Exactly this distinction between framed (closed) and non-framed (open) forms can be shown in the paintings of Caspar David Friedrich and Phillip Otto Runge. An interesting example of the closed form is Runge's *Die Lehrstunde der Nachtigall* (The Nightingale's Lesson, 1802/4/5, Kunsthalle Hamburg), with its outer rectangular frame enclosing an inner tondo. The tondo itself encloses a thick woods through which we catch just a glimpse of an idealized world beyond. (See Plate II.)

PLATE II

Phillip Otto Runge: *Die Lehrstunde der Nachtigall*

Friedrich's closed types are numerous: within their innermost frames we find images of continuance or eternity (among his favorites were water and graves). See, for example, his now-famous *Frau am Fenster* (Woman at the Window, 1822) or *Gedächnisbild für Johann Emanuel Bremer* (Memorial Picture for Johann Emanuel Bremer, 1817) (Plate V). *Kreidefelsen auf Rügen* (Chalk Cliffs on Rügen, 1818) is typical: here the actual frame encloses a painted frame of trees, which encloses a frame of the chalk cliffs. In the center is the image of eternity, where two tiny boats sail out to a vast sea.[25] (See Plate III below.)

We note with interest that Schubert and Beethoven's frames function in the reverse from Friedrich's: i.e. with the unchanging, eternal imagery represented by the frames and the mortal imagery between. It hardly seems to matter, however. One might even argue that in Friedrich's pictures, dying and being buried, or sailing out to sea, are human events and actions, and that what surrounds them here (for example, the trees and cliffs in *Chalk Cliffs on Rügen,* the sides of a gate in *Friedhofseingang* (Entrance to the Cemetery)[26] (see Plate IV on p. 57) or a frame of trees in *Gedächnisbild für Johann Emanuel Bremer* (Memorial Picture for Johann Emanuel Bremer) (see Plate V on p. 57) is actually the immortal, the ever-renewable.

PLATE III

Caspar David Friedrich: *Kreidefelsen auf Rügen*

[25] Original in the Museumstiftung Oskar Reinhart, Winterthur.
[26] Original in the Stattliche Kunstsammlungen, Dresden

Thematic, Structural, and Temporal Imagination 57

PLATE IV

Caspar David Friedrich: *Friedhofseingang*

PLATE V

Caspar David Friedrich: *Gedächnisbild für Johann Emanuel Bremer*

Perhaps the greatest of Friedrich's open, non-framed paintings is *Der Mönch am Meer* (Monk by the Sea, 1809 or 1810).[27] Here the image of timelessness is represented by a seemingly limitless sea and earth, offering almost no sense of proportion except for one fragile human figure (Friedrich himself?) who traverses the sand:

PLATE VI

Caspar David Friedrich: *Der Mönch am Meer*

The great romantic dramatist Heinrich von Kleist found this picture highly disturbing:

> No situation in the world could be sadder and eerier than this – as the only spark of life in the wide realm of death, a lonely center in a lonely circle ... the picture appears like the Apocalypse ... and because of its uniformity and boundlessness, with nothing but the frame as a foreground, one feels as if one's eyelids had been cut away.[28]

Was the frame, either in its musical or literary form, important, then, to the sense of psycho-artistic well-being?

One of the literary counterparts of Friedrich's closed (framed) types is called a *Rahmenerzählung* (framed tale), a story within a story, which had a history in storytelling and literature centuries before it emerged as a romantic vehicle. We find a romanticized version of the straightforward narrative type in Clemens Brentano's village tragedy, *Die Geschichte vom braven Kasperl und dem schönen Annerl* (The tale of the

---

[27] Original in the Stiftung Preussische Schlösser-und-Gärten Berlin-Brandenburg.
[28] Heinrich von Kleist, "Empfindungen vor Friedrichs Seelandschaft," *Berliner Abendblätter* (hereafter *BA*), October 13, 1810, trans. Albert Boime in *Art in an Age of Bonapartism* 1810-1815 (Chicago, 1990): 582.

good little Caspar and the pretty little Anna, 1817). The tale that forms the inner story is actually a story within a story within a story, each increasingly focussed on the subject of honor. The main story tells of an old woman's quest for partial honor, to be bestowed posthumously on two doomed young lovers. It circumscribes the middle story of honor mocked and contested. Deeply imbedded in the narration, the innermost story, the lancer's tale, encapsulates honor in its purest manifestation. This inner window affords the reader a momentary vision of an idealized and unequivocal concept of honor. This perfect concept is a standard, a current that runs beneath the entire story, obscured by accounts of honor denied, delayed, compromised, or abandoned completely. Throughout the text we find songs and poetry framed in smaller contexts as well. (The text of this story is too long to reproduce here or in the Appendix, but it is easily available to the reader.)

Perhaps the best known closed-frame type in German romantic literature is the play within a play in Ludwig Tieck's *Der gestiefelte Kater,* familiar in English as "Puss in Boots." Here the goal was to deliver a satiric message safely tucked away within the heightened unreality of the fairy tale, a framed play about a talking cat. Tieck mingles the levels of his wit by allowing the spectators of the inner play to talk about that play during its progress. Thus by extension the real audience is encouraged to do the same. The total effect of *Der gestiefelte Kater* is not unlike that created by the characters in Friedrich's paintings who face into his pictures, reminding us that we, too, are looking into the larger picture. Tieck's play brings us little of the serious, cosmic vision of German romanticism, but more of the comic infinity of foible, the chaotic human to be found in all of us, revealed by a cat. Even so, the play's fairy-tale inner setting represents by its very nature a suspension of finite understanding.

The proper appreciation of myth, dream, and fairy tale requires more, however, than just a suspension of finite understanding; it requires also a suspension of time. Klingsohr's fairy tale in Novalis' novel, *Heinrich von Osterdingen* is a framed tale that seeks to suspend the narrative time of the novel. It functions as a quasi-independent section embedded within a larger structure, known as a type of mixed genre (*genre mêlé, genre mixte*), which frames it. The structural idea of the *genre mêlé* is manifold. A basic aspect is that frames mark various manipulations of time: past, present, and (theoretically) future. The most common manipulation in the superstructure of a literary work is the out-of-sequence return to the past, what later in cinema became the flashback. Another part of the idea of the *genre mêlé* is that within these frames different media can represent different concepts of speed and flow, as well as different degrees of emotion, affectation, and formality. Framing techniques also control various levels of spectator involvement with that emotion, affectation, and formality. The model for the idea lies in the drama, with its mixture of action, dialogue, soliloquy, and choral commentary. In *Heinrich von Osterdingen* Novalis represents the flow of real time and action in the narrative sections, saving the intervening dreams and fairy tales for the representation of timelessness beyond the scope of the narrative. Alice Kuzniar provides a succinct account of the technique:

> [The] initial chapter of *Heinrich von Osterdingen* establishes an exemplary structural pattern that is repeated at different intervals throughout the work. It initiates or generates a series of narrative insets, each of which attempts anew the process of encapsulation. The process of embedding is repeatedly broken by the reintroduction of the narrative, just as

Heinrich always awakens abruptly from his dreams. The end of a fairy tale or dream signals the sudden reentry of the frame whose ongoing narration stands in opposition to the closed, self-contained, timeless structure of the preceding account. Enclosure becomes nonclosure.[29]

"Enclosure becomes nonclosure:" not only does this tag suggest the existence of a larger continuum, an eternal flow on which the entire novel is overlaid, it reveals the common goal of two seemingly opposite techniques. Thus the German romantic novel – which, like its large-scale musical equivalents, has suffered extensive criticism for an apparent lack of dramatic thrust – provides us one more piece of the contextual puzzle of early nineteenth century approach to form and construction in all artistic endeavors.

A note on introductions and postludes

In the matter of introductions and postludes in Schubert's lieder, we find heavy editorial hands at work, early and modern as well. We quote from Crutchfield:

> Keyboard improvisation [in that period] was not limited to solo performances. Walther Dürr observes that the lack of piano introductions to many of Schubert's songs implies that the accompanist improvised a brief *Vorspiel.* Dürr theorizes that many of the piano introductions in the posthumous Lieder that are not provably composed by Schubert are derived from his improvisation: he characterizes these not as forgeries but as necessary complements (*Ergänzungen*) to the text in a printed edition for dilettantes. [30]

Why Crutchfield would support this point of view without testing it is unclear to us, but in any case, Dürr's implication cannot be taken seriously. The fundamental assumption that Schubert would go to the trouble of writing out a whole song but forget – or not bother (and in only select cases) – to include an introduction because he could count on it being "improvised" in performance is patent nonsense. Like Dürr's approach to ornamentation, this assumption is an example of a pre-existent theory in search of corroborating facts. Note that Dürr can say such a thing only about the *posthumous* lieder, for even he must sense that Schubert would not have allowed someone to publish their own version of a *Vorspiel* to a work of his while he lived to object. Secondly, how was a publisher who added an introduction to a Schubert song long after Schubert's death supposed to have remembered *or even known* how it had been improvised – if indeed it had been? To our knowledge, Diabelli (the chief culprit here) had not been present for most (or any?) of Schubert's performances. Furthermore, many of the song accompaniments were premiered by other pianists.

Let us test Dürr's reasoning. *Nachtgesang* D119 and its companion *Trost in Tränen* D120 both sport unauthenticated introductions (however brief). To our knowledge, the Diabelli firm published D120 in 1835, 21 years after it was written, and D119 in 1850, 36 years after it was written. We have no record of a performance of either song while Schubert lived, and yet the publishers were supposed to have "reconstructed" these introductions from Schubert's "improvisation"! Further: *An den Mond* D259 was written in 1815. Again we have no record of a performance, and again the publishers "reconstructed" Schubert's "improvisation," this time 35 years later, an impressive trick!

---

[29] *Delayed Endings: Nonclosure in Novalis and Hölderlin* (Athens: Univ. of Georgia Press, 1987): 108.
[30] Crutchfield cites *NSA*/1a through 5a, p.xiv: IV/6-7, p.xii.

Apart from Diabelli's precedent, another cue for the modern addition of introductions to the lieder appears to be the existence of multiple versions, where Schubert himself added introductions to later versions (never the case in reverse). This fact would constitute an argument for addition only if we could view each subsequent addition as a stepping stone in the compositional process, culminating in a "final" version. This may not always be the case, however. One might argue, for example, that in *An Emma* D113, Schubert had not made up his mind about the basic meter. But even here he composed the second version in 6/8 to its end before returning to the 2/4 meter of the third version. None of these versions is a "final" conception, and each retains interesting features lacking in the others. In fact, Schubert published both the second and the third versions of *An Emma*. If we wish to examine the compositional processes that led to finished works, then we must begin with the hundreds of fragments, autograph torsos and first drafts that he left behind, but not always with completed versions.

How, for example, would we decide which of the two versions of *Selma und Selmar* D286 to regard as the "authoritative" one?

EXAMPLE 2.12

Since one of the autographs of this work is lost (the Deutsch-Aderhold *Thematic Index* calls it the "first autograph"), we have no way of knowing which of the two versions came first.[31] In such cases (and cases of undated manuscripts as well) the catalogue places the version with the introduction last. Such placement is a mere theoretical conceit, for it is perfectly possible that Schubert had given the earlier version the introduction. The same caveat applies, for example, to the five versions of *Die Forelle* D550, only one of which has an introduction. In any case, performers with a true sense of history need follow only two simple rules: 1) do not mix versions; and 2) do not assume that Schubert preferred one version over the other, chronology notwithstanding. This last principle may be difficult to accept, for we have been taught since childhood about the "creative struggle" towards a final masterpiece – characteristic, principally, of great nineteenth-century composers. Composers of all periods, however, would attest (or would have attested, we think) to the frailty of such a concept, for without the right to change one's thinking, creativity would soon be saddled with the responsibility of achieving lasting perfection: a journalistic notion at best.

---

[31] Otto Erich Deutsch, *Franz Schubert: Thematisches Verzeichnis seiner Werk in chronologischer Folge*, ed. Werner Aderhold (Kassel: Bärenreiter, 1978).

Having tried to soften the "immortal composer" image for Schubert (at least from his point of view), we still must agree that for a man who averaged some 50–60 significant compositions per year, to take the time to rewrite a song or even completely reconsider the setting of its text (often numerous times), bespeaks a constant state of compositional creativity. Indeed Schubert revised or recomposed many of his songs several times. In most cases we can assume that he found a form with which he could live *at that time* (after all, he stopped rewriting at some point), and in such cases he prepared a final version, with or without an introduction, postlude or interludes. In this regard it is interesting to note that in all of Schubert's manuscripts (including his first drafts), not a single introduction is added afterwards, say, at the end or elsewhere in a manuscript. If Schubert decided that a song could use an introduction for some reason, he wrote out the entire song again. This fact alone should deter us from the somewhat presumptuous notion that we as performers might be able to judge when a song without an introduction should receive one gratis from our own (generally less practiced!) hand.

For the convenience of singers and pianists who perform from older editions, the following is a list of some well-known songs (based on the Bärenreiter catalogue) often printed with unauthentic introductions. In cases of lost autographs, other introductions printed by Diabelli may be unauthentic as well:

D119 *Nachtgesang*
D120 *Trost in Tränen*
D255 *Der Rattenfänger*
D259 *An den Mond*
D403/1 *Ins stille Land*. First version (of 4) published with Diabelli's spurious introduction. This mishap is odd and unfortunate in that versions 3 and 4 have authentic introductions.
D492 *Zum Punsche*
D530 *An eine Quelle*
D564 *Gretchen im Zwinger*. Material added at the end.
D623 *Das Marienbild*. Introduction has been added again at the end.
D847 *Trinklied*. The entire accompaniment has been added.
D875 *Mondenschein*. Although Schubert wrote an accompaniment, the publisher substituted a spurious one.
D912 *Schlachtlied*. The publisher released this work for "voluntary accompaniment by pianoforte or physharmonic," possibly an idea of Ferdinand Schubert's.

One cannot help but note again that every work listed here was published by Anton Diabelli during the latter's supervision of the firm. The saddest fact is that each of these unauthenticated *Vorspiele* is derived utterly from the accompaniment of the song which it precedes. We cannot help but observe that any amateur pianist who has accompanied his or her church choir for more than a month has learned to do likewise. Are we dealing with a real composer of genius here, who knew what he wanted, or merely a musical amateur who needed help at every turn? In Diabelli's case, the frivolous addition of selected introductions smacks of sales-interests, as well as the limited imagination we might expect from a composer of his ilk. Franz Schubert, on the other hand, appears to have understood the difference in impact between starting a song with an introduction, and not. Readers may wish to compare the four Novalis Hymns D659–662, obviously written as a group within the same creative burst. Here the first and last hymns are provided with short introductions and the middle two begin directly with the text:

EXAMPLE 2.13 a/d

(Novalis Hymns incipits)

a. Hymn I: *Wenige wissen das Geheimnis der Liebe*

b. Hymn II: *Wenn ich ihn nur habe*

c. Hymn III: *Wenn alle untreu werden*

d. Hymn IV: *Ich sag es jedem, daß er lebt*

Perhaps Diabelli would have argued that the songs that he touched up were not part of cycles, but were independent. Thus he was merely offering his buyers a contextual bonus, not unlike an art dealer who throws in the frame with the painting. The difference, of course, is that art dealers, even the slipperiest of them, do not paint their frames directly onto the canvasses.[32]

    Having said all of the above, however, we must mention that in concerts and musical evenings of that day, unlike the more stylized variety of our own day, some form of "preluding" (as it was then called) between songs occurred; this practice served either as a bridge between songs in unrelated keys, or simply to establish a key for the singer where a song had no introduction. On the subject of "preluding" or improvisation in general, none of the Viennese tutors mention a practice of extracting a section from the song or work to follow. After all, music-making in the salon was not the same as hymn-singing in church.

---

[32] Why was Diabelli so selective in adding his introductions? Why did he not add them to: D197, 217, 218, 219, 263, 280, 290, 321, 432, 434, 508, or 632, for example? The answer must lie, somehow, with his probable percepton of their "lesser" commercial value.

* * *

Through the comparative analysis above we hope to have placed Franz Schubert firmly in the company of the greatest painters and writers of his time, and to insure that those who perform and hear his music today are aware of his place in the development of artistic ideas. Biographical history shows us clearly that he himself was not cognizant of his own importance to the larger romantic picture, but this fact merely redoubles our zeal to grant him this distinction posthumously. Although not every Schubert score reveals the radical, transformative ideas that we have discussed above, the spirit of romantic intellectualism appears to have permeated his imagination from the middle teen years of the nineteenth century to the end of his days. In his mind this startling romanticism appears to have existed simultaneously with older classical precepts. For this reason, also, we must trust Schubert in his choices of framed and unframed lied settings, taking each version of each work on its own terms. It was his job to work through such ideas, and not ours to impose upon his works in hindsight.

The single most important performance hint to be derived from the rich artistic metaphors of time and temporal manipulation we find in Schubert's music is that the distinction between "finite" (local) and "infinite" (universal) time lines can be maintained only when one of them remains in a constant tempo, while the other supports the humanly expressive plasticity for which the composer has made ample allowances. Often, and especially in cases of the great musical warhorses, the maintenance of this interesting dichotomy will be uncomfortable to those of us who have learned these pieces in ways consistent with late nineteenth-century practices. Nevertheless, if we can overcome such prejudices, we will learn to understand a profoundly new and different Franz Schubert.

Chapter III

Reading Schubert's Music

Assessing editions and choosing scores

Nothing is more crucial to performance than a good score, and beyond that nothing is more important than the ability to decipher it. Unfortunately, in the case of Franz Schubert's music we are compelled to fight uphill battles on both accounts. Let us begin with the concept of a good score. Franz Schubert surely must have performed his own music often from manuscript, although he and the friends who played his music probably preferred to read from the published versions where available. Today, of course, for almost any of his works we can purchase what we assume to be a well-edited, printed score. We base our preference on the reputation of the publisher (often we look for so-called "urtext" editions), the attractiveness and usefulness of the layout, not to mention, of course, the price. Our responsibilities as interpreters begin at this point, then, with the most careful possible choice of scores.[1]

    How do we really know what to expect, however, from a good Schubert edition, one that represents an accurate account of his written legacy? Few performers have access to autographs, even in facsimile, for comparison. Even fewer have acquired the experience necessary to sort out the seemingly enigmatic and often-conflicting musical statements that Schubert left in manuscript. Therefore, we rely almost completely upon editors, whose job it is to create useful scores out of the myriad scratches, pokes, strokes, circles, ovals, arches, slashes, hatchings, smears and other markings that comprise the totality of Schubert's music in its autograph state, not to mention the information garnered from early prints and corrections. Even among experienced editors, however, the results that must emerge from this process as finished documents are not self-evident.

    For comparison, we offer four "urtext" prints of the opening measures of the F-minor Impromptu D935, each brought out by a highly respected publishing firm: Breitkopf und Härtel (*GA*), vol. ed. Julius Epstein; Henle, ed. Walter Gieseking; UE, Schott: Wiener Urtext Edition, ed. Paul Badura-Skoda; and Bärenreiter (*NSA*), vol. ed. Christa Landon† / taken over by Walther Dürr. We found eight major points of difference in the space of the first eight measures, affecting stem direction, beaming, dynamics, slurs, other articulation,

---

[1] Cf. Elmar Budde, "Bemerkungen zur Problematik praktischer Ausgaben" in *Schubert–Kongress Wien 1978: Bericht*, ed. Otto Brusatti (Graz: Akademische Druck- u. Verlagsanstalt, 1979).

and even pitch: an average of one major disagreement per measure among only four editions. Had we examined the some dozen different editions that modern players still use, the results would have been significantly more daunting. If, then, to this complexity we add the fact that most performers take or leave what they want from any given edition (a process often confused with "interpretation"), we can hold out little hope to musicians with a genuine interest in discovering Schubert's ideas and intentions.

EXAMPLE 3.1a/f

a. Breitkopf und Härtel (*GA*), vol. ed. Julius Epstein

b. Henle, ed. Walter Gieseking

c. UE, Schott: Wiener Urtext Edition, ed Paul Badura-Skoda

d. Bärenreiter (from *NSA*), vol. ed. Christa Landon†/taken over by Walther Dürr

All four editors have taken the autograph materials and/or the first edition as sources, yet their interpretations reveal significant variance. Some of the differences arise from layout decisions about beaming, stem direction, note distribution between staves, placement of dynamics, number of measures to the system, etc. Generally, these things are regulated according to house policies and have little bearing on performance. But sometimes they can have a direct effect on a musical gesture: consider the different layout decisions reflected in m. 3, descending right hand line, which will serve as our first point of conflict:

1) In example a. the editor shifts the right-hand line to bass clef at the beginning of the bar; in b. the editor waits until halfway through the new measure to shift; in c. the editor shifts at the beginning of the measure, but also drops the whole line into the lower staff; and in d. the line is allowed to remain in treble clef and on the top staff all the way down.

Editors a.-c. might argue, reasonably, that modern players have learned to "read through" changes of clef, and that such layouts have little effect on the actual phrasing, which in any case must be consciously thought out by the player. Editor d. might argue just as reasonably that an unbroken visual pattern of descent helps the player to arrive at that decision, and that any help an editor can give should be appreciated. Before we discuss the relative merits of these arguments further, let us consider other editorial decisions which are more demonstrably crucial to artistic interpretation:

2) In measure one, a.–c. show a *fp* followed by a *decrescendo*, whereas d. shows *fp* plus an accent, but no *decrescendo*. To muddy the waters further, editor c. (Badura-Skoda) suggests that *fp*⎯⎯ be read as *f*⎯⎯*p*.

3) In measures one–three, a. and b. break the overhead slur into two measures plus one, but c. and d. allow it to span the entire three bars of right-hand descent.

4) In measure two, a. alone has not connected the left hand's top whole-note "f" to the half note in measure three.

5) In measure three, a. alone gives a separate slur to the last two beats of the left hand.

6) In measure four, a. and b. show no articulation marks in the first two beats, whereas c. shows a *staccato* dot for only the right hand in beat two; d. gives *staccato* strokes (most likely presuming a sharper treatment) for both hands, but only for beat one.

7) In measure seven we see a replay of the accent-vs-*decrescendo* hairpin.

8) In measure eight b.–d. disagree about the lower pitches in the turns, whereas a. offers no opinion: on beat one b. gives E♮ in the first beat, whereas c. and d. recommend E♭. On beat two, b. and d. agree upon D♯, E♮ but c. is not sure. On beat four b. recommends B♮, E♮ whereas c. and d. leave the player to follow the rule of succession, producing a B♭.

Because all four of these prints are advertised as "urtexts" (and there are more!), those poor conservatory students who are packed off to the music store to buy "the *Urtext*" must settle for the proverbial pig in a poke. The cleverest among them will have done just as well to save their money and check out the old nineteenth-century Peters edition from the library. It is a pastiche, of course, but where's the difference?

e. Peters, ed. Louis Köhler[2]

[2] Print No. 9397, later edited by Adolf Ruthardt and others.

What then, is the serous Schubert performer to do? Is it all guesswork and intuition, or can we establish some guidelines for a decison? For this Impromptu the answer to the last question is yes. We have four principal sources: a sketch (Raab, see Deutsch Catalogue), a completed autograph *(PPM)*, a copy *(GMF)*, and the first edition, brought out in 1839 by Diabelli. Sketches are not documents of final intent, thus we can only use this sketch as a check source for difficult decisions (the value of this will be demonstrated in the discussion of D887, below). The *Abschrift* in the *GMF*, originally part of the Witteczek-Spaun collection, is just that, a copy. One always hopes for a first edition brought out during the composer's lifetime and approved by him, for even with some printing errors it is likely to represent a generally clear statement of intent at that time (one must always allow a composer to change his mind later). Here we can virtually dismiss the first edition, for it was prepared without Schubert's approval and, worse, by Diabelli, who after Schubert's death exploited, changed and added to Schubert's scores at will. (His bastardized edition of *Die schöne Müllerin* (see pp.198ff) is sufficient proof of his avarice, and his addition of piano introductions to other lieder indicates his indifference to the material.) Our main source, then, is the autograph, and most decisions about this work should reflect its notation. Let us compare the autograph (see facing page) with the four editions, following the points as enumerated above:

1) Only edition c. follows the source. Indeed Schubert himself is unconcerned with the shift to bass clef and the lower staff. Editor d. has allowed himself to be influenced by his own choice of a three-measure slur, which is also incorrect: cf. 3) below.

2) Editions a., b. and d. follow the source. The reader can see clearly from the reproduction of the autograph below that the sign is a hairpin fade (reaching over three beats!), and by no stretch of the imagination an accent as proposed by c. Accentuation has already been provided by the *fp*.

Reading Schubert's Music

f. autograph

3) Only a. and b. follow the source. We understand that c. and d. might have imagined a connection between the end of the slur in m. 2 and the beginning of the slur in m.3, the first slur broken off because the pen might have run out of ink. But a closer look at the end of the first slur shows no such occurrence, and even after another dip of ink Schubert easily could have resumed the connection directly from the end of the first slur. Instead, he clearly and firmly began again in the next measure. A comparison with mm. eight and nine confirms the gesture for the second half of the period. Furthermore, we know that Schubert rarely wrote a slur over a longer stretch than could reasonably be played by a violinist on a single bow (see this chapter, below, for exceptions in the piano music). One might raise questions, however, about the slur that stretches over mm. 115/116 and possibly further (here the page ends), for on first glance it appears to be one of the exceptions to the rule. If, however, editors c. and d. had tried to make the first slur match the second (or vice-versa), then they have not allowed Schubert the freedom of change and development in his recapitulation. The great Heraclitian principle has been sacrificed to the little god Uniformity.

4) Only b.–d. follow the source. Editor a. has missed the tiny slur to the top F.

5) This is a difficult call, and it is possible that none of the editions has followed the source. The lower slur in m.. 3 appears at first glance to stretch over three notes, not two (as in a.) and not four (as in b.–d.). We see otherwise that in this score Schubert is generally careful about the number of beats covered by his slurs, often stopping fractionally short of the end of the last beat. The slur in measure two appears to begin with the "a♮" and extend slightly beyond the "c" to the downbeat, producing two successive inner phrases independent of the upper phrasing and each beginning on beat two. Knowing Schubert's propensity to conceive voices as if they were string parts (this left hand part is by no means pianistically notated), this solution strikes us as highly probable.

6) Only a. and b. follow the source.

7) Editions a., b. and d. follow the source. Cf. 2) above.

8) Only a. is correct. Editors must learn to withdraw from matters of performance practice unless they can (and do) demonstrate clear rules of the day, corroborated by the appropriate pedagogical sources and other historical documents. Merely offering an opinion, even backed by one's reputation, is not good enough in such matters.

Compiling the results, then, a rough estimate based on these eight measures shows the *GA* and the Henle editions to have an edge over the Wiener Urtext, and that all three of these editions are more accurate than the *NSA*. Between the *GA* and the Henle editions, then, the choice rests on convenience of layout, and whether or not the pianist wants the built-in fingering suggestions provided by Gieseking.

Most players, however, even the most responsible ones, do not have the time or the skills to carry out such comparisons as we have made above. In many cases, the buyer of an *urtext* must be satisfied with a list of the sources upon which it was based (usually listed in a foreword). Generally speaking, those editions based upon single sources, such as an autograph or a first print from Schubert's lifetime, prove to be the most unified and thus the best. The use of multiple sources as the basis of an edition is most likely to (but must not necessarily) produce an unuseable pastiche, depending on the editor. If the editor picks one of the multiple sources as the prime basis and merely consults the other sources as checks against possible errors (reporting them carefully in the critical notes), the buyer has had good luck. Furthermore, if the editor has refrained from interpolating his own ideas about performance practice (cf. the turns in the Impromptu above), the buyer has had even better luck.

We do not wish to belittle the role of editors, but to alert users of modern editions to the hidden uncertainties with which we all are faced from the outset. Editors exercise an enormous influence over performance, and the consequences of their interpretations can linger on for generations. For more than a century, for example, dutiful Schubertians made an extended but utterly non-contextual volume fade on the final note of Schubert's C-major Quintet D956, simply because the editors of the first publication (Spina, 1853) and later the editors of the *GA* (as well as several major performing editions) had read Schubert's expressive mark as a hairpin *decrescendo* instead of an accent designation. But no context for a *decrescendo* exists; no other Schubert *allegro* movement or finale ends with a *decrescendo*, whereas many end with an accent. In recent years the *NSA* volume editor, Martin Chusid, restored the accent, and some ensembles finally have begun to respond to the logic.

The *NSA* (W. Dürr, gen. ed.) and the *GA* (E. Mandyczewski, gen. ed.) are, of course, the two principal study editions of Schubert's works. Undertaken in the late nineteenth century, the *GA* was an astonishing achievement, considering the disorganized state of the available materials and the (then) merely formative recognition of Schubert as a great composer in the same sense in which one already regarded Bach, Mozart and Beethoven. The *NSA* (begun in 1964) introduced certain refinements: over-and-under instead of left-and-right layouts of the four-hand works for easier analysis, a more complete presentation of alternate versions and sketches, fuller editorial reports (in the *Quellen und Lesarten*), and facsimile pages at the outset of many volumes. The available input from modern scholarship—including such recent trends as "paper studies", but also some extremely important work such as Alexander Weinmann's monumental cataloging of Viennese publishing houses,[3] not to mention the contributions of twentieth-century musicologists who have devoted most of their careers to Schubert – has lent the *NSA* the cachet, at least, of state-of-the-art presentation. One of the greatest overall problems with this edition, however, is that it was designed not purely as a study edition, but also with an eye towards further commercial distribution in the form of playing editions. Thus rather than reflect Schubert's autographs more or less literally, the *NSA* has added substantial editorial interpretations, some of them size-reduced, bracketed or italicized, to be sure, but others with no particular warning to the reader. This conflict of purpose has diminished its usefulness in both capacities: it is neither fish nor fowl.

All of the editions mentioned above have their advantages, disadvantages and, as we have seen in the example of the F-minor Impromptu, their peculiarities. As we move now from the general to the specific we will try to point out further strengths and weaknesses in the context of the performance issues themselves. It would be impractical to extend this consideration to the various commercial editions as well, but even by the end of the next chapter readers will have gained a sufficient grasp of the problems to continue the search for good texts on their own.

Schubert's notation

An intriguing observation, if one has not made it already, is that almost nothing in Igor Stravinsky's basic notation would have been unintelligible to Franz Schubert. Whether Schubert would have cared for Stravinsky's music, or whether Stravinsky really understood Schubert—these are other matters, imponderable and unimportant. Actually, allowing for special circumstances surrounding the development of instruments, as well as for the symbols for the gestures that represent the emotional conceits of each successive age, almost nothing of notational essence has changed since the baroque. Certainly, within a hundred years or so, every composer would have been able to decipher every other composer, at least on paper. Beethoven could read Bach, and Bach could have read Beethoven.

Before examining Schubert's place within this notational continuum, we must ask ourselves exactly how he came to know the music that he obviously knew: Haydn, Mozart, Beethoven, etc. Clearly he was enraptured by Mozart's G-minor Symphony, but where and how often had he actually heard it? How many times would it have been played at concerts he could attend? How often were the Beethoven symphonies actually played at concerts he might have attended? Did he learn these works principally in concert, or did he study the scores? And if his truest knowledge of the literature was gained through scores, how did he acquire them? Full scores were expensive and probably hard to find. He certainly had no money to purchase them. Perhaps the Konvikt was a source, but we know almost nothing about its library. Perhaps he borrowed scores from older musicians. As to string quartets,

---

[3] *Beiträge zur Geschichte des Alt-Wiener Musikverlages.* Reihe I/II: ca. 30 volumes printed by various publishers from 1948ff.

smaller orchestral works and large choral pieces, we know he learned them in his capacities as a string player (first in his family ensemble as violist, and later at the school as second violinist) and as a royal chorister. Still, he would have learned these works from the perspective of his own part, except when he was conducting, and even then he may not always have had a full score in front of him.

"Hook or crook" was the method by which he must have gained his early knowledge of the literature, and if so, then it was also the method by which he learned his notation. Obviously he learned to read music at home, but probably only from a performer's standpoint. Still, he must have been quite fluent by the time he came to the Konvikt. If Michael Holzer could not help him much further, Salieri certainly would have required him to convert this passive, performer's knowledge of notation into a compositionally active and useful one. We might gain some true insight into Schubert's development during this period if we would explore Salieri's notational habits in more depth, a project yet to be carried out at this stage of Schubert research.

Various changes in Schubert's compositional handwriting have been explored by Ernst Hilmar,[4] and the development of his musical style by many other scholars. Still, musicology has not paid much attention to Schubert's actual notational development *vis-à-vis* the music itself: at what stage did he solve this or that technical problem, and how did he come upon the answer, etc. Nevertheless, we still can identify some isolated moments of progress as he rounded certain conceptual corners. We can calculate, for example, the time period in which he learned to write the figure (♩ ³ ♪). Up to this point he had dealt with the problem of 12/8 vs. 4/4 within a single movement by laborious metrical juxtaposition, as in *Trost an Elisa* D97 (1814):

EXAMPLE 3.2a
Schubert's notation

[4] "Datierungsprobleme im Werk Schuberts" in *Schubert-Kongress Wien* 1978: 45-60.

This passage could have been written far more easily with two-note triplet notation:

EXAMPLE 3.2b

Trost an Elisa in a simpler notation

In fact, within a short time of having written *Trost an Elisa* Schubert clearly discovered the usefulness of the two-note triplet notation, for *Geisternähe* D100 (April 1814) is heavily laden with it, as if it had been a brand new toy:

EXAMPLE 3.3

And from this point forward, Schubert used the two-note triplet notation as needed.

Lingering myths about Schubert's notation

Over the course of some years, various musicians and editors have advanced suppositions to the effect that 1) Schubert's notational capability was and remained inadequate for his true musical intentions; 2) that he was unsure how best to notate certain works; and 3) that his notation was often inexact and inconsistent. These accusations have no basis in fact, for Schubert was far more painstaking about his notation than his reputation to date has allowed. Some of these misconceptions have arisen in the wake of nineteenth-century scholars who assumed that because Schubert wrote quickly, he must have been careless about details. This notion went hand-in-hand with another myth, to the effect that Schubert wrote directly in fair copy and rarely revised. Both of these assumptions are false. Indeed we will find some ambiguities in his scores: the occasional failure, for example, to provide a tempo marking after a ritard or an accelerando, or here and there the omission of a slur or some other mark of articulation. These, however, are minor oversights that cannot be compared with the almost systematic notational failures imagined by even highly respected scholars and performers today.

MYTH: "notational deficiency". This notion arose in the context of the assimilation issue, which we will discuss shortly. In Paul Badura-Skoda's edition of the Impromptus he stated that he had never seen the two-note triplet notation ♩ ³ ♪ in Schubert's music, and thus he had to assume that Schubert intended the figure ♫ to serve the triplet capacity as well. Our subsequent look through Schubert's works, however, revealed hundreds of examples of the requisite triplet notation (including several in Badura-Skoda's own edition of the *Wanderer* Fantasy), a fact that we pointed out in a 1991 symposium in Chicago, chaired by Eva Badura-Skoda. Forced to acknowledge Schubert's fundamental capacity to write such a notation (i.e. Schubert's knowledge of its function), Badura-Skoda persisted nevertheless in his viewpoint, arguing now that Schubert had not written the two-note triplet figure *enough* times throughout his works to be taken seriously![5] He continued to believe that the dotted eighth-plus-sixteenth figure equals (sometimes, or perhaps even more often) the two-note triplet figure shown above. As do others who support this rather subjective theory (Malcolm Bilson, for example),[6] Badura-Skoda appears to decide such matters only on a personal basis. He does not explain how he is able to know which of Schubert's dotted figures are "real" and which are merely "disguised", nor how Schubert merely could have "forgotten" to write triplets instead of the dotted figures.[7]

Even before Badura-Skoda's original statement that he had never seen the triplet notation in Schubert's music, Franz Eibner already had described it in a 1962 article. But Eibner, too, had failed to grasp its significance, deciding instead that Schubert was notationally even less responsible and clear than before for having introduced the new notation[!]:

> The very early song *Geisternähe* [D100] shows not only that Schubert (1) used various notations for the same rhythms, but inversely, in some circumstances (2) used the same notation for various rhythms.[8]

We read similar accusations of notational inadequacy and / or ambiguity concerning this notation throughout the gamut of music from Bach to Brahms, regardless of its increasingly widespread appearance in scores throughout the nineteenth century. Some theorist-performers of the past, including even Rudolf Kolisch, were simply unaware that the notation really existed. Presumably they would have altered their perspectives on the subject in light of new discoveries.[9] But even such a tireless and thorough researcher as the late Frederick Neumann allowed himself to subscribe to the theory of assimilation (probably because he had not turned his full attention to it), although his basic stance always had been to take a composer's notation seriously in the absence of contrary evidence: for example, in the fa-

---

[5] "Triolenangleichung bei Schubert—ein noch immer ungelöstes Problem?" in *Üben & Musizieren* (1992, hereafter *UeM*): 12-13.
[6] See David Montgomery, "Triplet Assimilation in the Music of Schubert: Challenging the Ideal" in *Historical Performance* 6/2 (1993, hereafter *HP*): 79-97 and the ensuing exchange with Malcolm Bilson in *HP* 7/1: 27-31.
[7] Badura-Skoda, "Triolenangleichung:" 8-14.
[8] "The Dotted-Quaver-and-Semiquaver Figure with Triplet Accompaniment in the Works of Schubert", trans. Maurice Brown in *The Music Review* 23:282 (hereafter *MR*).
[9] Conversation: "Zur Theorie der Aufführung", ed. Berthold Türcke, in *Musik-Konzepte* 29/30.

mous controversy over overdotting in French overtures.[10] Such has been the power of unsubstantiated suggestion concerning Schubert's notational capabilities.

Finding the proper perspective on this issue is not difficult: the reason that the two-note triplet figure occurs more often in Schubert's music than in Bach's, and more often in Brahms's music than in Schubert's, and so on, is not that notation was developing, but that musical style itself had changed. Bach's style called for the notation only rarely, Schubert's more and more, and Brahms's relatively often. Among great composers, musical ideas generate notational advances, not vice-versa.

MYTH: that alternate versions of certain works provide proofs of intention for the original versions, and vice versa. The reasoning goes something like this: "The composer created version a, and then he created version b; therefore we may take what we like from version b. and read it into version a. If that fails to please, we may take what we like from version a. and read it into version b." Such strange reasoning has misled many a baroque scholar, for example, to regard singly-dotted works as if they should be doubly-dotted in performance. The two versions of JS Bach's French Overture BWV 831 are often cited as proof:

EXAMPLE 3.4a/b
a.

b.

However, the B-minor Overture does not constitute a more accurately notated version of the C-minor Overture, but a separate piece in a separate context. Frederick Neumann's conclusion that these two versions constitute in essence two different works is in our mind the only acceptable approach to this material.[11]

Scholars appear particularly eager to view Schubert's alternate versions as proof of an inability to capture his music properly on paper. Eibner cites two rewritings of *An Emma* D113 (Example 3.5), for example, as proof that Schubert could not come to terms with the

---

[10] "The Dotted Note and the So-Called French Style" in *Essays in Performance Practice* (Ann Arbor: UMI, 1982): 71/2.
[11] "Rhythm in the Two Versions of Bach's French Overture, BWV 831" in *Essays:* 99–110.

Reading Schubert's Music

proper metrical notation for this song, which, as Eibner would have it, must already have been established in Schubert's mind as a kind of *Ding-an-sich*.

According to Eibner, Schubert was merely trying to decide whether 2/4 or 6/8 should dominate. Since version c. was chronologically the last setting, it would appear to be Schubert's clear preference. Nevertheless, Eibner reasoned that in order to honor Schubert's labors we were obliged to help him out by cavalierly incorporating certain elements from version b. into version c!

EXAMPLE 3.5a/c

The versions a. and c. are composed in 2/4 time, whereas b is in 6/8 time. The six-quavers-per-bar in the accompaniment of b. are written consistently in a. and c. as two-quaver triplets. From a comparison we can now deduce how Schubert, with such an accompaniment, wanted the notations in question to be performed in 2/4 time ... [!] [12]

---

[12] Eibner: 282.

In performance, then, certain duple figures should be taken, somehow, as triplet figures. This astonishing bit of reasoning rests again on the confusion of musical ideas with their notation. Schubert's problem here was not to find a satisfactory notation for an already fully conceived musical setting, but to find a satisfactory musical setting in the first place! No *Ding-an-sich* existed, and posthumously we must allow Schubert to change his creative mind. Alternate versions of works do not constitute internal evidence for performance practices. They merely constitute evidence of a concerned and continuing creativity.

MYTH: that Schubert's notation in general was often inexact and inconsistent. This notion has been propounded mostly by editors who have prepared his music for publication. As to inexactitude, we point out again that Schubert's notational signs are not unusual; we find them in all other music of his time. Generally we regard Beethoven as the most exacting composer of his day, but do we find notational signs in his music that do not appear in some similar form in Schubert's music? Apart from Beethoven's elaborate German verbal instructions, the answer is no. The difference between Schubert and Beethoven has nothing to do with notation, but with musical style and the formation of their ideas. Schubert's notation serves his style as well as Beethoven's notation serves his own style.

What is inexact about Schubert is his handwriting (should we discuss Beethoven's handwriting?), which has led some editors to the mistaken accusation of notational inexactitude. For example, in Schubert's autographs we find open-close hairpins that can be taken for accents as well as for *decrescendos*. This does not mean that they are interchangeable (as Walther Dürr has suggested for many cases),[13] or that Schubert was inexact in his use of them. This is merely a calligraphic issue, and the problem is to sort the two signs out correctly, relying upon musical analysis as a final check.

Along with the notion that accents and *decrescendo* hairpins might be interchangeable signs, Dürr also applies his theory of inexactitude to another aspect of Schubert's notation. Remarking rightly that in Schubert's scores the term "*diminuendo*" (as opposed to "*decrescendo*") occurs with unusual frequency at structural joins or closures, Dürr speculates on the possibility that for Schubert this term might embrace the idea of slowing as well as growing softer.[14] To date, however, we have been able to find no contemporaneous theoretical evidence that "*diminuendo*" meant anything other than growing softer. In fact, examples such as the one below would appear to constitute a direct refutation of the idea: the first (D459A/2,: mm.71–74) because Schubert clearly uses the term *dim.* here along with *decresc.* in a place where no speed change is appropriate. Fundamentally, *decrescendo* is one of a pair of instructions (*crescendo* being its antonym) and is often used in that context, as in the third measure of the example below. Like hairpins, *crescendo* and *decrescendo* can be used in tandem or separately. *Diminuendo* has no antonym among the technical terms of music, however, and it is used most often in the softer volume regions. Naturally, then, it is bound to appear quite often at the end of *andantes* and *adagios*, where things remain soft and where performers tend to slow down anyway. In the example below, however, we are squarely in the middle of an ongoing, virtuosic passage where Schubert uses

---

[13] *Schubert Handbuch*: 95.
[14] Ibid:98.

dim. as an extension of the *decrescendo*; it takes us down to **pp** just before the left hand begins its upward rush.

EXAMPLE 3.6

In the next example (D557/2: mm 65–71;), in addition to *dim.* Schubert offers a specific speed modifier, *rit.*, a superfluous instruction if *dim.* truly included "slowing" in its meaning.

EXAMPLE 3.7

We cannot even argue that in Example 3.7 the final *dim*. might indicate a slackening of speed for a seamless transition from the 32nds into the final 16ths, with a continuing *ritardando* to the end of the gesture, for a seamless *ritardando* was not Schubert's goal. Had it been, he easily could have left the entire passage in 32nd notes and marked it *molto ritardando*. He clearly wanted a sudden drop in values from 32nds to 16ths (at ***ppp*** incidentally, from the implication of his second *dim*. instruction), otherwise he could have used the standard intervention of triplets between the faster and slower values, as in this passage from the first movement of the *Wanderer* Fantasy D 760:

EXAMPLE 3.8
mm. 108–112

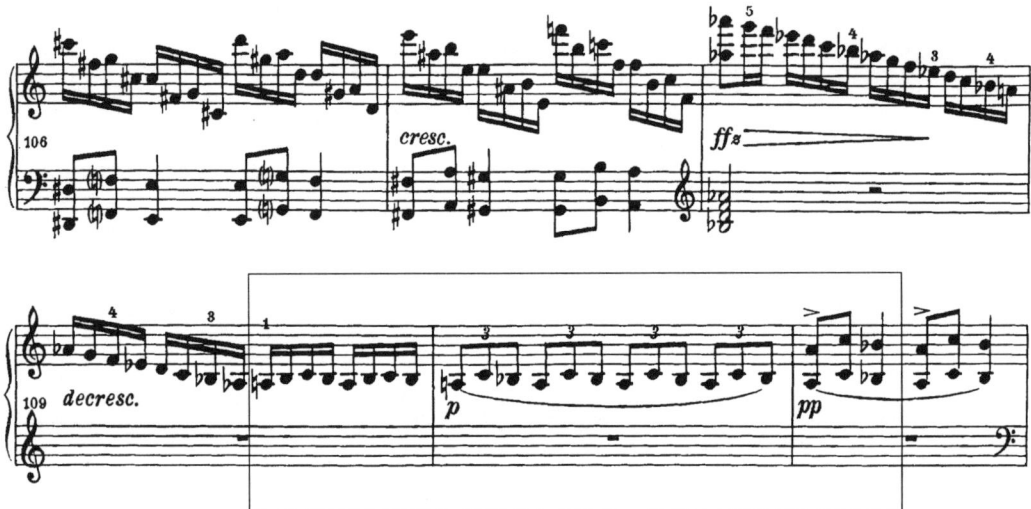

Obviously certain structural turns or endings might use an (unmarked) gentle relaxing of the tempo in conjunction with (marked) dynamic softening, but those situations are coincidental. We find plenty of structural junctures where only one or the other application is appropriate. In the course of "de-mystifying" Schubert's notational symbols, then, we must take care not to give multiple meanings to integral signs – especially where no theoretical tradition existed to support such an interpretation.

Even with Schubert's complex signs, such as *fp,* we must take care not to read more into them than was intended, and especially not to invent new meanings to suit preconceived interpretations. As we mentioned above, in the preface to the Wiener Urtext edition of the Impromptus Paul Badura-Skoda suggests that *fp*⎯⎯ is often to be read as *f*⎯⎯*p*. Again, as with his theory of triplet assimilation, Badura-Skoda does not tell us how and when to distinguish between this reading and the literal reading. His reasoning, apparently, is that *fp* cannot (should not?) be followed by a *decrescendo*, although in light of the fact that Schubert's lower dynamic end reaches to ***ppp*** (and, as shown above, by implication to ***pppp***), we can find no problem with such a *decrescendo*. Furthermore, examples of *f*⎯⎯*p* are numerous in Schubert's scores. Badura-Skoda cites the opening of the F-minor Impromptu as one place that might bear out his interpretation of the dynamic sign, but he gives no others in support of the idea. Indeed, as we have seen in the previous chapter, Badura's reading of this opening is far superior to Walter Dürr's (*fp* topped by an accent, with no *decrescendo*). Nevertheless, to dismantle the *fp* sign into its individual components artificially with a *decrescendo* between them, as if it were some sort of enigmatic and highly personal shorthand, brings us no further towards an understanding of Schubert's intent.[15] Finally, and significantly, we can find no contemporaneous evidence for such an unusual reading among theorists: Viennese, German or Italian. Why would Schubert feel the need to develop new meanings for his symbols, especially while the standard meanings served him quite well?

Literal vs. contextual values in Schubert: the historical background

Most of the remainder of this chapter deals with face-value aspects of Schubert's notation. By "face-value" we do not mean that the topics discussed are either self-explanatory or accepted unilaterally among scholars and performers, for indeed they are not. We mean, simply, that no research or analysis to date has uncovered true cause to second-guess Schubert's written notation in these areas. Nevertheless, to judge by public performances and recordings, Schubert interpreters as a group have developed specific, personal, and often even eccentric ideas about the interpretation of his metrical and rhythmic notation.

Critical reports, musicological essays, and musical correspondence confirm that a dispassionate discussion of these ideas is difficult to maintain. A few years ago we placed one aspect of note values and rhythmic interpretation in Schubert, the practice of assimilating dotted figures to triplets, under the public microscope, and from the reactions and replies by players and musicologists alike we were astonished to learn how sensitive and even private such matters were considered to be.[16] It was one of many times that this subject had been broached to the general musical public; the last major controversy occurred in London in the early 1960s following a concert by Benjamin Britten and Peter Pears, and the reaction at that time was just as heated.[17] In this realm, apparently, performers reserve the right to certain freedoms and idiosyncracies, as well as the right to discuss and defend them on a wide range of grounds, some of which extend even beyond the boundaries of art.[18]

---

[15] Perhaps Badura-Skoda got this notion from Robert Donington, (*Baroque Music: Style and Performance* / NY: Norton, 1982): 31/32), citing Mylius: "In 1686 Mylius [Möller] gave us the valuable warning that dynamic markings for successive levels may be indications not for sudden but for gradual changes, where 'one should not fall suddenly from piano into forte but gradually strengthen the voice, and then let it drop'. Thus *p* followed by *f* followed by *ff* quite probably (though not of course necessarily) means *crescendo poco a poco,* and *ff* followed by *f* followed by *p,* quite probably means *diminuendo poco a poco...*". Mylius's point, however, does not concern complex signs, but individual signs spread out so that between any two of them one indeed might have room for a *decrescendo* or a *diminuendo,* an entirely different matter. "Mylius" was W.M. Mylius (Möller), the author of *Rudimenta musices, das ist: Eine kurtze und gründliche Anweisung zur Singe Kunst* (Gotha).

[16] See Montgomery in *HP* 7/1 exchange (see fn 5 above).

[17] See Desmond Shawe-Taylor, "Schubert as written and as played" in *London Sunday Times,* 30 June 196 (hereafter *LST*), and subsequent forum in the *Musical Times,* September 1963 (hereafter *MT*).

[18] See Montgomery in *HP* 7/1 exchange (see fn 5 above).

Perhaps the best way to begin, then, is with the simplest of subjects: the value of notes and rests. Almost every musical tutor from the seventeenth century forward begins with a discussion of basic note and rest values and their duple divisions, often followed by the substitute values (triplets, for example). In the century preceding Schubert's birth and the two following it, no changes have occurred in the way we understand these values and their relationships one to another. Lately, however, we have heard and read suggestions that Schubert's music constitutes a special case wherein these values and relationships were more flexible, and thus more open to personal interpretation.[19] Although to date the proponents of this theory have advanced no relevant period evidence to support it, enough controversy has arisen to demand putting the issues in an overall perspective, particularly for a younger generation of performers who will be responsible for presenting Schubert's music to listeners in the years to come.

The flexible dot

Some of the misunderstanding about Schubert's notation appears to have arisen in connection with dot values, which in many tutors of the eighteenth and nineteenth centuries are introduced directly after the initial explanation of note and rest values. Indeed, in German galant sources we read about flexible dot values for expressive purposes. The practice of "overdotting" and "underdotting," to use their common names, is a matter of increasing or decreasing voluntarily the notated disproportion between two different rhythmic values which, combined in the duple meters, form full beats, beat divisions, or multiples:

EXAMPLE 3.9a/b

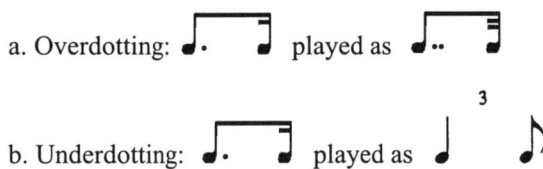

Overdotting

We must make a clear distinction between the twentieth-century convention of overdotting in baroque overtures (which has no documentable basis in historical practice) and the well-documented practice of overdotting in German galant- and classical-period solo playing.[20] The latter has been described by a number of writers, including J. Quantz (1752), C.P.E. Bach (1753, 1787), F.W. Marpurg (1755), L. Mozart (1756), J.F. Agricola (1757), J.A.P. Schulz and J.P. Kirnberger (in Sulzer, 1771-74), D.G. Türk (1789), J.G.Tromlitz (1791), H.C. Koch (1807). Koch published in the nineteenth century, of course, but we must remember that his dictionary is based on earlier sources and reflects a period of at least a decade or two previous to publication. German sources continued to describe overdotting until the last quarter of the nineteenth century, although, as we shall see, for reasons irrelevant to Schubert's music.

[19] Ibid.
[20] Neumann, "The Dotted Note": 73–98.

Let us compare the last of the Galant-period descriptions (Koch's) to a truly nineteenth century one:

> Where the interpretation must keep its roundness and its precision, there are cases in which the dot must be held out longer than its regular length. To these cases sometimes belong, for example, those dotted notes which in a slow and steady tempo are followed by fast sliding notes, as in Fig. 99. To these cases also sometimes belong combinations of similar notes in a passage of serious character and moderate tempo in which the first, third, and fifth notes, etc. are dotted, as in Fig. 16.[21]

EXAMPLE 3.10a/b
a. Koch's figure 99

b. Koch's figure 16

Koch's description of overdotting tallies with those of his late eighteenth-century colleagues and predecessors, all of whom observe that the appropriateness of overdotting depends upon the character, or affect of the music.

Our nineteenth-century source, August Leopold Crelle, speaks also of affect in the old sense but also introduces a new caveat, missing in previous tutors, that tallies with Spohr, Czerny, and others of the nineteenth century. He states that serious composers, at least, left little to chance, and that their notation was to be taken at face value:

> If a composer makes a figure with one note in it larger than the other, perhaps even if without altering the harmony and the modulation there is still room for another shorter note, one supports him in this purpose and does not shorten the long note. The performance prospers if in general, insofar as is consistent with the affect, the long note is lengthened even more. The performance suffers otherwise. For example, the place in Fig. 25 can prosper under certain circumstances when played as in Fig. 26, but suffer when played as in Fig. 27. But if the notational practices of the composer in question are very correct, one must play Fig. 25 exactly as it is written. Often the character of a piece forbids deviations that are allowed only in those pieces that need a passionate or unbridled and elegant performance. In great sonorities, as in serious fugues and strict, contrapuntal movements the exchange of Fig. 25 for Fig. 26 is not recommended.[22]

---

[21] Heinrich Christoph Koch, *Kurzgefasstes Handwörterbuch der Musik* (Leipzig: Johann Friedrich Hartknoch, 1807): 285.
[22] *Ausdruck und Vortrag:* 76/7. (See App. IIA, 1823).

EXAMPLE 3.11
Crelle's examples 25–27

Crelle was writing from Berlin – the heart of "overdotting country" – but his tutor also is one of the first to mention the performance of Beethoven's music during the latter's lifetime. We may speculate safely that had he known Schubert's great instrumental works he might have classed them with those of other "very correct" composers. And despite some modern notions to the contrary, Schubert had learned his craft well.[23] He took some pains, in fact, to guide performers.[24] The great spectrum of tempo differentiations that he developed, plus the care that he took with rhythms and expressive markings reveal a concerned, demanding musical nature. A composer who would go to the trouble of writing six versions of a single song (*Geistes-Gruß* D142), and two or three versions of many others, cannot have been characteristically happy about taking his chances in the performance arena. A composer who had no problem conceiving 9 against 8 (*Die Stadt* D957/11) or the double *alla breve* of the G♭ Impromptu was no one's notational "Schwammerl."[25]

---

[23] John Reed's statement concerning Schubert's notation in *Wasserfluth* D911/6 is typical, but fully unfounded: "A thorough insistence on maintaining the dotted rhythm [as Schubert wrote it against the triplets] is likely to sound mannered and jerky. [Assimilation] would have been perfectly consistent with Schubert's conservative notational practice," *The Schubert Song Companion* (New York: Universe Books, 1985): 447. Elsewhere he writes: "True to his conservative bent, Schubert never found any occasion to modify the conventions of musical notation he learnt from Salieri. There was nothing in him, as Sonnleithner said, of a musician of the future; the saying applies as much to his notation as to his attitude to the trend of public taste. So it is that in playing his music the performer is often called upon to make the same use of his interpretative skill as he would in playing Mozart and Haydn." Reed attempts to substantiate his notion of Schubert's and / or Salieri's "conventions" through now long-familiar but erroneous readings of various dotted figures in Schubert's music. Cited from *Schubert: The Final Years* (London: Faber, 1972).
[24] For a fuller account of his usage of the triplet analogue in order to clarify and specify his wishes, see Montgomery, "Triplet Assimilation:" 89.
[25] This nickname ("little mushroom"), perpetuated in sentimental biographies by amateur historians who saw Schubert as Vienna's good-natured but helpless little savant, was apparently the invention of his drinking acquaintances – some of whom were not above taking advantage of him personally while he lived, and of his memory after his death. Cf. Christopher Gibbs, " 'Poor Schubert' : images and legends of the composer" in *The Cambridge Companion:* 36–55.

As we have mentioned in connection with Spohr (Ch. I), nineteenth-century Viennese sources make a distinction between "serious" and "brilliant" or popular works. For the latter they document, even if not in abundance, a flexible treatment of the dot according to the character of the music. Heinrich Backofen's clarinet method of 1802/1809[?] is amusing. In the section *Vom Vortrage* (On Performance), he gives tips on good musicianship, recommending overdotting in "manly works," such as a "good march," and in dance music. In 1826 Hummel (p. 76) allowed a "piquant execution" of a dotted affect, but did not specify much further. We must keep in mind, of course, that Hummel's examples, with only several exceptions, are taken from his own music in the brilliant style. Finally, we have a similar but only small hint from Czerny, in op. 500 to the effect that one might sharpen certain dotted rhythms.[26] Czerny occupies himself principally with two kinds of musical delivery: the one appropriate to serious composers (Beethoven, Mozart, etc), and the other appropriate to music written by virtuoso pianists of the 1830s (many of whom were Czerny's own pupils).[27] Czerny's recommendation for rhythmic sharpening, then, is meant for what he and Spohr both call the "style brillant" (concertos, showpieces). Schubert wrote almost no music in this style, for he belonged to a different group of musicians than those who appeared in the public concerts.

One of the traditional notions proffered by those who favor overdotting in French overtures is that the double dot was yet not known in notation, and thus it is we who now must decide, somehow, where a composer wanted his dots lengthened and where not. This part of the "French overture theory" can be ignored, for double-dotted passages certainly were known and written, if not frequently, in various ways (also using rests instead of dots) in the eighteenth century. By Schubert's day, the double dot was a commonplace notation, recognized in every basic tutor. Schubert was perfectly capable of double-dotting in pieces whose character demanded this sharp delivery, and thus we have no reason to second-guess him concerning his single dots.

Still, however, we hear performances of certain works where voluntary overdotting has grown almost traditional. Often, the major stumbling block to achieving the proper rhythmic affect is an inappropriate tempo, almost always one that is too slow. Performers also overdot in response to a notational complexity such as a metrical conflict. An example that leaps to mind is the first movement of the B♭ Trio D898. Here the basic written affect is the 4–3 conflict between the sixteenths which follow singly-dotted eighths and the smaller notes of the two-note triplet pattern shown above. Performers may think that to overdot in this movement is to strengthen the affect by separating these elements even further, but instead, this practice merely removes the delicacy from the written rhythmic conflict.[28]

---

[26] Richault edition, 15th Lesson: 432 (See App. IIA).

[27] To be sure, Czerny writes about Mendelssohn and the Schumanns, and he has insightful things to say about performing the young Chopin's music. He even acknowledges Schubert's existence as a composer of four-hand works and sonatas, but does not discuss the performance of Schubert's music. In the Supplement (Pt IV), Ch. 1 Czerny discusses performance styles for Thalberg, Döhler, Henselt, Chopin, Taubert, Willmer, and Liszt. In the next two chapters he focusses on Beethoven alone.

[28] Cf. Isaac Stern, Leonard Rose and Eugene Istomin (SM2K 64515 in Isaac Stern: A Life in Music, Box III: Sony SX12K 67195).

EXAMPLE 3.12
a. as written:

b. as often mistakenly played:

The affect is strong enough as Schubert has written it; the trick is to deliver the conflict with elegance by de-emphasizing the smaller values, and not by rhythmic exaggeration.

Underdotting

Performers often seek, on the other hand, to remove such 4–3 conflicts entirely, by "underdotting", i.e. placing the smaller note of the dotted figure exactly with the smaller note of the triplet figure. Thus we are back, once again, to the assimilation theory advanced by Badura-Skoda and others, this time through a different doorway. Since this problem continues to surface in modern performances (sometimes instinctively but, often as not, backed by various aesthetical confessions) it might be appropriate to review it historically.

In keyboard tutors of the mid-eighteenth century and later we begin to find short discussions concerning the execution of mixed rhythmic figures in direct conflict, three-against-two, three against four and six-against-four. Some pedagogical authors (Quantz, Tromlitz, Löhlein 2nd ed, Türk) abjured the pupil to learn to play such figures properly as they were notated. Others, such as C.P.E. Bach and Marpurg, suggested a makeshift remedy *for those who could not learn to play them properly*. The remedy, whereby the two notes of a duple or a dotted figure would be played directly with the outer two notes of the conflicting triplet, is referred to as the practice of "assimilation" (*Angleichung*).

EXAMPLE 3.13a/b
a. as written: 3-vs-2, 3-vs-dotted, 6-vs-dotted or double-dotted

b. as assimilated by the pupil

Logically, these figures were a problem only for keyboard players, for they were a matter of coordination. Furthermore, Bach and Marpurg were writing for harpsichord players, not pianists. The difference is important, for the two conflicting smaller values cannot be managed with such elegance on the harpsichord, especially by beginners. For this reason Bach complained that the execution of the mixed figure sounded clumsy and needed a better solution (assimilation).[29] Despite the fact that the problem began as a keyboard issue, we find discussions of it even in non-keyboard methods such as those by Quantz and Tromlitz, with the effect of lending the entire assimilation question a purely aesthetic demeanor. Quantz and Tromlitz, incidentally, spoke out against assimilation, but by opening up the question to the realm of theory instead of practice, they unwittingly invited a horde of twentieth century readers to judge the alleged problem from their own musical perspectives. By now, in any case, modern performers are virtually forced to take these issues on aesthetic grounds, for no professional player today would admit that he or she could not execute a simple mixed rhythm at the piano.

Uncomplicated as such figures might appear to good modern players, they presented apparent difficulties for beginners and amateurs well into the nineteenth century. The most common of the rhythmic problems mentioned above is the successful presentation of duplets against triplets. To judge by pedagogical methods from C.P.E. Bach's day until well into the late nineteenth century, this execution was thought to be more difficult than the others, especially in slow tempos. The execution of dotted figures against triplets or sextuplets, on the other hand, was thought (rightly) to be most difficult in fast tempos. For professionals, neither of these rhythmic notations should be of intrinsic interest, for they have to do only with a practical solution to a widespread problem among beginners. With this thought in mind we turn now to the appropriate period evidence for Schubert.

The Viennese sources

The pedagogues of Schubert's day mentioned the assimilation problem in various sources, the most important of which is Beethoven's:

> [Ludwig van Beethoven], Notes to Cramer's Études (ca. 1818).
>
> Ex. 6 [referring to the sixth study, marked Vivace, 2/4, quarter = 108]. The rhythmic accent should fall on the first note of each triplet. Herewith, however, are the rhythmic configurations to be observed, which are sometimes longer, sometimes shorter: otherwise one would hear a false melodic progression. The movement is 4-voiced until the 15th measure. Beethoven.[30]

---

[29] C.P.E. Bach I:128. "Since the advent of the constant use of triplets in the so-called "bad" [common] or 4/4 meter, as also in 3/4 or 2/4 meter, one finds pieces that would be more comfortable if they had been written in 12/8, 9/8 or 6/8 instead of in these [common] meters. One measures the notes according to the other voice, as shown in Fig. XII. In this way the after-stroke, which is often unpleasant and always heavy-sounding, can be avoided."

[30] The annotations are possibly in Schindler's handwriting, but if so they were probably taken directly from Beethoven, either from another copy in Beethoven's possession, or from dictation. The annotations would not have been written before 1816, when Beethoven became Karl's legal guardian, and they probably date from a year or two afterwards. Karl would have been 10 in 1816 and possibly not yet proficient enough to have tackled the Cramer Études. In a handwritten note on the edition Schindler mentions an article about metronome marks in the *AmZ*:37 (1817). Perhaps, then, 1817 or 1818 might be the most accurate period in which to place these annotations.

EXAMPLE 3.14

This statement is the most important early 19th-century observation we possess on the subject of mixed meters, representing the wishes of the greatest master of his day. These annotations were written with Beethoven's nephew Karl in mind. Perhaps the most revealing part of the quotation is the last sentence, which emphasizes the independence of the voices. Readers should note carefully that although according to conventions of the day these rhythms are printed with the small notes aligned, Beethoven calls for a true distinction between the dotted rhythms and the triplets.

In a study of Schubert's last three piano sonatas, Arthur Godel makes a similar point about the desired complexity of texture vis-a-vis the question of assimilating a double-dotted eighth-plus-thirty-second-note to a sextuplet figure in the C-minor Sonata D958 (Cf. next section in this chapter):

> If double-dotting [against sextuplets] serves the differentiation between voices ... then one must also not assimilate in the case of triplets.[31]

Godel does not follow up his idea with any consistency, however, and we find him condoning assimilation in other places, but with no particular logic or documentation.

Beethoven's pupil Carl Czerny does not discuss the niceties of voice-leading, but approaches the assimilation issue on practical grounds:

> When triplets are combined with dotted figures, the note following the dot should be played after the last note of the triplet.[32]

In order to show that assimilation was a matter of expediency, not musical ideals, Czerny gives a second example with the tempo doubled, preceded by the following comment:

---

[31] Godel: 97.
[32] Translated from the Richault edition: Pt. I, p. 78: "Quand les Triolets se trouvent combinés avec de tels passages de notes pointées la note qui suit le point doit être jouée après la dernière note du triolet".

Reading Schubert's Music

> In very quick times, the note which follows the dot may be played with the third note of the triplet.[33]

Note that Czerny says, "may be played", and not "should be played" with the third note of the triplet. In the supplement, Czerny is quite specific about not assimilating in the first movement of the Moonlight Sonata, op. 27/2:

> The sixteenth is to be played after the last triplet underneath, but it is important to note that the triplet accompaniment must be played legato and evenly.[34]

J.N. Hummel does not mention assimilation of dotted figures to triplets, but on the issue of 3 vs. 2 he is quite clear about the reasons for making rhythmic compromises. We can well imagine that his explanation of the dotted / triplet problem might be similar:

> Johann Nepomuk Hummel, *Ausführliche theoretische-praktische Anweisung zum Pianofortespiel* (1826, pub. 1828)
>
> Often three notes in one hand are played against two notes in the other; but since it is too difficult for the beginner to play these together in strict rhythm, he is allowed to strike the second note of the duple together with the third note of the triplet [see example above]. If the beginner becomes more rhythmically secure and his fingers become more dexterous, the awkwardness between the two opposing relationships in performance will gradually disappear by itself.[35]

EXAMPLE 3.15

According to Hummel, then, assimilation was allowed for technical reasons only. This is precisely how we must look upon the problem today.

Josef Czerny, one of Schubert's publishers and a piano teacher in Vienna, also allowed assimilation of simple duple figures to triplets and sextuplets for the lower grades of piano playing. His *Wiener Clavierlehrer* (1825) is a basic guide for students and amateurs:[36]

EXAMPLE 3.16a/b

a.

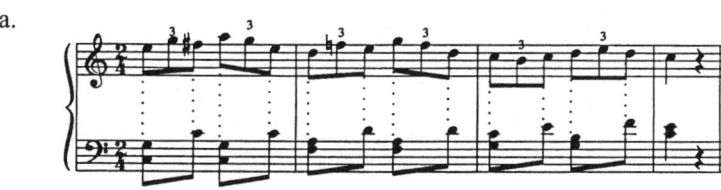

---

[33] Ibid: "Cependant ceci n'a lieu que dans les mouvements lents. Lorsque la mesure est rapide le note qui suit le point peut être [emphasis ours] jouée avec la dernière note du triolet". [Cf. English version: I:92]
[34] Czerny, *Pianoforte Schule* (German language edition): IV: 51.
[35] *Anweisung zum Pianofortespiel*: 33/ (See App. IIA,1826)
[36] Vienna: Anton Strauss (See App. IIA, 1825).

b.

Frankly, Schubert's piano music in general has almost no technically insurmountable difficulties in this regard for the professional player. Perhaps an exception might be seen by some pianists in the dotted / triplet passage from D567 only because it must be executed with one hand, but with some practice even this problem can be overcome.

EXAMPLE 3.17

Although few of the slower passages with mixed figures in Schubert's piano music are unplayable, we find occasional passages in *Allegro* that are difficult indeed. No one could fault a pianist for assimilating in the following passages from the coda of the *Klavierstück* D459A/3, which certainly appears unmanageable as written:

EXAMPLE 3.18
(Allegro patetico)

Dotted figures against sextuplets

The problem of dotted figures against sextuplets appears rare for Schubert's style. The upper figures in Exx. 3.17 and 3.18 are beamed as sextuplets, but in actuality they are pitted against the dotted figures in triplet divisions, in essence far more difficult to manage than a single dotted figure against the sextuplets. In Ex. 3.18 if one were to omit the middle two notes of each dotted figure and concentrate on placing each of the last 32nds between each of the sextuplet groups, the passage could be played without assimilation, even in *Allegro*.

The only statement we have in the Viennese sources concering simple sextuplets against dotted figures was made by Friedrich Starke, who allowed for compromise in such passages as well:

> Here the new, famous composers do not take the counting too exactly. The note which is written after the dotted note is calculated [by pianists] in performance situations to occur with the last note of the sextuplet.[37]

Starke does not present assimilation as a compositional ideal, but merely as an expediency. His term, "new, famous composers" is a bit puzzling. It cannot refer to Schubert, who was neither a "new" nor, in terms of piano music, a "famous" composer. (Starke never mentions him.) Likewise, it cannot refer to Beethoven who was 1) not lax about his notation; 2) against assimilation; and 3) not a "new" composer. Nor can it apply to Hummel, who, as we know, took his counting exactly. Perhaps Starke is referring to the "new, famous" virtuoso-pianist/composers of the Herz/Steibelt/Hünten ilk, who do not concern us here.[38]

The alignment theory

One of the chief arguments for assimilation, adopted over the years, rests on the fact that in many Schubert-period prints we often find the small notes of dotted figures aligned with the ends of triplets. In Paul Badura Skoda's preface to the Impromptus he writes:

> In this volume, triplets are clearly intended in the third variation of the Impromptu in B flat major D 935 (Op. 142), No.3. Until about 1860 all Viennese publishers took this into account in the graphical layout of their editions. Anton Diabelli even went one step further in his first edition of the Impromptus (1838), and printed:[39]

---

[37] *Wiener Pianoforte-Schule*, Pt I:8. (See App. IIA, 1819).

[38] In that Beethoven allowed Starke to teach Karl about the time that Starke wrote the *Clavierschule*, the pedagogue's principles were probably to the composer's liking, and, as we see from the example above, Beethoven was against assimilation. A few years later, however, when Stephan von Breuning asked Beethoven to recommend a piano method for his son, Beethoven chose neither Starke's, Czerny's nor any other Viennese method. He chose Clementi's method instead (*Introduction to the Art of Playing on the Piano Forte:* London, 1801). Beethoven ordered the German language version, entitled *Einleitung in die Kunst das Pianoforte zu spielen* (Vienna, Cappi et C. / Mollo, 1810?). "Czernis Klawier-schule nehm nicht, ich erhalte nährere Auskunft dieser Tage über eine andere" (21 January? 1826). Later: "Liebe werther! Endlich kann ich meiner Windbeuteley entwinden, hier folgt die versprochene Clement. Klawier schule für gerard, wenn er sie gebrauch, wie ich ihm schon anzeigen werde, es wird sie gewiß guten Erfolg leisten" (20 September 1826). [Ludwig van Beethoven. *Briefwechsel Gesamtausgabe,* ed. Sieghard Brandenburg; Munich: Henle, 1996):VI:207 (§2107) and 281 (§2203)].

[39] *Wiener Urtext*: preface, p.VII.

EXAMPLE 3.19
(the dotted lines are Badura-Skoda's)

Badura-Skoda is only partially right in his observation, for not "all" Viennese publishers achieved such neat layouts. Diabelli, for example, was rather inconsistent and unsystematic, as the following example from his edition of the *Müllerlieder* (*Ungeduld*) demonstrates. M.1 shows us a left-hand triplet eighth note aligned perfectly with the last note of the triplet above it. However, in the last beat of m. 8 it is a duple eighth which is placed with the last note of the triplet. In the first beat of the following measure the singer's sixteenth is placed clearly after the last note of the piano's triplet, whereas in the next beat (on the word "in"), the singer's sixteenth is placed more or less with the end note of the piano's triplet. To complicate matters even further, in the last beat of m. 10 the note setter has missed the proper alignment of the singer's eighth note entirely, placing it not before the final triplet in the piano, but well after it!

The only consistency we find in terms of triplet vs. sixteenth endings in this print is that the text appears to have dictated the spacing of the notes, and that alignments between the parts were of secondary interest. In general, alignments were preferred for readability, of course, but not always achieved.

EXAMPLE 3.20

Reading Schubert's Music   95

Actually, the workmanship in many Viennese publications was so haphazard in this regard that the short notes of dotted figures often were printed even to the left of the last notes of such triplet figures! Only an extended visit to the Heuringer wine district, however, could inspire us to take such things as performance hints.

Elsewhere Badura-Skoda points out that Schubert's autographs also reveal alignments of the last notes of mixed figures, but again he is only partially right.[40] Schubert's "horizontal" sense—i.e. his calligraphic style *per se,* plus the apparant habit of sometimes writing out a voice or part for a number of measures before adding the next one below or above it—often produced alignment, but just as often did not. And, just as in some printed editions, we even find the 16th note placed before the end of the triplet figure, as in the opening passage of the *Klavierstück* D946/1[41] (see Example 3.21 on p. 96). Even in the face of such evidence Badura-Skoda and others continue to support assimilation on the basis of orthography and printing practices.

Orthographical arguments fail for the fundamental reason that in those days alignments did not represent simultaneity, either in autographs or in print. If the first and last notes within beat groups happened to be aligned (by fortune, intent, or both), it was for

---

[40] Montgomery, "Triolenangleichung."
[41] See also the autograph of *Wasserfluth* D911/6: m.10, beat 1; m.11, beat 1; m. 13, beat 3; or m. 25, beat 1 (*PPM*, NY and Dover reprint: 23, see Youens, App. IIB).

clarity and ease of reading the beat groups as such. Furthermore, it hardly mattered what transpired in manuscripts, whether, as in Schubert, alignments were haphazard because of his horizontal-linear manner of working, or as in Chopin, whose alignments were as neat as his handwriting in general. Manuscripts were meant for the printer, not for the performing public. In printing, the alignment convention for grouping beats lasted even longer than Badura himself says, for at least one note setter's manual (J.H. Bachmann's) shows it to be still in force at least by 1865[42] (see Example 3.22 on facing page).

> The second quarter of the upper line consists of a dotted eighth and sixteenth. The corresponding quarter consists of a triplet in eighth-note values. Thus the upper figure involves two notes, and the lower figure three. Here not only the beginning, but also the end of these two equal-valued figures should be aligned.

EXAMPLE 3.21

---

[42] J.H. Bachmann, *Schule des Musiknoten-Satzes* (Leipzig): 59.

EXAMPLE 3.22

By the time this manual was written Lizst was 54, Verdi was 52, Wagner also was 52 and had already written *Tristan und Isolde,* Gounod was 47 and had finished *Faust* six years before, Brahms was 32 and well into his career, Saint-Saëns was 30 and celebrated across Europe, and even Giacomo Puccini and Gustav Mahler were alive. Does this mean we should assimilate in Liszt, Wagner, Verdi, Gounod, Brahms, and Saint-Saëns? Certainly not. The problem here is that adherents of the alignment theory may be looking at an old convention through modern eyes without adjusting for that fact. By the last two decades of the nineteenth century, most printers no longer aligned the end notes within beat groups artificially, but allowed all alignments to assume the meaning of simultaneity with which every modern musician is now unconsciously familiar. Looking back at other layout systems requires other eyes and other understanding, but indeed it is what one is expected to do when dealing with historical issues.[43]

The power of the printed page is so enormously influential, especially today, for reasons just stated, that editors must strive to remain impartial in these matters. Schubert editors, unfortunately, have not achieved such restraint. In the *GA*, for example, Eusebius Mandyczewski purposefully aligned the ends of certain mixed figures in the attempt to influence players, for whom alignment was by then binding for performance. Wielding a powerful visual tool, then, he misled generations of Schubert performers.[44] The oddest part of Mandyczewski's agenda is that he aligned only certain mixed figures, in the song *Wasserfluth,* for example, but not in all works with mixed figures. Thus the luxury of subjectivity, which still marks the thinking of many prominent modern interpreters, was introduced long ago under the aegis of scholarly reliability. In retrospect, it is little wonder that Schubert interpretation has suffered so much since from the *'mal so, 'mal so* (sometimes this way, sometimes that way) syndrome.

In the *NSA* Walther Dürr corrected the artificial alignments to an approximation of their proper proportions by modern expectations, but then in his commentary he cancelled his corrections throughout by recommending the practice of assimilation! Dürr is not alone in such confusing intervention; in an otherwise excellent edition of *Winterreise,* Dietrich

---

[43] The development we describe here is partially analogous to the rise of linear perspective in the late Renaissance. To view alignments in Viennese prints of the early nineteenth century as representative of modern time lines is just as erroneous as to view smaller adults in some Medieval paintings as if they were standing further away from the picture plane. Linear perspective played no role here: they were portrayed as smaller because they represented less important people.

[44] Montgomery, "Triplet Assimilation": 89–91.

Fischer-Dieskau and Elmar Budde not only promote the well-worn assimilation argument for the song *Wasserfluth,* but attribute its necessity to technical problems.[45] These "technical problems" have nothing to do with the original reasons for assimilation, namely, a young harpsichord player's lack of coordination. Budde / Dieskau's reasoning is that the singer would have difficulty in placing a sixteenth note after the triplet. We have encountered singers, of course, for whom such eventualities have proven undeniable. However, we must point out that *Wasserfluth* is marked "Langsam," and that any singer for whom such a problem exists at this slow tempo does not belong on the stage. In any case, the explanation makes no sense: no singer would wait expectantly during each beat for the pianist to complete a triplet and then try quickly to sandwich in his sixteenth note afterwards – what a jolly mess this would produce! The song is designed so that the singer may proceed upon his way independently of the pianist, who does the same in a slightly different rhythmic pattern. The oddest aspect of the Budde / Dieskau statement is that instead of recognizing the misleading idealist position that has influenced them, they have based their recommendation on opposite grounds— practicality— precisely where practicality plays no role.

Assimilation as a contextual choice

We have noted that the original purpose of assimilation, namely, as a remedy for awkwardness, has long since been relegated to second place. Assimilation is now discussed for its inherent "musical" merits, and some musicians argue (in hindsight, of course) that it must have been a compositional ideal of the period. Adherents of arbitrary assimilation in Schubert as a musical ideal often maintain that the dominant affect, or rhythmic context, of a work is a decisive factor in favor of adjusting dotted figures to match the triplets. The most common work invoked as evidence is the C-minor Impromptu D899/1, which begins with dotted figures that are sometimes softened to match the triplet accompaniment when it enters:

EXAMPLE 3.23a/c

[45] *Winterreise,* ed. Elmar Budde and Dietrich Fischer-Dieskau (Frankfurt, 1975): preface, p.3.

Reading Schubert's Music

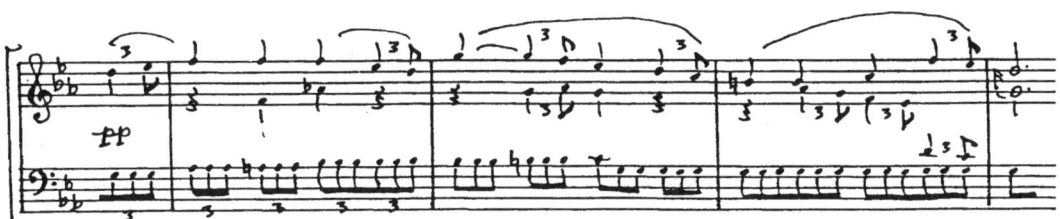

c. with all duplets assimilated to the triplets

The trouble with this argument (beyond the fact that the issue of assimilation should never have gotten this far) is that the dominant and contextual rhythm of this work is not the triplet accompaniment but the dotted figure, as defined by its prominent melodic character and the choice of 4/4 as the fundamental meter! Strictly speaking, triplets are mere "guests" in this meter, appearing from time to time but not remaining for the duration. At best, when the triplets enter after many measures of strictly dotted figures, we might say that the corporate affect then becomes the conflict between the two rhythmic ideas, but by no stretch of analysis can it be identified as dominated by the accompanimental triplets.

In some cases, modern performers would avoid even the simple 3–2 conflicts in Schubert's music on aesthetic grounds, as Paul Badura-Skoda advocates in the preface to his edition of the Impromptus (cited above). Since a pianist of Badura-Skoda's eminence cannot claim technical difficulty in such cases, his argument is automatically an interpretational one. Badura-Skoda does not discourage all such conflicts in Schubert, but only those which he himself appears to find unmusical. But such selectivity, instead of strengthening his position, demonstrates merely that the governing principle involved is performer-based instead of composer-based.

Taking the issue of assimilation out of the context of piano playing, where it originated, and into the larger realm of music-making has caused confusion among performers ranging from lieder singers to symphony conductors. The *Wasserfluth* case has become a cause célèbre, at least in Schubert circles. Only one other Schubert song, *Erstarrung* D911/4 has been singled out in this manner or with this frequency. Here the argument revolves around the forced configuration:

EXAMPLE 3.24

This notation arises simply through the collision of lines. In the past, Schubert scholars have presumed a softening of the dotted figure to be unavoidable. But as we have demonstrated elsewhere in detail, just the opposite is the case.[46] As in the C-minor Impromptu discussed above, the dominant rhythm here is by metrical definition the dotted figure, and the corporate affect is the struggle between the figures. What must give way here is the triplet, which also remains accompanimental throughout.

---

[46] Montgomery, "Triplet Assimilation:" 91-92.

Fermatas

In Schubert's music, and indeed in all music of his time, we find one notational value that cannot be quantified with certainty, the *fermata*. At least we should say that the proper length of a note under a *fermata* cannot be quantified successfully. The *fermata* is the most neglected notational sign in the pedagogical works of Schubert's day. August Swoboda appears to be the only Viennese theorist of this period to elaborate even slightly upon it. Swoboda, who is happy to quantify other values, for example, dots and strokes, apparently grants the *fermata* an inherent contextual plasticity:

> One often finds a dot over one note, covered by an arch. One calls this sign *Ruhepunckt* [point of pause], *Ferma, Couronne, Haltung* [hold], *General-Halt* [general hold]. It signifies that the note carrying it (or in cases of more than one, each note over which the sign stands) can be held as long as the musician desires. The musical meaning of such holds [can be] a question, a cry, a [moment of] reflection, etc. For example, one might perform the note
>
> a) loud, sharply attacked and long, gradually decreasing the volume until at the end it sounds ethereal like the aeolian harp; or
>
> b) imperceptibly and soft at first, growing in volume to a high point, at which it is suddenly and sharply broken off; or
>
> c) soft at first, growing to the loudest volume, and then growing soft again, until the tone can no longer be heard. If the word "Fermata" is written next to the sign, one may introduce an appropriate figure of his own choosing.* However, he who does not understand the spirit of the piece, and thus cannot enhance that spirit through [his figure], had better be satisfied with just holding out the tone. The best alternative would be if each composer would write out what he wanted.[47]

When Swoboda speaks of "*Fermata*" written next to the arch sign, of course, he means cadential caesure in concertos and arias. In any case, he hedges his bets on the subject of length, and does not even broach the two major side issues connected with this sign: 1) when, if ever, does one *ritard* before the *fermata*; and 2) when, if ever, does one leave a space after the *fermata* before continuing? Perhaps we cannot answer these questions systematically, but we can propose some contexts for the answers. Let us imagine four kinds of *fermatas*, their functions defined by their placement within a movement: "introductory" *fermatas*, "inline" *fermatas*, "cadential" *fermatas* and "closing" *fermatas*.

1) Introductory *fermata*. This type of hold occurs at the very beginning or near the beginning of a movement and is annunciatory in nature. It can occur several times until the movement gets underway. (See Example 3.25a/b)

For the Fourth Symphony, of course, there is no question of a *ritard* into the *fermata*, only questions concerning length and space afterwards. For the wind players no problem exists concerning length (within reason), but string players can manage *ff* only so long on a single bow. Unless we believe in bow changes on single notes in that era, we can calculate

---

[47] *Allgemeine Theorie der Tonkunst:* 30–32. (See App. IIA, 1826)

Reading Schubert's Music   *101*

EXAMPLE 3.25a/b
a. Fourth Symphony D417/1

b. *Die Zauberharfe* Overture D644

the length by watching the concertmaster. (More often than not, the concertmaster would have been leading the orchestra anyway.) In the middle of the previous century Leopold Mozart had spoken out against bow changes on single notes, but in doing so he confirmed, of course, that some soloists did change bows for occasional effects (see Ch. IV, fn. 57). It does not seem to have been a normal practice even as late as Schubert's day, and thus we truly might be able to rely on the capability of the bow for our length. As to a pause after the *fermata,* some break must occur if for no other reason that to save the lives of the wind players. Exactly how long the break lasted must have ranged from the minimum length of the concertmaster's retake to the time required for the flautists' faces to change color from red to reasonable.

For *Die Zauberharfe* another question would have been about *ritards* into the *fermatas*, but rarely would one have reason to *ritard* at the beginning of a work. First, to slow down into such *fermatas* appears to have no rhetorical basis, and second, orchestra leaders of that day were not trained in the flexibilities that all modern conductors take for granted. The only other question is whether or not to take Swoboda seriously about the possible volume changes on *fermatas*. We note that he says, "the musician" and not "the musicians;" thus he still must be talking about soloists or singers. Certainly no orchestra leader of that day was technically sophisticated enough to achieve such effects, and pianists, of course, had no control over a note or chord once struck.

2) Inline *fermata,* type A. We have borrowed this term, with apologies, from our technical friends, the plumbers and electricians. These holds can occur in any measure of a movement, from the second to the penultimate, and should not be prepared in any way. Their rhetorical efficacy lies in surprise, or better said, their sudden, momentary existence, followed by an equally sudden resumption of tempo with no break to hinder their flight. They can be used as markers, as in the openings of Beethoven's Symphonies Five and Six (see discussion of frames in Ch I/VI). Schubert gives us several good examples in the Sonata in A minor D537/4:

EXAMPLE 3.26

Does this example conform to Swoboda's type A, "loud, sharply attacked and long, gradually decreasing the volume"? Played on the pianoforte it must conform, for the tone decays by itself if held out long, and the motion resumes on the next measure in ***p***.

Inline *fermata*, type B. Sometimes we find cadential inline *fermatas* that should be looked upon as unmeasured, expressive *tenutos* over the course of several notes. They are found most often in Schubert's operas. The following example occurs in No. 27 of *Alfonso und Estrella:*

EXAMPLE 3.27
Alfonso und Estrella: No. 27, mm. 56-61, as written

The *NSA* editor (Dürr) speculates that this *fermata* should be filled out with an ornate lead-in in the style of Italian opera, and provides a sample at the bottom of the page:

EXAMPLE 3.28
Alfonso und Estrella: No. 27. mm. 60-61. execution as imagined by the *NSA* editor

Relying on apparent scholarship, as advertised in this edition, the unsuspecting singer and conductor might be tempted to use this rather clumsy and invasive lead-in, or another one like it, unaware that the editor has failed to distinguish between two basic styles: the florid Italian and the more straightforward German with its *singspiel* origins.[48] We cannot assert that Italian-trained virtuoso singers of Schubert's day would not have indulged in such ornaments at every opportunity, but we can assert that these things were not consistent with the character of Schubert's works. As we will learn in Ch. V, Schubert's music requires no voluntary ornamentation. This *fermata*, then, may be taken to indicate a moment of tempo flexibility, spread over four notes as controlled by the singer.

Schubert gives us an excellent example of a single *fermata* stretched over several notes in his instrumental writing, also from *Alfonso und Estrella:*

EXAMPLE 3.29
Opening of No. 30, specifically mm. 1, 3, and 5

Where Schubert feels the need for a few small notes during one of these extended *tenutos* he is perfectly capable of notating them himself:

EXAMPLE 3.30
Alfonso und Estrella: No. 4, mm. 65–69

---

[48] Not only does Dürr's lead-in prohibit spontaneity (the two singers would have to practice it beforehand in order to coordinate the turn and the inner hold), but it introduces an *appoggiatura* on the following downbeat that is absent in Schubert's score. Thus it falls into the category of "recomposing" Schubert's music, an exercise in scholarly arrogance.

In Ch.V we will learn from Louis Spohr that composers of the day had begun to incorporate most of their desired ornamentation (or what had once been ornamentation) into the written fabric of their melodies. Example 3.30 bears out this theory, for it is nothing more than a notated turn. Schubert gives it to only one of the singers, thus emphasizing its simplicity and avoiding any extended and monotonous planning between the two singers.

3) Cadential *fermata*. This is what Swoboda describes as a *fermata* with the word itself written next to the sign, or a cadential *caesura* in concertos and arias. Its principal harmonic orientation, but not necessarily its only one, is on the dominant (i.e. the tonic 6/4 chord). C.P.E. Bach had spoken years before of a *ritard* during the approach to this *fermata*, and we have no reason to believe that this practice had ceased. Basically, this *fermata* is not a part of Schubert's language, in that he wrote little or no music in the concerted, brilliant style.

4) Closing *fermata*. This type occurs almost always on the final note of a movement, and no rules can be derived for an approach to it. Certainly one tires of hearing the final "Luftpause-plus-pooh" invented by modern Baroque experts, and one hopes, at least, never to hear such a thing in Schubert. In structural terms, a non-*ritardando* approach to most final cadences puts more trust in the power of the *fermata* itself, which, after all, was developed to signal the end. In effect, the dramatic, heavy-weather endings favored by conductors of the early twentieth century were developed in the middle-to-late nineteenth century in response to the sense of long musical journeying engendered by major orchestral compositions of those times—from the expansive scores of Schumann and Berlioz to the massive productions of Bruckner and Mahler. None of this is necessary in Schubert's music.

Notational shorthand: implied vs. explicit

Probably the most perplexing question concerning dynamics, accentuation, articulation, pedalling, etc. for all music in the Viennese Classic and Romantic tradition, is when, if ever, to extend such expressive markings beyond the measures or parts in which they are actually notated. We use the term "shorthand" to characterize the initial markings in passages where we believe they are meant to be extended, but used in this sense it is a misnomer. What we really mean to say is "implied shorthand," as opposed to the explicit shorthand in the form of written instructions that Schubert and others often used for this purpose: *sempre staccato, simile,* etc. to continue an articulation for an ongoing motive without having to mark each note. Another example of real shorthand is the autograph of the Octet D803, where Schubert extends the dotting on its own to remind himself to fill in the notes of the *portando-Bebung* pattern on the fair copy:

EXAMPLE 3.31

Reading Schubert's Music 105

Perhaps the most common category of explicit shorthand for printers consisted of the slashes that indicated the unvaried continuance of an established pattern: for example, single slashes flanked by two dots (. / .) or double slashes for continuing groups of 16th notes, etc. As J.H. Bachmann later stated in his *Schule des Musiknoten-Satzes* (1865: 298), printers used their discretion concerning the appropriateness of such shorthand:

> Abbreviations [shorthand entries] in musical notation can be found in almost every manuscript, because composers use them to bring their thoughts more quickly onto paper. To transfer them intact into printed scores for distribution is not a laudable decision. First, the room that they save is minimal. Second, because of the swift overview with which one must interpret them on the spot, their proper execution demands a musical education which not every musical amateur possesses [...] [However,] in truly artistic compositions, whose musical worth can be recognized without any extra indications, they indeed are entered as follows [Bachman gives examples]. The executive person in such cases is the notesetter, who may actually [... using his own discretion ...] introduce such abbreviations into a printed score, even where not indicated in a manuscript.

Bachman, of course, was writing in Brahms's day, not Schubert's, but we know that the standard forms of shorthand he describes—particularly for basic flagging, grouping and note values—remained intact from a period even before the turn of the century.

A shorthand for indicating ongoing articulation was also known. D.G. Türk's *Clavierschule*[49] had implied its existence and stated that a performer should continue a *legato* style where slurring was marked only in a few measures at the beginning of a movement, and that the delivery should change only where a new articulation was marked. The shorthand instruction in the third edition of Leopold Mozart's *Violinschule*[50] was even more specific. Having prescribed emphasis on the "good" parts of a measure, Mozart went on to describe a typically simple accompaniment to an aria or concerted work, dominated by repeated eighths or sixteenths. He showed his readers a model pattern, saying that composers often showed the articulation / accentuation for a few measures and then made a tiny mark (Mozart used a *custos*, placed at the pitch of the coming downbeat) to show that the pattern should continue "until a change occurs:"

EXAMPLE 3.32

The very young Schubert was given shorthand rules similar to those of Türk and Mozart, at least where simple motivic situations were concerned (and without the *custos*, which he never used for that purpose). He could have read about such rules in those two tutors, but more likely he learned them from his own teacher, Antonio Salieri. In the *Romanze* from *Fernando* D220 (1815) the *portando* dotting in m.2 was apparently meant

---

[49] *Clavierschule* (1789:VI, §38:355)
[50] *Violinschule* (1787:§12:262)

to continue in the second violin and viola parts. Schubert even specified that the little voice-leading *crescendo*s and off-beat patterns (m. 5) are to receive a uniform *portando* (which they otherwise would not, because of more aggressive bowing). Finally in m. 6, after having modelled his articulation, leaving nothing to chance, Schubert discontinued the dotting entirely. Apparently his rule of thumb here was that shorthand modelling held good only where a motive or pattern continued relatively unchanged. The *crescendos* and off-beat patterns constituted changes in his mind, and so they too needed marking. After all three models had been established, it was no longer necessary to mark each one as it occurred in changing situations.

EXAMPLE 3.33

The *Fernando* autograph, where Schubert signed himself as a pupil of Salieri's, is quite clean, almost as if it were copied out as an important assignment from the master. Although the work was clearly written for the limited vocal and instrumental forces typically at Schubert's disposal at the *Stadtkonvikt*, it may not have been fair-copied merely for purposes of performance, and certainly not for publication. Orchestra parts from this time certainly would tell us more about Schubert's early concept and use of shorthand, or at least his training in this regard.

We cannot draw conclusions about Schubert's later shorthand use from *Fernando*, not merely because it is a student work, but also because of its older style. The kind of simplistic, single-affect movement in which accompaniment motives remained relatively consistent for long stretches was characteristic of the eighteenth century, about which Mozart and Türk wrote with authority, but that kind of orchestral language would not remain characteristic even a few more years into Schubert's career. More importantly, Schubert's demands upon performers were to become far more complex, more difficult to execute and certainly more specific to his style. He continued to use notational shorthand, however, principally for reminders to himself in first drafts, and for certain kinds of reminders to copyists and printers. Although much of his shorthand was not intended to get as far as the printed page, some of it indeed appears to have made its way into the public eye and consciousness. For example, even in fair copies he often marked voice and piano parts in the lieder with a single dynamic, most often confining the marking to the accompaniment; and this custom was taken over by his publishers.

In orchestral music Schubert sometimes marked dynamics only once for entire groups of instruments, particularly in drafts. Here, because we know his general tendency towards across-the-board dynamics, we can assume the same volume level for the other instruments in a group, at least conceptually. For example, the autograph reproduction of the first page of the *Alfonso und Estrella* overture (Example 4.27a, m. 1) shows *ff* for the violins, flutes, cellos and basses, but we can assume *ff* as a general dynamic for all the other instruments as well. Thus the *NSA* has interpreted this score correctly in print (ex. 4.27b). Still, it would have been more responsible for a scholarly edition to have left Schubert's dynamic markings exactly in their original state, offering a note in the preface concerning the implied shorthand. The *NSA* editorship (perhaps for reasons commercially favorable to the Bärenreiter company) remains, apparently, unwilling to distinguish between a study score and a performance score for the wider market.

In matters of articulation, Schubert's shorthand was meant mostly for copyists and printers. Occasionally, however, it has found its way mistakenly into printed scores for the general public. In the *Moments musicaux* D780 we find two such cases, both probably the result of printing from a first draft (the autographs for these pieces are lost). The autograph of No. 4 in C♯ minor is quite interesting. It was probably a first draft, wherein Schubert appears to have started the dots for five measures to instruct the copyist and / or the notesetter to continue the articulation for the duration of the opening left hand pattern. The words "*legato*" and "*staccato*," on the other hand, appear to have been directed at the performer (i.e. meant to have been printed) in order to emphasize the difference in articulation between the hands. For some reason, the publisher, M.J. Leidesdorf, allowed the manuscript to be printed as it stood, setter's instructions and all (See Example 3.34). By this point, Leidesdorf had lost his partner (Ignaz Sauer), and the business had substantially failed. Surely he had lost all interest in the quality of what he published. Leidesdorf himself absconded from Vienna shortly thereafter, and one would not be surprised if he had taken Schubert's score with him.[51]

In No. 5 of the *Moments musicaux* (F minor) Schubert's shorthand modelling for the copyist / note setter is also clear. Here, the dots in the second half of the first measure provide a model for the rest of the eighth-note pairs. Schubert renewed the dots in m. 5 because of the octave drop, the new voicing and the new dynamic. Again, the score was in the dubious care of M. J. Leidesdorf (See Example 3.35).

---

[51] See Hilmar / Jestremski: 269.

EXAMPLE 3.34

EXAMPLE 3.35

Reading Schubert's Music   109

In cases where Schubert's own fair copies were used as the basis for publication, it seems logical and wise to take the printed articulation at face value.[52] For example, in the manuscript of *Die Forelle* D550 (version 5) we see that Schubert went to some trouble to dot each of the eighth notes of the accompaniment figure. Here he easily could have employed some form of instruction (*sempre staccato,* for example) but he clearly did not wish to leave the matter to chance:

EXAMPLE 3.36

[52] Perhaps one of the oddest violations of this principle we have heard in recent years occurs throughout *Der Leiermann* D911/24 in a recording by Roman Trekel, baritone and Ulrich Eisenlohr, piano (Naxos 8-554471). Here the pianist takes the grace notes in the two opening bars as a model for the entire song, placing them laboriously on the beat as well (see Ch. IV on short graces at the beginning of movements). Not only is Schubert's lovely "tuning up" image at the beginning rendered meaningless, but the insistent graces throughout (particularly as played here) mar the simplicity of the song as a whole. Schubert notated his grace notes accurately and systematically in terms of value, number and placement throughout entire movements or songs, thus the addition of further ornaments constitutes *willkürliche Verzierung,* which has no place in his music (see Ch. IV). We cannot say whether this interpretation was conceived as a mere novelty, or whether the artists, like so many others of late, have been misled by recent speculative "scholarship" and / or editing. In any case, it is regrettable.

In general, we should take Schubert at his word, despite what may seem, on cursory examination, to need second-guessing. In the G-major Sonata D894, which was published during Schubert's lifetime and most likely proofed by him, we find first-movement passages that appear to be marked with shorthand, but probably are not. For example, we might ask ourselves, "Should we repeat the right-hand accents and hairpin dynamics of mm. 27/28 in mm. 29/30?" Our immediate response might well be, "Yes, of course, because the second phrase (mm. 29/30) is the balancing answer to the first:"

EXAMPLE 3.37

This analysis seems fair enough, given all that has been drilled into us about classical form and musical rhetoric from our student days. Let us suppose that we have guessed right, and that Schubert intended for us to play the second two bars in a fashion similar to the first two. We then must ask ourselves, "Why does he take such care to mark or differentiate the second half of each measure here (mm. 29-30), but not the first half?" In this light, we see that Schubert has specific plans for each of his phrases (note also the differences in articulation between this passage in the exposition and in the recapitulation), and that to standardize them would be to deprive his rhetoric of its richness.

Where Schubert himself did not prepare a fair copy for publication, and most especially where he abandoned scores at various drafting stages, performers often are faced with substantial interpretational difficulties. The first variation of the second movement of the String Quartet in D minor D810, *Der Tod und das Mädchen* provides an example. Based on Schubert's working draft (now in the Pierpont Morgan Library, hereafter *PPM*), the half-measure marked with *portando* triplets-cum-sextuplets (the bow moving in the same direction in sixes) in the second violin and viola would appear to constitute a model for the rest of the variation. According to the rule of the non-changing motive, we might assume this articulation to hold good for the entire variation. In a fair copy Schubert might have marked *simile* or *sempre portando* for the note setter. Interpreted in this manner, the accompaniment triplets and sextuplets of D810/2 would provide a softly undulating sea of sound, while the first violin fragments toss delicately to and fro above the waves, occasionally joining in with the *portando* bowings. This bowing style would constitute a notated render-

Reading Schubert's Music   111

ing of the old bow-vibrato (*Bebung,* Ch. IV). Such techniques are no longer practiced by modern players, apparently, for all string quartets now bow this entire accompaniment figure back-and-forth – most often off the string. Interpreted in a true *portando* (single bows for the threes and sixes), however, the passage would be an almost perfect demonstration of the principle that serious composers of Schubert's day incorporated ornaments of the past into their music first via sign, and eventually, as in the present case, by notating them bodily (cf. Spohr's description of this process in Ch. V).

EXAMPLE 3.38
D810/2, 1st variation, m. 25

Jean Dane proposes the possibility of a different but interesting bowing for the first measure of this passage, taking Schubert's notation (*portando* vs. non-*portando*) literally. She points out that the single half-measure of *portando* (beginning with a downbow, with which she would impart a slight agogic *tenuto* on the first of the sextuplets) brings the bow nicely to the tip for the rest of the passage. Thus, although the notes are bowed back and forth, the bow stays at the tip throughout the passage, creating an equally impressive accompanimental murmuring or undulation in *pianissimo*.[53] We can find no context for such a technique among Schubert's other works, however, and in light of the fact that this autograph was abandoned at a working stage we are inclined to view the marking as Schubert's shorthand reminder to himself to add similar markings throughout the passage at a later stage. In any case, both of these solutions are superior to current common practices among string quartets, most of whom simply ignore Schubert's marking in the first place, scraping away comfortably in the middle of the bow, and inevitably too loud.

[53] In conversaton with the author, fall 1999.

It is not only sad, but vexing that so much of Schubert's instrumental music remained unpublished during his lifetime. He prepared or supervised fewer fair copies than any other major composer of the Viennese school, and he corrected relatively few advance prints. His greatest completed symphonic work, the C-major Symphony D944, presents complex problems in this regard. While Schubert clearly submitted the score to the *GMF* in order to have parts prepared for a reading, it was no fair copy, nor do we believe that he had much to say about the parts themselves. Here again, in certain places he merely notated models for the articulation, probably as a reminder to himself or to a copyist to finish the dotting at a later time and / or in a fair copy. Surely the triplet passage beginning at m. 61 in the Introduction is one of these places:

EXAMPLE 3.39

Reading Schubert's Music 113

The triplets remain unchanged in character for nine measures, at which point a *crescendo* begins. There, of course, the strokes must become longer as the passage builds to *ff*. Dynamic change usually brings an articulation change with it in Schubert's scores.

In the opening section of the Scherzo of D944, we find articulation carefully marked except for the strings in mm. 25–26. Although many performances simply continue the articulation for these measures as if a shorthand instruction were in effect, we must ask ourselves, "Why would Schubert go to the trouble to write out articulation for the majority of measures, and then simply forget to mark these bars?" Clearly Schubert made no mistake here. A *crescendo* begins at this point, and Schubert the violinist (and we are still speaking of transition bows and unreinforced instruments) knows instinctively that *detaché* is the best bowing with which to build the passage. Through the changed articulation he also lets us know that something is happening here as the *crescendo* gets underway:

EXAMPLE 3.40

The following example gives the dynamic change in reverse. In the transition to the second group of the first movement Schubert takes us from the *ff* sextuplets of the first group to the woodwind entrance of the new group in only two measures. In the first measure he starts the *decrescendo* and in the second he prepares the new accompaniment through a new articulation. The editor (R. Fiske) of the edition shown below (new Eulenberg) has supplied further dots in brackets, as if Schubert either forgot to continue them, or as if the initial dots were a form of shorthand for the following measure as well. Neither supposition is correct, however, for Schubert has indicated merely what must transpire in the bowing style between point A (where the dots begin) to point B (where the second group begins).

EXAMPLE 3.41

Considering that in string music Schubert exchanged his *staccatos* for full-length notes to prepare for and execute *crescendos* and *decrescendos*, and considering that the *decrescendo* in the excerpt above starts already in m. 132, we probably will find that a steadily lengthening bowstroke from *staccato* to full *détaché* between mm. 132–134 is the proper approach to these two measures. No notational conventions existed to indicate such an idea, but it comes so naturally that one can hardly ignore the possibility.

The articulation problems in D944 are widespread, but because we have addressed them in a separate article we shall not go into further detail here.[54] We can only hope to make the reader aware that most conductors and orchestras still approach this work in warhorse fashion, and that many of its finest details have yet to be made clear to listeners. (See example 3.41 above).

That we have grown so used to hearing and interpreting Schubert's music as if he were forgetful or helpless in such matters is a sad fact indeed. Let us return to the D-minor Quartet D810 for a final observation. We may be used to hearing its scintillating finale

---

[54] "Performance concerns and criteria for Franz Schubert's Symphony in C major D944" in *Die Brille* 24 (2000).

Reading Schubert's Music

with a gratuitously homogenized articulation (cf. the editor's *simile* in m. 5), but this is certainly not how Schubert wrote it.

EXAMPLE 3.42

D810, Finale: *Presto* (Bärenreiter, ed. W. Aderhold)

We may have forgotten that Josef Czerny published this work in 1831, the last two movements, at least, from some other manuscript than the one in the *PPM*.[55] This manuscript may also have been a draft, for the finale is not entirely furnished with the proper dotting. Nevertheless, the changing articulation modelled via shorthand in the opening pages alone are enough upon which to base an intelligent performance. The ensemble that would take the trouble to differentiate his articulation in this movement according to this modelling would also discover in Franz Schubert a musical wit quite the equal of Haydn, Mozart and Beethoven in their most brilliant moments. If this statement is true, then, for a score with such interpretational problems, just imagine how easy it would be to create stunning performances based upon the Schubert scores in our libraries we know to be correct and non-problematic.

---

[55] A similar situation exists with the "Trout" Quintet D 667, also published by Josef Czerny, where now in manuscript only Albert Stadler's alternate version of the piece exists in parts. According to all modern editors, Czerny's print (1829) is the best source, and yet no "urtext" to date (including the *NSA* print) has managed to reproduce it without serious but senseless meddling based on Stadler's variants.

CHAPTER **IV**

Expression and Expressive Devices

In order to talk about expression we are forced to isolate a number of expressive devices from their modern contexts, which have grown to be combinative and complex in nature. Necessary as this procedure is, it may appear somewhat dry and even arbitrary at first. *Rubato* and agogic accentuation, for example, are regarded by many modern Schubert players as phenomena quite inseparable from the natural shaping of a phrase, not to mention the fact that such means of expression are believed to arise spontaneously and intuitively. Exactly how, technically speaking, these things operate in Schubert's music constitutes the secret of each performer's personal approach, perhaps gloriously unclear even to him or her. For this reason, they have taken on a slight analytical taboo, even among players who teach other players; thus, the entire topic tends to be avoided in any but the vaguest terms. A sure signal of this thinking is the reliance upon intangible but still widely-circulating catchwords such as "musicality," "taste," or "touch." To be fair, these words can be read in almost any tutor of Schubert's day as well. The difference is that musicians of Schubert's day were much closer to the issues at hand than we are now, the better part of two centuries later. Even so, Schubert probably did not want his music to be subjected to commonly understood notions of "taste" or "musicality," any more than composers today might want to rely upon such concepts in the modern concert hall.

Rubato

Although the concept of an expressive rhythmic freedom within a context of fixed tempo and measured note values may be older than the modern barline, theorists from Pietro Cerone in the early seventeenth century to Pier Tosi in the eighteenth and to Hugo Riemann in the late nineteenth have provided surprisingly meager enlightenment as to its application. Compilers of dictionaries have been even less helpful, for throughout the years many of them simply have borrowed their definitions from earlier compilers, often word for word and with little regard for changing musical realities. Where Schubert is concerned we automatically can weed out some descriptions of *rubato* (or "*tempo rubato*," in the older nomenclature). In cases where *tempo rubato* denotes an ornament in the Baroque sense (see Galliard's fanciful example in Rubato Overview, App. I), or even an ornamental passage (full metrical displacement, see discussion, App. I), we can reject it. Schubert's notation is reasonably complete, including the proactive indication of ornaments when and where required.

[Author's note: Because the elusive and changing concepts of *"rubato"* and *"tempo rubato"* present conceptual problems even today, we have included a short overview of the subject in Appendix I. The rest of this discussion proceeds as if the reader already were familiar with the information contained therein, or has just read it.]

For a long time, the paradigmatic modern description of historical *tempo rubato* types was contained in a 1918 article by Lucian Kamienski, and it remains useful even today as a basic chronological study.[1] Boris Bruck's 1929 dissertation is not so well known but perhaps is even more informative. Bruck was the first to establish a typology, identifying three main categories of *tempo rubato*: (1) as freedom in the rendering of rhythmic quantities; (2) as freedom in the rendering of rhythmic "qualities" (inversions and contrasts of dynamics, etc.); and (3) as freedom in the treatment of tempo itself.[2] Recently, Sandra Rosenblum has identified at least four different techniques. She cites two "contrametric" eighteenth-century models: the strict German displacement type, and the melodically freer Italian type. She describes another *rubato* technique in terms of tempo flexibility. Finally, she identifies an agogic accentuation that made its effect through a lingering on single, important notes, and, in the nineteenth century, in combination with tempo flexibility.[3] Here we would depart from her models only to grant separate status to these last two concepts, agogic accentuation and tempo flexibility, even for the nineteenth century. True, they are often combined one with the other, but viewed as separate components, each can also be combined with other techniques as well. Also, in recent times the concept of "agogic" accentuation has been expanded and refined in pedagogical practice. Now, in addition to a lingering on specific notes (with the emphasis necessary to sustain them, at least on the keyboard), it also refers to a slightly delayed, caressed attack.

Building partially upon Rosenblum's *rubato* classification and partially on our own we can identify two basic types, *tempo rubato* (older) and *rubato* (modern), which we can sort out into five techniques:

Classic *Tempo rubato* A and B

A. Free contrametric (Italian)

B. Strict contrametric (German)

    1. syncopation by anticipation

    2. syncopation by delay

    3. hemiola-sesquialtera displacement

Early 19th-century *Tempo Rubato* in transition to *Rubato* adds:

C. General tempo change

---

[1] "Zum 'tempo rubato'" in *Archiv für Musikwissenschaft* I (1918/19, hereafter *AMW*):108–126.
[2] *Wandlungen des Begriffes Tempo rubato,* Inaugural Dissertation, Friedrich-Alexander Universität Erlangen (Berlin: Paul Funk).
[3] *Performance Practices in Classic Piano Music* (Indiana University Press, 1988): 362-392. Also see her article, "The Uses of Rubato in Music, Eighteenth to Twentieth Centuries" in *Performance Practice Review* 7/1 (Spring, 1994, hereafter *PPR*):33–53.

It begins to blur or abandon types A and B, which even in Mozart's time had begun to be written into the music itself. Later 19th-century *rubato* adds:

D. Agogic accentuation

E. *Tenuto* on single notes

either independently or in various combinations with type C.

Frederick Niecks researched Chopin's Viennese debut, which occurred in the year following Schubert's death:

> Often, no doubt, people mistook for tempo rubato what in reality was a suppression or displacement of accent, to which kind of playing the term is indeed sometimes applied. The reader will remember the following passage from a criticism in the *Wiener Theaterzeitung* of 1829:[4] "There are defects noticeable in the young man's [Chopin's] playing, among which is perhaps especially to be mentioned the non-observance of the indication by accent of the commencement of musical phrases."[5]

This passage has several possible interpretations. Niecks seemed to think that the Viennese critic referred to the old German-style *tempo rubato* by syncopation. But if so, why would such a time-honored device be considered a defect, especially in Vienna? The critic does not actually say that Chopin failed to stress the beginnings of measures, but only that he did not stress the beginnings of phrases. This distinction could point more to a changing treatment of larger melodic lines, attributed to Chopin and others, or it simply might be evidence of a superior basic musicianship.

When we read in August Swoboda's rather up-to-date (to judge by the musical configurations) *Theorie der Tonkunst,* 1826, that *tempo rubato* is "stolen time" [entwendetes Zeitmaß], "taken from another meter," [6] we can see that in formal terms even he has not progressed much further than Agricola or Marpurg in the century before him. Swoboda still uses the original *rubare* metaphor, but crystalizes it into what we call *tempo rubato* B3 (see categorization above).

Friedrich Starke also characterizes *tempo rubato* as stolen time in the older German sense:

> Generally with this term one indicates a kind of shortening and lengthening of the notes, or a displacement of them [i.e. *tempo rubato* B1/2].[7]

The remarkable passage at mm. 78-85 in the second movement of Schubert's D-major Sonata D850 might appear to be a good example of this kind of *tempo rubato*, only notated instead of improvised:

---

[4] By this year it would have been called the *Allgemeine Theaterzeitung und Unterhaltungsblatt* ... (see List of Abbreviations).
[5] *Frédéric Chopin as a Man and Musician,* 2 vols. (London/NY: Novello, Ewer, 1888):102.
[6] "Tempo rubato: entwendetes Zeitmaß, eine aus einer andern Tactart entwendete Bewegung." (148).
[7] "Tempo rubato: gestohlenes Zeitmaß. Gemeiniglich versteht man darunter eine Art von Verkürzung und Verlängerung der Noten, oder ein Verrücken derselben."

EXAMPLE 4.1

But in addition to the fact that *tempo rubato* was improvised and not notated, we would suggest that the syncopation in this passage is no mere expressive ornamentation (remembering that *tempo rubato* of all kinds were still described as ornamental in Schubert's day, at least in theory). Instead, it is a stunningly beautiful compositional outcropping of a syncopated motive that has occurred throughout the movement. Schubert sets up the syncopations from the beginning by structuring his main theme in 6/8 (emphasized via accent), but calling it 3/4. If this constitutes a notated analogue to *tempo rubato* (and indeed as such it would correspond exactly to the requirements as set out by Marpurg, C.P.E. Bach, D.G. Türk, etc.), then it is an entire movement's worth!

EXAMPLE 4.2

Expression and Expressive Devices 121

Are there passages in Schubert where an improvised syncopated *rubato* might be applicable? What about the first movement of D784 (A minor), for example, where Schubert presents his second group in simple halves and quarters, offering no real deviation from the pattern? Can we apply a tasteful bit of classical *tempo rubato* to even one single measure, say m. 87, in order to bring this rather uniformly-shaped rhetoric to a little high-point?

EXAMPLE 4.3

[rubato variant, mm.87-88]

The answer is no. The reasons concern both Schubert's local and long-distance thinking. Locally, he has pitted the serenity of the measures marked *p* against the power of those marked *ff*, and to ruffle that serenity would defeat his purpose. In long-distance terms, we merely need look ahead to the recapitulation, where we understand, finally, that Schubert himself has prescribed exactly what he wants in terms of a variant. Indeed, we begin to understand that his rhetorical message is quite large-scale in its unfolding:

EXAMPLE 4.4

Expression and Expressive Devices 123

Despite suggestions to the contrary, we search in vain, even in early Schubert, for movements in which he himself has not notated sufficiently expressive devices for his own purposes. Schubert's music, then, does not require assistance in the form of *rubato* types A and B—which, although they are still "on the books" (Swoboda, Starke), have long since been either incorporated into the music itself as a fundamental characteristic (D850) or would not be appropriate to Schubert's own long-range planning. We move on, then, to a consideration of *rubato* type C.

Hummel, at about the same time, speaks also of *tempo rubato*, but describes it as "willkürliches Dehnen" (voluntary holding-back, i.e. type C).[8] Hummel's is the first treatise dedicated entirely to the brilliant style (which does not affect Schubert, although this style of playing flourished during his lifetime). If, on the Hummel evidence, we accept type C as a *rubato* type for Vienna of this period, then we must turn our attention to discussions of tempo maintenance and tempo change, whether they might have been characterized in Schubert's day as "*rubato*" or "*tempo rubato*." In Ch. VI, under Tempo Fluctuation, we discuss structural and regional tempo changes; here we limit matters to local fluctuations.

Spohr, writing well after Hummel, is still quite precise about the difference between *tempo rubato* and general tempo change:

> The Accompanist must be careful not to hurry or retard [sic] the Solo-player, though he must instantly follow the latter, whenever he slightly deviates from the time. This, however, does not apply to the tempo rubato of the Soloist, during which, the accompaniment must continue its steady, measured course.[9]

Spohr made a distinction between true chamber music and solo works, the latter being written to show off the technical equipment of a virtuoso. Clearly the citation above refers to solo works and can have no bearing on Schubert.

Czerny advocates strict tempo for "classic authors" such as Bach, Mozart, or Beethoven, except where otherwise indicated. He does not mention Schubert, but stylistically we can place Schubert in this category. In *Letters to a Young Pianist*, Czerny writes:

> In every composition the expressive signs, (*f, p, cresc, dim., legato, staccato, acceler., ritard.,* etc.) are so exactly written out by the composer that a player can never be in any doubt about what to play softly, *cresc.* or *decresc.,* slurred or *staccato,* faster or slower.[10]

---

[8] Pt. II: Ch. I, p. 26, "Vom Vortrage überhaupt."
[9] London edition: "On Orchestral Playing and on Accompanying:" 234.
[10] "In jeder Composition sind die Zeichen des Ausdrucks, (*f, p, cresc, dim., legato, staccato, acceler., ritard.,* u.s.w.) so genau vom Tonsetzer bezeichnet, dass der Spieler nie im Zweifel seyn kann, was er stark oder

This passage would seem to state Czerny's position quite clearly. However, a now-famous passage from his *Pianoforteschule* Part III (cited in the Laaber *Handbuch* and elsewhere), would indicate a contradiction concerning strict tempo:[11]

EXAMPLE 4.5

If we consider Czerny's remarks on Chopin in Pt. IV, however, we finally understand that the example above has to do only with the newer style of piano playing.

> Although Chopin's compositions are difficult to learn, they are not calculated to make brilliant effects, as are those of the three composers discussed thus far [Thalberg, Döhler, Henselt]. The character of Chopin's works is of the highest sentiment, and also mostly melancholic. Their performance is best based upon purposeful tempo-change: ritardando, accelerando and all of the performance techniques discussed in Pt. III of this method.[12]

The tempo changes mentioned by Czerny, then, are decidedly not for Schubert and Beethoven's classical-related sonatas and smaller piano works, but for the newer school of pianism that built upon the style of Hummel, Field, *et al*, and that developed into a new and quite fashionably cosmopolitan movement. Although the little four-measure example cited

---

schwach, wachsend oder abnehmend, gebunden oder gestossen, beschleunigend oder zurückhaltend vortragen soll." (31)

[11] p. 295.

[12] Czerny, *Pianoforte Schule* IV: 19. "Chopin's Compositionen sind nicht so sehr auf brillante Effekte berechnet, wie die der früher besprochenen Tonsetzer [Thalberg, Döhler, Henselt], obwohl sie bedeutend schwierig einzustudieren sind. Ihr Character ist höchst sentimental, auch meist schwermüthig. Der Vortrag ist vorzüglich auf zweckmässigen Tempo-Wechsel durch Ritardando, accelerando, und alle übrigen, im dritten Theile dieser Schule besprochen Mittel des Vortrags berechnet."

Expression and Expressive Devices   *125*

(or composed?) by Czerny might appear to be written in Mendelssohn's more conservative language, thus apparently closer to Schubert's world, we must remember that the newer school took just this classical language (often in a most harmonically repetitive and melodically banal simplicity, apparently borrowed from Italian *bel canto* opera) as a basis for their pianistic freedoms and variants. Readers who care to examine Czerny's next musical examples from this point in the *Pianoforteschule* will see that they reflect the style of Hummel and the virtuosic international school which succeeded him. (Readers have merely to consult the Laaber *Handbuch*, under "Musikalische Interpretation," pp. 296-7, to find a reproduction of the pages following the example reproduced above.)[13]

Generally speaking, *rubato* types D and E, agogic (delayed) attacks, and lingering on single notes, appear to fall into the domain of the newer school of pianism. Nevertheless, we will see that Schubert also developed a limited form of the agogic *rubato* type D (single note *rubato*), which we will discuss under "Accentuation" later in this chapter.

Schubert and "Viennese" rhythm

Although the peculiar mannerisms in Schubert performance that sometimes still parade under the banner of "Viennese" style are dying what we hope to be a graceful but decisive death, we still cannot help but assist them in this latter enterprise. It was not long ago, and it still occurs from time to time on concert stages, that Schubert, in his role as the quintessential little Viennese composer was and is subject to the strangest pushes, pulls, holds, and leaps in the history of musical classicism. For example, in the C-major Quintet, D 956, how many ensembles, even today, can eschew the unmarked *ritard* and late-Viennese *Schrammelmusik* hiccup in the following passage:

EXAMPLE 4.6
Mm. 42-51 as printed and as often played

---

[13] Here we are not discussing the natural shaping of phrases and larger structural periods that attends all communicative music-making. Professional instrumentalists tend to group these concepts under rubrics such as "breathing" or "turning a phrase", etc., and as long as these subtleties are not confused with purposeful *tempo rubato* or general tempo change, then all is well. A good rule of thumb is that as long as such "breathing" or "phrase turning" remains neither predictable nor noticeable, it cannot be considered excessive.

The members of string ensembles often smile contentedly at each other during and directly after such moments, convinced that they have done something quite *gemütlich* together (indeed, why not simply light up a cigarette?). Many musicians remain blissfully unaware that such mannerisms arose in late nineteenth-century Austro-Hungarian café music and had little to do with Franz Schubert.

One still hears Schubert's waltzes, *deutscher*, and *ländler* played (apparently indiscriminately, i.e. not according to genre) with marked elements of this *Schrammelmusik* style, presumably in the belief that it derives from inherently Austrian or even specifically Viennese classical rhythmical tendencies. One can trace certain of these mannerisms (often connected with specific musical tunes and types) to Alpine country dancing, particularly of the more extroverted sort. Here, the interplay of such factors as complex thigh-slapping and legwork, intermittent yodelling, the pull of gravity upon generously-proportioned human mass, coupled with the effects of strong drink all around, surely must have taken its toll on rhythmic regularity. Country folk are quite proud of such things (in Austria and elsewhere), and we easily can see how "circumstance" might have evolved into "tradition." Schubert played his dance music, of course, for a quite different sort of gathering. First of all, he lived in Vienna, already a more sophisticated atmosphere, and the balls, weddings, and other celebrations for which he played were attended by the highly educated upper-middle class, the minor nobility, and, of course, cultivated professional artists. In this world, the waltz had descended from the courtly minuet, not from the barnyard *Strampel-Ländler.*

It is questionable whether even the Strauß waltzes—of which the later ones were actually written in the *Schrammelmusik* era—should be subjected to the sentimentalized style which we can hear each year in the Vienna Philharmonic's New Year's Concerts. Perhaps we never shall recapture the original, simpler spirit of the *Blue Danube Waltz* (and perhaps we shouldn't even try), but we might note, at least, that its composer was not always happy with the kind of rhythmic and tempo mannerisms that even his own brother applied to the waltzes:

Johann Strauß Jr to his brother Eduard, 17 October 1894

Dear Eduard! Your orchestra played excellently last Saturday ... *Fledermaus* Overture, Ballet ... Everything was very well executed except for the first part of [the *Jabuka* Waltzes, op. 455 "Ich bin Dir gut"]. Play this piece strictly in waltz tempo without ritardando, except for the upbeat, and even that should be played only a little bit slower, so that the public can tell the difference between the introduction and the beginning of the waltz. For percussion, trumpets and even woodwinds, use a strictly metrical waltz-rhythm, which does not work in a slower tempo. At the very end you should treat the first part of No. 1 more as a waltz for dancing, the moreso that the melody is written in longer note values and is thus in need of rhythmic assistance, which can be found only in the accompaniment. If this also becomes slower, then the effect is compromised.[14]

---

[14] From Johann Strauß's critique of the 50-year jubilee concert given in his honor, 14 October 1894, in the Großen Musikvereinssaale, in *Johann Strauss (Sohn): Leben und Werk in Briefen* VII, ed. Franz Mailer (Tutzing: Schneider, 1998): 276/8.

Eduard Strauß is said to have been influenced by the *rubato* concepts of Wagner, Liszt, and Bülow, and it may be from him that the world has inherited the peculiar mannerisms now sadly inseparable from the only stylistically-consistent compositional tradition to extend from the recording age back to Schubert's Vienna.

Trillo, Bebung, tremolo, vibrato, ondeggiando, etc.

Parts of the following discussion agree with Frederick Neumann's article, "The Vibrato Controversy."[15] Of course, we may never be able to answer satisfactorily certain questions concerning the rise of modern *vibrato* as a performance norm: i.e., a fundamental, pitch-changing undulation on most tones except for fast-moving notes and others chosen specifically for a non-*vibrato* effect. Most writers on this subject are content merely to speculate along time lines, furthering the rather vague notion that the use of a continuous *vibrato* increased, somehow, until by the mid-nineteenth century it no longer was an unusual phenomenon. This theory does not account, however, for the strong evidence that *vibrato* as we know it today reached well back into the previous two centuries and probably beyond.[16] In this last regard, two well-known citations from W.A. Mozart need reexamination:

> Letter to Leopold Mozart, 12 June 1778 concerning the bass Joseph Nikolaus Meißner:
>
> As you know, Meißner has the terrible habit that with purposeful effort his voice shakes, marking off long notes in quarter and even eighth-intervals. I have never been able to abide this in him, and it is also really abominable. It is completely contrary to Nature to sing like that. The human voice trembles without help, but in such a manner and proportion that it is beautiful, that is the nature of the voice.[17]

This passage is usually translated from the original as a description of Mozart's *opposition* to a continuous *vibrato*, but of course it is no such thing.[18] At the very worst, it would seem that poor Meißner was trying to count off his long notes, using his gullet instead of his foot to keep time. It might appear that he was after something in the way of a *Bebung* (something quite distinct from *vibrato*), but lending it no elegance. Despite this apparently justified criticism of Meißner's clumsy ornamentation, Mozart appears to have been otherwise

---

[15] *PPR* IV (1991):14–27.

[16] Will Crutchfield relies on this chronological concept when he makes such statements as "The gradual transition to continuous vibrato took place during the 19th century and was a subject of much debate" [*Performance Practice:*296]. Crutchfield then refers his readers to a later chapter (p. 459), where we read, "Vibrato [he apparently means the *use* of vibrato] increased gradually as an expressive device".

[17] Bauer, W.A. and Deutsch, O.E., eds, *W.A. Mozart: Briefe und Aufzeichnungen* 4 (Kassel / Basel, 1963): 377/8, cited in Greta Moens-Haenen, *Das Vibrato in der Musik des Barock* / Graz: Akademische Druck- u. Verlagsanstalt, 1988: 17. "Meißner hat wie sie wissen, die üble gewohnheit, daß er oft mit fleiss mir der stimme zittert – ganze viertl – ja oft gar achtl in aushaltender Note marquirt – und das habe ich an ihm nie leiden können, das ist auch wircklich abscheulich. das ist völlig ganz wieder die Natur zu singen. die Menschenstimme zittert schon selbst – aber so – in einem solchen grade, daß es schön ist – daß ist die Natur der stimme."

[18] Crutchfield translates "zittert" (see fn above) as "vibrates" and omits the definitive part of Mozart's statement, where the composer explains that Meißner purposefully marked off his long notes in quarter and even eighth-intervals [*Performance Practice:*296]. "Vibrates" is clearly the wrong translation in this context.

satisfied with the natural *vibrato* that arises in vocal production. In his mind it would seem that any further ornamental *vibrato* effects were to be executed with elegance or not at all.

Mozart's criticism of the oboist Johann Christian Fischer's *messa da voce* and its normatively attendant *Bebung* is similar:

> Letter to Leopold Mozart, 4 April 1787
>
> ...sein Ton ist ganz aus der Nase – und seine tenuta ein tremulant auf der Orgel [His tone is nasal and his tenuta [tenuto] is like the tremulant stop on the organ.][19]

The term "*tenuta*" refers to a long note to which a *messa da voce* or a *Bebung* (or both together) would have been applied.[20] Technically speaking, what Mozart describes in both Meißner's and Fischer's style is not the pitch-changing *vibrato* now practiced almost universally by singers, string players, many woodwind and some brass players, but something akin to the expressive *trillo* inherited from Monteverdi's day and obviously still practiced (at least by older musicians) in Mozart's time. By now, in the German language it was called "*tremolo*" ["tremulo"] and / or "*Bebung*", but not "*vibrato.*"[21] String players could imitate it almost exactly with regular pulses of bow pressure or by a vigorous shake of the left hand (see below), flutists through pulsed breath control and / or key manipulation and *Fingervibrato*.[22] Additionally, almost every good organ had a tremulant stop whose mechanism interrupted the airflow at continuous intervals as long as the key remained depressed. Organs were built to simulate instruments and voices, and the *tremulant* stop was surely an imitation of a vocal technique (not *vibrato* but *Bebung*). The mechanism was used in the actual *vox humana* stop as well. Furthermore, there existed various *céleste* combinations

---

[19] *Briefe und Aufzeichnungen* 4:41, cited in Moens-Haenen: 124.

[20] Moens-Haenen (124) writes that the exact meaning of this quote is not clear, but that "arguably, Mozart opposed (excessive) vibrato on long notes." But Mozart was describing a *Bebung;* not a vibrato, and we point out that Moens-Haenen has copied out the word "*tenuta*" mistakenly as "temata," a term that does not exist and that Mozart did not use. We have consulted with Prof. Dr. Ulrich Konrad, of the Musikwissenschaftliches Institut in Wurzburg, who kindly has traced this citation for us through early editions of the letters (the autograph is lost), and has discovered that the word indeed should read "*tenuta.*" "*Tenuta*" (*tenuto*), of course, is a real term and carries with it the idea of a *messa da voce* (long swell and attenuation, with *Bebung* at the highest point). *Gedanken über die Nachahmung der Griechischen Wercke in der Mahlerey und Bildhauer-Kunst* (1754): Das allgemeine vorzügliche Kennzeichen der Griechischen Meister-stücke ist eine edle Einfalt, und eine stille Grösse, so wohl in der Stellung als in Ausdruck. So wie die Tiefe des Meers allzeit ruhig bleibt, die Oberfläche mag noch so wüten, eben so zeiget der Ausdruck in den Figuren der Griechen bey allen Leidenschaften eine grosse und gesetzte Seele.

[21] Although much ink has been spilled on the subject, widespread confusion still exists concerning the concepts "trillo," "vibrato," and "tremolo" and their notational symbols, even among adherents of the historical performance movement. Perhaps one of the most comical examples can be heard on Sony Classical's Vivarte label (S2K 66289) where in the first movement of J.S. Bach's Fifth Brandenburg Concerto the solo flute line at mm. 97ff (marked with what is usually taken for a trill sign) has been musicologically reinterpreted as an unusually slow and wide pitch undulation for the duration of the sustained values of each measure. This astonishing decision was based on the apparent discovery by one or more of the interpreters and / or the producer that similar wavy lines in some pedagogical works (unfortunately after Bach's time) were often used to demonstrate places for *Bebung* (which may still have been correct, but which was then further confused with a modern vibrato of the most sultry and eerie sort). The total effect is not unlike an eerie wail at a midnight Halloween party.

[22] See Moens-Haenen on Tromlitz, 113–116.

Expression and Expressive Devices 129

(perhaps not yet known by that term), whose pipes were deliberately but slightly mistuned against each other so as to create regular *Schwebung* (beating). In cases where such *Schwebung* combinations did not exist as such on the instrument, the player could create them easily by pulling out two solo stops together, one drawn not quite so fully as the other. Even the clavichord could produce *Bebung*.

Common to all the above-mentioned methods of "shaking" was the regular interruption of some sort of continuum: either an airflow, a bowstroke, or, in the case of *Schwebung,* a combinative soundwave pattern through mutual cancellation. The rule of thumb that, in the Baroque, a marked undulation should be used only on longer notes is a modern agreement that may reflect the aesthetic characteristics of *Bebung,* but certainly not those of pitch *vibrato*. This agreement is no more valid than the one which has set an almost universal standard among period instrument enthusiasts for tuning a half-tone lower than modern pitch for Baroque music. In the early eighteenth century Roger North's opinion of the wrist-shake [precursor of modern *vibrato*] had been that it served

> ... all [musical purposes] alike, upon Every note that gives time for it, and altho' it doth not stop the tone, yet being allwais ye same in manner & measure, whatever time ye musick bears it must breed some fastidium, which If sometimes used, and conforme to time, and sometimes forborne, would be prevented, but as it is an Exquisite action, it hath an Excellent grace ... [23]

Where the conservative Roger North was ambivalent about the overuse of shaking, Francesco Geminiani (1751) was rather enthusiastic about it, saying that it "may be made on any Note whatsoever." He was echoed by J. Sadler (1754), who wrote that "it may be made on any Note that is long enough to allow it."[24] Even Robert Bremner, writing about orchestral players, noted (with disapproval) that "Many gentlemen players on bow instruments are so exceeding fond of the tremolo, that they apply it wherever they possibly can." [25]

A major difference between *Bebung* and *vibrato* is that *Bebung* can be controlled, switched on-and-off and speed-regulated easily. Leopold Mozart identified two basic speeds: fast (per eighth) and slow (per quarter), plus a changing speed (from slow to fast, and in the reverse as well) that was used on certain long notes in the spirit of *messa da voce* (see the *Versuch* p.240, where Mozart shows the opening long notes of sample cadenzas):

EXAMPLE 4.7
Leopold Mozart's *Bebung*

§. 5.

Man muß aber die Bewegung mit einem starken Nachdrucke des Fingers machen, und diesen Nachdruck allemal bey der ersten Note iedes Viertheils; in der geschwinden Bewegung aber auf der ersten Note eines jeden halben Viertheils anbringen. Zum Beyspiele will ich hier einige Noten setzen, die man sehr gut mit dem Tremulo abspielet; ja die eigentlich diese Bewegung verlangen. Man muß sie in der ganzen Applicatur abgeigen.

---

[23] Moens-Haenen, 173.
[24] ibid, 174.
[25] ibid, 251. It is interesting that in the article on *Bebung* in Johann Georg Sulzer's *Allgemeine Theorie der schönen Kunste* (Leipzig: 1771–74), shaking is recommended for every note possible.

Common to *Bebung* and *vibrato* both in singing and string playing was the idea of regular undulation, i.e. changing pitch. *Bebung* distinguished itself from simple *vibrato*, however, in that it was sharply marked-off at the peaks, as Leopold Mozart explains at the beginning of §5 in the excerpt shown above:

> To the undulating motion [rocking back and forth on the string, support compression and pitch variation in vocal production] one must impart a strong pressure-accent [mit einem starken Nachdruck] with the finger, at the beginning of each quarter value and in faster motion at the beginning of each eighth value.

The effect that the elder Mozart describes here corresponds exactly with Wolfgang's description of Meißner's "purposeful effort." Note the generation gap: the worldly young Wolfgang did not seem to care for the device, whereas his more conservative father still described it as an aesthetically viable ornament. On the other hand, Wolfgang apparently had no objection to pure *vibrato*, which is and was, as he pointed out, a natural phenomenon in singing. If the evidence (or lack thereof) in tutors is sufficient proof, vibrato as such was not even taught. Certainly it was less subject to voluntary, conscious control than *Bebung*. *Vibrato* can intensify with increased volume and vice-versa, but it cannot easily be turned off and on, or its speed closely adjusted. Thus it could not have been considered an ornament, for an ornament must have a noticeable and characteristic profile that stands out against the general sonic background and / or the immediate melodic contour.

Bebung's growing disadvantage lay clearly in the aesthetic realm. Eventually it died out or, as Spohr says about ornaments in general, may have been transformed into or taken over into notation proper. In any case, only *vibrato* was to remain, and perhaps flourish, as the dominant expressive characteristic of vocal production. The question is: when and how did *Bebung* die out? By the nineteenth century its use appears to have become quite limited, and in the case of string playing it may even have been transformed into *vibrato* proper. If it existed in certain outdated styles, it now applied only to especially important longer notes in declamatory singing (and was employed only by the older singers) and perhaps still at the outset of cadential figures in "brilliant" instrumental works.

Expression and Expressive Devices 131

Beethoven still knew or remembered *Bebung* in its vocal context, however, and imitated it in the recitative of the Piano Sonata, op. 110 (1821/2):

EXAMPLE 4.8

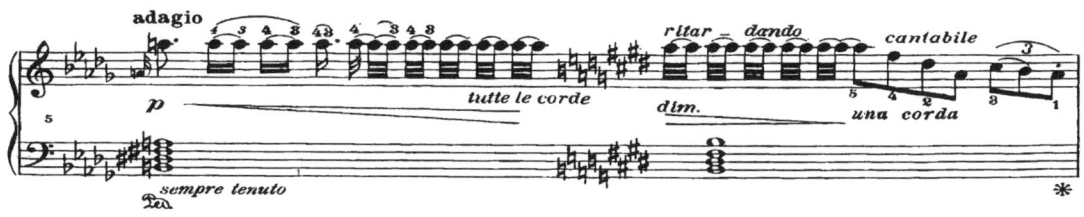

Some four years later (1826) August Swoboda still described *Bebung* as a known ornament in his tutor's dictionary. But his description is now problematic for us, because while it included the aspect of wavering pitch, it failed to mention the strong *Nachdruck* peaks.

> *Bebung*, or in Italian "tremolo", is a performance ornament for stringed instruments. One understands this term to indicate a soft, varied-speed back-and-forth motion made by the fingers as they press upon the string, whereby the exact pitch tends to waver (higher and lower) in its changing vibration.[26]

Fortunately, we are able to turn to a practitioner, for six years later (1832) Ludwig Spohr also failed to mention the *Nachdruck* peaks:

> To the class of embellishments belong also the tremolo, and the changing of the finger on the same note. The Singer in the performance of passionate movements, or when forcing his voice to its highest pitch, produces a certain tremulous sound, resembling the vibrations of a powerfully struck bell. This, with many other peculiarities of the human voice, the Violinist can closely imitate. It consists in the wavering of a stopped note, which alternately extends a little below and above the true intonation, and is produced by a trembling motion of the left hand in the direction from the nut to the bridge. This motion, however, should only be slight, in order that the deviation from purity of tone may scarcely be observed by the ear. In old compositions this trembling is sometimes indicated by a dotted line [....] or by the word tremolo; but in modern ones its employment is left entirely to the player, who, however, must guard against using it too often, and in improper places.[27]

Nominally, what Spohr describes here is the older *tremolo* or *Bebung,* especially where he

---

[26] p.104. "Bebung, italienisch tremolo, ist eine Spielmanier bey Saiten-Instrumenten; man versteht dadurch ein sanftes, mehr oder minder schnelles Hin-und Herwiegen des auf die Saite aufdrückenden Fingers, wodurch die genau bestimmte Höhe des Tones in eine sich wechselweise auf und absärts neigende Schwebung modificiert wird."
[27] p. 163.

talks of "dotted lines" and belltone waves (an image that he takes directly from Leopold Mozart).[28] In reality, however, it is probably nothing more than *tremolo*, softened into a form of *vibrato*. The biggest hint that Spohr gives us in this regard is his otherwise confusing statement that older composers specified such things (*tremolo*), but that modern composers left them to the player. If at this point Spohr had been talking about *tremolo* as a voluntary ornament à la the eighteenth century, then his statement would have been historically backwards. Voluntary (*willkürliche*) ornaments were once the province of the player, but now written into scores by modern composers, as Spohr himself stated earlier in the tutor. As it happens, his description of tremolo comes at the end of the section on essential (composer indicated) ornaments. Thus his statement would appear simply to mean that where undulation had once been a notated ornament, now it was a general and ubiquitous technique. That Spohr recommended it only on certain notes has at least two reasonable explanations: to begin with, for string players, there existed and still exists no "natural" *vibrato* as enjoyed by many singers. String players (especially violinists and violists) must learn to vibrate, sometimes with great effort.[29] For the string family the natural stopped tone is a "straight" tone. Even today the majority of notes played upon the violin are played *senza vibrato,* if only because the majority of notes in most scores occur in shorter note values than those which state the tunes. Secondly, the pedagogical model for the violinist's *vibrato* appears indeed to have been the *tremolo* instead of the natural vocal *vibrato*. This should not surprise us, for *vibrato* was not mentioned in previous pedagogical works, and

---

[28] Leopold Mozart:238. "Der Tremulo ist eine Auszierung die aus der Natur selbst entspringet, und die nicht nur von guten Instrumentisten, sondern auch von geschickten Sängern bey einer langen Note zierlich kann angebracht werden. Die Natur selbst ist die Lehrmeisterin hiervon. Denn wenn wir eine schlaffe Seyte oder eine Glocke stark anschlagen; so hören wir nach dem Schlage eine gewisse wellenseise Schwebung (ondeggiamento) des angeschlagenen Tones: Und diesen zitternden Nachklang nennet man Tremulo, oder auch den Tremulanten."

Readers will find the bell image, plus a strikingly similar description of *tremolo* [tremulo] in Giuseppe Tartini's *Regole per arrivare a saper ben suonar il violino.* We do not know for sure whether Mozart borrowed from Tartini or vice-versa, but whatever the case may be the description could not have been new even at that time. Mozart also used the bell image for a different purpose: "Wie der Klang einer Glocke, wenn sie scharf angeschlagen wird, sich nach und nach verlieret;" cited in Robin Stowell, "Leopold Mozart Revised" in *Perspectives on Mozart performance,* ed. Larry Todd and Peter Williams (Cambridge: CUP, 1991): 140. Spohr took over almost all of Mozart's [Tartini's?] concepts, as we can read in the following passage – each aspect of which [except the last, which also can be inferred in Mozart] can be traced directly to the earlier pedagogue[s]: "In cases corresponding to those in which, as above stated, this trembling is observed in the singer, the Violinist may also avail himself of it: hence, it is employed only in an impassioned style of playing and in strongly accenting [accented] notes marked with *fz* or > . Long sustained notes may likewise be animated and reinforced by it; and should a swell from *p* to *f* be introduced on such a note, a beautiful effect is produced by commencing the *tremolo* slowly and gradually accelerating the vibrations, in proportion to the increase of power. If a *diminuendo* occur on a sustained note, it likewise produces a good effect to begin the *tremolo* quick and gently decrease in velocity. The *tremolo* may therefore be divided into four species: 1st the quick *tremolo*, for strongly accented notes: 2nd, the slow, for the sustained notes in passages of deep pathos: 3rd, the slow commencing and gradually accelerating, for long notes played *crescendo*: and 4th, the quick commencing and gradually slackening, for such as are played *diminuendo*." (London ed., p. 163).

[29] Some players learn the arm *vibrato* more easily than the wrist *vibrato* used by many professionals, and some can manage only to master the finger *vibrato*. This problem is not so acute in cello playing, of course.

Expression and Expressive Devices 133

Spohr as an author (despite his true place as a progressive musician and composer) leaned quite naturally on pedagogical dogma of the past. One has only to recall his direct, "boiler plate" incorporation of Leopold Mozart's bell imagery, which had been printed some eighty years before.[30] And as we can see in the example below Spohr also takes over Mozart's old speed of "vibration" categories for *Bebung,* although they are no longer associated with fixed notation values such as eighths or quarters.[31]

EXAMPLE 4.9
Spohr, *Violin School* (London ed., p. 164)

[30] Swoboda and Spohr are not the only pedagogues to confuse us in this regard, for such dogma was passed on far into the century. C.G. Nehrlich's *Gesang-Schule* (Berlin, 1844, based on his *Methode,* 1841) mixes together scraps from earlier tutors and also fails to mention the measured *Nachdruck* that is so central to *Bebung.* Along the way he also repeats the ancient adage that this technique (whatever it is) should not be applied to every tone : "Das Tremolare del tuono, auch schlechtweg Tremolo genannt, oder das Beben des Tons besteht darin, dass man einen Ton mit Sicherheit ergreift, dann mit erzitternder Stimme bis zu der höchsten Stärke, deren ein gebildeter Ton fähig ist, antreibt und endlich ebenso wieder abnehmen lässt. Das Vibriren oder Erzittern wird durch das schnelle Wachsen und Drängen der Schallwellen erzeugt, darf aber ja nicht bei jedem Tone angewendet werden, wie es so oft der Fall ist. Dieses Beben des Tons können sich durch Studium alle diejenigen aneignen, die eine Messa di voce mit grossem Tone auszuziehen vermögen, denn es ist hauptsächlich Sache der Willenskraft und erfolgt von selbst, wenn man sich so lebhaft in den Charakter des Stücks versetzt, dass gleichsam alle Muskeln von der Willenskraft und dem Drange des Verlangens angespannt werden...." (p. 104).
[31] It is interesting that nineteenth-century violin teachers, with the dying model of *Bebung* in their consciousnesses, began to impose speed controls upon *vibrato* itself as if it were an ornament. By the early twentieth century at least a general rule had emerged to the effect that in the lower registers the *vibrato* should move more slowly than in the upper registers. More specific teachings concerning *vibrato* and expressivity have varied from school to school, but the great and inevitable influence of recordings has had a standardizing effect on *vibrato* as it is now used among singers and string players.

To this point we have looked at evidence for *vibrato* leading up to and into Schubert's time. The Viennese instrumental methods of Schubert's lifetime and shortly thereafter offer hints and information outlined above. As to *vibrato* in singing, we have to look beyond Vienna for pedagogical help. Since Schubert's lied style was principally a German-, Czech-, and Austrian-oriented phenomenon, we can eliminate French and Italian treatises, which in any case were devoted almost exclusively to opera singing. This last caveat is also true of German language treatises (which also included a number of beginning methods for schools), but at least the interested researcher might come closer to the mark in examining them for general expressive traits in singing. Among them we might mention:

1800?	Johann Friedrich Schubert, *Neue Singe-Schule* (Leipzig)	
1802?	Karl Friedrich Ebers, *Kurzgefasste aber doch vollständige Singschule* (Mainz)	
1805	Johann Friedrich Döring, *Anweisung zum Singen* (Görlitz)	
1809	Johann Michael Pfeiffer, *Die Pestalozzische Gesangsbildungslehre* (Zürich)	
1810	Johann Michael Pfeiffer, *Gesangsbildungslehre nach Pestalozzischen Grundsätzen pädagogisch begründet* (Zürich)	
1810	Hans Georg Nägeli and Johann Michael Pfeiffer, *Vollständige und ausführliche Gesangschule* (Zürich)	
1811	Bert. Rotweil, *20 Versuche, einer elementarischen Gesanglehre für Volksschulen* [& *20 Singstücke zur Rotweilschen Gesanglehre*] (RC)	
1812	Carl Zelter, *Practische Gesang-Lehre* (ms. SBB)	
1813	Bernhard Christoph Natorp, *Anleitung zur Unterweisung im Singen für Lehrer in Volksschulen* (Essen?)	
1815	Ambrogio Minoja, *Über den Gesang*	
1817	Hans Georg Nägeli and Johann Michael Pfeiffer, *Chorgesangschule* (Zürich)	
1817	Hans Georg Nägeli and Johann Michael Pfeiffer, *Gesangsbildungslehre für den Männerchor* (Zürich)	
1820	Peter von Winter, *Vollständige Singschule* (Mainz)	
1821–23	Johann August Heinroth, *Gesangunterrichts-Methode für höhere und niedere Schulen*	
1822	August Ferdinand Häser, *Versuch einer systematischen Übersicht der Gesanglehre* (Leipzig)	
1822	Joseph Hoerger, *Kurze und faßliche Sing-Anleitung* (Augsburg)	
1824	Carl Zelter, *Gesang-Übungen sowie 2 und 3 Cursus der Compositionslehre* (ms. SBB)	
1826	Karl Loewe, *Gesanglehre für Gymnasien, Seminarien und Bürgerschulen* (Stettin)	
n.d.	Karl Loewe, *Lehre des Balladengesangs* (ms., see Karl Anton in *Zeitschrift für Musikwissenschaft* I, Oct. 1919, hereafter *ZMW*)	
1826	Adolf Bernhard Marx, *Die Kunst des Gesanges* (Berlin)	
1827	Johann Jakob Wachsmann, *Gesangfibel: Versuch ein methodisch Lehrganges beim Zifferngesang* (Magdeburg)	
1827	A. Häfele, *Einstimmige Übungsbeispiele für den Gesang-Unterricht an räparandenschüler Seminaren* (Speyer)	

1827	Joseph Hiensch, *Über den Musik-Unterricht, besonders im Gesang auf Gymnasien* (Berlin)
1827	Johann Christian Markwort, *Gesang- Ton- und Rede-Vortraglehre* (Mainz)
1828	Wilhelm Häser, "Andeutungen über Gesanglehre" (in *Cäcilia* VII–IX, hereafter *Cä*)
1829	Bernhard Hahn, *Handbuch beim Unterricht im Gesange für Schüler auf Gymnasien und Bürgerschulen* (Breslau)
1830	Franz Blatt, *Kurzgefaßtes theoretisch-praktische Gesangschule* (Prague)
1830	M. Waldhör, *Neue Volkgesang-Schule, oder gründliche Anleitung den Gesang ... zu lehren* (Kempton)
1831–38	Heinrich Carl Breidenstein, *Praktische Singschule* (Bonn)

If we wished to establish a perspective from the other end of the time scale, looking back upon Schubert's era, we might consider one further fragment of evidence, provided by Gustav Walter's turn-of-the-century recording of *Am Meer* D957/12.[32] In this deeply moving recording Walter employs a continuous, modern *vibrato*, albeit slim and perfectly controlled. Walter, the oldest of the recorded Schubert singers, was born in 1834, only 6 years after Schubert's early death. Knowing as we do that singers rarely rebuild their basic techniques as they grow older, we can safely assume that Walter learned that *vibrato* in the 1840s (depending upon how his voice developed), not too long after Schubert's day. In any case, Walter's *vibrato* of the 1840s was unlikely to have developed as the result of a sudden new fashion, but rather represented an established practice reaching at least into Schubert's time. Unfortunately, we possess no corroborating recorded evidence from singers of Walter's age or older.

In any case we must reconsider our current application or non-application of *vibrato* according to an historical time line. It well may be that vocal music always was susceptible to *vibrato* and that instrumental *vibrato* came into its very own only after *Bebung* was dropped or transformed as a means of musical beautification. Where Schubert is concerned, the odds are that the application of *vibrato* as we know it today (perhaps with some restraint and far more flexibility) would not have been unfamiliar or unattractive to him.

Dynamics: ranges, levels, and layering

Schubert's dynamic markings range from ***ppp*** to ***fff*** and even further, by inference from certain *crescendo* and *decrescendo* markings from these extremes. Only the written ***mp*** is rare. In orchestral and chamber music (including lieder, where the dynamics are mostly, but not always exclusively, in the piano part) Schubert generally assigns across-the-board volume levels, as did many of his classical predecessors. Nevertheless, from his earliest compositions forward he made certain distinctions, which we can separate into categories.

The first type has to do with dynamics in conjunction with accentuation and / or articulation. Most often the distinctions arise naturally between voices in the course of an

---

[32] G & T 042097, 1904, reissued in EMI's collection, Schubert Lieder On Record 1898-1952, RLS 766.

EXAMPLE 4.10

imitative passage, but sometimes Schubert writes them for calculated effect. For example, the finale of the E♭-major String Quartet D87 (see Ex. 4.10 above) begins with a tiny explosion in the two outer parts, and Schubert wants the motor provided by the inner parts not to interfere with that effect. Furthermore, as a violinist he knows that to give the *fp* to the inner parts as well would impede their initial forward motion.

The second type of differentiation consists of contrasting expressive melodic gestures from accompanimental ones. For example, the *Andante* of the D-major String Quartet D74 opens with a swell–fade hairpin in the upper voice. Here the idea is to differentiate between the fluid expressivity of the melody and the quiet, unrelenting forward motion of the accompaniment.

EXAMPLE 4.11

We find many examples of this highly expressive type throughout Schubert's music. In m.5 of the G-major Quartet D887 we see the reverse of those swells in D74. This time the melody is left in *p* while the counter line in the two violins is graced with a small swell-fade.

Expression and Expressive Devices 137

EXAMPLE 4.12

The third major type of differentiation found in Schubert's multi-instrument works is a general dynamic contrast between solo line and accompaniment:

EXAMPLE 4.13a/b
a. Fourth Symphony D417/2

b. C-major Quintet D956/1

Where Schubert has left us to balance dynamics (and / or articulation and accentuation) in chamber, vocal and orchestral music, we must consider carefully how to present the sound. Ex. 4.14 would imply that in a nearby passage with no solo dynamic indication the two voices carrying the corporate "line" (viola and first cello) should be treated equally and that together they should be played slightly fuller than the rest, despite the fact that all the voices are marked *pp*. Schubert himself contributes to this interpretation by marking the second cello *pizzicato* (thus thinning the sound) and requiring a soft *portando* stroke from the violins. Note that in m. 326, only the melodic duet is marked with a swell-fade:

EXAMPLE 4.14

Allegro ma non troppo

m. 321

We can balance most of Schubert's dynamics on the simple principle that in music of the Viennese classic-romantic era, melodies and counter melodies are more important than accompanimental textures. (If readers are tempted to regard this as self-evident, they may wish to attend the next concert on which Beethoven's Violin/Piano Sonata in A major is billed. The chances are that the pianist's initial two-note melodic snippets will be overwhelmed by the average violinist, happily whacking away at his accompanimental "umpah-pahs" as if he were the only player who was going to be paid that evening.)

Expression and Expressive Devices

In Schubert's lieder, dynamics are found mostly in the piano part. The singer must and should take many of his dynamic cues from that context. On the heels of the melodic dominance principle just stated, this circumstance may appear odd at first. However, as we have said before, the piano parts of Schubert's lieder often cannot be described as "accompaniment," and in some cases they probably constitute the main event, the story itself.

Accentuation

Apart from some special problems that we will discuss shortly, Schubert's accentuation is clear in its intent, and reasonably classifiable:

1. The simple accent sign [>] : Schubert uses this universal mark to create the web of basic stresses that guides us through each of his scores.[33] In his manuscripts it is easily confused with the hairpin *tenuto* sign described above. The accent sign *per se* mostly serves Schubert's grammatical purposes, and is only nominally an accent in the sense that we have come to understand that term. Dynamically, it can be interpreted as only one level above the context in which it is written. Where it indicates phrase shaping more than actual accentuation it may not even reach an entire level above the context. [>] appears most often where the general dynamic is soft or medium, and in this context can border on the purely expressive.

Sometimes, Schubert uses [>] not to show basic *buona-cattiva* stress patterns, but to reveal deviations from (cf. mm.15–16 in the example below) those patterns.

EXAMPLE 4.15a/c
a. *Marche caractéristique* D968B/1, opening / primo

---

[33] This is one point on which we may agree completely with Clive Brown, who writes: "Schubert, who often employed *sf* and sometimes *sff*, and who used > very frequently, undoubtedly intended the latter marking primarily to designate where the expressive stress in the melody should fall. Sometimes he reinforced the message of the slurring with > and sometimes he overrode it . . . Such passages imply that, for Schubert, > corresponded with the normal degree of emphasis that a good singer would naturally give to the stressed syllables of the text or to musically important notes." *Classic and Romantic:* 113.

b. Piano Sonata D894/4, mm. 143-147

c. A-minor Quartet D804/1, mm. 44–49

He also uses the accent mark to indicate how his larger metrical regroupings function, as in the opening of the *Wanderer* Fantasy. Here the accents (in *ff*) mark off Schubert's extraordinary phrasing in 3/2, superimposed upon an actual metrical marking of 4/4.

EXAMPLE 4.16a/b
a. First movement opening

Expression and Expressive Devices 141

The grammatical structure of this opening is echoed at the outset of the Scherzo:

b. Scherzo opening

We can often glean valuable information about tempo and character from the occasional accented measure. In the example below the two accented measures confirm that the rest of the passage should be phrased in segments of at least two measures each in a fast tempo.

EXAMPLE 4.17
Fifth Symphony, finale

Likewise, Schubert writes accents not in every measure, but in every other measure of the opening of the finale of the *Great* C-major Symphony in order to achieve forward motion, clarity and large-phrase thinking (see Example 4.18 on p.142).

In the notes to the score from which the excerpt on the facing page is taken, the editor Roger Fiske writes:

> ... [Schubert] came increasingly to believe that accents were all-important in the performing of his music, and he peppered his later scores with the kind found in the horn solo at the beginning of this Symphony. There are quite a number of these accents in his earlier symphonies,

EXAMPLE 4.18

mm. 1-13

but literally thousands in this one. When Schubert's muse was in full flow such accents get bigger and bigger until they become indistinguishable from his diminuendo symbols.[34]

As an example of Schubert's "peppering" in "bigger and bigger" dimensions Fiske reprints the last page of the autograph, which shows, however, only a single accent. Certainly we see no calligraphic escalation here.[35] In fact, we must look back through the last two pages of the score (19 measures) to find the last accent before this one, and 13 measures before that for the previous one, etc. Indeed, Schubert accented where necessary to reveal the expressive grammar of his music, and if we consider the probable state of Viennese orchestras in his day, this could not have been a bad idea. But one cannot speak seriously of "peppering," a term which conjures up the random enthusiasm of an amateur chef. The accents in the opening horn part, for example, occur only once per measure, in order to insure a forward flow; and now that in recent years scholarship has reestablished the fact that the meter for this opening is *alla breve,* the accents (grammatical in nature) make even

---

[34] Preface: XII.

[35] On principle it is a mistake to confuse the musical escalation represented in a score with the actual mood of the composer when he notated it. These two phenomena might coincide, and again, they might not. He might not even have written it in its final order.

Expression and Expressive Devices

more sense. In fact, if we compare the accentuation of this opening motive with the accentuation of its reappearance at the end of the movement, we will find stresses on the same notes, written this time in 2/2 and in a context of *ff*. Schubert, at least, knew what he wanted. If there is any random "peppering," it comes from the editor, who with no reasonable explanation adds "[*simile*]" to a number of passages in order to continue accents and other markings in places where Schubert does not (and does not mean to) write them. (See Notational Shorthand, Ch.III).

[>] often appears simultaneously with other accentuation signs. In the A-minor Sonata D845/1, for example, we find a passage that culminates with [>] over the top D and *fp* directly underneath between the staves (m. 162). The accent signs [>] are grammatical, possibly even *tenuto*-agogic hairpins, and apply mostly to the melody, whereas the *fp* sign is independent and applies (in theory) mostly to the lower three voices.

EXAMPLE 4.19
mm. 158–163

Incidentally, the accent signs that follow the *fp* signs in mm. 159/161 are almost certainly misconceptions or misprints and should be read as *decresc.* hairpins. Two different accent signs horizontally joined in this way on a single note or chord have no meaning. If one mentally removes the top line from this passage, Schubert's intention becomes much clearer.

[>] is the only integral accentuation sign that Schubert used. The often-repeated notion that the vertical stroke [ı], for example, was another form of accent in early nineteenth-century Vienna cannot be corroborated, either for Beethoven or Schubert (see discussion on Fiske below). The rest of Schubert's accentuation signs (2.–7. below) are combinative, and various elements (for example, Italian prefixes and specific dynamic indicators) can be added to, changed, or subtracted from them as the need arises.

2. *fp* / *ffp* / *fffp:* Clearly, a strong dynamic followed somewhat directly by a softer one on the following note or, if no note follows it immediately, further into the same note. Swoboda (p.68): "If *fp* (*forte piano*) is written, one plays the first tone loud and the next one softly. The reverse is true where *pf* is written."[36] In loudness, the *forte* of *fp* is only two levels above the *piano*, and this relationship should not be stretched. Schubert has provided *ffp* and *fffp* for such contingencies.

We encounter *fp* mostly in soft contexts, but not always. In the following example, one simply drops to *p* on the B♭ of the third beat of m. 68:

---

[36] "Steht *fp* (d.i. *forte piano*), so gibt man den ersten Ton stark, und die folgenden schwach an, und umgekehrt, wenn *pf* steht."

EXAMPLE 4.20
Sonata D279/1: mm. 67-70

On the pianoforte, *fp* is most successful in a situation such as in ex. 4.20, where *forte* and *piano* are to be played on separate notes. In a situation such as the following passage, the marking cannot be executed literally and the player must reckon with natural tone-decay for his effect:

EXAMPLE 4.21
Sonata D279/1: mm. 40–42

In a context such as the *Andantino* of the Sonata D959, m. 5, the *fp* is almost theoretical. In the relatively fast tempo of *Andantino* no real decay can set in; the best one can do is to play the second beat of the left hand softly, as well as the first beat of the next measure in the right hand. On a period instrument one is marginally more successful, but the gesture remains elusive. In Ch. I we noted that the sketch for this movement indicates such exotic instructions as *crescendos* on individual melodic tones, a pianistic impossibility, and we suggested that Schubert was thinking more like a violinist. Applying this suggestion to the problem of accentuation, we can imagine that a violinist playing Example 4.21 would merely use a faster bow stroke on the *forte* of the note and slow the bow suddenly for the *piano*. Indeed, *fp* on single notes throughout Schubert's music should serve to remind us of his linear-melodic orientation as a string player.

If we return briefly to the problem of the opening of the F-minor Impromptu (Ch. III and above), we find a similar theoretical (idealistic) marking. Again, we find that it was Schubert the lyrical, linear thinker who notated this gesture, not Schubert the professional pianist. This situation does not call for a change of his notation (Dürr) or a reinterpretation of the symbol (Badura-Skoda), for such makeshift solutions do not address the central issue. Nominally, Schubert may have written this piece for the piano, but his mind was

Expression and Expressive Devices

operating on a higher, more theoretical plane. This is one of the features that makes his music so wonderful and so challenging to play.

That Schubert thought fundamentally as a string player becomes abundantly clear as we consider the following passage from D568/3 (E♭). Here, in Schubert's compositional mind, the "2nd violin," "viola," and "cello" are required to execute the dotted halves with *fp* markings, as in the second version below (fast-slow bows on single notes), while the "first violin" dances around above them:

EXAMPLE 4.22
mm. 49–54 as written

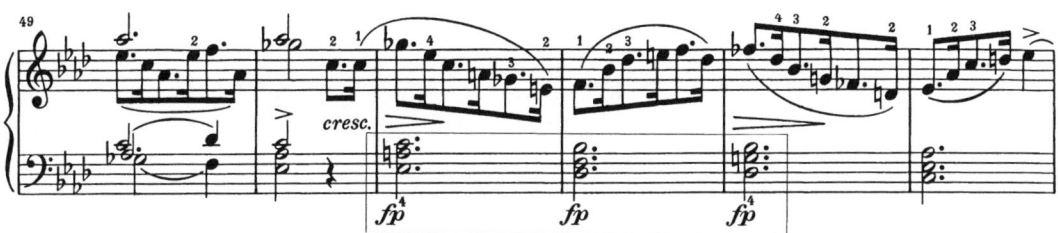

Pianists cannot do such things, but this fact did not stop Schubert from writing them.[37]

3. *sf* (Swoboda: "*Sforzando*, or *Sforzato* indicates that a note should be given particular strength, but the marking applies only to the note on which it is written.")[38] Schubert appears to use *sf* only when a movement is already underway. For opening notes (opening "events"), he seems to prefer *fz, fp, fzp*, etc.

4. *sfp* (D568/4 mm. 25–27). This marking is almost identical with *sf;* with the added *p* Schubert merely specifies the second dynamic.

5. *fz / ffz / fffz:* (Swoboda: "*Forzando*: begin the tone with great strength, but decrease the strength right away".)[39] Whereas *fp* and *sf* sometimes indicate a dynamic change on the very next note, *fz* always indicates a dynamic decrease on the initial note itself. *fz* indicates a more vigorous attack than does *fp*, and occurs most often in louder contexts. Example 4.23 from the E♭ Trio D929 makes the relationship clear: (See p. 146.)

6. *fzp* (opening of slow movement, G major Quartet D887/2, see Ex. 4.12) / *ffzp* (D537/3, m. 266). This marking is almost identical with *fz;* with the added *p* Schubert merely specifies the second dynamic.

7. *rf* (Swoboda: "strengthening, getting louder").[40] Although this marking may appear to belong to the accent family, in reality it represents the beginning, if perhaps a marked beginning, of a new dynamic level. In the E♭ Piano Sonata D568 Schubert writes a passage

---

[37] Oddly enough, on the modern grand piano, one can execute a kind of *sfzp* with a clever mid-rise catch of the key, but the technique surely was not known or practiced in Schubert's day.
[38] "Sforzando, oder Sforzato zeigen an, dass der ton mit besonderer Stärke angegeben werden soll, bezieht sich aber nur auf jenen Ton, bey welchem es steht."
[39] "Forzando: den Ton sehr stark angeben, aber gleich wieder nachlassen."
[40] "Rinforzando: verstärkend, anschwellend."

EXAMPLE 4.23

with expressive accentuation in single right-hand patterns, the last of which is an octave leap that should be strengthened in preparation for the octaves to come:

EXAMPLE 4.24
D568/1: mm. 147-154

Hairpin accents vs. decrescendos

Of all the ongoing and new expressive effects of Schubert's time that we as modern performers must interpret, perhaps the most elusive are the various forms of accentuation. Here again, we must isolate these effects and determine their individual meanings for Schubert. This project alone would constitute the basis of an entire dissertation, but here at least we can begin to raise the proper issues. Musicology has not yet focussed much attention on the details of accentuation (nor on articulation) in Schubert, and in most cases it has dismissed thorny issues merely with speculative half-answers. As we noted in the last chapter, Walther Dürr believes it often doesn't matter whether Schubert's open-to-close hairpins are printed as accents or *diminuendos* (he clearly prefers accents, as in the opening of the F-minor Impromptu), because in his opinion they can mean the same thing.[41] Although he has no grounds for such a remarkable assumption, it has been accepted, tacitly, at least, by his readership, and exemplifies a modern tendency towards homogenization.

The discrepancy in m. 1 between the Bärenreiter edition of the F-minor Impromptu and its two competitors, mentioned at the beginning of the previous chapter, is not confined to that single example, but represents a disturbingly consistent reinterpretation of Schubert's *decrescendo* hairpins as simple accent marks. All Schubert scholars and most players are familiar with this issue, which cannot be solved on the basis of calligraphy alone. Indeed, if we relied solely upon the autograph evidence, we could haggle for years about Schubert's intentions. Certainly no simplistic rules of thumb concerning Schubert's handwriting will serve us here. The familiar suggestion, for example, that partially vertical hairpin signs in Schubert's scores indicate accents whereas horizontal ones indicate *decrescendos* brings us no systematic enlightenment. Theories about placement of signs over or under notes have proven equally untenable. Jaap Schröder points out rightly that performers (who are largely untrained in musicological problems) have been forced to draw their own conclusions about such markings, a situation that can lead us only further along separate paths and by no means towards a deeper general understanding of Franz Schubert's way of thinking.[42]

The need to discover other principles and larger contexts for this problem has not always been self-evident. For years string ensembles were cowed (even if unsatisfied) by the final note of the C-major Quintet, where the *GA* and other publishers printed a *decrescendo*, based upon the original edition. In the late nineteenth century, editors appear not to have asked themselves whether this gesture was truly characteristic of Schubert's style, or whether it had any meaning in the larger Viennese style. Reassessing the score for publication in the *NSA* in recent years, Martin Chusid applied the proper logic and sense of style to this problem (after all, why would a responsible composer suddenly rob his listeners of the impact of a final chord after such a dramatic and lengthy musical journey?), and now the sign reads correctly as an accent.

Chusid's decision in this matter is satisfying, but curiously at odds with the apparent policy of the general editorship of the *NSA*. Apart from such isolated decisions the *NSA* appears to have reverted to a simplistic approach, opting almost dogmatically to interpret open-left to closed-right hairpin signs as accents in problematic autographs. This inexplicable preference appears to stem directly from the general editorship, and is backed, of course, by the power of a well-known and highly respected press. In our estimation, however, it constitutes a lamentable and now-uncorrectable flaw in the edition, rendering countless passages stylistically nonsensical. Consider the following example from the first movement of the B♭ Trio D898, where in m. 268 the strings have swell-fade hairpins with the

---

[41] *Schubert Handbuch*: 95, "[Das Akzent-Zeichen] ist oft nicht leicht von Decrescendo-Gabeln zu unterscheiden. . . , und ist nicht einnmal sicher, ob es überhaupt von ihnen unterschieden werden soll. [!]

[42] CD booklet notes to the Octet D803, performed by the Atlantis Ensemble (Virgin Classics 791120-2):8.

clear objective of regaining **p** and softer at the beginning of the next bar (marked in all three parts). Astonishingly, however, the editor has read the fade part of the hairpin in the piano as an accent, thus defying logic as well as the general principle of across-the-board dynamics in Schubert.

EXAMPLE 4.25

We can think of no reason for the piano to remain louder than the other voices in the second measure of this example (not to mention the obtrusive accent at the top of what should be a gentle swell in all voices). This reading would require a *subito* **p** from the pianist at the beginning of the next measure, where the left hand would suddenly drop in volume in the middle of a scalar sweep and then begin a *decrescendo* on the very next beat (in *Allegro*)!

Two other examples may suffice to convince the reader of serious problems in the *NSA*. The first concerns the opening of the C-major Fantasy for Violin and Piano D934, where in mm. 2 and 3 Schubert makes a hairpin swell followed in m.4 by a hairpin fade—and the same process in mm. 7 and 8. The *NSA*, however, has printed the fades as accents, thereby introducing disturbing peaks where we should hear gentle billows in a general context of **pp**. In m.5, the violin enters **pp**, but according to the *NSA* the piano accompaniment has made a *crescendo* plus an accent and thus remains louder than the melody (ditto for m.8): dynamically speaking, a case of the tail wagging the dog.

EXAMPLE 4.26

Expression and Expressive Devices 149

Rudolf Kolisch taught his chamber music pupils that in the music of Beethoven a double hairpin of the convex type, as the example above rightly should read, with no other marking attached (such as a *fp* in the middle) indicated an expressive swell-fade within the general dynamic of a particular passage. We will find that this interpretation applies to Schubert's works as well. Schubert used the single hairpin to move out of one dynamic and into another only where the transition was a relatively fast one. Otherwise he wrote in verbal instructions such as *cresc.* or *decresc., dim.*, etc., for the practical reason that hairpins could not stretch over long sections of the score without causing or encountering graphical conflicts.

As a further example of the *NSA*'s enigmatic stance concerning hairpins, we might consider one in the concave fade-swell shape. Unlike the convex combination, the concave type does not always remain within the confines of a general dynamic. Often it constitutes a gesture of a most dramatic nature, as in the opening measures of the Overture to *Alfonso und Estrella* (mm. 2/4, for example). Here, the autograph (*SBB*) calls for fade-swells acccented with *fp* (not a literal sign, see "accentuation," below) at their beginnings, falling to *p* (see m. 2, violin I, ex. 4.27a) and sweeping dramatically back up to *ff*, all on a single bow (or in one breath, as the case may be). A comparison of the manuscript with the *NSA*

EXAMPLE 4.27a/b
Overture to *Alfonso and Estrella*, p.1
a. *SBB* autograph

version (W. Dürr, volume editor), however, is eye-opening. The *SBB* autograph must be considered the main source for this overture. In the notes to the *NSA* Dürr names multiple sources as his basis, including string parts from an unknown copyist, but as we noted in Ch. III (Assessing editions and choosing scores), such riches can lead ultimately to poverty. From these various sources Dürr seems to pick and choose his dynamics, articulation, and even the tones themselves apparently according to whim, resulting in a confusion and inconsistency far more grievous than that of which Schubert himself is often accused. Dürr has changed the first halves of these concave hairpins to accents and would have us execute simultaneously two kinds of accents at the beginning of mm.2 and 4, etc.: ***fp*** and [>]. Dürr clearly does not mean that his new accent sign be taken grammatically, but as a true accent.

b. *NSA* print

Expression and Expressive Devices

Indeed, the beginning of the second and fourth measures (*fp*) are not to be attacked as sharply or as heavily as beat 3 of the first and third measures (*fz*) and so a grammatical accent combined with *fp* would be contradictory (and just as pointless as a literal accent on top of the *fp*)!Nothing except a hairpin fade following the *fp* makes sense here (and as we see in the *SBB* autograph, m.2 the violin parts, which Schubert probably wrote out first and most carefully, are unmistakeably marked with a long hairpin. Incidentally, Dürr, clearly influenced by his other sources (see the copyist's violin part, for example, reproduced in the *NSA* volume), has simply removed Schubert's slurs in mm. 2 and 4, etc. In doing so, he has also removed evidence about tempo (without a bow change, these measures can be played only in a true *andante* in four beats instead of the wildly slow eighth=92 marked by someone other than Schubert) and evidence about the beginning of trills (slurred from the preceding notes, the trills must start on the main notes). Lastly, in terms of the tones themselves, we cannot understand why Dürr would depart from the autograph (see his note at the bottom of Ex. 4.27b) in such a manner that the first trombone is the only player who fails to participate in the dramatic octave drop in the second half of the first measure.

We see that beyond the pure consideration of Schubert's autograph, the correct interpretation of this opening depends upon a systematic knowledge of his tempos (and in fact of playable tempos in general), a knowledge of contemporaneous bowing practices (and of bowing in general), an intimate familiarity with the meaning of Schubert's accentuation signs (which to date have not been codified properly), not to mention a practical knowledge of instruments and an overall grasp of Schubert's musical intentions for this opening (cf. the lone trombone part). Furthermore, all of this must be checked against early nineteenth-century style, and the result measured against logic,in order to avoid producing what in this case we can most generously characterize as a regrettable pastische.

Schubert's accent markings constitute one of the least understood aspects of his notation, as well as that of the nineteenth century in general. The dominant opinion appears to be that his markings were too inconsistent for classification, and that he called for more than a sufficient number of accents in his scores (see Fiske quotation on pp. 141-142, concerning the C-major Symphony D944). Here we must reiterate that such thinking is indicative, at the least, of insufficient analysis and, at the most, of rationalization in support of an ever-growing affinity for highly personal Schubert interpretations among modern performers. In fact, Schubert's method of accentuation was not only reasonably systematic, but in many works, beautifully enlightening. Here, too, he was a master, and clearly not the legendary notational dabbler with a pen in one hand and a wine glass in the other.

Perhaps the most important key to understanding Schubert's accentuation lies in his own notational idealism: simply put, the striving within the confines of one medium to reach the plateau of a higher medium. For example, in Ch. I we pointed out this aspect of Schubert's piano music, where his ideal model was the string quartet. In the piano music this idealism is evident in the phrase lengths (corresponding to bowstroke capacities) and the distinct four-part textures, and also in the dynamics and accentuation. In Ch. I we mentioned an example of an impossible *crescendo* on a single, sustained piano tone (A major Sonata, op. post.), and readers can easily find many similar places in his music. Let us look now at an early example of his accentuation in this light. (See Example 4.28 on p. 152.)

Where in the passage mm. 164–174, Schubert based the main notes of his melody on traditionally strong parts of the measures, at the melodic tag where he merely echoes and summarizes his melody through singly-placed, accented notes over the same harmonic pattern in m.175 he opts for a kind of notated *tempo rubato* type B2. Here, then, the accents apply to the delayed melodic half notes. It is the extraordinary pianist who can accentuate this top line without including the other right hand notes that occur simultaneously.

The first thing for modern pianists to remember about such accents in Schubert is that on period-style instruments they often were executed more successfully as slightly agogic accents than as percussive ones, particularly in situations like the one above. This is also true of some orchestral instruments as well, the clarinet, for example, and particularly the flute. (As we shall see, *fz / ffz / fffz*, by contrast, were more easily rendered with the rhythmic and metrical sharpness that suits their expressive purposes in his scores.) In this light the passage above is not particularly pianistic, but in its individualized voicing looks far more like a keyboard arrangement of a string quartet. If we think about how a violinist would execute these accented tones—with a faster bow and a sweetened *vibrato*, in the course of which the center of their sound may occur marginally later than usual—they suddenly begin to make sense to us. The pianist who keeps this sonic picture in mind will find the right character for this passage.

EXAMPLE 4.28
D279: mm. 175-181

The tenuto-agogic-hairpin

Actually, the hairpin signs in Example 4.28 were officially recognized as *tenuto* markings. Both Friedrich Starke and August Swoboda describe an open-to-closed hairpin, shorter than a *decrescendo* mark but longer than an accent mark. Starke calls this middle-length sign a "kleine Anschwellungszeichen" [literally, a "small swell sign"]. He tells us that its efficacy lasts as long as the length of the sign itself (i.e. a *tenuto* sign in the modern sense), but offers no further interpretation.[43]

> [Note to the reader: In our first assessment of this description (*Die Brille* 24) we assumed that Starke must have misnamed the sign, for visually it goes from open left to closed right: i.e. a

---
[43] Czerny, *Pianoforte Schule:* 14.

Expression and Expressive Devices 153

"small attenuation sign" rather than a "small swell" sign. Subsequent reflection leads us to believe that Starke meant what he said, that indeed the sign called for a small swell, or at least a small reinforcement of the sound, particularly in that Swoboda later says the same thing in other words. Obviously, in order to achieve a *tenuto* on the piano one must reinforce the sound at the outset. Starke is describing the actual attack.]

Swoboda calls the sign a "short *crescendo*" sign and states further that when it is placed over single notes, it carries a special significance: He shows his Fig. 118 (reproduced below) and adds, "if it is written over a single tone." Then he adds the most interesting observation of all: "We also often understand '*tenuto*' to mean that one makes it possible to hear the oscillations [Schwingungen] of a tone; i.e. that the performer must cause the oscillations to be 'felt' aurally" ["dem Gehöre fühlbar"].⁴⁴

EXAMPLE 4.29
Swoboda's Kleine Anschwellungzeichen

§. 95. Oft findet man die Sylbe ten., welches die erste Sylbe des Wortes tenuto (halten, aushalten) ist, über einer Note, und durch diese wird angezeigt, daß der Ton mit einem besondern Nachdruck ausgezeichnet werden soll.

Fig. 117.

Dieselbe Bedeutung hat auch das kleine Crescendo-Zeichen

Fig. 118.

wenn es sich nur auf einen Ton bezieht.

Unter ten. versteht man oft auch, daß man die Schwingungen eines Tones hörbar, d. i. dem Gehöre fühlbar machen soll.

Here the word "Schwingungen" cannot be interpreted in the modern acoustical sense, for the behavior of sound waves would not have been of interest to the reader of this manual. In any case, how would a pianist, for example, make the oscillations suddenly more audible to the listener? Clearly, Swoboda is talking about *vibrato*, for which no standard terminology yet had developed. He has focussed on string players and singers here, and, in modern parlance his instruction would call for a "sweetened" (faster, more intense) *vibrato* on such notes, probably combined with an agogic delay and a slight lingering on the tone. Likewise, wind instruments with *vibrato* possibilities can execute this *tenuto* in a similar fashion, but those for whom *vibrato* is not appropriate must rely on the agogic delay and lingering for the effect. The opening of the unfinished oratorio *Lazarus* D689 provides an example in the clarinet part, particularly in mm. 9 and 10. Here it seems clear that Schubert had something particularly expressive in mind, for in addition to the extremely

---

⁴⁴ Swoboda: 44.

soft dynamic (***ppp*** with a *diminuendo*!) we also find a rare general phrasing slur above the smaller binding slurs, as shown in the section of the autograph facsimile:

EXAMPLE 4.30

Pianists can approximate this kind of "sweetening" only through the agogic execution, whereby the attack is slightly emphasized but delayed, and the tone held out as long as possible without destroying the rhythmic context: another case where pianists aspire to the condition of a higher medium. In German this technique is called *Nachdruck*, and it corresponds to a form of single-note *rubato* later developed extensively by Liszt and Chopin.

For singers the hairpin *tenuto-rubato* is an especially important sign. Normal accents as performed by instruments are not typical of singing styles, and where we find a left-open to right-closed hairpin in Schubert's vocal music (where it occurs comparatively rarely) we are dealing almost certainly with a classic hairpin-*tenuto*. Again, the fullest part of the attack is agogically delayed, as is surely the case for the hairpins shown in Example 4.31 (from the autograph copy of the first tenor part of *Frühlingsgesang* D740):

EXAMPLE 4.31

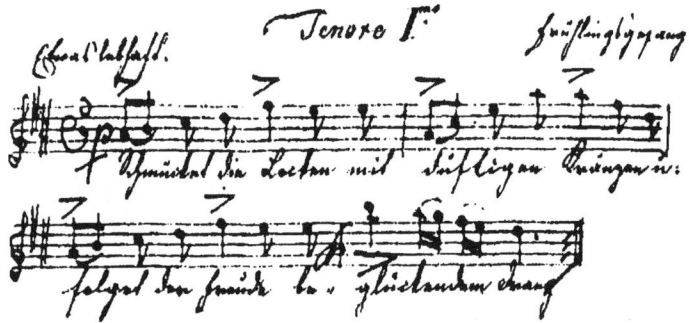

A thorough reassessment and new taxonomy of Schubert's hairpin signs based on the information above will take some time to complete (in this respect his handwriting remains difficult to interpret). In terms of instrumental music we can suggest immediately that one look for such *tenutos* not only among the strong beats, as shown in *Frühlingsgesang*, but just as often among the weak-beat stresses. In such contexts, these stresses relate to earlier forms of *tempo rubato*. For example, in Example 4.32 (first movement, second group of the

Expression and Expressive Devices 155

C-minor Sonata D958), the hairpin sign surely must call for a *tenuto-rubato* rather than a simple accent. The accents in mm. 39 and 42 might appear merely grammatical to the analyzing eye (the first on what appears to be a hemiola pickup and the second on a downbeat), but to the ear they can no longer be heard as such. In m. 39, one half of a "6/8" measure following a pause gives us no graspable context for a hemiola effect; and in harmonic terms the accent on the downbeat in m. 40 occurs not on the outset of the main phrase (which indeed would be a strong beat), but at the beginning of the answering phrase on a subdominant chord. Thus, these two accents can be looked upon as expressive in nature, to be played with the slight agogic delay and lingering described above.[45]

EXAMPLE 4.32
mm. 39–54

Perhaps even more decisive for Schubert's notation is the possibility that in many cases where we find a hairpin augmenting a *fp* or similar stress, the hairpin should be interpreted most wisely as a *tenuto-rubato* rather than a conflicting and superfluous accent. *Wandrers Nachtlied* D224 provides an excellent example. Here one can interpret all the hairpin signs

EXAMPLE 4.33

[45] Also see Elmar Budde," Akzent, Nachdruck und Sforzato" in Musica 34/4 (1980, hereafter *Mu*): 366/7.

(which occur only in the piano part) as *tenuto-rubatos,* particularly the weak-beat stresses in mm. 3–4. Above all, however, the hairpin sign in m. 5 must be seen as a *tenuto-rubato*: theoretically it coincides with a *fp* but Schubert's separated notation shows us clearly that he intends the *fp* to apply only to the inner voices in the right hand (*f* on the first beat and *p* on the second) and that he reserves the hairpin for the top voice (see Example 4.33 on p. 155).

The pure tenuto

Unlike the *tenuto-rubato* described above the pure *tenuto* has almost nothing to do with attack, but merely with the length of a note. In its verbal form the *tenuto* instruction was known in Viennese music well before Schubert's time (for example, the marking at the beginning of the slow movement in Beethoven's Sonata in A major, op. 2/2, 1794 or 1795). C.P.E. Bach had discussed it in his *Versuch*.[46] We find this verbal instruction in Schubert's works as well. It tells players to extend these tones just as if Schubert had written a horizontal stroke over the notes. Until recently it was thought that Schubert never shortened this verbal instruction to the horizontal stroke familiar to modern players. However, the first version of *Sehnsucht* D310/1 ("Nur wer die Sehnsucht kennt," 1815) shows us not only that Schubert used the *tenuto* stroke early in his career, but that he made a distinction between its extended length and the normal length of a dot under a slur. To our knowledge this notational distinction to that point had not been made even by Beethoven, another refutation of the ill-considered but still widespread prejudice that Schubert's notation was conservative and / or simplistic (cf. Reed, Ch.III, fn. 23 or Keller, below under Articulation).

EXAMPLE 4.34

[46] Part One, Section III, item 22.

Expression and Expressive Devices 157

The autograph of the *Klavierstück* D946/3 presents an even more progressive notational specification for the period. Under the bracket in Example 4.35a we find four measures, originally eight measures in an earlier concept, wherein the quarters are to be played either increasingly longer (the most progressive interpretation) or at least from a certain point longer (the literal interpretation). The articulation begins with dots under slurs, the longest separated articulation in use at that time, and by the fourth quarter it lengthens unmistakably into modern *tenuto* strokes. For extra insurance, Schubert has written out the verbal instruction "*tenuto*" at the beginning of the passage.

Unfortunately, despite Schubert's clear call for an increase in the *tenuto* quality (Example 4.35a), modern editors and printers have simply ignored his instruction. Laboring perhaps again under the impression that he was too conservative and/or simplistic for such subtleties, they have printed his markings instead as uniform dots (*NSA*, Example 4.35b) or strokes (Henle, Mies, Example 4.35c). We shall never really know how an editor or a *Stecher* (note setter) of Schubert's day and place might have read this passage because the work was first published in 1868, well into another era of notational understanding.

EXAMPLE 4.35a/c
a. autograph

b. *NSA*

c. Henle
(Allegro)

If our reading of this autograph is correct, it would indicate a rising need (at least on Schubert's part) to show more finely-graded transitions in articulation, duration (speed), and other elements than the reasonably fixed relational hierarchy of notational signs in early nineteenth-century Viennese musical orthography could offer.

Articulation: dots, strokes, slurs, tenutos, bowing vs. phrasing marks, pizzicatos

It must be clear that to discuss articulation as a subject separate from the others in this chapter—accentuation, *rubato*, *vibrato*, dynamics—constitutes an overly clinical activity. Still, clinics have their uses. As our medical friends might put it, the good news here is that articulation signs in Schubert are numerous and expressively various. The bad news is that until now not everyone has become fully aware of the good news, and those that may have done so are still puzzled by it.

In abstraction (i.e. before application to specific instruments and voices), the articulation issue concerns note length. Although for Schubert it has never been dealt with in depth, it has been discussed and debated hotly for the earlier Viennese classical style in general, often with the unsatisfying conclusion that composers were not particularly consistent in their notation. Most writers of the past have assumed (possibly influenced by popular historical reportage of the nineteenth and early twentieth centuries) that composers such as Mozart and Schubert wrote with enormous speed and were not particularly concerned with rewriting, nor with correcting their first editions. On the basis of this and other remarkably faulty assumptions, Hermann Keller, for example, writing on the subject of nineteenth-century articulation as late as 1955, simply dismissed the subject with the statement that articulation "did not develop beyond that of Mozart and Beethoven." His assessment of Schubert was not only correspondingly uninformed, but demeaning as well:

> In Schubert we find a limitless source of magnificent melodies, true wonders of harmonic imagination. But his carefree attitude [geringere Anspannung], which had such negative consequences for his existence in general, also revealed itself in a carefree sense of musical form and often in a dull ["stumpfen," dumpy] articulation.[47]

[47] *Phrasierung und Artikulation* (Kassel: Bärenreiter, 1955): 81.

Expression and Expressive Devices 159

Nothing could be further from the truth. Sadly, Keller's prejudice still prevails, and many contemporary scholars today dismiss Schubert's notational problems and challenges in similar ways, offering instead the sadly inadequate instruction that contemporary players must use their own "taste" and "experience" to decide upon each problem for themselves.

Generally speaking, eighteenth-century composers had not standardized much of their notation, but this problem had come a long way towards being solved by the first decades of the nineteenth century. On the subject of note length and staccatos, for example, we possess several clear period Viennese statements, all of them in agreement. Johann Wenzel's *Pedal- und Hackenharfen-Schule* (1808) was one of the earliest Viennese sources to distinguish between dots and strokes, and by the middle of Schubert's career this distinction was made in almost all major treatises.

J.B. Cramer, *Practische Pianoforte-Schule* (ca. 1819): p. 33:

The slur over or under two dots signifies mezzo staccato (half-sharp attack). The notes should not be so sharply attacked as if they were notated as follows [here Cramer shows staccatos and wedges].[48]

Friedrich Starke, *Wiener Piano-Forte Schule* (1819–1821), describes three different attacks:

1) The short, sharp attack that is indicated by strokes, where every note receives a fourth of its written length-value; 2) the half-sharp attack indicated by dots, where the notes receive one half of their written length-values; and 3) the carrying (appoggiato) ["tragende," portando] attack that is indicated by dots under a slur, where every note receives three quarters of its written length-value.[49]

Ernest Krähmer's *Czakan-Schule* (1821), p.8, tells us that:

strokes (ıı) or dots (··)[over a note] signify separate attacks, but the strokes require a sharper treatment than the dots. The carrying of tones [Das Tragen der Tön, portando] is indicated by dots under slurs, whereby the notes are indeed bound to each other, but nevertheless each receives a small, separate weight [Nachdruck].[50]

August Swoboda (*Allgemeine Theorie,* 1821) is not only clear, but meticulous in his treatment of dots and strokes:

The opposite of binding (legato) is shown by a dot over a note:

---

[48] "Der Bogen über oder unten zwei Punkten bedeutet mezzo staccato (halbabstossen). Die Noten dürfen dann nicht so scharf abgestossen werden, als wenn sie, wie folgt, bezeichnet wären: [Cramer shows strokes and dots]."
[49] Starke: 110.
[50] Enest Krähmer, *Neueste theoretisch-praktische Czakan-Schule* (See App. IIA, 1821): p.8 "Striche (ııı) oder Punkte]. . .bedeuten, dass die Noten sollen abgestossen werden; jedoch verlangen die Striche eine schärferer Behandlung als die Punkte. Das Tragen der Töne wird durch Punkte, über welche ein Bindungsbogen gezogen ist, angezeigt; wodurch zwar diese Noten aneinander gezogen, doch jede aber einen kleinen Nachdruck erhält."

EXAMPLE 4.36a/c

a. (Swoboda's Fig. 75)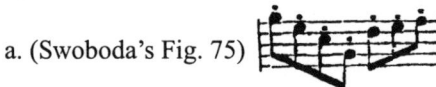

It means, namely, that the beginning and end of each tone can be heard particularly clearly, and further that each tone must be separated in equal measure from the previous and following one. One calls this kind of expression . . .(stoßen). . .staccato . . .When each tone is meant to be played particularly short, one writes, instead of dots, little vertical strokes over the notes.

b. (Swoboda's Fig. 76)

One often finds slurs over the dots [the example shows strokes, however], in which case one must separate the notes as if there were no slur, except that singers and wind players must perform them in a single breath, violinists in a single bow stroke [*bebung*], and pianists in a single swing of the hand in the desired direction ["nach der jedesmahlig einzuschlagenden Richtung hin"].[51]

c. (Swoboda's Fig. 77)

Strokes vs. wedges, not discussed here, is not an important issue, but merely a matter of calligraphic and / or printing style. Schubert rarely, if ever, used wedges in his manuscripts, but he used strokes and differentiated clearly between them and dots:

EXAMPLE 4.37
Grand Duo Sonata D812, autograph secondo part, mm. 215-221

Questions may arise about the value of a relatively long note (half or whole, or even the quarters in the example above) under a stroke or printed wedge, a notation that we find often in Schubert's music (see Example 4.38 on facing page).

If we were to go strictly by Starke's quantification for a note under a stroke, then the half would equal an eighth plus dotted eighth rest (Starke does not mention wedges over half notes). If this solution is correct, Schubert could have written the same thing as a quarter under a dot plus a quarter rest. We feel certain, however, that this literal quantification, or even a more generous one such as halving the value, cannot be correct. In any case, Schubert took the time in other passages to write out such note-and-rest alterations, and it does not seem logical that he would grow lazy in this regard only at certain times. Our biggest conceptual problem here is the unnatural conflict between the long value and the

---

[51] pp.29-30.

EXAMPLE 4.38
Rosamunde D797/1, Entre-Act nach dem 1. Aufzug
mm.12-17, string parts

stroke-as-sharpest *staccato*. This conflict alone might lead us in another direction: for example, back to the suggestion that the stroke sometimes served as an accent mark. Again we can eliminate this possibility, not only because Schubert had at his disposal (and employed) the entire range of accent marks already described (notice the accents that follow the first wedged notes in the example above), but also because not a single pedagogical author of Schubert's Vienna even alludes to such a possibility.[52] The most reasonable solution to the problem, we believe, is in this case the most widely-practiced one:. i.e. to think of such notes as true halves, but to perform them with the most generous detachment.

In the preface to the Eulenberg edition of the *Great* C-major Symphony D944 Roger Fiske tells us that in Schubert's music the stroke "implies an emphasis and occurs only in loud passages."[53] He is mistaken on both counts. As we have mentioned, no contemporary evidence, pedagogical or other, exists to support the first theory (which Fiske shares with Dürr and others),[54] and the presence of separate accentuation over notes marked with strokes throughout Schubert's works further discourages it. As to strokes occurring only in loud passages, a quick look at Schubert's keyboard music, for example, the passage from the F-minor Impromptu D935/4 (Example 4.39 on p. 162) refutes the notion completely.

---

[52] Robin Stowell writes: "the dot later [in the eighteenth century] seems to have gained preference [to the dash]—Wolfgang [Mozart] certainly appears to have employed dots more freely in his mature years—so that the dash (or wedge) denoted either a normal staccato or an accent, or a combination of the two, generally, but not exclusively, in forte contexts." ("Leopold Mozart Revised" in *Perspectives on Mozart Performance*, R. Larry Todd and Peter Williams, eds. Cambridge Univ. Press, 1991; p. 135). Stowell does not explain how he came to the conclusion that Mozart's more frequent ("freer") use of dots, if indeed this is so, must suddenly have added "accentuation" to the meaning of dashes.
[53] op. cit: XIV.
[54] *Schubert Handbuch:* 98

EXAMPLE 4.39

In terms of orchestral music, Fiske appears not to have noticed the examples of strokes in *piano* marked in his own edition of the C-major Symphony:

EXAMPLE 4.40
D944/2, m.m. 212-214

If we look a bit further we will find many other soft passages with strokes over the notes, as in the B-minor Symphony fragment D759/1:

EXAMPLE 4.41

Expression and Expressive Devices 163

This is not to mention the extraordinary appearance of strokes over notes marked both *pp* and *pizzicato* at the end of the exposition of the first movement of this symphony, a phenomenon which brings us to the most interesting part of the present discussion.

In the passage below (from the variations in D810), the cello line, marked *pizzicato*, presents two interesting enigmas: first, if it is to be played *pizzicato*, why does Schubert mark it *staccato* as well; secondly, in the first and second endings of the second half of this variation, how is the cellist supposed to play a *portando* sextuplet *pizzicato*? Schubert marks *arco* at the beginning of the next variation, so we can assume that the entire variation is *pizzicato*. These questions are rarely raised by editors, and certainly never answered.[55]

EXAMPLE 4.42

[55] Roger Fiske mentions the existence of dots over *pizzicatos* in the C-major Symphony D944 (Eulenburg No. 410, print 6742: XIV), but remarks merely that he is "uncertain of their purpose."

In the past these *portando* markings appear to have been ignored or even suppressed. The Eulenberg score (EE 1111), for example, gives dots but omits the slurs. The *NSA* restored the *portando* slurs, which we find clearly marked in the autograph. (Furthermore, Aderhold also has corrected the traditional quintuplet reading of m. 39, cf. Eulenberg and others, which was patently wrong. Here Schubert did not remove a note, which indeed would have created a quintuplet over two beats, but simply changed a note):

EXAMPLE 4.43
D810/2 autograph from m. 34

Throughout this book we have and will continue to emphasize Schubert's sonic, structural, and notational idealism. Our codification of Schubert's articulation can point only in this same direction. How many of us, for example, have truly considered the significance of articulation markings (dots, strokes, etc) over *pizzicatos,* as in the example above? Surely such markings must be superfluous! They are not, however. The fact is that

Expression and Expressive Devices

in the chamber music and symphonies of his last years Schubert came to write at least four different kinds of *pizzicatos*, and assigned them even further distinctions through the various note values over which they were marked (mostly quarters, eighths and sixteenths):

1. *Pizzicatos* in three denominations without further articulation.

2. *Pizzicatos* in three denominations with *staccato* dots (D956/2: quarters, eighths, sixteenths. D759/2, D804/4, D810/2, D887/1, D944/1: quarters, eighths).

3. *Pizzicatos* in triplet eighths with *staccato* dots under slurs, i.e. *portando* (D810/2). By inference, he could have notated this variety in quarters and sixteenths had the need arisen.

4. *Pizzicatos* in quarters under strokes (D759/1). By inference he could have notated this variety in eighths and sixteenths had the need arisen.

Thus we have eight actual types and four more by inference. When we factor in differences in tempo (say between a quarter in the slow movement of the Quintet and in the first movement of the B-minor Symphony) and loudness, we are presented with a true array of articulated *pizzicato* types: all in all, perhaps several dozen distinctions. Occasionally we have seen some of these differentiated types in music after Schubert's time, but not in music prior to his time.[56] Schubert appears to have provided the watershed in this regard.

Is this notational arsenal merely theoretical? Perhaps in some extremes it is. We cannot imagine that many string players of Schubert's day took great care to differentiate their *pizzicatos*. Certainly the cello's *portando* measures in the D-minor String Quartet must have prompted a raised eyebrow from the first player (Linke?) who read through it. Clearly in Schubert's "mind's ear" the cellist's *portando* figure commented on the violinist's *portando* in m. 46 and prepared the way for the next variation. It is doubtful, however, that Linke could or might have made this distinction in performance, nor have we heard it made in modern times. Of course all string players know how to make slight differences between *pizzicato* types: using the length of the thumb to pluck the string produces a fuller sound than using the fingertip; also, releasing the left hand directly after plucking the string renders the *pizzicato* much drier than usual. But whether we can manage eight fundamental differences (not to mention the extra factors mentioned above) is another matter. Frankly, what we have here is Schubert the idealist, who in any case wasn't hearing much of his great instrumental music played, and / or certainly not with much understanding. Why shouldn't he, like Beethoven, write what he could hear and not merely what a Linke could play or understand? If we can regard Schubert's piano music as a kind of striving towards a higher, more complex medium, and certainly we have seen enough "idealistic" keyboard notation to support this concept, then we can regard his string music in a similar light. Only this explanation can account adequately for the thinking of a man who could conceive the glorious *Andante sostenuto* of the B♭ Piano Sonata or the *Adagio* of the C-major Quintet.

---

[56] *Pizzicato* markings reinforced by dots above the noteheads can be found, for example, in Puccini's scores (cf. the string parts n the "Humming Chorus" from *Madama Butterfly*) and probably in those by other composers of the late Romantic- early Modern period.

Bowing, slurring, and breathing

Readers who wish to familiarize themselves with normative bowing practices and theories inherited by musicians of Schubert and Beethoven's Vienna may wish to consult Robin Stowell's article "Leopold Mozart Revised," in which the author has traced bowing and other articulation issues of the late eighteenth century through the various editions of Mozart's famous violin tutor (into the nineteenth century) and compared them with other period sources.[57] Schubert may not have used Mozart's tutor, but the internal evidence of his scores reveals a firmly classical training: in most of his earlier works slur lengths – and this holds true for all the instrumental genres – are no longer than a bow might manage in a single stroke. This rule of thumb seems to have been his guide in writing wind lines as well. We find few indications of bow changes on single notes[58] and none of the progressive bowing styles of post-Paganinian Europe, etc.

Eventually Schubert developed some longer slurs, often with expressive accentuation built in, as in this phrase from D804/1 (first two measures with pickup, answered by cello), which even with the modern bow is often played in two strokes:

EXAMPLE 4.44
D804/1, mm. 121–125

or, quite dramatically, this passage from the end of D804/1:

EXAMPLE 4.45
D804/1, mm. 283–290

---

[57] Op.cit: 126-157.
[58] Concerning the extension of final cadenza trills, Leopold mentions disapprovingly the habit of prolonging them through an extra bow stroke (1787 edition, see Stowell, p. 150). Thus the habit was known, but in what other kind of situations it might have been indulged is unknown.

Expression and Expressive Devices

Such slurs were still unusual for Schubert, even in piano music. We have already mentioned the example at the beginning of the F-minor Impromptu D935, and we also find several in the C-major Symphony D944/4. In the example below, the contrabasses and cellos of Schubert's day were unlikely to have been able to manage the long slur on a single bow, especially beginning at *ff*:

EXAMPLE 4.46

Double slurring (expressive slurs above bowing slurs) remained rare. We find what appears to be an example in D804/2, m. 76. Here, on paper, the larger slur looks like an expressive slur above the inner bowing slurs, but in fact it is not. On the second beat violin 2 is expected to take both 16th pairs in the same direction. This is not true of the viola, which has joined the violin at the last minute and which will initiate the new articulation on beat three. Typically, Schubert changes over from the lyrical bowing to a more aggressive one (also for violin 2) as the *crescendo* begins in m.77 (similar changeovers at the beginnings of *crescendos,* often moving from dots to *detaché,* can be found throughout the string quartets and symphonies).(See Example 4.47 on p. 168.) One rule of the past, that upbeats required upbows and downbeats downbows, is clearly no longer applicable in music of Schubert's day, for the simple reason that the rhetoric of music had grown much more complex. Even as early as 1751 Geminiani (whose treatise also came out in Vienna in the

EXAMPLE 4.47

mm.75-77

late eighteenth century) had declared that rule to be a "wretched" one.[59] Still, Viennese critics remained conservative (stubbornly uninformed?) on such subjects, as we can infer from the critical reaction to Chopin's "non-observance of the indication by accent of the commencement of musical phrases" in 1829 (see *Tempo rubato,* above).

For singers, the issue of phrasing and slurring is intimately connected with breathing practices. Unfortunately, we possess little pedagogical information from Schubert's Vienna concerning breathing. Even so, Friedrich Starke's little nine-page singing tutor, the *Kurzgefaßte Gesang-Methode* (ca. 1820), provides us with some general rules:

A. Taking a breath is not allowed:

    1) in the middle of a word, except where indicated on a syllable drawn out over several measures;

    2) where an article, an adjective or a pronoun would be separated from its corresponding noun or verb;

    3) after the short part of a measure [after an upbeat?, nach einem kurzen Tacttheile]. One always breathes after the long part of the measure [after a downbeat?, nach einem langen Tacttheile];

    4) between a suspension [Vorhalte] and the following note, or likewise between two notes bound by a slur.

B. On the contrary, breathing is allowed:

    1) at the beginnings and ends of phrases [bei Absätzen (Ein- und Abschnitten)];

    2) during rests;

    3) after *staccato* notes;

    4) before a syncopated note;

    5) at unaccented parts of the measure;

---

[59] *The Art of Playing on the Violin* (London, 1751): 4.

Expression and Expressive Devices 169

6) ["bei": before, between?] three equal notes, for example 3 eighth notes in 3/8, or ["bei": before, between?] triplets, etc.

Some of these rules make common sense: not taking a breath in the middle of a word, or not separating an article from its noun. Others are more difficult to grasp. For example, if we interpret A.3 correctly, what is the real difference between it and B.5? And whence comes the rule about breathing at or before three equal notes? These are only a few of the many still unanswered questions related to the subject of breathing and phrasing in vocal music during this period. Taken together with the subject of vocal delivery in general (Ch. I), they constitute the stuff for a separate research project, which perhaps might be of interest to a young scholar of the future.

Pedalling

Schubert wrote pedalling into many of his scores for piano or involving piano. None of these markings appear to have been made for technical reasons (i.e. to help the pianist smooth out difficult *legato* connections) or to support a general concert hall ambience. Schubert's pedalling, like Beethoven's, appears calculated to achieve specific atmospheric or rhetorical effects. In Ch. I we discussed pedals in general, as well as the atmospheric effect of the pedalling in the *Nachtstück* D672, meant to reveal a hidden sonic world to the listener. As rhetorical pedalling we might cite the *Andante* of the A-minor Sonata D784. Here the pedal is lifted (*sordini*) in m. 4 (and *passim*) to sharpen that motive in relationship to the opening measures, in effect, to further clarify the musical dialogue:

EXAMPLE 4.48
mm. 1-16

Interestingly enough, this pedalling is clearly meant to begin at the outset although it is not so marked. Only when we come upon the instruction *sordini* (with dampers) do we see that the rest of the movement should be played *senza sordini* (with no dampers). Considering the remarks we find in the pedagogical sources that pedals were developed especially to enhance *adagios* (i.e. central slow movements) and from the fact that the *sordini* instruction in this movement is clearly the exceptional marking, we could infer reasonably that Schubert expected pedal to be applied in his other slow movements as well, even though not marked. This expectation would apply, of course, only to slow movements of a particularly *legato* character, especially where he supplied the extra marking: *ligato* or *molto ligato*. Here we do not mean to imply that *ligato* is an instruction to pedal, but merely that it reveals the places where pedal occasionally might enhance the character of the passage.

Where a character conflict exists, Schubert also supplies the resolution: in the *Allegretto quasi andantino* of D537 he marks the right hand *legato* and the left hand *staccato* – and here no pedal would be wanted, for it would obliterate the left-hand articulation. Later, in the B♭ Sonata D960/2, he wants a similar but more subtle interplay between *legato* and *staccato*. This time he insures the *legato* of the right hand with the instruction *col pedale* and the complex articulation of the left hand in other ways. As we noted in Ch. I, the pedal is not meant to drench the movement, but merely to enhance the central duet in the right hand without losing the possibility of articulating the left. On modern grands one must thin out the sound by fluttering the pedal in order to achieve the desired effect.

In movements other than slow ones or lieder (Schubert writes few *adagios*, mostly *andantes*, *andantinos* or *allegrettos*) we also find a few models for pedalling. Here, however, we have no pedagogical evidence that the *sostenuto* pedal was developed or intended for faster movements. Nevertheless, as we said, it would be the courageous pianist who would try, say, the opening of the posthumous B♭ Sonata completely without the aid of the pedal. Still, this work and many others tend to drown somewhat in pedal, for pianists are fond of creating their own ambience. This approach may be appropriate for the opening measures, but with the trill and first *staccato* in mm. 8/9 the pedal must be lifted. Almost no one takes the wedge in m. 9 seriously, but the entire gesture of trill plus sharp cut-off is meant to foreshadow its aggressive "military drumroll" reappearance in the first ending:

EXAMPLE 4.49a/b
a. D960, mm. 6–9

b. D960, mm. 118-121

Expression and Expressive Devices 171

The same precaution must be taken with the pedalling as the movement evolves into the articulated figuration. Schubert's lively sense of figuration evolved from the eighteenth-century models, and much of it can be obliterated by the pedal. Mm. 22 and 52 (below) show clearly that the pedal must not be engaged, otherwise the difference in articulation between the two hands could not be effected:

EXAMPLE 4.50a/b
a. D960, mm.21-22

b. D960, m.52

Likewise, the bass-note *staccatos* in mm. 27–32 are imperative, if the *pizzicatos* string imagery described in Ch. I is viable and if we are not to sleep through Schubert's passagework:

EXAMPLE 4.51

We find few, if any, pedalling marks in the four-hand works, not even the F-minor Fantasy D940. This is not because Schubert forgot to mark in his pedalling wishes, but mostly because in four-hand playing the pedal is less essential. Certainly the upper player cannot pedal, unless he or she is intimately acquainted with the harmonic foundations of the bottom part. In many passages the upper player is freed from "harmonic duty" and can mould the melodic lines and figuration quite well without pedal. The lower player, on the other hand, often has less such figurative responsibility and can provide the motors and harmonic foundations with far more fluidity than in a two-hand score. Indeed, in order to achieve Schubert's wonderfully rich articulation and individuation of voices, four-hand teams should avoid pedal wherever possible. Even the F-minor Fantasy, normally drenched in pedal for the sake of ambience and "musicality," will reveal wonders when towelled off a bit.

CHAPTER V

Essential and Voluntary Ornamentation

Essential ornamentation

By Franz Schubert's day the variety of ornaments in sign had dwindled from the rich internationally-individuated stock of the Baroque down to a handful of general types: trills, turns, shakes, *appoggiaturas*, and grace notes (single, multiple and combinative). This does not mean that Schubert wrote fewer ornaments than his predecessors, for his music is filled with them. In fact, he and other serious composers of his age (principally Beethoven) may have written more ornament signs than had many of their predecessors, in keeping with a newer spirit of explicitness and control on the part of the composer. After Schubert, however, ornaments in sign grew fewer and fewer as composers began to develop the melodic styles of the mid-nineteenth century, which demanded a different set of interpretative skills from performers.

The pedagogical rules for executing many of the surviving ornaments in the first decades of the nineteenth century were still partially in agreement with past pedagogy. Even the later Viennese sources – Swoboda (1826), Hummel (1826), Spohr (1832), Czerny (1839) – still repeated certain venerable wisdoms: for example, concerning long *appoggiaturas*, which take half the space of the long note in duple values and two-thirds in triple values.[1] Commensurate with the reduced variety of ornaments in use in early nineteenth-century Vienna, however, the newer theoreticians also simplified and shortened the instructions for executing them. Furthermore, some statements in Viennese tutors of Schubert's time point (if somewhat vaguely) to the changes that must have been taking place rather rapidly: for example, trills beginning on main notes, and, if we read carefully between the lines, *appoggiaturas* as pre-beat ornaments (grace notes).

---

[1] Almost all theoreticians imitate their predecessors to a degree. Indeed, parts of some of the tutors of the past were lifted word-for-word, like boiler-plate legal language, from earlier tutors. Nevertheless, Walther Dürr's instruction (*Schubert Handbuch:* 105) for Schubert players to consult Türk's *Klavierschule* (1789) on grace notes and *appoggiaturas* would have us reach back too far. Türk was summational and thus conservative even for his time; later theoreticians who leaned on him simply perpetuated what was already out-of-date even for him. As we have pointed out in several articles (cf. "Modern Schubert Interpretation" and "Franz Schubert's scores"), it is high time to consult Viennese theoreticians of Schubert's day.

Schubert wrote signs or small notes for the following ornaments:

I. Trills.
- A. With afterstrokes (*Nachschläge*)
    1. Starting with the upper auxiliary note
    2. Starting with the main note
- B. Without afterstrokes
    1. Starting with the upper auxiliary note
    2. Starting with the main note

II. Long *appoggiaturas* (*lange Vorschläge*) in various denominations, on-beat.
- A. quarter note
- B. eighth note
- C. sixteenth note

III. Short *appoggiaturas* (*kurze Vorschläge*) in various denominations, pre-beat (grace notes, slides, etc.), on-beat and after- or inter-beat (*Nachschläge*).
- A. single *appoggiatura* with half the value of the main note
    1. eighth note
    2. sixteenth note
    3. thirty-second note
- B. single *appoggiatura* with one fourth the value of the main note
- C. multiple *appoggiaturas* in all the above denominations

IV. *Acciaccaturas* (rare)

V. Shakes, mordents

VI. Turns, with or without instructions for the accidentals

VII. Arpeggios (not really additive ornaments, like the others, but direct performance instructions)

Trills

J.N. Hummel's treatise (1826, pub. 1828) is usually credited as offering the first theoretical documentation of trills beginning on main notes, but the changeover had taken place long before. In 1811 the Kapellmeister of St. Stefans, Joseph Preindl, published a *Gesang-Lehre* with examples by Schubert's teacher Antonio Salieri, and already here we find the trills beginning on main notes.[2] If Salieri were up-to-date on this issue, then naturally he would

---

[2] From what we know about the time lag between writing and publishing, caused by the censorship process in Vienna, this source may represent practices already established in the previous decade, i.e. during Schubert's earlier childhood.

Essential and Voluntary Ornamentation

have taught Schubert the newer style as well. In any case, by Schubert's heyday main-note trills had become a standard part of the composer's language along with pre-beat graces. Thus, because in general Schubert was careful about his notation and because main-note trills were a standard part of his language, the simplest conclusion to be drawn in this matter is that all trills without upper-note starters were intended to begin on the main note. Trills beginning on upper notes were exceptions, which he took care to notate. The biggest mistake for us to make would be to take the trills with written starter notes as models for those without, rationalizing, somehow, that Schubert had forgotten or was too busy to write starter notes, or that he was inconsistent in his notation.

Nevertheless, in the *Schubert Handbuch* Walther Dürr shows the opening trills of the first act of *Alfonso und Estrella,* noting that each of them should have a starter note corresponding to the first one (the only one so marked):

EXAMPLE 5.1

Dürr speculates that the first one has a starter note because Schubert wanted to show that the upper tone of the trill should be altered chromatically.[3] Indeed, the entire opening passage is cast temporarily in the minor and the upper note should be G♭ but this is surely not the reason why Schubert added the starter note. He added it here and no further because it was the opening note and needed a kind of attention-getting bite to it. The successive trills should be played without starter notes. A passage from the A-major Sonata D959 is enlightening. In m. 87 Schubert gives the trill a starter note (chromatically altered), but two measures later he omits the starter note (also chromatically altered). Obviously he wants "bite" on the first trill, and he wants the second one to join it unobtrusively. The pattern repeats in mm. 96/98; this time the starter note is given but it is not to be altered chromatically. Schubert went to some trouble to differentiate the beginnings of these trills, and we must take care not to ride roughshod over his details, especially in this case, because we have solid evidence that main-note trills were well-established by Schubert's time. As we emphasize throughout this book, Schubert was not notationally deficient. If he felt the need to indicate a chromatic alteration to the player, he could do so with a sharp or flat beside, above or below the note in question, just as he might do for turns (*Doppelschläge*). Afterstrokes (*Nachschläge*) to the trills (or the lack thereof) also should be taken at face value.

Appoggiaturas

We can expect, probably, that the young Schubert learned the rules of long and short *appoggiaturas* (both in main notation and in sign) not from a book, but directly from Salieri. If so,

---

[3] op. cit:106.

he learned from an active, practical composer, not a theorist, and his own use of *appoggiaturas* is likely to reflect this approach. Nevertheless, *appoggiaturas* had been developed partially for cosmetic purposes, so that composers could have their dissonances, but still show theoretically correct harmonic consonance on strong beats. In this respect, Quantz's remark about them is revealing:

> Appoggiaturas ... are not only ornaments but actual necessities ... if a melody is to have a refined appearance, it must always have more concords than discords.[4]

No such cosmetic necessity existed in early nineteenth-century Viennese music, however, except perhaps in the most anachronistic of sacred styles. Nevertheless, it is useful to remember that the origins of the long *appoggiatura*, at least, were rooted deeply in vocal music of the past. Thus, the long *appoggiatura* occurs most frequently in Schubert's vocal music, and we must keep its lyrical nature in mind. If Schubert's long *appoggiaturas* do not always look like vocal ornaments on paper, it is because he did not always slur them to their fundamental notes. But as C.P.E. Bach had pointed out many years before, it made no difference whether an *appoggiatura* was slurred to the main note or not: the slur was implied.[5]

The long appoggiatura

Walther Dürr theorizes that Schubert intended two basic types of long *appoggiature*, "melismatic" and "syllabic."[6] In 1924 Ernest Walker had given these two types functional names in English: "halving" and "eliminating" *appoggiaturas*. Here we shall call them "half-replacing" (melismatic) and "full-replacing" (syllabic) *appoggiaturas*.[7]

EXAMPLE 5.2

Of these two types, however, the syllabic or full-replacing *appoggiatura* appears to have no currency in Schubert's style. Viennese tutors of Schubert's day distinguished between long and short *appoggiaturas* only, with no subcategories. According to common rules still in effect, the long *appoggiatura* took up half of the main note in a duple value, and two-thirds of the main note in a triple value. The stress was placed on the ornament itself. These tutors mentioned neither the full-replacing *appoggiatura*, nor the kind of cadential formulas discussed above (also see fn. 11). In terms of long *appoggiaturas* Schubert calls specifically for the half-replacing variety, indicating the exact length of each one by the value of the preceding small note, almost always one half the length of the main note. Nevertheless, we still find the majority of modern singers dutifully making full-replacing *appoggiatura*s, exemplified here in *Halt!,* No. 3 of *Die schöne Müllerin:*

---

[4] From the *Versuch einer Anweisung die Flöte traversiere zu spielen* (Berlin, 1752): 77, trans. Robert Donington in *NG* 13 (1980): 830.
[5] *Die wahre Art I:* 57.
[6] *Schubert Handbuch*: 104.
[7] See the multi-author article "The Appoggiatura" in *ML* 5: 132-144. In *Ornamenting Mozart* (*passim*) Frederick Neuman calls the "syllabic" or "full-replacing" type an "overlong" *appoggiatura*.

Essential and Voluntary Ornamentation 177

EXAMPLE 5.3

There exists no contemporaneous theoretical backing, however, for the interpretation shown above in the variant directly above the vocal staff (recommended by the *NSA*). A full-replacing *appoggiatura* cancels the immediate, expressive ornamental effect; the audience can hear no difference between it and the rhythms in the measure directly before, for in actual sound they are identical. Clearly, Schubert wanted something different on the word "blinken" (and *passim:* "singen," "traulich," "Bächlein").

To illustrate this point further we might look at a recurring passage in *Lob der Thränen* D711, where in m. 17 ("Scherz") one sings the *appoggiatura*, according to all rules, as a quarter note (i.e. half-replacing *appoggiatura*). Two measures later, if one opts for a full-replacing *appoggiatura,* as do most singers, it produces exactly the same length as the one in m. 17. What, then, would have been the point of writing an *appoggiatura* in the first place?

EXAMPLE 5.4

Most composers of Schubert's day had been trained, of course, in strict old-style counterpoint (Schubert, apparently, not so systematically), and in that context they once may have encountered some form of full-replacing *appoggiaturas*. The question is, "what sort"?[8] C.P.E.

---

[8] Concerning Haydn, see David Montgomery, "Notation and Performance in Schubert".

Bach, Quantz, and Leopold Mozart traditionally had provided the standard pedagogical wisdom concerning *appoggiaturas*, and they recognized the full-replacing variety only for two particular situations (culled here from Quantz):

> 1) When in 6/4 or 6/8 time two notes are tied, and the first is dotted ... hold the appoggiatura the complete length of the first note including its dot [cf. Bach's Fig. VI/4, below].
>
> 2) When an appoggiatura is attached to a note followed by a rest, give the whole length of the main note to the appoggiatura, and give the length of the rest to the main note. [cf. Bach's Fig. VII, below][9]

Neither of these situations has much to do with Schubert's lied style, created more than sixty years later. C.P.E. Bach was even less specific than Quantz; he merely offered several concrete examples of what he called "unusual" *appoggiaturas*:

EXAMPLE 5.5

We might search the eighteenth-century theoretical works devoted specifically to singing, but there we also will not find the full-replacing *appoggiatura* described in the way that some modern singers apply it to Schubert lieder.

Johann Adam Hiller's singing treatise of 1780 demonstrates two kinds of full-replacing ornaments (one stepwise, one at the perfect fourth), used in cadences in operatic styles where two notes on the same pitch occur on a downbeat.[10] Lacking the prescriptive small notes (or other form of *appoggiatura* signs), however, both of Hiller's examples (see example 5.6 on facing page) fall into the category of voluntary ornaments, which do not apply to Schubert.

---

[9] Trans. Donington in *NG* 13:830.
[10] *Anweisung zum musikalisch-zierlichen Gesange,* cited by Will Crutchfield in *Performance Practice:* 298.

Essential and Voluntary Ornamentation 179

EXAMPLE 5.6

Clive Brown reminds us of Haydn's *Applausus* letter of 1768, however, wherein the composer does indeed provide the small note in an example. Haydn requests that the following figure:

EXAMPLE 5.7a/c

be sung as

and not as

Indeed, this example is proof of the continuing use (at least until the late 1760s) of a full-replacing stepwise *appoggiatura* indicated in sign. The mere fact that Haydn was compelled to make this request, however, shows us that the full-replacing realization was one of at least two apparently standard methods of interpreting the long *appoggiatura* sign before two equal notes, the other being the more modern half-replacing ornament which he did not want for that particular text.[11]

If the full-replacing *appoggiatura* still had currency after Haydn's time, it appears nevertheless to have been on its way out, except, perhaps, in some opera recitatives and sacred works in older styles. Frederick Neumann demonstrates that W.A. Mozart largely avoided it, even though his own father had advocated it.[12] One has difficulty, then, with the

---

[11] See David Montgomery, "Notation and Performance in Schubert: A Discussion and Review of the Relevant Sections from Clive Brown's Classical and Romantic Performing Practice 1750–1900" in *Die Brille* 27.
[12] See Frederick Neumann on the 'overlong' *appoggiatura* in *Ornamentation and Improvisation:* 18–22.

notion that Franz Schubert was using it a full thirty years later. Brown, however, not only believes that he used it in abundance, but theorizes that Schubert even developed a special notation for it:

> Where two syllables of this kind occur in Schubert's vocal music, he generally indicated the desired appoggiatura with a small note before the first of the pair, but wrote the small note with only half the intended value of the appoggiatura.[13]

Perhaps Brown has been influenced by the *NSA,* where the editorship has supplied realizations above each of Schubert's signed *appoggiaturas*, showing them almost uniformly (but with no theoretical backing) as full-replacing. It is practically as if the *NSA* had planned deliberately to present Franz Schubert as an old-fashioned composer. We can find no reason and no defense for such unilateral misrepresentation.

Brown tries his best to fit Schubert into this conservative picture as well, this time through a reverse argument:

> [continuing from above]: If Schubert required the figuration that his appoggiaturas seem to indicate [the value as given], he wrote it in full.

EXAMPLE 5.8
Brown's ex. 13.12

This statement is simply misleading. To begin with, Brown's example above does not show two equal notes. It shows (in the second full measure) a quarter value (two eighths) followed by a half note. In any case, for every written-out half-replacing *appoggiatura* Brown might find, we in turn can find an example of a written-out full-replacing *appoggiatura*, such as the following one, for example, in *Der Tod und das Mädchen* D531. Readers will have no trouble finding many others:

EXAMPLE 5.9

[13] *Performing Practice:* 465-466.

Essential and Voluntary Ornamentation *181*

Brown seeks to bolster his theory with an imaginary notation system, which he asks us to accept without a single article of proof:

> [continuing from above]: Where *appoggiaturas* occur before single syllables (or in instrumental parts before single notes), however, [Schubert] generally gave them the value with which he intended them to be performed, but since he did not use minim [half-note] small notes this is not the case before notes longer than a minim.

In Brown's imagination, then, Schubert practiced a rather complicated and fanciful notational system for his long *appoggiaturas*: for some of them (full-replacing) he gave the small note at half-value, for others (before single notes) at full value, except before whole notes or larger, which he gave again at half-value! We can only point out that no composer with a desire to have his works performed (never mind performed to his satisfaction) would invent such a labored, personal and convoluted method of communicating with performers.

      Brown proves to be just as unflattering to Schubert as are Dürr, Reed, Keller, Badura-Skoda *et al.* Otherwise, why would Brown automatically attribute the absence of half-note *appoggiatura* signs to a supposedly inconsistent notational system, rather than to Schubert's advanced melodic style and compositional preferences?[14] Spohr tells us that recent composers had begun to incorporate much of what previously had been ornamentation into the melodic fabric of their music itself, and we can have no reason to doubt him:

> In former times, it was usual for the composer to write the melody in a very simple manner, leaving the embellishment of it to the player or singer. Hence, a multitude of Graces were invented, and which one player learned from another. But as succeeding performers constantly endeavoured to surpass their predecessors in embellishing, by the addition of new invention; there at length arose such freedom and consequent tastelessness in this particular, that composers found it advisable to prescribe the required embellishments themselves. At first, this was done in small notes, the division being left to the player; but afterwards, in notes of the usual size, with a strict divison of the bar.[15]

Brown's best argument for interpreting Schubert's *appoggiaturas* before two equal notes as full-replacing appears to be that the accompanying instrumental lines in certain passages from the operas coincide with the vocal lines only if the latter are supplied with full-replacing *appoggiaturas*, thereby avoiding moments of heterophony. Brown cites *Fierabras,* which to our knowledge has not yet been brought out in a modern scholarly edition. Nevertheless, we will accept the passage as he gives it:

EXAMPLE 5.10
Brown's ex. 13.11:

---

[14] In any case, such long values would be the mark of a fairly ancient and outdated notational system, wherein many of the main notes would have to be wholes and double wholes.
[15] *Violin School* (English edition): § XIII:142: "On Graces or Embellishments".

182 *Schubert's Music in Performance*

Here Brown joins those theorists who find a necessity for strictly tidy and homogeneous agreement among musical voices. The Dolmetsch / Donington school had advanced a similarly unfounded theory that would change and unify the written values of diverse pickup notes in French overtures, so that they all would be sounded at the same time. Another group still argues, equally without proper backing, for the assimilation of the short notes of dotted figures to match accompanying triplet figures (see Ch. III). Such theories would seek out the lowest common denominator of rhythmic expression, simplifying, reducing, and limiting (in essence, "dumbing down") all complexities to single levels of interest. Each of these theories contains a cleansing element that is strongly antithetical to the potential splendor and intricacy of Western composition, just as in the context of larger culture it has proven disastrous to the human race.

Schubert appears to have been comfortable with simultaneous layers of rhythmic and melodic complexity, as the following passage from the D-minor Quartet D810 shows:

EXAMPLE 5.11
Andante con moto, mm. 136–147

Essential and Voluntary Ornamentation

He was also given to a delightful heterophony where voices and ornaments were concerned:

EXAMPLE 5.12
Alfonso und Estrella, No. 25, mm. 43-46

Even the editorship of the *NSA* declines to honor the cleansing argument at times:

EXAMPLE 5.13
Alfonso und Estrella, No. 27, mm. 46–47:

If Spohr was right in remarking that modern composers were incorporating what formerly were ornaments directly into the melodic fabric of their music, then the remaining ornaments in sign must be looked upon as something special, something expressive, something above the melodic norm. What could fit this description better than a beautiful moment of non-conformity, of uniqueness, of heterophony?

The signed, long *appoggiatura* in its half-replacing function, then, represents a wisp of freedom from the normal melodic / rhythmic context of Schubert's music. This idea suggests that the ornament be sung with an added inflection, in a manner that would reflect its status as an ornament. Perhaps we are talking about an infinitesimal moment of *tenuto*, extra volume, less volume, etc. Such things cannot be set out in rules, for they depend upon the meaning and emotional power of the word that is graced by a given ornament.

Short appoggiatura

The short *appoggiatura* takes two theoretical forms: accented and unaccented, i.e. on-beat and pre-beat. The latter are grace notes. According to period rules (which we take here from Swoboda),[16] an *appoggiatura* is taken as short and on the beat if:

---

[16] *Allgemeine Theorie:* 52–54.

1) it occurs before a series of repeated notes;

EXAMPLE 5.14a

2) it occurs before a series of equal-valued notes;

EXAMPLE 5.14b

3) it occurs before staccato notes;

EXAMPLE 5.14c

4) it occurs before disjunct intervals;

EXAMPLE 5.14d

5) it occurs at the beginning of a movement, phrase or other independent musical thought;

EXAMPLE 5.14e

6) it occurs before syncopated notes;

EXAMPLE 5.14f

7) it occurs before short dotted notes;

EXAMPLE 5.14g

Essential and Voluntary Ornamentation 185

8) it occurs before triplets, sextuplets, etc.;

EXAMPLE 5.14h

9) it must spring to the main note.

EXAMPLE 5.14i

In reality, however, there was and is a conflict between taking an *appoggiatura* short and on the beat at the same time. Only in two cases was there no conflict: 1) the intentional Scotch snap or Lombard rhythm where the *appoggiatura* is marked with an accent (melodically alone, or in combination as *acciaccaturas*, both rare in Schubert) and 2) the first in a series of fast, equal valued notes, where the written (first) main note typically is twice the value of the others (found mostly in the early works closer to the purely classical style), as in the first movement of the Fourth Symphony:

EXAMPLE 5.15
C-minor Symphony D417/1, mm. 39–40

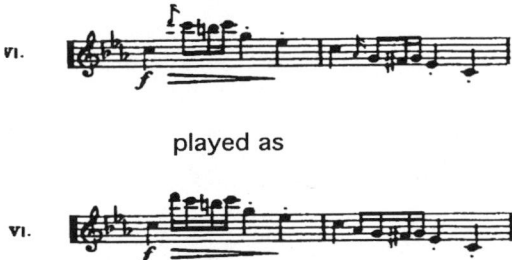

Indeed for the late-eighteenth and early-nineteenth centuries, the most interesting historical question about essential ornamentation concerns the emergence of most short *appoggiaturas* as non-accented, pre-beat phenomena. Each scholar appears to have his or her take on this matter, and understandably so. In our estimation, one of the main secondary sources on this subject is Frederick Neumann's *Ornamentation and Improvisation in Mozart,* which takes a progressive stand on the issue.[17] Neumann's argumentation and evidence points strongly to the probability that even by Mozart's day many single-note graces started before the beat, and without a stress.

---

[17] To gain an overview of the entire issue, one should read reviews, replies, and counterreplies to this work by a number of authers in various journals of the late 1980s. Neumann was often willing to revert to his own "musical" arguments, a stance which we discourage, but he never wavered from the central proposition that modern theories of period ornamentation must explain practical realities as well as pedagogical rules and other mere "paper" evidence.

When one examines the Viennese pedagogical sources of Schubert's period, one expects, then, to find this new principle firmly established for all music and perhaps taken over even in new contexts for special cases. Surprisingly, even allowing for the conservatism of pedagogical treatises, this is not the case. Essentially, in reexamining the sources, we learn little that we did not know already from Preindl (1811), Junghanns (1818), Starke (1819), Hummel (1826), Swoboda (1826), Spohr (1832), or Czerny (1839): all of them theoreticians of Schubert's period and/or slightly thereafter. As we stated above, the measuring stick here is placement and accentuation, and all of our Viennese theoreticians show the old-style on-beat placement and accentuation, even for grace notes with slanted strokes through the flags or stems. (In any case, to our knowledge, Schubert does not use strokes through the stems of his small notes. The ones shown in Example 5.16 have been added by the editor.)

Considering the gulf between this theoretical consensus, which reaches from the beginning of Schubert's career to well after, and the reality of modern Schubert performance, we all must admit that a conceptual problem exists and that it appears to be of significant proportions. Let us take the sources literally for a moment. Are we truly to believe that the small notes of the following passages are to be played on the beat?

EXAMPLE 5.16
D810, finale opening

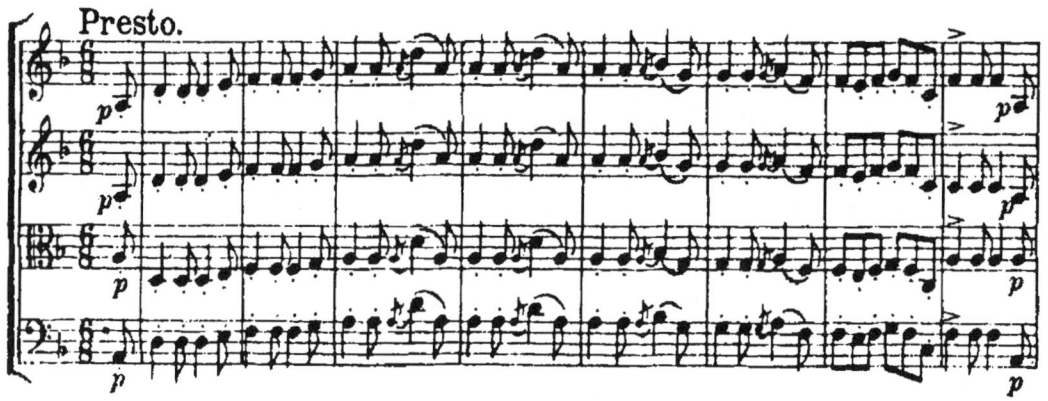

Neumann begins his discussion of grace notes by demonstrating unquestionably that pre-beat *appoggiaturas* were not only known but recommended in certain cases. He cites Quantz (1752), for example, who states that *Vorschläge* preceding notated *appoggiaturas* should be played as pre-beat graces:[18]

EXAMPLE 5.17

---

[18] Neumann, *Ornamentation:* 42.

Essential and Voluntary Ornamentation 187

How is it, then, that some three quarters of a century later, theorists still failed to honor the pre-beat placement of graces, even Czerny, whose section on ornaments applies at least partially to the emerging mid-century performance styles and whose graces show the newer-style strikes through their stems? We cannot simply chalk up this discrepancy to Viennese conservatism in general, or even to the specific conservatism of Schubert's Vienna. It is more likely that some sort of ideal still existed to the effect that short *appoggiaturas* should retain their original spirit and gesture, even in the face of changing musical practices. Spohr, for example, tries to have it both ways:

> As the appoggiatura always falls on an accented part of the bar, it is given with greater emphasis than the note before which it stands, with which however it is always united in one bowing; because, as an appoggiatura, it belongs to this note, and in it finds its resolution. The short appoggiatura (which as such, should always be marked with a cross stroke, in order to distinguish it from the long one) deprives the note before which it stands, of scarcely any of its value. With this note, it is quickly and lightly connected in one bowing.[19]

"Lightly" is the key to realizing this ornament, as Spohr says, but one cannot play it lightly and expect it to be accented at the same time. Neumann's argument is that as the perception of accent is shifted to the main note, the perception of the barline shifts as well, effectively producing a pre-beat grace.[20] One might try playing the graces in D810 with Spohr's (and Neumann's) compromise in mind. The execution may be difficult at first if the mind is too fixed upon the barline itself, but it can be done, and eventually with a noticeable freedom of spirit. This middle-ground solution may be theoretically untidy, but it works. We should say, it works in proportion to the denomination of the notes and, of course, the tempo. The less time available, the shorter and thus more sharply barline- or beat-oriented the execution will become: the more time available, the more *rubato*-like and melodically flexible. These last two characteristics are important expressive characteristics of Schubert slow movements, of course, and so we cannot be entirely unsatisfied with such a solution.

Multiple-note interbeat and afterbeat ornaments are not uncommon in Schubert, and as a rule they are played as graces, i.e. unaccented and before the beat.

EXAMPLE 5.18

Multiple-note pre-beat ornaments (mostly two-note slides, or *Schleifer*), however, were still treated theoretically as if played on the beat, as in these examples from Swoboda and Spohr (confirmed by Junghanns and others):

---

[19] *Violin School:* 159.
[20] Neumann, *Ornamentation:* 8.

EXAMPLE 5.19a/b

a.

b.
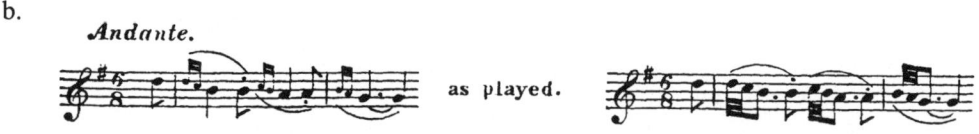

Nevertheless, as Neumann points out about short single note *appoggiaturas*, these ornaments also tend to displace the beat so as to function virtually as pre-beat graces. Tempo, of course, plays a major role. For example, if cellists were able to find the proper *Andante con moto* in 2/4 for the middle movement of the E♭ Trio (a feat we have not yet heard, cf. discussion in Ch. VI), they might find themselves placing the ornament somewhat earlier, and with less of the traditionally lugubrious accentuation:

EXAMPLE 5.20

often mistakenly played as:

In any case, by the end of Schubert's career (when this work was written) he certainly meant such figures as highly flexible, predominantly pre-beat graces.

Shakes, turns and arpeggios present no particular interpretational problems. Shakes in Schubert are simply the opposite of mordents (in fact, Czerny's translator calls them "mordents" in the French edition): one-note flips to the upper tone and back. Turns follow the known conventions of mid-century practice; if a chromatic alteration was necessary (and not obvious) Schubert was capable of indicating it as such. Schubert's arpeggios are started from the bottom unless notated otherwise (rare), and they vary in speed according to context.

Voluntary ornamentation and improvisation

The following pages of this book should never have needed to be written, for, to state the situation bluntly, improvisation and voluntary ornamentation are not appropriate for Schubert's music. In general, by Schubert's time 1) serious composers had long since begun to indicate their desired ornamentation by sign; 2) notated it more fully; or 3) incorporated it in other ways into the fabric of their music (cf. the adapted *tremolo* in the first variation in the string quartet D810, above). We can confirm these statements not only through writings of the time, but by careful stylistic analysis as well.

Recently, however, some adherents of the performance practice movement have begun a trend to ornament and embellish Schubert's instrumental music in the manner of the eighteenth century and through spontaneous impulse (as it has been described to us) to add additional musical material to the lieder and piano sonatas, not to mention altering Schubert's scores harmonically and melodically. In some cases the "improvisations" (as they have been described to us) have been captured permanently on CD, causing them to be repeated literally with each playing. Thus, to the unwary modern listener, they effectively become part of the music itself, i.e. Schubert recomposed. Apart from misrepresenting Schubert's wonderfully worked-out musical ideas, not to mention using his scores as a kind of platform from which to promote the compositional talents of the performer, the larger historical problem with such invention is that it runs counter to the new direction taken by serious music—and Schubert's music specifically—during the early nineteenth century. Since we take such strong exception to these practices in the performance of Schubert's music, we feel compelled to offer the reader an overview of the subject in the hope of clarifying and correcting some of the operative misconceptions which have been popularized of late.

Improvisation

The spirit of extemporaneous creation that formed such a central part of Baroque and galant musical thinking, survived, although somewhat reduced, among virtuosos in the first quarter of the nineteenth century. Perhaps the most sensational event along these lines was given by the eleven-year old Franz Liszt (billed as nine), demonstrating his powers to an enthusiastic Viennese audience in his first public concert in 1822. As often happened at such concerts, he saved his big improvisation for last, adding to the impression by asking the audience itself to suggest the motives and themes. Keyboard players of the past had improvised for long stretches, and not just in the manner of "preluding," or pleasant arpeggiation and related figuration, but in far more elaborate and impressive ways. They were not alone in this tradition: virtuoso flutists, clarinetists, violinists, cellists and others once improvised brilliant variations on set harmonic patterns as part of their stock in trade.

Until recently, scholars assumed that in the course of the early nineteenth century a sharp decline occurred in the formal teaching of improvisation, evidenced by a corresponding lack of published treatises. Alice Mitchell begins her English translation of Czerny's [Systematische] *Anweisung zum Fantasieren,* op. 200 (ca. 1827) by noting a "paucity" of similar treatises and stating that "the only attempt at formal instruction other than Czerny's op. 200 was a manual on preludizing by A.E.M Grétry that appeared around 1800."[21] This last statement is not exactly accurate, as the following summary of Viennese sources alone indicates, and yet Mitchell's sense of a decline may not be far-fetched.[22] Let us modify it, however, because what may truly have been the case is that the formal teaching of improvisation concentrated more and more upon organ playing alone (where figured bass also enjoyed an after-life), while training in improvisation for pianists confined itself gradually (if actual practice was any indication of training) to theme-and-variation and certain kinds of free fantasy *à la* Parisian salons of the 1820s, '30s and '40s.

In Vienna we can point to a continuing pedagogical tradition concerning improvisation leading up to Czerny's work and passing beyond into the early 1830s. Ambros Rieder's *Kurze Anleitung zum Präludiren auf dem Orgel oder Pianoforte* (1826, dedicated to Ferdinand Schubert) demonstrates the expectation that both organists and pianists should be able to master at least the simpler level of spontaneous creation. J.B.Wanhal's *36 Cadenzen, oder Übungen für die Orgel, oder Forte-Piano wo allmögliche Intervallen vorkommen* (1806?) gives us examples of typical modulation formulae that were part of such improvisations. Likewise, Johann André's *Instruktive Variationen über 5 Töne* (1807) was aimed at pianistic improvisation in the spirit of eighteenth-century models by C.P.E. Bach, Georg Benda and others. Organ treatises, *per se,* continued to instruct the student in improvisation, as stated specifically in the title of Joseph Drechsler's *Fortschreitende Generalbassübungen, nebst Anleitung und Beispielen zum Präludiren auf der Orgel* (1816). Drechsler (whose general bass treatise Schubert may have studied) later published the *Theoretisch-praktische Leitfaden ... phantasiren oder präludiren zu können* (1834) as well. Emanuel Förster's *Praktische Beyspiele* (1818/1830) also showed a series of sample prelude formulae for organ improvisation, as well as some instructive fugues. Rieder's *Anleitung zum Fugiren* (before 1825), an organ treatise, also would indicate an ongoing training in the improvisation of more complicated forms, although it is sometimes difficult to tell whether actual improvisation was the message as opposed to a mere understanding of the form in the abstract.

Czerny's *Anweisung zum Fantasieren* (Pt. II as *Die Kunst des Präludirens,* op. 300) is a novelty among its fellow treatises. It purports to take the piano student through the most advanced and well-worked out forms for improvisation. If we examine its table of contents, we find preludes of simple types (arpeggiated filler for chords in longer note values) and more elaborate varieties, cadenzas and fermatas, improvisation on single themes, improvisation on several themes at once, potpourris, variations, strict fugal improvisations and capriccios. Despite Czerny's contention that Beethoven improvised the finale to op. 10/3, he does not elucidate sonata form in the treatise, nor do we read anywhere about the sonata as an object of improvisatory display. Although Czerny's examples are often melodically as elaborate as the highly figurative passages in Hummel's concertos, perhaps none of these types match his ex. 50, "Fughetta," in difficulty of conception:[23]

---

[21] *A Systematic Introduction to Improvisation on the Pianoforte* (New York: Longman, 1983): ix.

[22] Mitchell does not supply us with titles of earlier treatises for comparison, but our own overview of the sources indicates at least that pedagogical interest in this subject dropped off sharply after Czerny's time. See Montgomery, *Musical Tutors,* for titles and dates.

[23] Czerny claims to have heard Beethoven improvise in complete sonata forms, saying that in a first move-

Essential and Voluntary Ornamentation   191

EXAMPLE 5.21
Czerny's ex. 50

Despite reports about the young Liszt (we do not know what form his improvisations actually took), it is unlikely that anyone might have been capable of creating such a polished work on the spot. Czerny himself was not known as an improviser (an ironic fact, considering that he was the author of the most comprehensive work on the subject), and we cannot

---

ment form or finale-rondo form Beethoven would close off the first section normally, having introduced a "middle" (2nd) theme in a related key, but that he would render the second half freely—always developing the motive according to his fullest inspiration. Specifically, Czerny claims that Beethoven improvised the finale of Op. 31/2 (which Czerny designates as Op. 29/2), inspired by a galloping rider (*Pianoforte-Schule* IV:56). But a period method for learning to improvise sonata movements has not turned up, and we must assume that such "advanced" information might have been imparted by word of mouth or grasped, perhaps, by sheer gift.

imagine that his examples arose extemporaneously. It is more reasonable to look upon his entire treatise as a highly idealized summary of a bygone tradition. In any case, his treatise was not only singular in its exhaustiveness, but the last of its kind.

The great era of improvisation in strict forms as described by Czerny clearly had been dealt a major blow when Beethoven ceased to play in public, and probably was well-outdated by the middle of Hummel's career. What remained of it was practiced by pianists and operatic singers who performed in the popular, "brilliant" style, wherein figuration was designed to bring maximum glory to the performer in the eyes and ears of an increasingly middle-class (and decreasingly sophisticated) public. Within this style and its corresponding repertoire of potpourris, operatic themes for decorative variation, and unabashed bravura extravaganza, even those pianists who were not capable of improvisation in stricter forms were still expected to provide free cadenzas at the end, say, of first-movement concerto forms, and lead-ins at minor *fermatas*.[24] Similarly, in Italian operas (always the vogue in Vienna), singers still provided *coloraturas* (*passaggi*), lead-ins at *fermatas* and cadenzas at larger stuctural caesurae. Whether these performers conceived their elaborations in mid-air or worked them out on the ground, or something in between, cannot be established with certainty, but a number of period sources exist to document the results.

Until this point, however, we have not discussed a tradition relevant to Franz Schubert. He was no virtuoso of the brilliant style, he wrote no concertos, and his operas, even in their grander moments, were conceived in the German style, not as showcases for virtuosity. His lieder (with some exceptions) were principally text-related expressions developed from a simple Austrian, German, and Czech tradition. Schubert himself was not known to the public as an improviser (his harmony and counterpoint training seems to have been directed toward composition, *per se*), with the possible exception of his dance music.

Deutsch speculates that the first of the Schubertiades must have taken place on 26 January 1821, and he goes on to describe such events as "gesellige Abende in befreundeten Familien, an denen ausschließlich Schubertsche Musik gemacht wurde; wenn die Damen dabei waren, erlangen auch Tänze, die Schubert, der nicht tanzte, selbst am Klavier spielte und oft improvisierte." (fn, p. 115). Deutsch offers no documentation of Schubert's improvisation, but his supposition is not illogical. When we read that on 17 September 1826 Schubert played for dancing at the wedding of Leopold Kupelwieser and Johanna Lutz, and that "Er ließ niemand anderen an das Klavier heran," we can assume that he improvised at least part of the time.[25] We cannot imagine that he brought with him an entire evening's worth of written-out occasional music, although on another evening with Joseph Gahy he seems to have provided plenty on paper.[26] In any case, his characteristic little binary dance-forms would have been easily tossed off on the spot. This does not mean, however, that his notated dances require further improvisation, for in notated form they are complete.

---

[24] With exceptons, such as when performing Beethoven's Fifth Piano Concerto, where even the cadenzas are written into the music.

[25] *Dokumente:*376.

[26] See Fritz v. Hartmann's description of an evening at Spaun's, 10 February 1827. "... Die Musik war herrlich, da sie nur aus Walzern von Schubert bestand, zum Teil vom Komponisten selbst, zum Teil von Gahy gespielt ..." *Dokumente:* 408.

Apart from these dances, however, most of Schubert's music arose through the meticulous and complex process of composition, by which we mean not only the inspired heat of first drafting but also the reflective stages of correction and recomposition (alternate versions). This maxim applies even to the "external" structural sections in his songs. Here performers have been misled to add introductions (often said to have been improvised or to represent typical period introductory improvisations) following the regrettable example of the publisher Diabelli (see Ch. II). Significantly enough, Diabelli seems not to have dared such liberties while the composer lived. Finally, we would repeat our supposition that written additions are no proof of improvisation. In fact, they point in the opposite direction.

Improvisation and ornamentation in the opera

The art of extended improvisation, as discussed above in the context of piano playing, was not limited to instrumental music, but is said to have pervaded musical performance in the theater as well. We might have begun this chapter with improvisation in the context of vocal music, considering what is generally taken to be its historical precedent. "Passage embellishment" (*passaggio, coloratura*), a specifically operatic device, is the substitution of decorated lines for a composer's written melody, ranging in length from the value of a single note to entire sections of music. August Swoboda not only defines the word "*coloratura*," but specifies the genre in which it is used: "we understand this [term to indicate] passaggi, progressions, roulades, etc., which one brings particularly to bravura arias on single syllables of the text." To the present time, Schubert scholars have devoted surprisingly little attention to singing styles at the various theaters in Vienna in the early nineteenth century. It is likely that the Italian-trained singers who dominated those stages applied embellishment freely to Italian operas, at least, but to date we have discovered next to nothing about how they treated Schubert's operas and other German-language stage works.[27]

In general, it is difficult to believe that singers once were capable of smooth, spontaneous passage embellishments as elaborate as those notated by the pedagogues Pellegrini-Celoni, Garcia and others.[28] The underlying command of harmony and counterpoint essen-

---

[27] One cannot imagine that the vocal lines in *Fidelio* were ornamented by the singers, at least not in Beethoven's presence. Even in concertos, the pianist's equivalent of an opera singer's aria, Beethoven seemed not to tolerate embellishment and additions to the text. Ries reports: "I recall only two instances in which Beethoven told me to add a few notes to his composition: once in the theme of the rondo of the Sonate Pathétique [Op. 13], and again in the theme of the rondo of his first Concerto in C major, where he gave me some passages in double notes to make it more brilliant" (Franz Wegeler and Ferdinand Ries, *Biographisches Notizen über Ludwig van Beethoven,* p. 106/7, trans. Thayer: 367). "In playing he would give a passage now in the right hand, now in the left, a lovely and absolutely inimitable expression; but he very seldom added notes or ornaments..." (Wegler / Ries:100, trans. Thayer:367). Carl Czerny recalled Beethoven's heated reaction to his (Czerny's) experiments with ornamentation in the Piano / Wind Quintet, op. 16: "Beethoven quite rightly took me severely to task in the presence of Schuppanzigh, Linke and the other players. The next day I received the following draft ... 'Dear Czerny! Today I cannot see you, but tomorrow I will call on you myself to have a talk with you.– I burst forth so yesterday that I was sorry after it had happened; but you must pardon that [kind of behavior] in a composer who would have preferred to hear his work exactly as he wrote it, no matter how beautifully you played in general." *WamZ,* 20 September 1845, trans. Thayer: 640/1.

[28] Anna Pellegrini-Celoni, *Grammatica, o siano regole de ben cantare* (Rome, before 1800) and Manuel Garcia, *Traité complet de l'art du chant,* Pt. I (Paris, 1840).

tial to such prowess would not have been impossible to acquire, of course, but certainly it would represent an impressive musical education. Whatever the opera singers of former times were capable of, however, the entire art of spontaneous, extended embellishment in that same music no longer exists in theaters today. In any case, the limited scope of the present book has prohibited us from pursuing this line of research, and so we move on to a study of singing in the private sector: to Schubert's art songs, and to the more modest question of local ornamentation within that genre.

Ornamentation in the lieder

On the basis of general style, we believe that much solo song of the eighteenth century and before, with its relatively simple outlines, not only permitted spontaneous ornamentation, but required it. The composer's sense of invention in the basic construction was important, but a song's real success lay with the imagination of the singer. Styles changed, however, and the solo song, *das Lied,* gradually outgrew the trappings of mere entertainment, and began to take on the mantle of art. This meant that the major control of and responsibility for a song's emotional content and melodic shapes (including ornaments) shifted to the composer, and were then reflected by the performer. Harmony, and accompanimental texture took on more sophistication as well, so that all aspects of the song contributed to its impact. Schubert, at least, approached song in this manner, and from the very beginning of his compositional career regarded the *Lied* as a vehicle worthy of his finest powers.

The "Vogl" controversy, once again

Our present-day concerns with Johann Michael Vogl's interpretations of Schubert lieder address two separate issues: 1) reports concerning his histrionics ["dramatic" vs. "lyrical" delivery] and 2) reports that he embellished Schubert's songs. We have dealt with the first topic in Ch. I, where we hope to have made the point that an aging theater performer was bound to have brought something of his dramatic art into the drawing room, especially if it helped him to cover for a failing instrument. This does not mean that such delivery matched Schubert's ideals (or sometimes Vogl's, either). The tradeoff, a few vocal tricks in exchange for Vogl's genuine and important support, was clearly advantageous for Schubert, but this doesn't mean that he approved of it. Finally, we must not confuse "dramatic" (in the sense that the lieder singer takes on an actual role, or roles) with "declamatory", which describes a respectable and well-documented art of powerful and highly enunciatory presentation often required in Schubert's songs.

The second issue concerns reports that Vogl and others (possibly Carl Pinterics, for example) embellished Schubert's songs in performance and in writing as well. Thus, it breaks down into two opposing topics: spontaneous ornamentation vs. documentable text changes. As far as spontaneous ornamentation in performance goes, no one really knows how, to what extent, or even whether at all, Vogl embellished the songs in performance. When we separate out the chaff concerning Vogl's histrionics from any factual reports, we wind up with very little in hand. What we think we know about period embellishment or ornamentation of Schubert's songs as performed with him at the piano, or in his presence, is based upon reportage undertaken long after his death by his friends (Bauernfeld, Sonnleithner,

Spaun, for example). If we possessed even a single reliable and informative period description of ornamentation (spontaneous or not) in a performance of a Schubert song (which we do not), we might be a small step forward.

In lieu of direct accounts concerning ornamentation, the musicological community to date has relied upon a far more circumstantial kind of evidence in the form of embellishments, additions, and other changes to Schubert songs in some copies. In some circles, such alterations have been accepted as representative of a common practice for Schubert's time. Volume 80 of the Schubert *Abschriften* lists five songs that were designated as "verändert von M. Vogl:" *Antigone und Oedip* D542, *Der Fischer* D225, *An Emma* D113, *Jägers Abendlied* (II) D368 and *Gebeth während der Schlacht* D171.[29] John Reed lists two others: *Wer sich der Einsamkeit Ergibt* D478 and *Blondel zu Marien* D626.[30] Kreissle von Hellborn cites changes to *Der Einsame* D800 in the 1827 Diabelli edition, asserting that the latter were the worst of Vogl's additions (probably referring to the added high notes).[31] Walther Dürr also views such sources as the so-called "Tremier" Liederheft [32] as evidence of Vogl's approach to embellishment, but offers no proof that Vogl actually sang the songs with these ornaments. Lastly, Dürr has demonstrated his belief in Vogl's authority by reissuing Diabelli's publication of *Die schöne Müllerin* (Diabelli's so-called "second" edition, made after Schubert's death). This edition contains variants and embellishments said to have been based on a copy once in Vogl's possession, but now lost.[33] (The original edition, clearly approved by Schubert, had been brought out by Sauer & Leidesdorf in 1824.)

The Abschriften *(copies)*

One could hardly believe that Schubert approved of the amateurish, copious and obtrusive ornamentation that characterize the changes of the *Abschriften* in the Witteczek-Spaun collection. Schubert himself made many copies and transpositions of his songs, and in none of them do we find such careless deviation. The Witteczek-Spaun copies show small alterations, additions, and omissions throughout, mostly in the matter of dynamics, but in other areas as well. Of course, for this reason alone they cannot be regarded as serious sources for study. All such alterations—changed pitches, embellishments, added or forgotten dynamics, etc.— detract from the credibility of a source. Certainly, we cannot single out one kind of alteration (embellishment) and claim it to be useful to us, while ignoring the rest.

---

[29] Walter Dürr, ed. *Franz Schuberts Werke in Abschriften: Liederalben und Sammlungen, NSA* VIII: 8, Quellen II (Kassell: Bärenreiter, 1975).
[30] Reed: 68/434.
[31] H. Kreissle von Hellborn, *Franz Schubert* (Vienna: 1865): 121 fn. Schubert's part in preparing the copy for this edition needs some research. Even Diabelli, with his nose for opportunity, probably would not have dared publish an unauthorized version while Schubert lived.
[32] The private lieder book of Franziska Tremier, née Pratobevera. According to the *Dokumente* (op. cit:519) it was a wedding present from Josef Tremier to his bride. It contains a number of copies of songs, many by Schubert, and some Schubert autograph materials, including a transposition of Beethoven's *Abendlied unterm gestirnten Himmel,* WoO 150.
[33] *Die schöne Müllerin: Reprint der Diabelli-Ausgabe von 1830* (Kassel: Bärenreiter, 1996).

Perhaps it would be enlightening to examine one of these copies. In the *NSA* Dürr reproduces a passage from *Im Walde* D834 (*Abschriften* Vol. 31):

EXAMPLE 5.22a/b
a. *Abschrift*

b. *GA* print

To begin with, the overly-careful hand in the *Abschrift* is that of an amateur, unused to writing or copying music. He or she does not follow simple notational conventions such as proper stem direction and placement. In the second measure from the top the fourth beat of the piano's right-hand part is clumsy, for the copyist does not appear to know that the continuance sign [./.] would stand for the entire beat, including the eighth rest. The confusing notation and placement of dynamics and accentuation also belong to the amateur copyist's unpracticed manner. These details are unimportant, however, in relationship to the lack of musical knowledge revealed by the ornamentation. In the fourth measure, the singer's last eighth note is a B♭ filling in between the preceding D and the G of the downbeat. Here the copyist fails to note, however, that the underlying harmony has not yet changed from dominant to tonic! Only one choice would have been possible, namely the lower F♯. Our "embellisher" however, not only has missed this possibility, but chosen exactly the worst variant, namely a B♭ in direct conflict with the A of the piano's right hand! Vogl, a practiced professional, could not have taken part in this fiasco. Actually, it is no ornamention proper, but merely a poor example of "messing about" with Schubert's melody. If it were attributed to "M. Vogl," it can have been transcribed only in terms of what the poor copyist thought was the way in which the master (Vogl) would have rewritten Schubert's music.

DIABELLI's *MÜLLERLIEDER* EDITION

As we gather from reading the preface to Walther Dürr's 1996 reprint of *Die schöne Müllerin,* his belief that the embellishments came from Vogl rests entirely on a quotation from the singer Josef Gänsbacher, who in 1864 identified the alterations in this edition as "all those variants with which Vogl had so often sung [these songs]." Apparently, Gänsbacher also called them (and rightly) "cuckoo's eggs" that "Vogl had laid in the Müller songs."[34] Dürr does not explain why it took Gänsbacher 34 years to object to the edition, or with what authority Gänsbacher pronounced these embellishments to be Vogl's. Indeed Dürr might be hard pressed to do so, for Josef Gänsbacher (b. 6 October 1829 – d. 5 June 1911) was about one year old [!] when the edition appeared; he was a small child when Vogl stopped singing in public, and a little over 10 when Vogl died.

Furthermore, Dürr does not explain how or why Diabelli (himself a composer) would have needed Vogl's input in this matter. To begin with, editorial collaboration with a famous performer was still a most unlikely scenario for Viennese publishing practices of that day.[35] Secondly, if Diabelli were truly interested in authenticity, he would have done better to have approached Karl von Schönstein, to whom the cycle was dedicated. Schönstein appears to have sung and promoted the cycle many years after Schubert's death. We must not forget that Schubert had known Vogl since 1817, whereas the cycle was written in 1823 and appeared in 1824. Schubert well could have incorporated any "vöglische" embellishments at that time, had he so desired (which clearly he did not). Furthermore, considering Diabelli's undisguised greed for sales, such a collaboration would have been pointless unless Vogl's name appeared somewhere on the edition. This, too, is not the case. Lastly, only

---

[34] In "Recensionen und Mittheilungen über Theater und Musik," cited in the preface to Diabelli's edition, op. cit: viii, trans. J. Bradford Robinson. Cuckoos do not build nests, but lay their eggs in other birds' nests. Thus, when the eggs hatch, other birds are stuck in the role of surrogate parents, raising little cuckoos, often at the expense of the lives of their own offspring. Gänsbacher's metaphor still speaks volumes about certain ever-continuing traditions in the performance of Schubert's music!

[35] The practice of including the name of a celebrated out-of-house musician-cum-editor on publications in order to promote and legitimize the contents arose first in the late mid-century with the editions of Theodor Döhler, Clara Schumann, Julius Knorr, Louis Köhler and others.

several of the songs in this cycle show embellishments: but no transpositions, no falsetto markings, no spoken passages nor any other theatrical devices characteristic of Vogl's delivery. Such moderation does not correspond in the least to contemporaneous accounts of Vogl's lieder performances or his musical personality in general. It is difficult to understand, then, how one might detect Vogl's authority and influence in this edition, or his collaboration in any way.

No one yet has mentioned the most telling evidence against the notion that these ornaments were added by Vogl. As in the case of the *Alfonso* metronome markings (cf. Ch. VI), it is again quite simple: impracticality. Consider, for example, m. 29 (the second measure below) in *Mein!* D795/11, marked "Mässig geschwind" in *alla breve*:

EXAMPLE 5.23

We know that even by Schubert's middle years Vogl had long been over the hill as a singer. Is it possible for us to believe that he might have managed this intricate figure at a normal tempo in *alla breve*? We challenge any modern singer in their prime today, in fact, to execute this figure cleanly at the approximate tempo in which this song is usually taken!

The turn shown above was clearly added by a non-singer who could not judge its difficulty. If indeed these ornaments were added by Diabelli, they were doubly inopportune, for successful publishers of those days usually tried to avoid bringing out works with such difficulties. We see that in the passage preceding the figure shown above, beginning with "Durch den Hain," Diabelli has simplified Schubert's line (crassly removing the lovely G♯ on "Schalle"). Dürr rightly criticizes this variant, but still attributes it to Vogl, speculating that "perhaps the elderly Vogl, who was already experiencing serious difficulties with his voice [at this time], no longer wished to entrust a larger audience with Schubert's original text. Only singers suffering from the same problems should take variants of this sort as their guide." Here again, Dürr is on shifting ground. To begin with, why would Dürr imagine that just because Vogl could no longer manage such things, that among the "larger audience" there might not be someone who could? Secondly, why would Vogl care? But most importantly, this is not the sort of simplification that would present difficulties even for an aging voice: the *coloratura* is easy to manage and the highest note is an E. If anything, Vogl probably couldn't manage the soft glide over the F on "weiten:" note, however, that it is retained (see Example 5.24), as well as several instances of F♯ in full-voice, later on! Clearly these perplexing changes to Schubert's score are not by Vogl, but by an incompetent editor with no feel for musical difficulty—if not Diabelli himself, then possibly one of his employees. As if the lack of feeling for difficulty were not enough, these changes

Essential and Voluntary Ornamentation

EXAMPLE 5.24

reveal a predictable repetitiousness born of diminished imagination. Compare Schubert's original at the beginning with the editor's version.

EXAMPLE 5.25

Schubert himself had avoided any harmonic-melodic conflict until the "eure," where the sudden A♯ brings a delicious little twist to the end of the phrase.

EXAMPLE 5.26

The editor of the Diabelli print, on the other hand, simply dulls our expectation with his repeated and pointless *appoggiaturas*. In his print, the A♯ is practically meaningless by the time we reach it.[36]

The most telling flaw in this entire line of thinking, however, is that if embellishments were truly part of a singer's art, i.e. an improvisatory art, why would it be necessary to write them out? When embellishments are written out, they become part of a composition – or, more accurately, part of a "compositional-editorial complex" – and are no longer improvisational. Walther Dürr himself points out this fact in his reply to our observations on Schilling.[37] Why, then, does he accept written ornaments—worse yet, printed ornaments—as evidence of an improvisatory tradition in lied singing? Did Herr Vogl improvise or did he not? Did other singers improvise? Could almost everyone in those days improvise, even those amateurs in Schubert's circle who most often sang his music?

Of the nearly 100 other singers (many of them professionals) who are known to have performed Schubert's music during his lifetime (Ch. I), only Vogl is so often singled out for supposedly having embellished his music in performance. Nevertheless, Dürr and other scholars now identify Vogl's Schubert singing not only as representative, but also as exemplary. This conclusion is extraordinary enough, but Dürr and his colleagues further maintain that Vogl's treatment of Schubert's vocal music also has instructive consequences for the performance of the instrumental music.[38] Adherents of this view are simply in error, for here, as in the case of essential *appoggiaturas*, described above, vocal practices part company with instrumental practices. Actually we should say that "operatic" (nay, Italian operatic practices) part company with Viennese instrumental practices.

Ornamentation and embellishment in the instrumental music

> In the performance of [Beethoven's] works (and generally in all classic authors), the player must by no means allow himself to alter the composition, nor to make any addition or

---

[36] One is astonished by ever-renewed attempts to authenticate Diabelli's print. The latest such attempt is by Miklós Dolinszky, entitled "Die schöne Müllerin – eine authentische Fälschung? Neue Dokumente zur Vorgeschichte der Diabelli-Ausgabe" in *Die Musikforschung* 52/3 (1999, hereafter *MF*). Here the author refers to handwritten changes in several private music books (kept by Schönstein, Walcher, Leopold Sonnleithner, Henriette and Josephine Spaun, plus another book called the "Peterskirche Album") all of which show striking similarities and some exact notational agreements with the Diabelli edition. Dolinszky does not and cannot demonstrate that any of these changes come from Schubert. Indeed they do not, even if Dolinszky states (offering no proof) that they do. Nevertheless he allows himself to imagine that the Diabelli version still must have some standing, because by some magic, one or all of these "previous" sources must have been the basis for the "eventual" Diabelli version. Has it not occurred to him that if indeed Schubert went around writing all of these alternate versions in various private notebooks and at various times, that, instead of being so curiously identical, they more than likely would have been slightly different? The changes in these albums were made as a result of the posthumous Diabelli print (not vice-versa), and clearly not by Schubert. Cf. review in *Die Brille* 24: 178.
[37] Reply to Montgomery's letter "Exchanging Schubert for Schillings" in *EM* 26/3: 534. "I have emphasized again and again that printed ornamentation takes away the character of the improvised, of the spontaneous, and raises it to the rank of the composition itself ..." [!]
[38] See Montgomery, "Franz Schubert's Scores:" 81-82, 94ff.

abbreviation. [...] All embellishments, turns, shakes &c which the author himself has not indicated, justly appear superfluous, however tasteful they may be in themselves.

Carl Czerny
The Art of Playing the Ancient and Modern Piano Forte Works[39]

Although we may think of Franz Schubert as a "classic author" in Czerny's sense (and surely Czerny himself thought of him in that sense as a song composer), it is clear that Schubert did not enjoy that same reputation in the instrumental realm. For a number of years after his death, the bulk of his instrumental music remained practically unknown to the public. By the time that many of his major works were published the generation of Hummel was also gone and Czerny was active mostly as a teacher to an even newer generation. Czerny's pupils, among them Liszt, Thalberg, Heller, and Kullak, were fast creating new approaches to performance, not to mention the impact of Mendelssohn, Chopin, Hiller, Moscheles, and Clara Wieck-Schumann. Of the important pianists of Schubert's immediate circle, only Carl von Bocklet (1801–1881) was left. Among the famous singers who had known Schubert and championed his lieder Anna Milder had died in 1838, Johann Michael Vogl in 1840, leaving only Wilhelmine Schröder-Devrient (1804–1860). Schönstein sang on, but was known mostly for performances of the *Müllerlieder*. Neither Schönstein nor Schröder-Devrient wrote treatises. Louis Lablache, Heinrich Panofka, and Josephine Fodor-Mainville had known Schubert and promoted his songs, and all three later wrote treatises on singing—unfortunately none of them appropriate to Schubert. Two great losses among pedagogical documents, which might have discussed Schubert, are Joseph Leidesdorf's *Neueste wiener Clavierschule* announced for 1824 but apparently never printed; and Vogl's singing tutor, partly completed at his death but now apparently lost.

Viennese pedagogical sources of Schubert's day fail to mention him or his remarkable compositional style. However, they appear to offer a reasonable context for the performance of Franz Schubert's music. This last advantage is made possible through a special historical circumstance, which is reflected in the Viennese treatises. In the Introduction to this book we already have noted Alice Hanson's formulation of the two distinct directions taken by music in post-Napoleonic Vienna: the "serious" (Beethoven and a few others) and the "brilliant."[40] It is interesting that of all the German-language musical tutors of the period between 1815–1840, it is mostly, if not exclusively, Viennese authors who promote this distinction between popular concert music (in the "brilliant style") and serious composition. The reasons for this dichotomy appear to be that 1) for many years the greatest German-speaking composers had lived in Vienna (which gave rise in the first place to the distinction between them and merely fashionable composers); and 2) that financially, after the Napoleonic wars, the nobility no longer could support composers in the manner of bygone years, meaning that any musician with an overpowering yen for worldly remuneration was forced to cater to the most common tastes. This state of affairs clearly widened the margin between those who wrote specifically for the public and those who wrote for themselves with the mere hope that decreasingly sophisticated audiences still might learn to appreciate

---

[39] London edition, Pt. IV:32.
[40] Introduction, fn.2.

them. In terms of performance itself, Beethoven, for all his past success, was now living in a private, soundless world wherein his former public display as a virtuoso was no longer possible even had he desired it. Although he still presented new works, he was also beginning to be seen as a living monument, discussed by pedagogues during his own lifetime. Schubert had never been a virtuoso, and he died before he could prove himself as a composer to the small public who would still listen attentively to serious, demanding symphonies and chamber music.

It was not Schubert's wish to create works for a small isolated public, or particularly for the future. Schubert actively sought performances by the leading virtuosos, and he wanted them to happen while he lived. This is why, for example, the last three sonatas—now treasured as great spiritual documents by Schubert lovers—were meant to be dedicated to the popular virtuoso pianist Johann Nepomuk Hummel. Schubert wanted Hummel to play and promote them, just as he wanted Johann Michael Vogl and Anna Milder to sing his songs.[41] On the other hand, he had no intention of writing works specifically for the common taste. He wrote, simply, what he had to write, most of it beyond the musical grasp of garden-variety virtuosos in the first place. What a Hummel or a Vogl might have made out of his scores was a forced secondary consideration, although gradually—had Schubert lived a little longer—he might have gained enough authority to put his foot down on waywardnesses with his music. We do not wish to imply that his entire output was of the highest spiritual quality; we cannot expect this feat from any composer. Still in all, precious few of his works do not deserve to survive him.

One of the most reliable musical chroniclers of the period, Carl Czerny, defined the category of "serious composition" by remarking that it was the province of "classic authors" (in the quotation on p. 200-201), i.e. composers who wrote music of a quality that would secure it a place in the future.[42] Czerny contrasted serious composition with popular concert music, which he characterized as having been written in the "style brillant" – which demanded a corresponding performance style. Here we can place the bulk of instrumental music composed for the Viennese public concerts after 1815: concertos, potpourris, fantasies, rondos, variations on popular themes and the like. A large percentage of vocal music (Italian opera, for example) falls into this category as well. Under the rubric "Über das brillante Spiel" in Czerny's great method, he likened the performance manner appropriate for this style to "handwriting that one can read from afar." Compositionally, he illustrated the difference between the two styles by comparing Hummel's D-minor Septet (a "brilliant" work) to Beethoven's Quintet, Op. 15 (a "serious" work).[43] It is reasonable to assume

---

[41] Unbeknownst to Schubert, even during his lifetime he already had captured Felix Mendelssohn's interest. Siegrfried Dehn heard Mendelssohn accompany Karl Adam Bader in a performance of *Erlkönig* in November of 1827 and reported the occasion in *BamZ* on 5 December 1827. The Leipziger *Amz* (16 January 1828) reported the same concert, describing Mendelssohn's playing as "finished and powerful." The song itself did not fare as well. The reviewer compared it unfavorably to the settings of Reichardt and Zelter, throwing Schubert a small, dry bone by noting its abundant "modulation and bizarrerie."
[42] *Pianoforte-Schule IV*:31: "Das Wort klassisch, kann, nach seiner wahren Bedeutung, nur von denjenigen Compositionen gelten, welche sich, (auch nach dem Tode ihrer Verfasser,) durch eine lange Zeit ihre Dauer für die Zukunft gesichert haben."
[43] *Pianoforte-Schule III*: §9 (pp. 58–60).

that Czerny would have included Schubert among his "classic authors;" they had met personally, and Czerny appears to have known some of Schubert's finest works. As an Appendix to the *Vortrag* (not available in a modern edition; UE has published only Chapters II and III), Czerny offers a "Catalogue of the best and most useful Works of all Composers for the Pianoforte from Mozart to the Present." Of Franz Schubert's piano works he appears to have known a small sampling of the solo pieces, some of the better four-hand works and the two late piano trios.[44] We can assume that he knew the famous songs as well.

Each in its own way, the major performance treatises of post-Napoleonic Vienna (with one significant exception) documented the distinction between the two kinds of musical composition and delivery described above. The exception is Hummel's *Ausführliche theoretisch-praktische Anweisung zum Pianofortespiel*.[45] Its author had no inclination to make such a distinction, apparently, for almost the entire book is devoted to the *style brillant* in the first place. Except for a fugue each by J.S. Bach and G.F. Händel, all of the examples are by Hummel himself. Robert Schumann later referred to precisely these examples (through "Florestan," his extroverted self) as "lauter Hummelianis." In his maturity Hummel was not noted for playing what we now regard as the great classic masters, as did Karl Maria von Bocklet or Carl Czerny. Hummel made his living by promoting himself as a virtuoso, and as such he was one of the best and most celebrated. One of Florestan's earlier comments echoes Czerny's standards for separating a "brilliant" from a "classic" musician:

> Already with Hummel's piano method I formed the quiet suspicion that though an excellent virtuoso in his time, he might not be a teacher for the future.[46]

As to be expected in Hummel's virtuosic style (within which he was recognized as a player of "good taste"), he advocated limited voluntary ornamentation, but in *adagios* only.[47] We can exclude even this allowance, however, for Schubert's music.

In terms of performance styles, Friedrich Starke's *Pianoforte-Schule* (1819–1821) makes it clear that highly ornamented performances are for the mere "*Mode-Kenner*" (fashion hound), as opposed to more respectful performances appropriate to greater works. Like most pedagogues of the day, he makes a distinction between prescribed and voluntary ornamentation. Despite the fact that his tutor is principally for pianists his description of voluntary embellishment pertains mostly to operatic singers (and in many places he specifically

---

[44] *Pianoforte-Schule IV*: Anhang: 161 ff: Schubert's works in Czerny's catalogue: Sonata in D major, Op. 53; Fantasy in C major, Op. 15; 4 Impromptûs [sic], op. 142; Momens [sic] musicals, op. 94 (This is the spelling on the original Leidesdorf edition); Sonata (Grand Duo) in C major, op. 140; Sonata in B♭ major, op. 30; Fantasie in F minor, op. 103; Variations in E minor, op. 10 (dedicated to Beethoven); Variations in A♭ major, op. 35; 3 Heroic Marches, op. 27; 6 Great Marches, op. 40; 2 Characteristic Marches in C, op. 121; Trio in B♭, op.99; Trio in E♭ major, op. 100. Still, this is an odd list. Why would Czerny not have known the A minor Sonata D845, for example, or the first set of Impromptus?
[45] Haslinger, 1828. The method was written several years earlier, however.
[46] Gesammelte Schriften I: 11, cited by Andreas Eichhorn in the Preface to the 1989 facsimile publication of the second print of Hummel's method (Straubenhardt, 1989): "Schon bei der Klavierschule Hummels ... schöpfte ich einen leisen Verdacht, ob Hummel, wie er ein ausgezeichneter Virtuose seiner Zeit war, auch ein Pädagog für die künftige wäre".
[47] Chap. II: § 4 : 418. See Montgomery, "Modern Schubert Interpretation," op. cit: 109/110.

uses the word "singers"). He describes typical operatic *passaggi* of the Italian sort – made of "many notes, scales, and the like" – as opposed to the prescribed ornaments (trills, turns, slides, mordents, etc.) which he has excluded from voluntary use. However, he is careful to say that the music of the best composers needs no ornamentation unless at *fermatas* or cadences (i.e. cadenzas), by which terminology he appears to be talking about concertos or operatic arias:

> Sadly, in musical practice (as in politics and morality), fashionable taste and artistic taste are two different things. [...] In general, the greatest composers endeavour to write their own ornamentation so carefully into their piano works that the performer is left little in the way of voluntary ornaments and additions. Should the performer be left something to invent at fermatas and cadences he should always make it suit the character of the pieces, and, more specifically, remain faithful to the given harmony.[48]

In 1823 the pianist and teacher J.C.G. Junghanns, in his meticulous and inclusive *Theoretisch-praktische Pianoforte-Schule* restricted voluntary embellishment even further, admitting it only at cadences: i.e. for the improvisation of cadenzas in concertos.[49] In this section of the tutor, entitled "Von den Verzierungen (Manieren)," Junghanns does not mince words, but presents his basic exclusion of voluntary embellishment as a simple fact of modern performance life. This three-part method is almost never mentioned in discussions of Viennese performance practice during the early nineteenth century, and yet it is clearly an important and sophisticated source: an antidote, in a sense, to Hummel. Junghanns's examples reveal his primary interest in the "serious" composers, drawn from W. Bach, Haydn, Mozart, Beethoven and Méhul (and one from the celebrated Viennese guitarist Mauro Giuliani), but none from the *style brillant*. Sadly, Junghanns appears not to have known Schubert's instrumental music at this point (we do not know how long his tutor was held up by the Viennese censors). The *Wanderer* Fantasy D760, for example, one of Schubert's first important instrumental publications, had just been advertised in early 1823.

We cannot assume, of course, that the brilliant style automatically required voluntary embellishment. There exist plenty of show-stoppers in which the player would be hard-pressed to stuff in a single extra embellishment, not to mention those moments in every such work when simplicity itself might function as an ornament-in-reverse. Schubert wrote a few pieces which now have the word *brillant* in their titles: for example, the three movements on French themes assembled under D823, published as *Divertissement en forme d'une Marche brillante* D823/1 and *Andantino varié et Rondeau brillant* D823/2–3, or the *Rondeau brillant* in B minor for Violin and Piano D895. In all three cases, however, the word *brillant* appears only in the printed editions and was probably added by the publishers. Schubert also wrote fantasies, rondos and variations which might easily have pleased a crowd. But if we examine the style of these works carefully we find that they do not depart from the style of his other works.

Schubert's most cherished goal in terms of public recognition and success was not to entertain with occasional pieces or even concertos, but to produce grand symphonies (i.e.

---

[48] Friedrich Starke, *Wiener Pianoforte-Schule:* 18 (See App. IIA, 1819). For a fuller version of this passage see Montgomery, "Modern Schubert Interpretation": 106/7.
[49] Cappi & Diabelli, printed by A. Strauß.

Essential and Voluntary Ornamentation 205

for full forces and of substantial length). The oft-quoted remark in Schubert's letter to Leopold Kupelwieser, to the effect that through the production of quartets and other smaller instrumental things he would "pave the way" to the grand symphony, has been misunderstood by a number of modern authors.[50] It has been popular of late to discuss Schubert's "compositional learning process" in this regard, as if through composing string quartets he was preparing himself, somehow, to master the symphonic art.[51] The fact is, of course, that he already had mastered that art. What he was on to now was a more worldly scheme: namely, through the sale of chamber music gradually to interest his publishers in a symphonic project that would bring him public recognition and, most of all, a little money.

Musical structure and the argument for embellishment

In terms of musical structure, Arthur Godel tells us that "the strongest criticism brought against Schubert's sonatas concern the repetition of larger sections unchanged." This must be the criticism that has provided the impetus for the current trend toward embellishing Schubert. Godel continues, clearly not in favor of embellishment as an antidote:

> What is meant here are the recapitulations, the prescribed exposition repeats which occur up to and in the last sonatas, and the larger sequences in development sections. Concerning exposition repeats and unchanged recapitulations, if Schubert constantly employs such conventional [structural] means, then for him—the quick-change artist—they must have compositional meaning.[52]

As we have noted earlier on the "Vogl" issue, one of the chief spokesmen for embellishing Schubert has been Walther Dürr, Editor-in-Chief (now emeritus) for the *NSA*. Apart from Vogl, Dürr's other mainstay on the subect of voluntary ornamentation in Schubert is Gustav Schilling's *Musikalische Dynamik*. This book indeed repeats the venerable dichotomy between *wesentliche* (prescribed) and *willkürliche* (voluntary) *Manieren*. Dürr bolsters his approval of voluntary ornamentation and embellishment with passages such as the one cited below, which indeed foster the notion that literal repeats cannot be allowed to go undoctored:

> [Finally], a fitting place for free ornamentation would be in the repeats of a particularly long theme or movement ... and similarly, we find other forms and places where we can apply this kind of ornamentation, namely in what are called 'rondo-like' compositions. In such works, where the composer himself has not supplied ornamentation, the player can and must apply it himself rather than merely repeat [the material]."[53]

---

[50] 31 March 1824: In Liedern habe ich wenig Neues gemacht, dagegen versuchte ich mich in mehreren Instrumental-Sachen, denn ich componirte 2 Quartetten für Violinin, Viola u. Violoncelle u. ein Octett, u. will noch ein Quartetto schreiben, überhaupt will ich mir auf diese Art den Weg zur großen Sinfonie bahnen.— Das Neueste in Wien ist, daß Beethoven ein Concert gibt, in welchem er seine neue Sinfonie, 3 Stücke aus der neuen Messe, u. eine neue Overture produciren läßt.—Wenn Gott will, so bin auch ich gesonnen, künftiges Jahr ein ähnliches Concert zu geben." *Dokumente*: 235.
[51] Cf. L. Michael Griffel, "Schubert's orchestral music: 'strivings after the highest in art'" in *The Cambridge Companion to Schubert* (Cambridge: CUP, 1997): 201/2.
[52] Godel: 243.
[53] *Musikalische Dynamik:* 255 "Endlich bietet sich ein schicklicher Ort zu freien Verzierungen in den Wiederholungen eines namentlich längern Hauptgedankens oder Satzes dar [...] und eben so kommen auch in der Instrumentalmusik wohl Formen und Stellen, auf welche sich diese Regel betreff des Verzierten

Schilling's theory about embellishing major repeats derives straight from the Baroque, of course, applying to ABA operatic arias and related concerto movements of that time. Indeed, Schilling may be referring here to the performance of eighteenth-century music. In any case, what he has to say concerning the embellishment of rondo themes has no theoretical standing in nineteenth-century Vienna, nor does Dürr bother to provide evidence that it does.[54] He merely cites two examples of written-out *coloratura* in Schubert's sonatas, and then – with breathtaking reasoning – he declares:

> Schubert does not always write out such variants himself. Occasionally he leaves them to the player, who applies them to suit his particular abilities, the character of his instrument, the venue and perhaps even the expectation of his public. When in the sketches to the slow movement of his Piano Trio in E flat (D929) he writes "with more coloratura" (m. 86) or "varied" (m. 100), then indeed he reveals his thought that the player should add the coloratura here, and he [Schubert] has also done this [i.e. added the coloratura himself] in the final version.

Sensing, perhaps, the paralogism that he has just introduced, Dürr quickly repeats himself, at the end: "but it is to be supposed that Schubert did not always [sic!] notate [such colorature]."[55] But merely repeating this statement still does not make it come true. Why would Schubert imagine that a player would further embellish an already partially filigreed passage? By Dürr's own supposition, a player would only embellish a non-embellished passage. Secondly, this is neither a repeat, nor a rondo (cf. Schilling, above). If indeed these annotations in the sketch are by Schubert (there may be some doubt about the handwriting), they can only be notes written to himself as a reminder to flesh out these four bars in the next draft (cf. m. 86 / m. 90). We know, of course, that he did so in the final version. If the annotations are not by Schubert, then we know that they are 1) not written by a performer, for performers do not play completed pieces from first drafts; and 2) most likely written by a person with no respect for Schubert's manuscripts, but who nevertheless wished

---

Vortrags anwenden läßt, namentlich in den sogenannten rondoartigen Compositionen, in denen ebenfalls der melodische Hauptsatz in mehrmaliger Wiederholung auftritt, und wo nun dem Spieler gleichergestalt freistehen kann und muß, denselben auch in einer verziertern denn blos der einfachen Weise wiederzugeben, wenn solche Verzierung nicht von dem Componisten selbst schon ausgeführt und vorgeschrieben seyn sollte".

[54] As Will Crutchfield points out, Pellegrini-Celoni advised her readers to "adorn" the recurring themes of rondo-type arias. *Performance Practice:*303. We cannot assume, however, that even in eighteenth-century Italy this instruction remained good for instrumental rondos. As we have pointed out above, her guidance is based entirely on eighteenth-century Italian vocal principles, and certainly far removed from the world of Franz Schubert. Schilling may have borrowed the idea to embellish rondos from Pelligrini-Celoni in the German translation by Johann Gottfried Schicht (Leipzig, 1820). Schilling's colleague, G.W. Fink, even published a *Musicalische Grammatik* (Leipzig, 1836).

[55] *Schubert-Handbuch:* 110/111. "Nicht immer schreibt Schubert solche Varianten selbst aus. Gelegentlich überläßt er sie wohl dem Spieler, der sie seinen besonderen Fähigkeiten, dem Charackter seines Instrumentes, dem Aufführungsort und vielleicht auch den Erwartungen seines Publikums anpaßt. Wenn Schubert in den Skizzen zum langsamen Satz seines Klaviertrios in Es-Dur (D 929, op. 100) notiert » mit mehr Coloratur « (T. 86) oder » Variirt « (T. 100, s. NGA [*NSA*] VI, 7, S. 274), dann deutet das zwar darauf hin, daß er den Spielern die Coloraturen hier selbst anzugeben dachte und dies in der gültigen Fassung auch getan hat – es läßt aber auch vermuten, daß er sie nicht immer notiert hat."

to compare the draft with the completed version. The gravest error in the quotation above, however, is Dürr's assumption that where Schubert has not written out a passage in sufficient filigree, he expects the performer to do so for him. "Schubert does not always write out such variants ('Varianten') himself. Occasionally he leaves them to the player ... "[!] Why would Schubert leave himself to the whim and taste of a player at times? Why, indeed, would he do it at all? Dürr offers no enlightenment.

Schilling's text (published in Stuttgart in 1843) is a strange rehash of 18th-century sources and sentiments, mixed with information and aesthetics from the heyday of Mendelssohn, Schumann, Chopin, and Liszt. A quick look at the table of contents shows us several apparently modern genres, including *Die Sinfonie* (§ 120) and *Das Lied* (§ 131), but one cannot help noticing as well that the list of dance forms that he proposes to treat calls for nothing less than a powdered wig. (For Schilling's personal sake one can only hope that by the later mid-nineteenth century people were still dancing the *minuet,* the *forlane* or the *folie d'espagne* in faraway Nebraska, his final destination.)[56] The reason for this mixture of modern awareness with long outdated information is that Schilling borrowed heavily from early sources. The section to which Dürr refers most often (Chap. III: § 93–96, *Subjektive Verschiedenheit des musikalischen Vortrags oder über den einfachen und verzierten Vortrag*),[57] for example, reads as if it were lifted out of an early galant source; parts of it are, in fact, "liberated" from earlier works. As an example we might take Schilling's admonishment that "ripienists" [!] should not ornament their parts, couched in more or less the same terms that have been passed down from Rousseau's *Dictionnaire de Musique* (1764) to various turn-of-the-century sources (Koch, for example) and thus into the nineteenth century itself. Schilling's very use of the term "ripienists" is revealingly anachronistic, for by Schubert's day (and certainly by Mendelssohn's day, when Schilling's text was printed) this thoroughly Baroque description of an orchestral player was no longer used.

In the *Universal Lexikon* Schilling also borrows unabashedly from earlier models, sometimes not even bothering to change the language. In the article on *Manieren* he writes, for example, that "freie Manieren [...] bringen Licht und Schatten in das ganze Tonstück,"[58] a metaphor lifted directly from the corresponding article in G.F. Wolf's *Kurzgefaßtes Musikalisches Lexikon* of 1806, where we read that such *Manieren* [...] "bringen Licht und Schatten in den Gesang."[59] (Wolf himself borrowed this metaphor, for it had been used in Sulzer[60] and other eighteenth-century sources, originating from earlier discussions of painting. In any case, Wolf's own information on *Manieren* is far outdated.) Dürr admits that:

> One very often reads that what Schilling writes is twaddle, and that other music theorists of the time had more important and more original thoughts. In that sense Eggebrecht is entirely right

---

[56] In addition to being sued for fraud and plagiary concerning his writings, Schilling ran up a number of debts and was finally forced to leave Germany. See *MGG* (195-): "Gustav Schilling" (Eggebrecht).
[57] Preface, fn 9.
[58] Cited in *Schubert Handbuch:* 107.
[59] (Halle: Hendel): 185.
[60] Johann Georg Sulzer, *Allgemeine Theorie der schönen Kunste* (Leipzig: 1771–74): musical articles by J.A.P. Schulz and J.P. Kirnberger.

– the question is only what I expect from a music theorist of the 19th century. If I seek originality of thought, then Schilling is not the right address; but if I seek to learn the general consensus – widely held ideas – then I must orient myself precisely with people like Schilling (and with widely circulated reference works such as his *Universal Encyclopedia*), indeed even avoiding all too original ideas.[61]

This statement is remarkable; it is tantamount to saying that because in Schilling's day he repeated "widely held ideas" of his own day we now can take him seriously as a period source about the performance ideals and habits of a long-dead composer whom he never met (and never mentions in the *Musikalische Dynamik*), and about a city whose specific musical practices appear to have escaped his attention! But in one sense we must agree with Dürr, for we, too, have no interest in "original ideas" where research is concerned. We are far more curious about facts. Nor are we interested in "other theorists" of Schilling's time, but in theorists of Schubert's time.

To be fair, we must take two factors into consideration here. First, what Schilling actually has to say about ornamentation, regardless of where he got it, is more or less standard information. Unfortunately, however, it is standard information only for the eighteenth century. The same caveat applies to Rochlitz's information on ornaments. Of course, these gentlemen would not be the first musical authors to peddle long outdated information; among pedagogues, for example, A.F. Emy de L'Ilette published his *Théorie musicale* in Paris in 1810, blithely prescribing *notes inégales* and other eighteenth-century *galant* mannerisms which had gone out well before the French Revolution.) The second factor in this ticklish problem is that Gustav Schilling (like Rochlitz) was not a practical performing musician, and certainly not a teacher. He was an encyclopaedist, a compiler of information. Encylopaedists do not and did not necessarily discard older information, at least not in centuries past. A dependence upon earlier works goes with the territory (cf. Brossard–Grassineau, for example), and the less one knows about a given field, the more he is apt to borrow.

We wish to exit this chapter with a passage of some interest. Published a decade and a half after Schubert's death, it cannot count as authoritative for Schubert, nor even for his general period. One wonders, however, what its author might have written had he once talked with the composer, attended a Schubertiade or even heard the *Unfinished* Symphony.

> If we recall so many noble creations of Gluck, Haydn, Mozart, Beethoven and other really spiritual composers, and if we recall the sublime, inspiring feats of a Spohr, Rode, Field, Cramer, Hummel, Mara, Catalini ... and other deeply-knowledgeable masters in the art of playing and singing : [we must ask] how did it come about that in their great lives they managed to infuse their tones with such powerful, deeply-moving declamatory truth? – [answer]: through noble and sublime simplicity. Without much coloratura, without highly embellished fermati and cadenzi, without any richly-bubbling splendor of passaggi, but living in the full truth of expression and in the complete depth of their nature, their creations remain alive in our memories. Is it not just that which causes us to listen so gladly to this or that work of a composer, or to remember this or that performance of an interpreter, now nearly a half-century after their

---

[61] *EM* 26/3 (1998): 534.

Essential and Voluntary Ornamentation

creation, so long after they have flowered?

> Every true virtuoso abstains from all free ornamentation where the original notes on the page suffice to express the composer's intentions; and therewith he can be sure of having done the right thing, for mere external pomp – which is awakened by a single such ornament – contradicts one's true artistic responsibility and damages the expression more than it can serve it. One need not fear that monotony will ensue, for this is something different from simplicity. If a performer is compelled to hide a composition's simplicity with his ornamentation, then surely he lacks every deep spiritual feeling, and the various movements will appear only as an empty game of notes.

This passage is taken from Gustav Schilling's *Musikalische Dynamik*, Dürr's own source, only three pages past the discussion on ornamentation cited in the *NSA*.[62]

---

[62] §92–96, "Subjektive Verschiedenheit": 258.

CHAPTER VI

Tempo, Time, and Character

Although by 1812 the division and measurement of musical time had been so refined as to reflect a rather sophisticated gamut on Maelzel's metronome (48 bpm–160 bpm), to establish and maintain appropriate tempos in the performance of the music of the period remains one of the most difficult tasks demanded of a performer. Like all perceptions, our sense of time is subject to caprice, and for even the most experienced musicians the mere fact of having started a piece in a given tempo provides no guarantee of consistency even several measures into a work. Nevertheless, one of the continuing compositional characteristics of Viennese music in this period is its organization into large regions of regular metrical division with no notated change in tempo (particularly in the instrumental music), and all musicians interested in historically-informed performance must come to terms with the meaning of this organization.

Myriad schools of thought exist today concerning meter, tempo, and tempo adjustment in the music of Franz Schubert. One school maintains, for example, that Schubert was just as serious about his markings as was Beethoven, and that, within a limited range according to changing affect and passagework, and taking into account an emerging nineteenth-century *rubato*, the large regions of music mentioned above should be delivered in correspondingly consistent tempos. Another school maintains again that Schubert was just as serious as Beethoven about his tempos, but that for neither composer was consistency a part of this seriousness. One of the arguments advanced by this school concerns Beethoven's supposed note on the now-lost autograph of the song *So oder so* to the effect that his metronome marking applied only to the first few bars of the song (see App. IB for a reprint of this song).[1] Reports by period witnesses to Beethoven's unique and supposedly erratic playing style also add fuel to this particular fire, although the reports are conflicting and by no

---

[1] Thayer/Forbes 687, referring to Fischoff in the German ed. of Thayer, ed. H. Deiters/rev. Riemann/Leipzig 1907–17: IV:66:n.3). We wonder how many people actually have taken the trouble to examine this song. It is a straightforward strophic affair, but with a quirk. In several of the verses Beethoven instructs the performers to hold the tempo back and then to move forward – particularly in the last verse, where, after two lines in tempo he marks "Etwas verzögernd bis zum ersten Zeitmaß." The performers are to reach the "ersten Zeitmaß" only in the last line of the piece. Given such unusual instructions, one does not doubt that Beethoven could have made the reputed remark concerning tempo, but it cannot be taken as representative of his general attitude about tempo instructions. In any case, since the autograph is lost, we cannot speculate much further on this issue.

means reliable. A third school, represented, perhaps, by the majority of performers today, resists the idea of metronome markings and tempo consistency altogether (particularly in Schubert's case), arriving at such decisions through a personal, instinctive sense of history and musical understanding. Hundreds of variants and combinations exist, but common to all is the fact that Schubert's tempo indications have never been examined systematically, and his metronome markings, unlike Beethoven's, have never been taken seriously as the basis for historically-informed tempo choices.[2]

Schubert's earliest tempo and character indications for songs and instrumental music were in Italian and without metronome markings. He had been a pupil of Salieri, and the Italian orientation, at least in external terms, would have come naturally. By the middle of his career, however, he had grown accustomed to providing most of his vocal music on German texts (principally the songs) with German instructions and all instrumental music and operas with Italian instructions. Instrumentalists were used to instructions in Italian, which was the musical *lingua franca* in Europe (with the exception of France and possibly the low countries). On the other hand, Schubert wrote the songs mostly for his German-speaking friends, and intended them to be published for a German-speaking public.

We cannot compare Schubert's German and Italian tempos in absolute terms, for although we find almost one hundred metronomic additions to the tempo indications in both languages (for the early song publications, *Alfonso und Estrella* and the Deutsche Messe), we must reject the largest group of them, the *Alfonso und Estrella* markings, as unauthentic (see Absolute Tempo, p. 251). We do this with great reluctance, for had they been genuine we might have analyzed them along with the German markings to determine whether 1) each set is internally consistent; 2) whether they exhibit consistent external equivalencies (i.e. is *Mäßig* really the same as *Andante*?); and 3) if so, whether we can extrapolate further metronome markings from them as a single group, particularly for the instrumental works in general, and for vocal works with specific tempo problems.[3]

We cannot correlate even the cases where Schubert provided both German and Italian tempo-and-character indications for the same musical material (principally songs as the basis for later instrumental settings), for his concept and treatment of the original material in subsequent settings appears to have changed according to genre and musical need. The *Mäßig* of D531 (*Der Tod und das Mädchen*) is not precisely translatable into the *Andante con moto* of the corresponding movement in the string quartet known by that nickname. Likewise, discrepancies of meter, character, and tempo exist for the *Langsam* of *Sei*

---

[2] We can no longer entertain lingering doubts as to the accuracy of the early Maelzel metronomes. Years ago Rudolf Kolisch addressed this issue in his now-famous two-part article, "Tempo and Character in Beethoven's Music" in *MQ* 29 (1943): 165–187/291–312, and his logic has yet to be refuted. Kolisch's laconic tact, as we knew it, probably prevented him from printing what he really felt: that most artists of his day were put off by the metronome as anything other than a practice device for children, and that artists in general were unwilling to forego their own acquired tastes in favor of the results of historical inquiry where it proved uncomfortable. Kolisch was in the process of revising his article when he died, and thus we were saddened that in 1997 *MQ* simply reissued the article verbatim without consulting the few Kolisch disciples who might have shed light on a revised version.

[3] For a more exacting study see Waidelich, *Franz Schubert: Alfonso und Estrella*.

mir gegrüßt D741 vs. the *Andantino* of the C-major Fantasy D934. We find similar problems with the *Wanderer* material (*Sehr Langsam* in the song vs. only *Adagio* in the fantasy), the *Die Forelle* material (D550 *Etwas lebhaft* vs. D667/4 *Andantino*), and, by direct conflict between Italian markings alone, the *Rosamunde* material (D797/5 *Andantino* vs. the Impromptu theme of D804/2, *Andante*).

Still, we will seek to accomplish our goals with the limited information available, employing internal as well as external information.

Relative tempos

By "relative tempos" we mean, simply, the range and hierarchy of tempo categories applicable to any composer's music or to a general style and period. Long before Schubert's time pedagogues and theorists had begun to print tables of such relationships, some of them in the most fundamental terms (*Presto, Allegro, Andante, Adagio*) and others more elaborate with terminological equivalances between languages, often including measurable time divisions.[4] The following table shows tempo hierarchies and equivalancies from various Viennese theoretical works of Schubert's day, which we have compared to the general categories employed by Schubert.[5] We have also included a table for Beethoven, whose markings have been analyzed thoroughly by Rudolf Kolisch (see fn 2).

TABLE I

1756, L. Mozart

Prestissimo – Presto – Molto Allegro – Allegro – Allegro ma non troppo / Allegro moderato – Allegretto – Vivace – Moderato – Andante – Lento – Adagio – Largo – Grave

1779, Rigler

Prestissimo – Presto – Allegro con moto / Allegro brillante – Allegro molto / Allegro assai – Allegro – Vivace – Allegro moderato – Allegretto – Poco allegro – Molto andante – Andante – Andantino – Poco andante – Larghetto – Andante non molto – Poco adagio – Adagio – Adagio assai – Largo – Lento

1787, Petri

Prestissimo – Presto – Allegro molto – Allegro assai – Vivacissimo – Poco presto – Allegro – Vivace – Veloce – Allegro ma non troppo – Allegretto / Poco allegro – Poco vivace / Moderato / Poco Veloce – Poco adagio / Poco largo / Poco andante – Andantino / Larghetto / Moderato – Largo non troppo – Adagio – Largo – Lento – Adagio assai / Adagio di molto – Largo assai / Largo di molto – Lento assai

1811, Preindl

Prestissimo – Allegro assai / Allegro molto – Presto – Vivace – Allegro – Allegretto – Moderato – Andante – Andantino – Larghetto – Adagio – Lento – Grave – Largo

---

[4] Although many articles on the metronome have been written in recent years, Rosamond Harding's little volume, *The Metronome and its Precursors* (Henley-on-Thames, 1938), remains one of the clearest introductions to the subject of tempo and its measurement up to and through the advent of the modern metronome.
[5] Complete citations in App. IIA.

1812, Cramer

Vivacissimo – Vivace – Allegro – Allegretto – Andante – Adagio – Larghetto – Largo – Lento

1819 – 1821, Starke

Presto – Allegro / Vivace – Allegretto – Andante – Andantino – Adagio / Lento – Largo

1821, Krähmer

Prestissimo – Presto – Allegro – Vivace – Allegretto – Moderato – Andantino – Andante – Larghetto – Lento – Adagio – Grave – Largo

1823, Junghanns

Vivace – Presto – Allegro – Allegretto – Andantino – Andante – Larghetto – Lento – Adagio – Grave – Largo

1826, Hummel

Prestissimo – Presto – Vivacissimo – Allegro – Allegretto – Andante – Andantino – Adagio – Lento – Larghetto – Largo – Grave

1826, Swoboda

Prestissimo – Presto assai – Presto – Allegrissimo – Allegramento – Allegro – Allegretto – Andantino – Andante – Larghetto – Largo – Adagio – Adagissimo – Grave – Lento

1827, Bathioli

Prestissimo – Presto – Vivace – Allegro – Allegretto – Andante – Larghetto – Largo – Lento – Adagio – Andantino – Adagissimo

1839, Czerny

Prestissimo – Presto – Allegro – Allegretto – Andantino – Andante – Adagio – Larghetto – Largo

Beethoven (from Kolisch tables)

Prestissimo – Presto – Allegro molto / Allegro vivace – Allegro con brio – Allegro – Allegro ma non troppo – Allegretto – Andante / Larghetto – Adagio / Largo

Schubert:

Prestissimo – Presto – Allegro presto – Allegro molto – Allegro vivace – Allegro – Allegretto – Andantino – Larghetto – Andante – Andante molto – Adagio – Largo – Lento – Grave

This table reveals some significant disagreements from the outset: for example, in the varying concepts of *Andantino* (i.e. as faster or slower than *Andante)*. Czerny ranks it faster than *Andante*, which he calls "slow." Thus no consistency existed in the matter of diminutives, for *Allegretto* is by no means faster than *Allegro*. Concerning *Andantino*, Czerny and Schubert (along with Krähmer, Junghanns, and Swoboda) were in agreement, but were opposed by Rigler, Petri, Preindl, and Hummel). Beethoven does not use the term *Andantino*. In agreement with Beethoven, Schubert's *Larghetto* (practically an *Andantino*) was significantly faster than Czerny's, which was merely a brightened *Largo*.[6] On the other hand,

---

[6] Perhaps one of the most drastically misunderstood tempos in all of Beethoven's works is the *Larghetto* of the Violin Concerto, which over the years has acquired such a gravity of spirit as to remove it entirely from

Bathioli considered *Andantino* itself slower even than *Largo, Lento,* or *Adagio*! For Schubert, unlike Czerny and others, we can dismiss *Largo, Lento,* and *Grave* as separate categories (see discussion below). Schubert also employed the indications *Marcia, Marcia funebre, Walzer, Deutscher,* etc. which were commonly understood tempos in his day, their exact speeds determined by function and fashion. Here, however, we do not include them as categories, because their applications are so limited.

We can characterize Schubert's Italian tempo rankings as follows:

TABLE II

1. *Prestissimo* : the fastest speed, as fast as possible. No apparent conceptual disagreement between Schubert and his contemporaries. Nevertheless a rare indication for Schubert; only one example (early) among the major instrumental works.

2. *Presto*: includes *Presto vivace*, which can be taken as a step between *Presto* and *Prestissimo,* although a theoretical distinction at best. For the instrumental music, Schubert's *Presto* embraces mostly 2/4 and 3/4, specifically those types which are perceived as one beat to the measure or even several measures.

3. *Allegro molto / Allegro con brio / Allegro con fuoco / Allegro presto / Allegro vivace / Vivace.* Linguistically, *Vivace* is not a category, for it simply means "lively." But Schubert and others understood it as a category slightly under *Allegro molto* and *Allegro con brio*, especially for scherzos and finales. *Allegro presto* can be defined only because both terms pertain specifically to speed. A rare marking, which, like *Presto vivace*, remains theoretical at best. Only two examples exist, one early, one "late;" both can be understood as *Allegro molto* or *Allegro con brio*.

4. *Allegro*: along with *Andante* the most common category, carrying probably the largest range of metronome markings. Its modifiers range from *Molto moderato* through *Assai, Molto,* and *Presto* (see 3. above).

5. *Allegretto*: in the livelier half of the range, this diminutive is in itself almost a character indication (cheerfulness, etc.). It has no satisfactory translation from or into German.

6. *Andantino*: by all internal characteristics of music so marked by Schubert to be regarded in the middle of the range, one notch below *Allegretto*. Schubert employed two tell-tale markings: *Allegretto quasi andantino* and *Andantino quasi allegretto*, which, taken together, confirm the close proximity of *Andantino* and *Allegretto*. Cf. also the *Andantino con moto* of D50 with the *Allegretto* of D52:

EXAMPLE 6.1a/b
a. *Die Schatten* D50

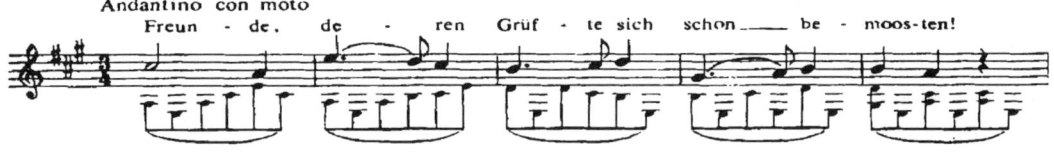

its true function as an entr'acte between the great outer movements. The violin part in this movement is an ornamental commentary on a simple tune, but usually is drawn out as if it were a great solo statement.

b. *Sehnsucht* D52

7. *Larghetto*: Schubert used this term in only a small handful of works. We may look upon it as equivalent to *Andante*, and in some cases even *Andantino*. Compare, for example, the following arias (*Alfonso und Estrella* Nos. 5 and 21). Note the similarities in shape and rhythm of the vocal lines, as well as the accompaniment patterns and general moods.

EXAMPLE 6.2a/b
a. No. 5, Aria

b. No. 21, Aria

In cheerful 6/8 secular works *Larghetto* is again indistiguishable from *Andantino*:

EXAMPLE 6.3a/c
a. D190

b. D647/6

and may even border on the character of *Allegretto*:

c. D528

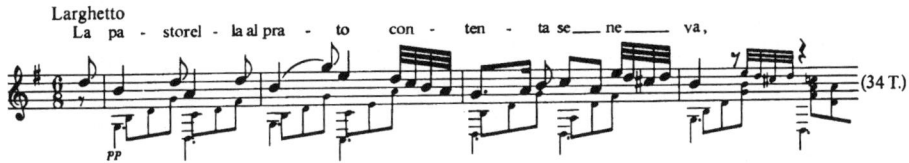

8. *Andante*: Along with *Allegro*, *Andante* is Schubert's largest category, and (again with *Allegro*) carries the widest range of modifiers. In his instrumental works, however, he follows Beethoven's example and rarely writes an *Andante* in 4/4.

9. *Adagio*: By Schubert's mid-career this concept evolved into his slowest category. It carries a number of modifiers, although not as many as do *Andante* and *Allegro*.

10. *Largo*: Schubert invoked this term only nine times (five times before D10), and with two notable exceptions (in the fragment of *Lazarus* D689 and the Fantasy D940) he used it only early in his career. After D383/1 we can assume that *adagio molto* became his standard expression for this tempo.

11. *Lento:* can be dismissed as a category. Only one example exists (D167/6).

12. *Grave*: Only five examples exist, four of them before D104. Afterwards, Schubert used some form of *Adagio*.

Schubert's fundamental German markings range from *Rasch* or *Sehr Schnell* (*Allegro molto*) to *Sehr Langsam* (*Adagio molto*). We have no German equivalent of *Presto* or *Prestissimo*, because his German markings applied mostly to the songs, which did not move at those extreme speeds. The following concordance is neither all-inclusive nor taxonomically precise; Schubert used many other German terms than we have listed, and sometimes he used the same term in several different contexts.

TABLE III: CONCORDANCE

Allegro vivace to *Allegro molto* : *Sehr schnell, Rasch, Feurig*
Allegro to *Allegro vivace* : *Schnell, Geschwind, Lebhaft, Frisch*
Allegro moderato / Allegro ma non troppo : *Etwas Geschwind*
Allegretto : *Bewegt*
Andante : *Mäßig, Gehend*
Andante molto : *Etwas Langsam* or *Nicht zu langsam* (see Thinking Down, Thinking Up, p. 234)
Adagio : *Langsam*
Adagio molto : *Sehr langsam*

From a purely linguistic point of view, these equivalencies present some problems. *Lebhaft*, for example, is not faster than *Geschwind*, and yet its closest Italian translation is *Vivace*. If Schubert's metronome markings are reliable, then *Mäßig* equals *Andante* instead of *Moderato*. And *Moderato*, as we will see, will turn out to be a modifier rather than a fundamental category. We have not attempted to compare Schubert's German terms with Beethoven's, as we did for the Italian terms. By the end of his life, Beethoven's tempo and character instructions had become so purposefully intricate (Op. 128: *Allegretto: Mit Lebhaftigkeit, jedoch nicht in zu geschwindem Zeitmaße und scherzend vorgetragen*) that Schubert's terminology would seem crude (which it is not) by comparison.

In the course of Schubert's fifteen career years his German terminology, intimately bound up with his non-operatic vocal music, never evolved from its original simplicity. By contrast, his Italian terminology, which he employed for his instrumental music, grew somewhat more sophisticated, if not in individual complexity, at least in variety. His predilection for closely-mixed categories (*Allegretto quasi andantino, Andantino quasi allegretto*, etc.) show his clear intention to refine his tempo wishes, i.e. not to leave them to chance. He introduced at least one new theoretical sub-category, *allegro presto*, which we can place a notch higher than *allegro molto*, but one lower than *presto*. As we explore his metronome markings in relationship to his Italian categories, we will find that the significant overlapping between them represents an even more sophisticated and complex tempo sense than a cursory overview of his terminology might initially have led us to assume.

Thus, Beethoven and Schubert had a common goal: to refine their written tempo and character wishes: the older man motivated probably by many bad performances of his music, the younger perhaps by a growing ambition as a composer of important instrumental works. The metronome, announced in 1813 and warmly supported not only by Beethoven but Schubert's teacher Antonio Salieri as well, was looked upon, at least initially, as a watershed invention. The general musical public was fascinated as well, and expressed itself both for and against the invention. Against it, for example, was G. A. Weber, who in a now-famous *AmZ* article published his objections to the invention, asserting that the traditional string with a weight on the end was far more reliable, not to mention more practical for those who could not afford the new machine. One wonders indeed whether if Weber himself had been included among the honored few who had been offered a metronome for initial trial he might not have supported it, but such, clearly, was not the case. For it, on the other hand, were authors of articles such as in the *AmZ Miszellen* section, wherein the unidentified writer pointed out the international problems of tempo interpretation:

> One notes ... how the tempi of even famous and characteristic pieces are taken in different places! For example, at the Guardason'schen Gesellschaft in Prague I heard Mozart himself rehearse his Overture to *Don Giovanni*. Later I heard it played in Paris, Vienna and Berlin. In Paris they took the Adagio a bit slower, in Vienna significantly faster, and in Berlin almost twice as fast as Mozart had done. In all three places the Allegro was more or less faster as well ... The need for a musical chronometer [Taktmesser] has long been felt.[7]

For better or worse, by the outset of Schubert's career the metronome was in the world to stay. It was not a general panacea, but it offered specific advantages. While a metronome mark was in one way not a completely satisfactory substitute for a categorization such as *Allegro* or *Andante* (which even without modifiers impart character meaning), at least it could give musicians in Prague, Berlin, Vienna, Paris, and even Philadelphia the same starting point for tempo decisions. The size of halls, the capabilities and temperaments of musicians, as well as any modifying instructions by the composer (*con fuoco, moderato*, etc) still played their traditional part in such decisions; but the wide swings described by the *AmZ* author (first quote above) might be avoided. Or was this indeed the case? Perhaps the following account is revealing.

---

[7] *AmZ*, cited in *WamZ* for 1813: 388.

Support for the metronome from Beethoven, the most celebrated living Viennese composer, was important for Maelzel, and, in retrospect, for us as well. But the first person, apparently, to recognize the historical use of the invention was Antonio Salieri, not merely for the preservation of his own intentions, but for that of others as well. His initial impulse was not to mark his own music, but that of two great heroes of the recent past: Gluck and Haydn. This service has yet to receive its proper recognition in recent inquiries into Viennese tempo matters. At the time, it was noted with some surprise and bewilderment:

> Herr Hofkapellmeister Salieri, motivated by his personal respect for the immortal composers Gluck, Händel, Haydn and Mozart, has pledged himself to mark their masterworks with indications taken from Maelzel's metronome. In this way the works can from now on be performed in their proper spirit, communicated to us with a direct knowledge which Maestro Salieri possesses better than anyone else.
>
> [...]
>
> Our readers might consider the extraordinary results of this undertaking. According to Herr Salieri's marking of Haydn's authorized tempo terminology in *The Creation:* the aria "Nun schwanden vor dem heiligen Strahle" is to be taken at 120 quarters to the minute, and the recitative "Im vollen Glanze" at 76 quarters to the minute. What a contrast! How slow the recitative seems, and how fast the aria! Both are marked *Andante alla breve.* Equally unreconciled [*mißlich*], are the choruses "Mit Staunen sieht das Wunderwerk" and "Des Herrn Ruhm,' which are both marked by the whole measure at *Allegro.* But [Herr Salieri] marks the first one 58 and the second one 120 to the minute: thus he means for us to take the tempo of the latter twice that of the former. These two examples should convince us that the greatest task in music today is to undertake a fundamental reform in matters of tempo, in which endeavor we should make use of Maelzel's metronome.[8]

Salieri's results were clearly unexpected, not only in their apparent inconsistencies, but in their absolute values as well. In the Viennese edition of this report the anonymous author remains respectful of the master's markings, but in the almost verbatim reprint in the Leipziger *AmZ* (which perhaps Salieri might not read) he adds the following disclaimer as a footnote:

> Herr Salieri's tempi deviate significantly from those taken by Haydn in these same works, a fact that I know and which others who know me and who also have heard Haydn personally in concert can corroborate.

As we know, Beethoven's metronome markings, too, never have been accepted in full by the performance world, although with the possible exception of the markings for the outer movements of the Piano Sonata in B♭, Op. 106, they are all playable.[9] But in the absence of

---
[8] *WamZ* 629, 1813.
[9] Susan Kagan, the leading authority on the Archduke Rudolph, has offered us a list of metronome markings made by him about the same time that Beethoven made his own. Among them are many markings for tempos which simply cannot be managed even by the greatest virtuosi:

> "Archduke Rudolph (1788-1831), who studied composition with Beethoven from 1804 until 1824, put metronome markings in three of his works, two of which were published by S.A. Steiner & Co. in Vienna : Forty Variations on a Theme by Beethoven (1819), and Sonata for Clarinet and Piano (1822). (The third work, unpublished, is a two-page

conflicting information we must give them our serious consideration. Performers' feelings do not count as "information," although the limits of their capabilities do, perhaps. The burning question concerning both Beethoven and Schubert is: if refinement, i.e. exactitude, were the goal, as apparently it was, why did both composers fail to provide the majority of their works from 1813 forward with metronome markings: especially Beethoven, in the face of his public support for Maelzel's invention? What was the purpose of their continuing experimentation with the vagaries of German and Italian instructions, an experimentation which lasted until the end of their lives? Perhaps by the end of this chapter, after all the evidence has been examined, we will have the basis upon which to approach this question, but to this point we have no reasonable answer.

The following table presents all metronomic markings traditionally associated with Franz Schubert's music:

TABLE IV

1. *Gretchen am Spinnrade* D118 (op. 2) Oct. 1814
    Nicht zu geschwind 6/8: dotted quarter = 72

2. *Schäfers Klagelied* D121 (op. 3/1) Nov. 1814
    Mässig 6/8: eighth = 120

3. *Rastlose Liebe* D138 (op. 5/1) May 1815
    Schnell, mit Leidenschaft 2/4: quarter = 152

4. *Nähe des Geliebten* D162 (op. 5/2b) Feb. 1815
    Langsam, feierlich mit Anmut 12/8: dotted quarter = 50
    [cf: 2a, *Langsam, feierlich mit Anmut* 6/8 Feb. 1815]

Capriccio for piano, ca. 1820). It should be noted that the autographs of all three works show corrections and emendations in Beethoven's hand. The metronome numbers written in by the Archduke range from reasonable (if slightly on the fast side) to virtually unplayable. The M.M. numbers for the first movement in the Clarinet Sonata, for example (Allegro moderato, 4/4: quarter=144) and the third (Adagio, 2/4: eighth = 84) are awfully brisk. The finale, a set of variations, is marked Andantino (4/4): quarter =108, and feels truly like an andantino tempo, with faster markings for some of the variations. In the Forty Variations, however, the tempos as marked require virtuosity beyond the abilities of most pianists. The opening Introduction is marked Adagio (4/4): quarter=84. Its character—ceremonial and filled with dotted rhythms—is belied by the metronome marking, which gives it more the tempo of an allegretto, although it is certainly playable. Similarly, Beethoven's Liedthema "O Hoffnung, O Hoffnung," etc., marked Andante (4/4) is quite fast at quarter =100. The following variations, mostly in 4/4 (a few are in compound meters) are assigned various numbers, from quarter = 96 (a variation based on thirty-second note rhythms) to quarter =104, 112, 116, and 138. Variation 36, a lengthy Adagio, sounds ridiculously hectic at its metronome marking of quarter =88; Variation 37 (Tempo di Marcia) is equally ridiculous at half =104, which is the same number given to Variation 40, the multi-sectioned Finale, marked Allegro agitato. Finally, the closing fugue, marked Allegro moderato assai, is metronomized at quarter =152; playable, but hardly an example of a very moderate Allegro tempo!"

Dr. Kagan assures us that the Archduke Rudoph was not the sort of person or composer to leave such markings to editors or assistants, thus they must come from him personally. And yet the Archduke was an accomplished musician, and would certainly not have wished to confuse other players with impossible demands. This mystery demands a thorough investigation, which unfortunately cannot be accomplished here.

Tempo, Time, and Character 221

5. *Meeres Stille* D216 (op. 3/2b) June 1815
  Sehr langsam, ängstlich ¢ quarter = 72
  [cf: 2a, *Sehr langsam, ängstlich* ¢ June 1815]

6. *Wandrers Nachtlied* ("Der du von...") D224 (op. 4/3) July 1815
  Langsam, mit Ausdruck C: quarter = 50

7. *Der Fischer* D225 (op. 5/3b) n.d.
  Mäßig 2/4: quarter = 60
  [cf: 2a, *Mäßig* 2/4 July 1815]

8. *Erster Verlust* D226 (op. 5/4) July 1815
  Sehr langsam, wehmütig C: quarter = 54

9. *Heidenröslein* D257 (op. 3/3) Aug. 1815
  Lieblich 2/4 : quarter = 64

10. *Erlkönig* D328 (op. 1/4) Oct. 1815?
  Schnell C : quarter = 152

11. *Der König in Thule* D367 (op. 5/5) early 1816?
  Etwas langsam 2/4 : quarter = 66

12. *Jägers Abendlied* D368 (op. 3/4) early 1816?
  Sehr langsam, leise 2/4 : eighth = 63

13. *Der Wanderer* ("Ich komme von...") D489 (op. 4/1c) n.d.
  Sehr langsam ¢ : quarter = 63
  [cf: 4a, 4b (Oct. 1816) *Langsam*]

14. *Am Grabe Anselmos* D504 (op. 6/3a) Nov. 1816
  Langsam 3/4 : quarter = 50
  [cf. 3a: 3/4 *Sehr langsam*]

15. *Die abgeblüthe Linde* D514 (op. 7/1) n.d.
  Mäßig C : quarter = 92

16. *Der Flug der Zeit* D515 (op. 7/2) 1817?
  Etwas geschwind 6/8 : dotted quarter = 112

17. *Der Tod und das Mädchen* D531 (op. 7/3) Feb. 1817
  Mäßig ¢ : half = 54

18. *Memnon* D541 (op. 6/1) March 1817
  Sehr langsam, schwärmerisch ¢ : quarter = 50

19. *Antigone und Oedip* D542 (op. 6/2) March 1817
  Langsam C: quarter = 54

20. *Morgenlied* ("Eh die Sonne...") D685 (op. 4/2) 1820
  Ziemlich langsam ¢ : half = 63

21. *Drang in die Ferne* D770 (op. 71) beginning of 1823 (republished 1827)
  Etwas geschwind 9/8 : dotted quarter = 76

ALFONSO UND ESTRELLA, D732, Sept. 1821 – Feb. 1822

22.   Overture: *Andante* 12/8: eighth = 92
23.   Overture: *Allegro* ¢ : half = 160

24. Overture: *Più mosso* ¢ : whole = 96
25. No. 1: *Allegro giusto* C: quarter = 144
26. No. 2: *Andante molto* C: eighth = 76
27. No. 2: *Larghetto* 6/8: eighth = 108
28. No. 2: *Allegro* C : half = 92
29. No. 3: *Allegro* 3/4: dotted half = 72
30. No. 3: middle section: *Andantino* C : quarter = 100
31. No. 3: *Andante maestoso* C : quarter = 52
32. No. 4: *Andante* ¢ : half = 58
33. No. 4: *Più mosso* C : half = 76
34. No. 5: *Allegro ma non troppo* C : quarter = 126
35. No. 5: *Larghetto* 3/4 : quarter = 80
36. No. 6: *Allegro moderato* C : quarter = 100
37. No. 6: *Più presto* C : half = 104
38. No. 7: *Allegro* 6/8: dotted quarter = 120
39. No. 7: *Allegro moderato* ¢ : half = 120
40. No. 8: *Allegro* C : quarter = 106
41. No. 8: *Allegro giusto* C : quarter = 160
42. No. 9: *Andantino* 3/4 : quarter = 88
43. No. 9: *Allegro* C : quarter = 160
44. No. 9: *Più mosso* C : half = 126
45. No. 10: *Tempo di marcia* C : quarter = 132
46. No. 10: *Andantino* 3/4 : quarter 88
47. No. 10: *Adagio* 2/4 : eighth = 72
48. No. 10: *Allegro assai* C : half = 116
49. No. 10: *Allegro moderato* ¢ : half = 116
50. No. 10: *Più moto* : half = 152
51. No. 11: *Andante con moto* 12/8 : dotted quarter = 66
52. No. 12: *Andantino* C : quarter = 116
53. No. 13: *Un poco più moto* [no marking]
54. No. 13: *Andante* [no marking]
55. No. 14: *Allegro moderato* 3/4 : quarter = 108
56. No. 15: *Andantino* C : quarter = 120
57. No. 16: *Allegro moderato* C : quarter = 138
58. No. 17: *Allegro agitato* ¢ : half = 144
59. No. 17: *Allegro assai* C : half = 104
60. No. 18: *Allegro molto* C : half = 160

Tempo, Time, and Character 223

61. No. 18: *Allegro* C : quarter = 160
62. No. 19: *Allegro molto* C : half = 112
63. No. 20: *Un poco più lento* : quarter = 160
64. No. 20: *Allegro molto vivace* C : half = 112
65. No. 21: *Andantino* 3/4 : quarter = 80
66. No. 22: *Allegro* C (recitative) : half = 88
67. No. 22: *Allegro agitato* 3/4 : quarter = 108
68. No. 22: *Allegro vivace* C : half = 120
69. No. 23: *Allegro* ¢ : half = 160
70. No. 24: *Allegro* ¢ : half = 160
71. No. 25: *Allegro assai* 3/4 : dotted half = 84
72. No. 26: *Allegro molto* ¢ : whole = 84
73. No. 27: *Andante moto* 3/4 : quarter = 84
74. No. 28: *Allegro moderato* C : quarter = 132
75. No. 29: *Allegro assai* ¢ : half = 138
76. No. 30: *Allegro* 6/8 : dotted quarter = 104
77. No. 31: *Allegro moderato* C : quarter = 96
78. No. 31: *Allegro* ¢ : half = 132
79. No. 32: *Allegro agitato* C : quarter = 104
80. No. 33: *Andante* ¢ : quarter = 100 [*GA* shows *Andante* C]
81. No. 33: *Allegro* C : quarter = 112 [*GA* shows *Allegro* ¢ : half = 120]
82. No. 34: *Allegretto* 6/8 : dotted quarter = 63
83. No. 34: *Allegro moderato* (offstage music and recitatives) : quarter = 120
84. No. 35: *a tempo* (Allegro moderato) C : quarter = 120
85. No. 35: *Allegro* C : quarter = 160
86. No. 35: *Andante* C : quarter = 50
87. No. 35: *Allegro molto moderato* : quarter = 84
88. No. 35: *Allegro* C : quarter = 160

DEUTSCHE MESSE D872, Summer or Autumn 1827
89. Zum Eingang: *Mäßig* C : quarter = 60
90. Zum Gloria: *Mit Majestät* C : quarter = 69
91. Zum Evangelium und Credo: *Nicht zu langsam* 6/8 : eighth = 80
92. Zum Offertorium: *Sehr langsam* 3/4 : quarter = 50
93. Zum Sanctus: *Sehr langsam* 3/4 : quarter = 56
94. Nach der Wandlung: *Sehr langsam* C : quarter = 56
95. Zum Agnus Dei: *Mäßig* 6/8 : eighth = 80
96. Schlußgesang: *Nicht zu langsam* 3/4 : quarter = 63
97. Anhang: Das Gebet des Herrn: *Mäßig* 6/8 : eighth = 80

Although the compositions themselves represent a span of about thirteen years, the markings allegedly were made between 1821 and 1827. The large lieder group above, written between 1813 and 1820, was published by Diabelli only in 1821, although some of the songs were copied into the *Liederheft* for J.W. von Goethe in 1816. We do not find metronome markings on the original autographs or in the Liederheft copies; the markings were conceived, most likely, at the time of publication in 1821. Maelzel's metronome had been announced for the market in the fall of 1813 (*Wiener Vaterländische Blätter,* October 13, hereafter *WVB*), but Schubert probably did not use one at that time.

Metronome markings for *Alfonso und Estrella* can be found in the autographs, but they are later additions not in Schubert's hand. They seem to have been accepted as genuine by the scholarly community, the explanation being that Schubert might have sat at the piano, playing through the score, dictating the markings to a friend, perhaps Josef Hüttenbrenner, whose handwriting was the most consistent with that of the markings.[10] Walther Dürr supports the supposed authenticity of the markings through his "red pencil" theory, in which he claims to identify (offering no technical explanation or calligraphic evidence) the actual pencil as the same one used by Schubert elsewhere in the manuscript. Are we to believe that each early nineteenth-century Viennese red pencil somehow left its own unmistakable trace?[11] Another serious problem with this entire line of thinking is that the metronome markings are patently not those of a young man, whether Schubert, Hüttenbrenner or anyone else. Furthermore, they appear to have been made by someone not entirely comfortable with notation, which again eliminates both of these young men. For example, the handwriting of the marking at the beginning of the second act finale

EXAMPLE 6.4

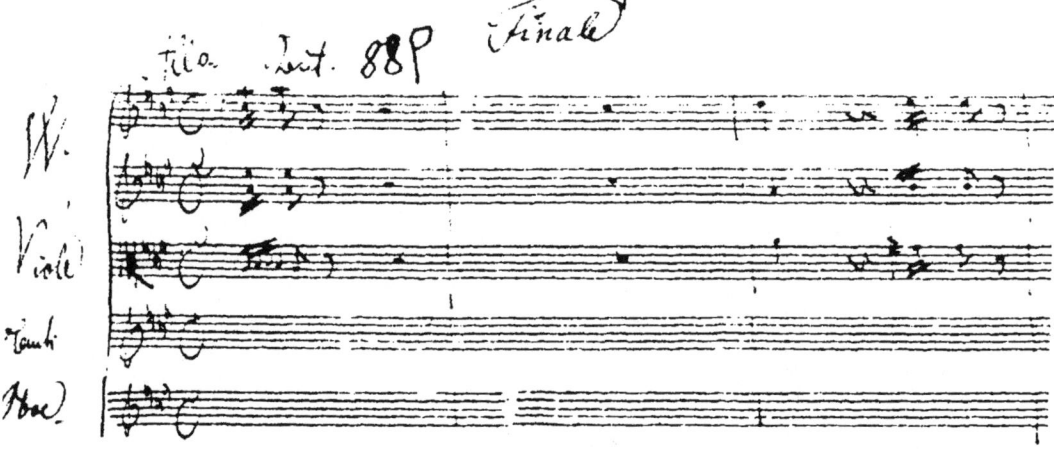

[10] The speculation that Josef Hüttenbrenner was involved comes from Kreißle von Hellborn (Franz Schubert: Vienna, 1865) and is supported by Ernst Hilmar and taken over in the *NSA*. Hüttenbrenner was still alive when von Hellborn's biography first appeared, and could have corroborated the speculation himself. It is interesting that he did not do so.

[11] *NSA* II:6a:xviii.

reveals not only the infirmity of advanced age, but an unfamiliarity with the appropriate direction of the half-note stem, particularly in relation to the opening of this number.

None of the authors who have occupied themselves with the *Alfonso* markings has confronted the most obvious and serious contradiction of their authenticity: the fact that all of these projected tempos in the upper ranges of *Allegro* C, *Allegro* ¢ and *Allegro molto* C are unplayably fast. They are not merely "uncomfortably" fast, as with Beethoven markings, but literally unplayable. A few people have noted that the upper range tempos are somewhat "fast," but no one has come right out and spoken the truth: that they are unrealistic and impossible. Anyone with the inclination to refute this statement might first want to sit at the piano and try playing through nos. 19 and 23 at the speeds marked.[12]

Schubert, who was eager to make a success as an opera composer, was never so witless as to propose tempos that in some cases were more than twice too fast even to manage, much less manage with clarity. We find other hints about the unreliability of these markings in the suspicious frequency of mm = 160 (the uppermost number on the machine), which conjures up a picture of someone with a new toy, *in modo* "machine over man" (Cf. numbers 41, 43, 60, 63, 69, 70, 85, and 88 in the chart above). Nor do the indications always make relative sense: for example, the *Allegro assai* of No. 17 and the *Allegro molto* of No. 18 should not be 56 notches apart:

59.   *Alfonso* No. 17: *Allegro assai* C : $\dotted = 104$

60.   *Alfonso* No. 18: *Allegro molto* C : $\dotted = 160$

The supposition that these markings were made at the time when the opera was being prepared for prospective performance results from retrospective historicism, i.e. from a modern perspective that has been superimposed upon an historic situation. Today's composers indeed provide their music with metronome markings from the outset, and the metronome long has been accepted for this purpose. When Schubert wrote *Alfonso und Estrella*, however, the metronome was still a novelty. Composers did not mark their autographs with metronomic indications for performance; such things were added by the publisher at the time of publication, mostly to increase interest in the item to be sold. Who would have

---

[12] If Dürr's theory is correct, whereby Schubert sat at the piano and played the music while Hüttenbrenner wrote down the metronomic indications, then one or both of them (Schubert and Hüttenbrenner) must have partaken of rather potent drink. If we consider further that at least one of these tempos was apparently mismarked by a copyist (see the violin part reproduced in the *NSA*), we have further cause to reexamine the whole thing from the beginning. If Ernst Hilmar's research is correct, then the handwriting is Hüttenbrenner's indeed. If so, this can only mean that the aging Hüttenbrenner was asked to supply the opera with metronome markings for a projected printing (it would have had to have been for Diabelli) many years after Schubert's death, and furthermore, that Hüttenbrenner did so "in his head" and not at the piano. In recent writings, Peter Brown ("Performance Tradition, Steady and Proportional Tempos, and the First Movements of Schubert's Symphonies" in *Journal of Musicology* 5 (1987): 297, hereafter *JMus*) and Clive Brown ("Schubert's Tempo Conventions" in *Schubert Studies*, ed. Brian Newbould; Aldershot, Ashgate, 1998:3) have accepted Dürr's evidence without qestion, physical impossibilities of performance notwithstanding. Clive Brown (p.3) concludes: "There can be little doubt . . .that the metronome marks derive from Schubert, and that they probably represent his own performance of the opera at the keyboard on a particular occasion."

requested Schubert, who was still relatively unknown and uninfluential, to mark his autograph in such a fashion for a performance? He himself was not in the habit of doing so, not even in his symphonies, or else we would have many more reliable metronomic indications than we do. In view of the complaints about the C-major Symphony raised by the GMF at the first reading, we might have expected to find a difficult tempo marking here and there on that score, or in the parts. But such is not the case. Were opera companies, orchestras, leaders, and singers in those days concerned particularly with "the composer's intentions," especially those of a young, not-so-famous composer? We seriously doubt it. In any case, Schubert would have been on hand in case a tempo needed clarifying.

We reject the *Alfonso* markings with great reluctance, for they would have provided us with an almost secure basis on which to construct a general tempo table for Schubert's works. We are left, then, with the metronome markings in the songs and those in the Deutsche Messe as the basis upon which to derive any absolute tempos for Schubert's works. We shall be able to consider certain metrical modulations or clearly-intended tempo relationships as well, but they will prove to be rare.

Tempo, meter, and character

TYPE A/ TYPE B

In reconstructing Schubert's tempos, we can hardly ignore the intimate and variable play between marked tempo and meter, plus the apparent character. We say "intimate", because we can determine an absolute tempo for a movement only in the context of its metrical organization and accentuation. We say "variable," because the faster the basic beat involved in the long path from *Largo* to *Presto*, the more we must distinguish between types, even where movements are marked identically. To wit, among the movements Schubert has marked with *Adagio* or *Langsam* we find few dramatic differences in expressive types, and thus also not in speed. But on the other end of the scale, between movements with virtually the same instructions (cf. *Allegro con brio, Allegro molto, Allegro vivace*) we find fundamental differences in type and tempo requirements. For example, although the finale of the Piano Sonata in A minor D784 and the scherzo of the Piano Sonata in A minor D845 bear identical meter and tempo indications (*Allegro vivace* in 3/4), they are not to be taken at the same tempo:

EXAMPLE 6.5a/b
a. Piano Sonata in A minor, D784/3: Finale: *Allegro vivzce,* 3/4

Tempo, Time, and Character

b. Piano Sonata in A minor, D 845/3: Scherzo: *Allegro vivace*, 3/4

Measured at the same denomination the finale of D784 is distinctly more measured in character and thematic content (cf. the second group) than the scherzo of D845, not to mention the impossibility of taking the last bars of D784 in one! The finale of D784, then, is taken at three to the measure, and the scherzo of D845 in one. At the higher end of the tempo chart (beginning with *Andantino*) we will find such basic types, which we shall designate as A and B. Thus in the following charts, "type A" movements are felt according to the metrical unit given, and "type B" according to the next general unit. For example, in 3/4 type A moves by the quarter and type B by the dotted half. In 2/4 type A moves by the quarter and type B by the half, etc.

The duple meters: ¢¢ , ¢ (variant: 6/4), 2/4 (variant: 6/8)

¢¢

This special meter occurs only once in Schubert's music, in the G♭ Impromptu. It can have been meant only to combine the idea of extreme internal speed (12 eighths to the beat) with an overall structural feeling of *Andante* (the long-short-short pattern in whole and half notes). The publisher, Tobias Haslinger, made a note to transpose the work to G major and cut its meter by half, and indeed it was later brought out in such a version. This supposed simplification (clearly a bone for the public) works against everything that Schubert took such obvious pains to achieve. Ironically, because of the orientation provided by the spaces between black key groups, the piece is actually easier to play in the original key than in G major.[13] The work is a duple-meter Type A movement, despite the preponderance of triplets. The prescribed meter of any Schubert work remains the dominant one, and all performance choices must reflect this fact. Thus, the basic beat speed for a work in C with many triplets (*Erlkönig*, for example) is faster than for a work in 12/8 marked with the identical Italian or German tempo instruction.[14]

¢

A fundamental question concerning the difference between *Alla breve* and 4/4 has occupied musicians involved with all modern artistic periods, to wit: is ¢ really twice the speed of C, is its basic beat only somewhat faster than C , or is the difference merely one of accentuation, phrasing and syntax? Actually, such distinctions are more appropriately applied to ¢ as opposed to 2/4, i.e. between two kinds of duples instead of between a duple and a quadruple construction. Comparing duple constructions, then, where the fundamental beat remains in two (instead of compressed into one, as in certain fast finale types), the beat speed is identical for identical markings. For example, between *Allegro molto* in ¢ and *Allegro molto* in

---

[13] The G-major version later achieved enough currency that the chief critic for the *New York Times* (hereafter *NYT*), Olin Downes once allowed the following remarks to appear in print.

> ". . . The little fatbacked, be-spectacled Schubert, whose shyness was an agony, produced these small pieces with the same spontaneity that he composed his songs, and with if anything less intellectual responsibility, being freed here from conformance to any poetic text. The first of the Impromptus of Opus 90 is the sustained melody in the key of G major (outrageously transcribed in one edition to the wholly inappropriate key of G-flat major) which could not be simpler in its form or harmonic facture."

This delightful blunder is excerpted from Downes's review of a Horowitz concert in 1948, and we are indebted to Dr. Susan Kagan for drawing our attention to it. Kagan comments: "The combination of ignorance, pretentiousness, and condescension displayed by the eminent critic is truly astonishing. By 1948, when these notes were written, the Breitkopf und Härtel *Gesamtausgabe*, with the Impromptu correctly published in Schubert's original key of G♭ had been in existence for more than half a century, ample time for him to know the sad history of the publisher Haslinger's outrageous mutilation of the Impromptu in the first edition in changing both the key and the time signature, presumably to simplify it." ("Kuriosa", in *Die Brille* 27, 2002).

[14] The rightful dominance of the stipulated meter is also the fundamental analytical argument against assimilation, as it has mistakenly been applied, for example, in the C-minor Impromptu against the left-hand triplets when they enter.

Tempo, Time, and Character

2/4 (where not taken in one), the basic beat speed remains relatively constant even though in ¢, of course, the actual quarter note speed has been doubled. As did most modern composers, Schubert chose ¢ or 2/4 (or even C) according to the character of a work, and particularly according to its harmonic motion.

It is important to concentrate on beat speeds instead of individual value speeds: for example, if we compared only the value speeds (say, of a quarter note) in *Der Fischer* D225 (2/4 *Mäßig,* quarter=60) and *Meeres Stille* D216 (¢ *Sehr langsam, ängstlich,* quarter =72), we would find the value speed of the latter actually faster than that of the former. The relative beat speeds of these two works is correct, however. In all cases Schubert (and certainly Beethoven) marked his tempos according to character and fundamental beat. For this reason many of the tempo charts of abstract values that we find in various nineteenth-century treatises are useless. Hummel's chart is slightly more sophisticated (see below), for he gives examples of value speeds in the context of meters. Unfortunately, he appears to

EXAMPLE 6.6
Hummel's Metronome Chart

Nahmen der Autoren.	Ursprüngliche Bezeichnung des Stücks	Zeitmass nach des Autors Willen und Angabe gemäss dem Metronom.		Im Zeitmass.
bei Paer	*Allegro moderato*	♩ -	50 Grade	C
" Paer	*Allegro moderato*	♩ -	80	C
" Mehul	*Allegro moderato*	♩ -	72	C
" Mehul	*Allegro moderato*	♩ -	88	C
" Clementi	*Allegro*	♩ -	54	C
" Clementi	— — — —	♩ -	50	C
" Cherubini	— — — —	♩ -	112	C
" Cherubini	— — — —	♩ -	126	C
" Cherubini	— — — —	♩ -	72	C
" Mehul	— — — —	♩ -	96	C
" Berton	*Allegro molto*	♩ -	176	C
" Spontini	*Presto*	♩ -	72	C
" Spontini	— — — —	♩ -	88	C
" Beethoven	— — — —	♩ -	152	C
" Beethoven	— — — —	♩ -	176	C
" Beethoven	— — — —	♩ -	224	C
" Clementi	— — — —	♩ -	96	C
" Cherubini	*Andantino*	♩ -	76	3/4
" Cherubini	— — — —	♩ -	164	3/4
" Cramer	*Moderato*	♩ -	63	3/4
" Cramer	— — — —	♩ -	116	3/4
" Cramer	*Allegro non tanto*	♩ -	138	3/4
" Cramer	*Presto*	♩ -	138	3/4
" Cramer	*Moderato*	♩ -	100	3/4
" Cramer	— — — —	♪ -	258	3/4
" Viotti	*Andante*	♪ -	52	3/8
" Berton	— — — —	♪ -	152	3/8
" Nicolo	*Andantino*	♩. -	52	6/8
" Catel	— — — —	♩. -	126	6/8
" Paer	*Andante*	♩. -	50	6/8
" Berton	— — — —	♩. -	100	6/8
" Cramer	*Più tosto moderato*	♩. -	92	6/8
" Cramer	*Allegro agitato*	♩. -	66	6/8
" Paer	*Lento*	♪ -	120	6/8
" Paer	*Andante*	♪ -	120	6/8
" Paer	— — — —	♪ -	112	6/8
" Berton	— — — —	♪ -	300	6/8

have been quite careless in preparing his chart; the speeds for Beethoven, which he certainly could have checked against the latter's own printed lists in the Steiner booklets, are simply wrong.[15] For example, the MM mark Presto: "224" in 𝄴 comes, we might assume, from the Septet, where it does not apply to the half note, but to the quarter!

2/4 (Type A: ♩)

A measure in 2/4 is not just half of a measure in 4/4, for if so it would have a strong first beat and a weak second beat. In A types the second beats receive almost as much stress as do the first, and in some cases equal stress. Schubert exploits this possibility in movements such as the *Allegro moderato* of the A-minor String Quartet D804 or the *Allegretto* of the *Divertissement à l'hongroise* D818:

EXAMPLES 6.7a/b
a.

b.

2/4 (Type B: ♩)

Here the second beat stress of Type A is dropped in favor of gliding lightly over an entire measure and sometimes even a group of measures (in which case even the first beat stresses are reduced as well) in a significantly faster tempo. For comparison we might take the finales of the *Grand Duo* Sonata D812 and the A-minor Piano Sonata D845, both marked *Allegro vivace*:

---

[15] *Bestimmung des musikalischen Zeitmasses nach Mälzel's Metronom* (First and Second Installments: Vienna, 1817)

Tempo, Time, and Character 231

EXAMPLE 6.8a/b

a. IV. Allegro vivace

b. IV. Rondo: Allegro vivace

6/8 (♩.)

The absolute tempo of a passage in 6/8 marked in any category from *Presto* to *Adagio* is meant by definition to be taken about a third slower than if it were a passage of 2/4, even if the latter were to contain triplets. The same comparative statement can be made about 9/8 as opposed to 3/4 and 12/8 as opposed to ₵. The reason is obvious: these uneven meters and analogues have one more eighth note per beat. The tempo range of the 6/8 meter is quite wide. Slower examples feature two almost equal stresses per measure, similar to the Type A cousin in 2/4. They might be illustrated with the finale *Allegro* of the A-major Sonata D664:

EXAMPLE 6.9

Allegro

6/8 (Type B: 𝅗𝅥.)

Here the speed and accentuation favor the full measure, as in movements such as the finale of the D-minor Quartet, "Death and the Maiden," or the finale of the posthumous C-minor Sonata, below. Of course, we find the B types almost exclusively in the upper ranges of the tempo spectrum.

EXAMPLE 6.10

The triple meters: 3/4 (variant: 9/8), 3/8 (3/2 is rare as a main meter indication)

3/4 (Type A: 𝅘𝅥)

What we have said about Types A and B in 2/4 applies equally to 3/4. Here, of course, Type A has a typical stress pattern of 1,3,2 in descending order of strength. The scherzo *Allegro vivace* of the D-major Piano Sonata D850 falls decidedly into this category, limited in speed because of its figuration, ornamentation (m. 3) and its heavy accentuation:

EXAMPLE 6.11

3/4 (Type B: 𝅗𝅥.)

Here the stress pattern drops any emphasis on beats 2 and 3, and sometimes even on beat 1 in the context of a group of measures. The Scherzo of the *Grand Duo* Sonata D812 is a good example:

EXAMPLE 6.12

Tempo, Time, and Character   233

9/8 (𝅗𝅥.)

In 9/8 (and in 3/4 with a basic triplet analog, such as in *Ungeduld* D795/7) we find mostly Type A movements.

3/8 (TYPE A: ♪)

This meter lends itself naturally to Type B (who would want to go to the trouble of writing out the 32nds and 64ths that might characterize a Type A movement in this meter?) And yet, we find at least one solid Type A among the instrumental works, the *Andantino* of the A-major Sonata for Violin and Piano D574:

EXAMPLE 6.13

Naturally, in the slowest tempo categories, only Type A is possible, and in the fastest categories, only Type B. In the middle categories (*Andantino* and *Andante*), both types are possible.

3/8 (TYPE B: 𝅘𝅥.)

In the *Andante con moto* D759 (equivalent to an *Andantino*) of the *Unfinished* Symphony Schubert left a marvelous example of a Type B, to be taken *quasi* in one. This movement, along with the first movement (also to be taken *quasi* in one), is one of the most misunderstood pieces in the orchestral repertoire, premiered at a time in the nineteenth century when "philosophically slow" was all the rage, particularly for the minor keys. In a faster tempo a good example of Type B is the finale of the A-minor Piano Sonata D537:

EXAMPLE 6.14

The quadruple meters: 4/2 (rare, no known variant), 4.4 (variant: 12/8)

𝄴 (𝅘𝅥)

The syntax of 𝄴 is quite different, of course, from that of either 2/4 or 2/2. Nevertheless, the value speed of a quarter in 𝄴 and 2/4 is the same except where 2/4 is to be taken in one (mostly in fast finales). The normal stress pattern of ȼ in Schubert is the same as that in all Viennese classical music: in descending order of strength, beats 1, 3, 2, 4.

$$12/8 \; (\text{♩.})$$

Here we find exclusively Type A works, such as the Overture to *Alfonso und Estrella,* with its spurious metronome marking of ♪ = 92 (which is far too slow). In this opening Schubert has provided extra stresses on the third beats, which have little purpose if the tempo is taken so slowly as to lose the perceptual grasp of entire measures.

EXAMPLE 6.15
Alfonso Overture incipit

Schubert's character modifiers (*espressivo, maestoso, sostenuto, furioso, spiritoso, con fuoco, con brio, gemäßigt, mit Gefühl, ruhig,* etc.) are numerous and clearly influential upon his tempos, but, with several exceptions, they do not define fundamental categories. These modifiers are difficult to rank and not all of them can be taken at face value. The "*agitato*" of *Allegro agitato,* for example, is often mistaken as a call for increased speed, but appears in fact to be a limiter — reflecting an increased internal activity in small values. The "*giusto*" of *Allegro giusto* is not even a tempo modifier, but merely a call for strictness. The same problems and conditions hold for Schubert's German markings.

Among the exceptions mentioned above are the "*vivace*" of *Allegro vivace,* the "*spirito*" of *Allegro con spirito,* the "*brio*" of *Allegro con brio* and the "*fuoco*" of *Allegro con fuoco.* These all seem to belong to the same category as *Allegro molto* and figure significantly among his movements—typically in fast menuets, scherzos and finales—although as modifiers they have to do with character. Linguistically, the German equivalent of *Vivace* is *Lebhaft* (sometimes *Frisch*), which in Schubert's German hierarchy appears to constitute a fundamental category as well. In that *Vivace* is actually short for *Allegro vivace,* it is necessarily faster than *Allegro. Lebhaft* or *Frisch,* on the other hand, is itself a fundamental conception, equivalent to *Geschwind (Allegro),* and it carries its own modifiers. Schubert confines himself to *Etwas lebhaft (Die Forelle)* and *Ziemlich lebhaft (Der Musensohn),* which limit its speed. That *Frisch* can be viewed as a parallel category with its own modifiers, can be seen, for example, in *Der Alpenjäger (Frisch, doch nicht zu schnell).*

Thinking down, thinking up

Having asserted so often throughout this book that Schubert's thinking and notation was and is far more specific and informative than the musical world traditionally imagines, we encounter one decidedly unhelpful habit whereby he reveals his concerns with fine-tuning

Tempo, Time, and Character 235

a tempo (*Con moto, Moderato, Molto moderato, Ziemlich schnell, Nicht zu langsam, Nicht zu geschwind,* etc.) but fails to give us the main tempo cagetory itself (*Allegro, Andante, Frisch, Lebhaft,* etc.). Taken alone, just how fast is "*con moto*" or "*nicht zu geschwind*"?

Among modern musicians, such markings are often believed to represent certain ineffable categories that had meaning to Schubert, but which now cannot be placed exactly in the tempo hierarchy.[16] Thus their true determination would appear to fall chiefly into the domain of the intuition. This assumption, however, is merely another unwarranted bid for more autonomy on the part of the modern performer, for at the moment that a choice is made (no matter how) and the music begins, all mystery vanishes: the tempo is indeed measurable. It seems clear that Schubert was either "thinking down" from some higher category (in the latter case it didn't have to be *Geschwind, per se)* or "thinking up" from some lower category (probably not from *Langsam*, but possibly from *Mäßig*, or equally possibly from *Geschwind*).

The most problematic of these cases tend to be those in the German language, in which Schubert never really developed an intricate tempo hierarchy. Where Italian instructions are involved, Schubert's "half meanings" are easy enough to decipher, for in this language the tempo hierarchy long had been established. If Schubert added a novelty here and there (*Allegro presto,* etc.) or left out a basic instruction ([?——] *con moto*), we still have enough information from movement placement, character, and from the instruction itself to determine the level and direction (down or up) from which he was thinking. We rarely see the instruction *Allegro con moto*, but often have seen *Andante con moto,* and so our probabilities concerning the D-major Piano Sonata D850/3 are easily determinable. Likewise, we rarely see the instruction *Andante moderato* (Schubert uses *Andante molto*), but we often have seen *Allegro moderato.* Thus we are well on the way toward a decision about the opening of the B♭ Sonata D960, where *the Molto moderato* is nothing more mysterious or precious than *Allegro molto moderato,* the more so because it is a large opening movement with Sonata-allegro characteristics.[17]

Schubert's German language instructions are more problematic because they apply mostly to lieder and other vocal works, each of which is singular in nature (i.e. they have no set contexts, and are text-dependent as well). This statement is true occasionally even for apparently standard terms such as *Mäßig* (which from the pedagogical sources we know as the equivalent of *Andante*). For example, in TableV, below, we have placed three movements (two marked "*Mäßig*" and one marked "*Nicht zu langsam*") in the *Sehr langsam* category, because their metronomic speeds and the fact that they are in 6/8 (i.e., slightly

---

[16] In addition to the above, we find oddities such as *Unruhig, klagend. Im Zeitmaße wachsend bis zur Haltung* (D196), which, like the marking in Beethoven's *So oder so* attest to Schubert's ingenuity but which have no bearing on or relationship to the basic categories.

[17] *Alfonso* No. 6 opens with *Moderato* followed by *Allegro moderato* (♩=100), a juxtaposition that would imply that *Moderato* alone was an independent marking. Here, however, Schubert refers to a difference in character: the first section is a recitative, requiring freedom of movement, followed by the same basic tempo in a stricter setting.

slower than their cousins in 2/4) demanded this decision. Thus in these special cases, *Nicht zu langsam* and *Mäßig* are relative to *Sehr Langsam (Adagio / Adagio molto)*.

TABLE V

2/4: *Jägers Abendlied* D368 (*Sehr langsam, leise,* ♩ = 31.5)

6/8: Messe D872, Zum Agnus Dei (*Mäßig,* ♩. = 26.7)

6/8: Messe D872, Anhang: Das Gebet des Herrn (*Mäßig,* ♩. = 26.7)

6/8: Messe D872, Zum Evangelium und Credo (*Nicht zu langsam,* ♩. =26.7)

> Note to the reader: The rather unusual-looking quantifications shown here and throughout (31.5, 26.7, etc) are expressed in these forms by the author and not by Schubert. The actual numbers with which Schubert expressed his metronome markings are unimportant; they have no bearing on the character or meter of given works. Of essence was the actual speed. Therefore, for comparative purposes, we have reduced all speeds to that of the quarter or dotted quarter note.

Much as we can learn or deduce about Schubert's written character indications, we still must look beyond them into the internal character of his thematic materials in choosing absolute speeds. The verbal instructions can be helpful, of course, but then again perhaps not. How could we choose a speed on the basis of a confusing instruction such as in the *Wanderer* Fantasy's first-movement: *Allegro con fuoco ma non troppo* (is this *Allegro* with "limited fire", or is it "limited" *Allegro* with fire)? In this work the thematic *Gestalt* (determined by accentuation, phrasing, syntax, plus the lack of motoric inner notes) points decidedly to a conception in half-values. Schubert marked the movement in ₵, however, and added *ma non troppo*. Nevertheless, the intended absolute speed of the quarter is clearly faster than in the last movement, an *Allegro*, also in ₵. The opening of the last movement shows no value smaller than an eighth note, and from a purely technical point of view the entire movement can be played faster than the first movement (a fact which many pianists seek to use to advantage, often as not to divert the listener's attention from the problems which he or she has had with the octaves at the end of the first movement).[18] The pianist who does so, however, is mistaken. For one thing, the articulation and accentuation of the second measure of the finale show clearly that the basic beat is in four. More importantly, the opening page of this movement is fugal, and thus vocal or horizontal in nature. As we might expect from an early nineteenth-century fugal movement, the tremendous accumulation of tension at the end depends not only upon the old stretto methods (confluence of voices, more frequent entrances of motives, etc.) but also upon a new use of accentuation and dynamic resources. Speed itself (*à la* the then-popular Rossini finale) was not a factor

---

[18] We reject the old conservatory rule of thumb which still provides so many teachers and performers with pat answers: "Look through the score, seek out the smallest denomination, and select your tempo to make that denomination comfortable to perform." The basic stance of a classical movement is determined at the outset. Afterwards it can do no harm for the performer to leaf through and find out what he or she is up against (cf. the octaves at the end of the first movement of the *Wanderer* Fantasy) but the process in reverse is merely self-serving.

for potency. In any case, the resultant sense of closure in the simple *Allegro* is more satisfying by leagues.[19]

In choosing absolute speeds for his works, Schubert, too, must have made similar analyses, although more instantaneous, surely, than ours. First, we know that he did not calculate his few metronome markings at the time of composition. Thus he chose them not in the same heat of inspiration in which he probably chose his original tempo and character instructions, but now rather as an observer of his own works. (This is surely true of the songs, and possibly of the Deutsche Messe as well.) He would have noted his own verbal instructions and the meter of each work immediately, of course, but it is unlikely that even in haste he would have made metronome choices based solely upon these factors. More likely, he was obliged to appraise the internal character of each work, its *Gestalt,* concentrating particularly on the opening material.

Of all the music we examine in this chapter, probably the Deutsche Messe D872 affords the clearest representation of character/ tempo relation verified in the verbal/ metronomic indications. As in much church music this work is three-speed in nature, the liveliest tempo assigned to the Gloria (*Mit majestät,* ♩= 69). The 6/8, 9/8, and 12/8 sections are marked with middling tempos (*Mäßig*). Most of the rest lies around a common tempo of about 50 to the beat, with the instructions *Langsam* or *Sehr langsam*. All of these tempos are ponderous, of course, befitting the solemn nature of the service. In addition to character, of course, a purely external reason for the relatively slow tempos of Schubert's masses in general concerns the acoustics of church architecture, which he clearly included in his calculations. Noting, then, that Schubert's liturgical music flows according to its own rules of tempo, we must acknowledge the resultant skew when comparing the tempos of the Deutsche Messe to those of the songs.

In terms of absolute speed, the lieder have their oddities as well, which we will examine shortly. First we must extend our discussion of musical character, examining the effects of contrasting musical affects and thematic areas on tempo.

Tempo fluctuation

The widespread characterization of Franz Schubert as a classic-romanticist, while not unwarranted, has brought with it certain performance problems, particularly some unclear principles concerning the maintenance of a basic tempo once established. The problem reveals itself in three specific areas: in romantic structural devices, in contrasting thematic

---

[19] In a 1985 dissertation, *Tempobezeichnungen in Franz Schuberts Liedern,* Ruth Schilz-Storck devotes a full chapter, the largest single section in her work, to relationships between tempo and character in the Diabelli lieder. Her goal is to prove that Schubert changed his verbal tempo indications to match the new internal *Gestalt* and/or affects of some alternate settings of his songs. Her basic assumption may be flawed, however, as evidenced by the number of Schubert's alternative settings (the majority) for which the tempo indications remain the same as in the older versons. The most celebrated example must be *Erlkönig* D 328, where in the piano part Schubert actually changed the triplet affect in order to make it possible to maintain his tempo! We must not second-guess Schubert's creative process, but allow him to change his mind about tempo as he will. Our task as performers is exactly the opposite: to find those tempos "from scratch." From this viewpoint, of course, Schulz-Storck's chapter makes provocative reading.

or affective regions of instrumental music and pictorial lieder accompaniments, and in the concept and application of *rubato*. The last of these areas involves only momentary, localized effects, discussed separately in Ch. IV along with other micro-rhythmic questions.

The lingering notion, still held by many professional musicians, that "classicism" (whatever that may be) involves an almost metronomic regularity of forward motion, contrasted with the supposed flexibility and freedom of "romanticism," has done enormous damage to Schubert's music in performance.[20] Anyone who has ever attempted to clock the speed of a performance of a Baroque or Classical work with the metronome knows that even the most controlled interpretation produces merely an impression of regularity. This impression masks a continuous and natural process of bunching and thinning out of the artificial divisions of temporal flow, which can be confirmed only theoretically by devices such as pendula or metronomes. It is the impression, then, rather than the supposed regularity itself, which is fundamental to the artistic pose known as musical "classicism."

The impression of regularity makes a surprisingly generous allowance for those habitual devices which belong naturally to music-making: accentuation, agogics, surprise attacks, *noti agitati,* slightly-pushed *crescendos* / slightly-pulled *decrescendos,*[21] ornaments which cannot be played strictly within the meter, physical breathing, etc. In the hands of judicious players and singers, the classical impression allows also for subtle kinds of structural delineation ("turning a phrase" or "turning a corner," as musicians put it), and even for *tempo rubato* of the proper sort (Ch. IV). For certain works, composers (Schubert among them) minimized the give-and-take of such effects with the simple marking, *giusto* (*Tempo giusto, Allegro giusto*, etc.), imparting thereby a certain strictness to the impression of regularity.

We move into the realm of romanticism not through the amplification, expansion, or exaggeration of the devices mentioned above, as is popularly believed and practiced. The exaggeration of almost any one of these devices damages the impression of classical regularity, which remained crucial to music long after the death of Franz Schubert. In order to clarify this statement, we shall somewhat widen the scope of our discussion.

---

[20] The idea can be traced to Johann Joachim Winckelmann's (1717–1768) metaphor of the ocean, whose calm depths (representing the fundamental classicism of the Greeks) remained undisturbed by the raging surface of modern culture (*Sturm und Drang*).*Gedanken über die Nachahmung der Griechischen Wercke in der Mahlerey und Bildhauer-Kunst* (1754): Das allgemeine vorzügliche Kennzeichen der Griechischen Meisterstücke ist eine edle Einfalt, und eine stille Grösse, so wohl in der Stellung als in Ausdruck. So wie die Tiefe des Meers allzeit ruhig bleibt, die Oberfläche mag noch so wüten, eben so zeiget der Ausdruck in den Figuren der Griechen bey allen Leidenschaften eine grosse und gesetzte Seele.

[21] Ries tells us that Beethoven maintained steady tempos, although he occasionally introduced *ritards* and *accelerandos* for expressive purposes: "He played this last rondo (C-major Concerto), in fact, with an expression peculiar to himself. In general he played his own compositions very freakishly, holding firmly to the measure, however, as a rule and occasionally, but not often, hurrying the tempo. At times he would hold the tempo back in his *crescendo* with *ritardando*, which made a very beautiful and highly striking effect. [Thayer/Forbes: 367] Czerny tells us that "extraordinary as his playing was when he improvised, it was frequently less successful when he played his printed compositions, for, as he never had patience or time to practice, the result would generally depend on accident or his mood..." [ibid: 368–9] Nor do we find evidence that Beethoven encouraged voluntary tempo deviations in the playing of his students.

Tempo, Time, and Character

As we know, the extreme intellectuality of the romantic generations (we speak of the gamut, from the literary figures of the early 1790s through the painters and composers of the early mid-1800s) relied heavily on precepts of classicism to provide a context for their new aesthetics. One might go so far as to say, even, that classicism itself was a romantic concept. In music, the impression of a regular metrical context associated with that classicism, then, remained vital and irreplaceable even to the young composers of the 1830s. This was true whether, as with Mendelssohn, a new tonal and coloristic language was merely superimposed upon that regularity; or whether, as with Schumann, Berlioz or Chopin, it became the contextual foil for sudden, irrational flights of fancy. Perhaps one of the strongest supporting arguments for this point of view is the marked increase in notated tempo fluctuations that sprang up in the decade following Schubert's death. Compositionally, both approaches grew out of the music of Beethoven and Schubert, but we cannot say the same for the performance habits of the new generation.[22]

For geographic reasons, Schubert's emerging romanticism, like Beethoven's, developed somewhat independently from the literary and painterly context of German romanticism.[23] But in both developments, the essential difference between "classicism" and "romanticism" had to do with the dramatic intrusion and superimposition of a new experiential meaning upon formerly abstract forms, producing new allegory as well as new structure. Beethoven and Schubert knew the German romantic literature, but probably not the painting. When Beethoven conceived the fragmented opening of the Sixth Symphony, he was almost certainly unaware, for example, of similar fragments (see Plates III–V, Ch. II), created by his contemporary, the North German painter Caspar David Friedrich.

EXAMPLE 6.16
Beethoven, opening measures of the *Pastorale* Symphony

The opening measures of Beethoven's symphony do not constitute an introduction to or preparation for the movement. They are a section of the work, theoretically already in

---

[22] The only major figure among the new romantic generation who possibly might have heard Beethoven play was Liszt in his extreme youth. In any case, Beethoven would not have been in his prime as a player at that point. Stories to the effect that Beethoven recognized the young Liszt's talent warmly do not make sense: Beethoven was completely deaf by the time he was said to have heard the boy. And as far as we know, no major figure of the new generation heard Schubert play or sing.

[23] A prime reason for this isolation was the heavy literary censorship imposed on both native writers and the distribution of foreign publications in Vienna in the late eighteenth century and the first half of the nineteenth.

motion. Just as Friedrich painted beyond the internal borders of his pictures, Beethoven composed beyond the sonic "border" of his own canvas (represented by the *fermata*). The small bit at the edge of the main work that we can see (Friedrich, left and right beyond the tree trunks, see Plate III) or hear (Beethoven, the first four measures) constitutes an inner frame created from a section of the work itself. In Beethoven's case, then, any *ritard* into the *fermata* would create merely the effect of an artifical preparation, rather than a true and rather startling effect of the frame.[24]

As we pointed out in Chapter II, Beethoven and Schubert also used a device now known as a "curtain" to open certain movements. In Example 2.10 we showed the device as used in the G-major Quartet D887, wherein the clearly set-off curtain fulfills its metaphorical function and is withdrawn. We also showed a type represented by the C-minor and B-minor Symphonies, wherein the curtain is reused for partitioning in the movement itself (Examples 2.11a/c). Here we can point to a related structural device, revealed in the openings of the first movements of the C-major Quintet and the G-major String Quartet, and in this case Schubert, not Beethoven, was the innovator.[25] Through manipulation of the harmonic motion, Schubert imposes the spirit of a slow introduction directly onto the main material of the *Allegro* with no tempo or meter change. Notice, at the beginning of the G-major Quartet, the harmony changes only every several measures (taking the tonic minor, of course, as part of the tonic complex; and the dominant minor similarly). Suddenly in m. 15, where the simulated main group begins, the harmonies not only begin to change once per measure but they move into unfamiliar territory as well (dropping to F major and eventually E♭ major in a whole-step sequence): all in all, a stunning effect:

EXAMPLE 6.17
D887

---

[24] Hermann Scherchen's recording of the Sixth Symphony with the Vienna State Opera Orchestra, released on MCF CD and Millenium, was one of the first to dispense with the *ritard*. Also available is a recording made in Lugano for Westminster in which Scherchen rehearses this symphony (in Italian), making a strict commentary to his players about maintaining the opening tempo.

[25] For extended discussion see David Montgomery. "For Once: Beethoven in the Light of Schubert? Realizing the Implications of Meter and Tempo Proportions between Slow Introduction and Allegro Sections" in *Die Brille* 25 (2000): 51-66.

Tempo, Time, and Character

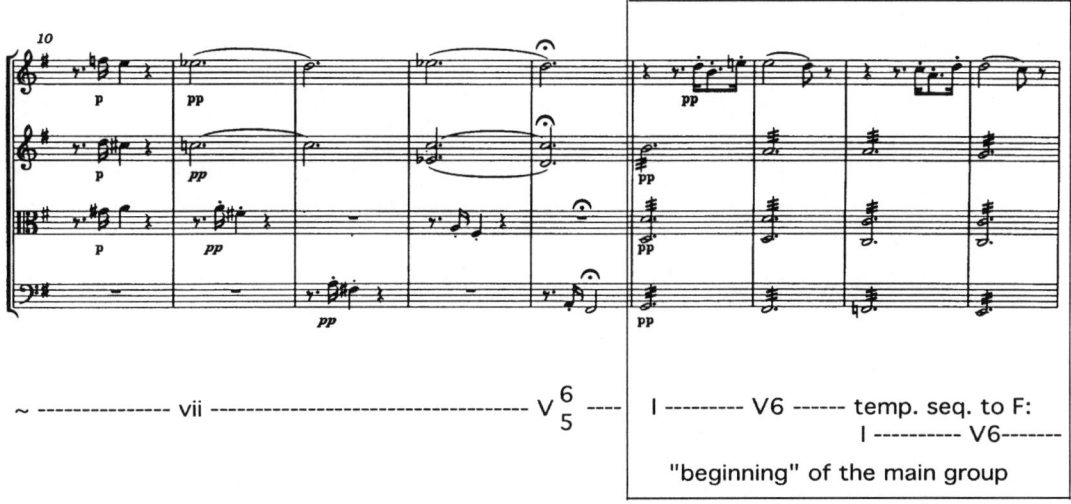

The Quintet mixes this technique of slow harmonic motion to simulate a slow tempo, with long pedal tones. After a long pedal on the dominant note "G" we arrive at the "main group," the simulation of which is strengthened through increased rhythmic activity in C-major:

EXAMPLE 6.18
String Quintet D956, opening

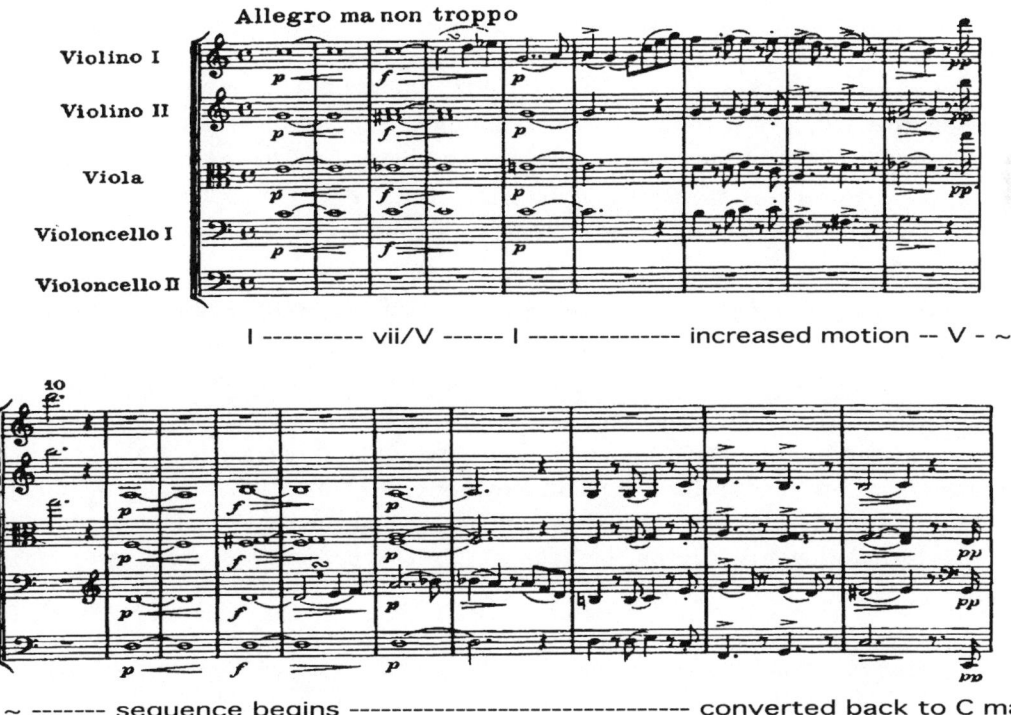

In these openings, any failure to achieve and maintain the main tempo directly at the outset would destroy the effect. Schubert had mastered other romantic structural techniques as well, such as the flashback. The end of the first movement of the C-major Symphony, D944, provides the best-known example (see p. 243). Actually, some measures before this flashback occurs, Schubert calls for a slight *accelerando*, but the general spirit of alla breve shared by the opening and the final quotation is not disturbed. The traditional voluntary reduction of speed for this passage is antithetical to the overpowering sense of thematic closure provided by the citation from the opening *Andante*.

The cause for the widespread misunderstanding of this passage lies partly in an initial failure to achieve a proper 1:2 relationship between the *Andante* and the following *Allegro ma non troppo*.[26] Many conductors still try to compensate for the disparity through a sudden drop in tempo to match the *Andante*. In such cases the lack of the 2:1 relationship has already forced the conductor to initiate an artificial *accelerando* into the *Allegro ma non troppo*. Another reason for the final tempo drop (usually accompanied by a rather heavy accentuation), however, lies in the belief that romantic elements—in this case the disruptive flashback—must be given special treatment, i.e. to be brought to the conscious attention of the listener by overflowing its written boundaries. Thereby, not only the "classical" content is suspended, but the "romantic" effect with it.

[26] See Jürgen Neubacher, "Zur Interpretationsgeschichte der Andante Einleitung aus Schuberts großer C Dur Sinfonie (D944)" in *Neue Zeitschrift für Musik* 1550 (1989, hereafter *NZM*): 15-21; and David Montgomery, "Franz Schubert's Music in Performance."(*CCS*)

Tempo, Time, and Character

EXAMPLE 6.19
C-major Symphony, movt.1, end

As in the case of structural devices, the problem of voluntary tempo changes for contrasting affective regions appears to be a matter of conditioning and tradition as well. It arises almost automatically in the treatment of trios, not only in minuets and scherzos, but in *deutscher*, *walzer*, and other dances as well. The contemporaneous literature on music offers little enlightenment on this subject. One might turn to the literature on dance, but it can offer no guarantees for Schubert, particularly in cases of dance forms within symphonies, quartets, and sonatas. In the absence of external evidence, then, one turns to the music itself. Here, however, even the internal evidence offers no particular reason to slow the tempo in trios, except in cases where marked specifically, as in Piano Sonatas D845 and D959 (A minor and A major), where the trio instructions read *Un poco più lento*, or in the Scherzo D459A/2, *più tardo*. The very rarity of such markings leads us to regard them as exceptions to the rule. Affective contrasts often tempt the romantically inclined Schubertian (and we speak now of the popular concept) to add to the contrast with a new tempo, and almost always a slower one.

Before leaving the subject of trios, let us consider the Piano Sonata D894/3 , where Schubert's expressive markings (***pp*** decreasing to ***ppp***, *ligato*), plus a change of modality to the major, often tempt modern players to take the trio slower than the *Allegro moderato*. But it must be clear that Schubert, having taken such pains to give this trio these expressive markings, could easily have marked a new tempo as well, had he wanted. The true romanticist, then, learns to make the difference with the tools that Schubert loans him: in this case volume, voicing, and coloring, and perhaps the use of the pedal. These are not insignificant tools, for the best fortepianos of Schubert's day were capable of enormous contrasts in these areas, especially within the dynamic range of ***p*** to ***ppp***.

EXAMPLE 6.20
Piano Sonata D894/3 Trio

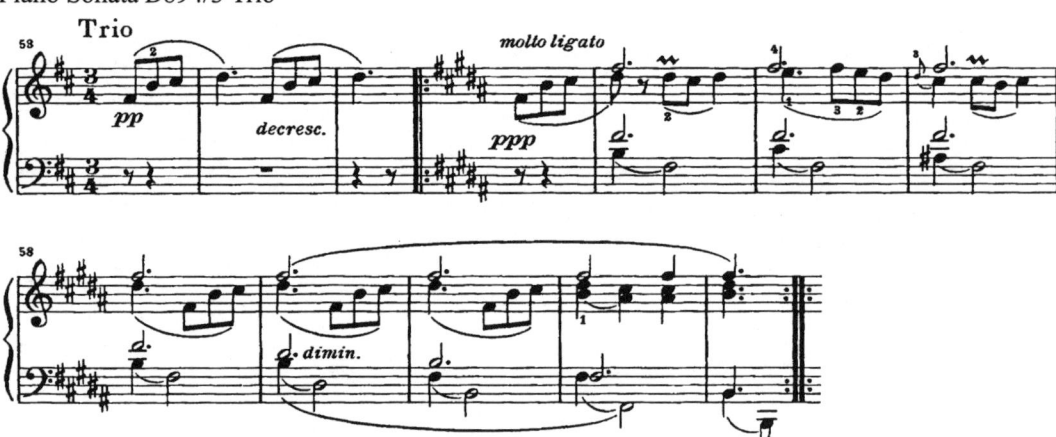

We can make the same statement concerning *minore* or *maggiore* sections: consider, for example, the *maggiore* verse of *Gute Nacht* D911/1 (see Ex. 6.21 on p. 245). Here a performance problem somewhat beyond our modern responsibility might be at fault, a problem that has warranted mentioning several times in the course of this chapter. One could make a case that, with an acquired overlay of about 170 years of changing traditions, theories and tastes, our essential musical sensitivities to the realities of times past may have become a bit dulled. A simple change of minor to major, as in *Gute Nacht*, may have been far more effective in Schubert's day than in ours. With all that has happened to tonality since then, we may feel a need to dress up such small differences with tempo changes, simply in order to experience the same degree of meaning. Those of us interested in real historical understanding, however, cannot remain satisfied with this dulled modern sensory-surfeit. We endeavor instead to return to the fresher perspective of the early nineteenth century.

Tempo, Time, and Character 245

EXAMPLE 6.21

In terms of tempo fluctuation, the normative modern treatment of *Gretchen am Spinnrade* also reveals a conflict between popular modern concepts of romanticism and the true romantic imagination: what we might call "mimetic actualization" vs. "mimetic metaphor." Traditionally, performers are encouraged by modern singing pedagogues to actualize the affect of the spinning wheel through certain traditional tempo fluctuations (although, considering the result, we might also ask ourselves if many modern pianists have actually sat at a working spinning wheel). Indeed, the spinning metaphor is merely supportive, for the musical essence and the structure of this song revolve around Gretchen's rising emotional state and its climax. Thus the song is still just a song, subject to its own laws (one high point, for such through-composed works) rather than the whims of musical impressionism.

We cannot say who might have been responsible for setting the *Gretchen* example for future performers. In addition to Sophie Linhart (who premiered the song), Anna Milder must have sung it, and it must have been in Wilhelmine Schröder-Devrient's repertoire as well. The tempo manipulations probably originated with a pianist of the mid- or late-nineteenth century, possibly someone as influential as Franz Liszt. Among other mid-century interpretative markings in Liszt's transcription, the passage beginning in m. 69 (directly after "sein Kuss!"; see Example 6.22) is marked *poco riten.* for four measures before the pianist is instructed to resume the original tempo, a habit now almost unavoidable in modern performances. In considering the possible origins of such mannerisms we suggest a figure (such as Lizst) from the mid-century, rather than from Schubert's own day, because the entire traditional approach to Gretchen has something of that New-German-School heavi-

EXAMPLE 6.22

ness about it.[27] If the song were sung in this manner, Gretchen could as easily have been a character in one of Wagner's operas (one thinks immediately of Senta in *The Flying Dutchman*). In any case, one does not think of the simpler song style of Schubert's day, nor even of the Viennese-German operatic style of that time.

    The attempt to portray too much in Schubert's lied accompaniments through tempo manipulation and other effects arises not only through a misunderstanding of Schubert's underlying (if perhaps subconscious) ideation, but perhaps through historical misunderstanding as well. The eighteenth-century affective style from which nineteenth-century Viennese lied composers derived their accompaniment figuration had little, perhaps even nothing, to do with tempo alteration. In fact, just the opposite is probably true: because of a fixed tempo and repetitive motivic representation the composer was able to conjure up a certain mood or affect, often consistent for an entire piece or movement. This aspect of compositional control underwent little change in Schubert's music, and where it was necessary to change tempo he certainly was capable of an appropriate notational instruction. Perhaps one of the songs that has suffered most in this regard is *Geheimes* D719, where pianists imagine that a constantly changing tempo and / or gestural approach helps to sell the text. Actually, however, the fragmented vocal line is not enhanced thereby, but is actually obscured through such gestural inconsistency in the piano part.[28]

---

[27] In a letter to Sigmund Lebert (10 January 1870) Liszt made his position clear: "...the rubato may be left to the taste and momentary feeling of gifted players. A metronomical performance is certainly tiresome and nonsensical; time and rhythm must be adapted to and identified with the melody, the harmony, the accent and the poetry... But how to indicate all this? I shudder at the thought of it" trans. William Newman in "Freedom of Tempo:" 545.

[28] A rather exaggerated example can be heard in the Sony CD "Schubert Lieder" (SK53104, with Brigitte Fassbaender, mezzo-soprano and Cord Garben, pianist), which in other respects offers much that is good.

Tempo, Time, and Character

Related to the problem of affect (mimetic actualization vs. mimetic metaphor), as in the accompaniment to *Gretchen am Spinnrade* or *Geheimes,* is that of thematic change. Here, unfortunately, we possess no information concerning Schubert's own thoughts. In the absence of external or internal indicators we should be able to assume that tempo for a single movement remains constant, but in the face of significant resistance to this point of view—evidenced primarily in recordings—we cannot let the subject simply drop. Again, the main problem here appears to derive not from Schubert's era, but from the half-century following. Specifically, it concerns the Wagnerian dictum that every theme must have its own tempo and character. The following passages are taken from the central section of *Über das Dirigieren,* wherein Wagner conjures up Friedrich Schiller's "Über naive und sentimentalische Dichtung" (1795) to distinguish between an older classicism (naive) of Mozart and the newer classicism (sentimental) of Beethoven. He reveals an uncertain grasp of turn-of-the-century aesthetics, for Schiller's new "sentimental" art was far closer to the aesthetics of Mozart's generation (even if Mozart himself did not live to a full age) rather than the eventual "age of Beethoven" that Wagner evokes with the *Eroica* Symphony:

> By contrast [to the fixed-tempo concepts of Mozart's day], what characterizes the true Beethoven Allegro? How would the ... first movement of his "Eroica" Symphony fare if taken in the strict tempo of a Mozartian Overture-Allegro? We question, however, whether it has ever dawned on any of our conductors to take this movement other than in a single tempo from beginning to end. [...] Musicians with a feeling for performance must guard well how they come to grips with [the following passages]:

EXAMPLE 6.23
Wagner's examples from the *Eroica* Symphony

> Some musicians do not care, for they [imagine themselves to be] on "classical" ground, where everything runs together: *grande vitesse...* "time is music" . Truly we now have reached an important turning point from which to judge our entire modern music-making [...] The first thing we might do is to reveal this dilemma and explain ... that in terms of the treatment and performance of music since the advent of Beethoven a real change has taken place. What once were thematically isolated and self-sufficient forms [are now combined as complex forms with competitive inner themes], clinging to each other, and having developed out of each other at the same time. Naturally this state of affairs must be reflected in performance, and above all so that tempi would be adjustable [with a sensitivity that reflects] the individuality of the thematic webs themselves, whose inner motion reveals [their proper treatment].[29]

[29] *Gesammte Werke* (Leipzig, 192?)9: 290/1.

Wagner notes that conductors of Beethoven's own day took the first movement of the *Eroica* in a unified tempo, and we have no evidence that Beethoven was unsatisfied with this approach. Wagner would have taught him better, though, and here he goes on to discuss the variations of the *Kreutzer* Sonata (each of which must have its proper tempo), "organic" tempo-modulations in the C♯-minor Quartet, Op. 131, and then onto the *Freischütz* Overture.[30] Throughout the essay we read his objections to fast tempos in *Allegro* and his taste for extremely slow tempos in *Adagio*. Earlier in this work Wagner had made much out of the idea of "melos" [melodic *Gestalt*], with which he had set up his entire idea of self-sufficient thematic areas and great drama within the confines of a single form. These concepts are essentially operatic in nature, strongly bound up, in fact, with the leitmotif idea.

Thus Richard Wagner himself documents the superimposition of mid-nineteenth-century operatic ideas on early-nineteenth-century instrumental music. He doesn't mention Schubert, but we can assume that his treatment of Schubert's music would have been similar to his treatment of Beethoven and Weber. The *Unfinished* Symphony was introduced to the world at the height of the Wagnerian age (1865), and it can be no accident that the heaviness, slowness, and tempo modulations which still characterize traditional performances was a direct result. Wagner's own objections to the predominantly "straight" performances and fast tempos of the conductors of the past (Mendelssohn, for example) may provide us with a partial picture of music-making of the past, reaching as far back, perhaps, as Schubert's lifetime.

We possess no evidence that Schubert's music requires tempo adjustments for separate thematic areas.[31] His operas do not make use of leitmotifs, either formative or full-blown. Likewise, his instrumental movements fall well within the traditions and dictates of the classical style: contrasting thematic groups are distinguished one from another merely as contrasting harmonic areas in an otherwise unified (from the point of view of tempo and meter) musical outpouring. This statement is true for the Austro-German symphonic school through Brahms, and is one of the reasons why Brahms, too, is often dubbed a "classicist".

Reviewing the evidence supplied by Schubert's contemporaries, at least in terms of instrumental music, we find only scant traces of any pending Wagnerism. Hummel, for example, is clear on the subject of a consistent metrical context:

---

[30] On the whole, *Uber das Dirigieren* is a masterpiece of misconception (discussed above), arrogance (Wagner alone, apparently, understood the art of conducting; even Mendelssohn was merely a classical speed demon), and bigotry (Meyerbeer's themes were "too Jewish"). In order to add "ignorance" to the list, we merely need to mention Wagner's complete disregard of Franz Schubert.

[31] Are separate tempos for contrasting thematic areas an issue in Schubert's lieder? The case of *Erlkönig* springs to mind, of course, for not only has this song been treated operatically in the twentieth century (as in the 1930 recording made by George Thill, Henri Etcheverry, and C. Pascal, wherein the separate "roles" were taken by individual singers: rereleased, EMI RLS 766), but at least once in Schubert's day as well, when Vogl, Schubert, and others are reported to have dramatized the work in this same manner during a sojourn in upper Austria (cf. Stadler in *Erinnerungen:*130). Identifying and even separating the vocal personae of the *Erlkönig*, however, is a far cry from dissecting and reassembling the whole temporal framework within which these personae function. Also see reference to Adolf Müller's theatrical revision and production of *Erlkönig* in 1834, *Dokumente:* 330.

Tempo, Time, and Character 249

§3...[In *allegro*] the player should not allow the tempo to deviate in every bar, but should hold the required tempo from the first measure on ...

In the continuation of this sentence he acknowledges the kind of [voluntary] "turning of the corner" which marks expressive playing:

§3 continued: ... he can linger just before places of extreme lyricism ["Gesangstellen"] or just before *coloraturas*["*Passagen*"]).

EXAMPLE 6.24
Hummel: Concerto in A minor, op. 85: *Allegro moderato*

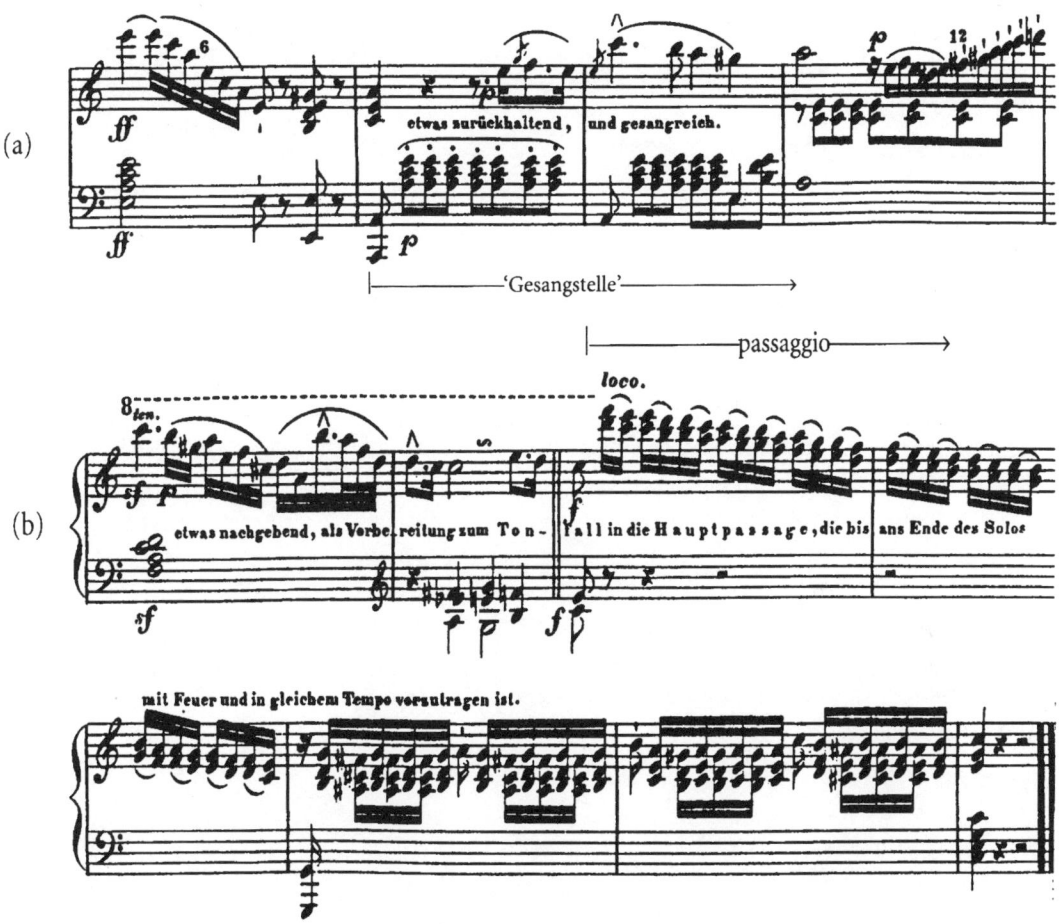

This kind of lingering is clearly subtle, lasting a measure or less in allegro, for Hummel notes the usually-prescribed "exception":

One can make an exception for places where a number of measures should go increasingly slower; usually the composer has marked such places with rallentando, or in the opposite case, with accelerando poco a poco.[32]

[32] p.418

EXAMPLE 6.25
Hummel: Concerto in A minor, op. 85: *Larghetto*

Weber, the most operatic of early nineteenth-century instrumental composers, shares with Hummel the tendency to offset contrasting thematic areas with individualistic and expressive instructions. One need only examine the contrasting themes of his piano sonatas to confirm this idea. In the first movement of Sonata No. 3 in D-minor, for example, we see at the outset, *Allegro feroce*, with an appropriately aggressive theme:

EXAMPLE 6.26

and at the elaborately-prepared second theme in the relative major, *dolce/tranquillo e lusingando*, followed 20 measures later by an episode marked *stringendo*. Still we cannot

Tempo, Time, and Character   *251*

prove or disprove that Weber, raised as a classicist, would have wanted a new tempo for the second theme, even though he clearly emphasized its autonomous nature through a long preparation and then a new character marking:

EXAMPLE 6.27

Through such highly distinct thematic areas Weber may indeed have inspired Wagner's more radical conceptions. Schubert gives us little or no hint of such thinking, not even in his last works. Even "turning corners" into different thematic and / or structural areas, as Hummel shows us above, remains unprescribed in Schubert's music. In the absence of such markings, then, we have no cause to apply tempo modulations, especially because Schubert provides other means of contrast. For example, at the second group in the first movement of the *Great* C-major Symphony the affect of the accompaniment remains unaltered, and the transition is made entirely through harmonic modulation and *decrescendo*. Furthermore, orchestral performances in Schubert's day were still led by musicians untrained in the art of conducting as we know it. The diverse and subtle manipulations of tempos to which we have grown accustomed in later times were, on the whole, probably not a part of the playing style of his age. Even Wagner admitted it.

Absolute Tempo

We come now to the primary evidence of "absolute" tempo, which, from Schubert's early career until the present time most musicians have measured in terms of Maelzel's metronome. The following table sorts the metronome markings reasonably attributable to Franz Schubert (30 in total) into large categories. Because thirty markings constitute a pitifully small sampling on which to base an overview that must account for several thousand individual songs, pieces, movements, etc., we shall not presume to offer the readers more than a projected tempo spread. Certainly we cannot hope to achieve the kind of thoroughness and detail that Rudolf Kolisch was able to bring to his famous work on Beethoven's tempos. Nevertheless, performers ultimately must choose specific tempos, right or wrong, and we offer here a systematic overview of the major works for comparison in making difficult decisions.

Each section shows tempos or tempo averages derived directly from the available Schubert models, indirectly through metrical modulations, or theoretically through extrapolation. Naturally, performers must adjust these numbers according to the specific character of any work. Because in general the specified beat (the quarter note in 3/4, the eighth note in 3/8, etc.) works out to be about a third faster in Schubert's B types than in his A types, the formula B=1.33A yields the tempo for a B type where the A tempo is known, and, vice-versa, A=B/1.33. The same relationship exists, of course, between the quarter notes of A types and the dotted quarters of the odd-value beats.

Where interpolation and/or derivation from metrical modulation is concerned, even one small but correctly-placed piece of a puzzle can lead to solid results: for example, knowing that the opening *Andante* ¢ of the C-major Symphony D944 (for which category we have a metronome mark from Schubert: *Morgenlied* D685, half = MM 63) bears an indisputable 1:2 metrical relationship to the following *Allegro ma non troppo* ¢, we can derive a tempo of MM 126 for the latter. From this tempo we can derive further markings for the mini-categories directly above and below *Allegro ma non troppo*. The relationship between these two sections is confirmed by Schubert's citation of the opening theme at the close of the *Allegro ma non troppo* material. Even allowing for the *Più moto* which has occurred in m. 560, the sudden tempo adjustment to "*molto maestoso*" taken by most conductors of the past (and still by many in the present) defeats the purpose of the citation. [33] Schubert does not call for it, and in fact the citation appears calculated to be decisive and compact rather than dramatic and nostalgic.

The finale of the E♭ Trio reveals a similar citation, this time from one movement into another. Here the relationship is even more strictly defined, for the theme of the *Andante con moto* is woven into the finale in such a way that the tempo cannot suddenly be adjusted to suit. Ensembles who have not established a true "*con moto*" tempo for the *Andante* typically find themselves forced to cite that theme at an entirely different pace in the finale: again, a solution which has no referential meaning.

EXAMPLE 6.28a/b
a. 2nd movement in 2/4

b. Finale in 6/8

---

[33] According to the recorded evidence, the first conductor to do away with this sudden *Maestoso* was René Leibowitz in the late 50s and early 60s (cf. recordings with the Vienna State Opera Orchestra on Whitehall WHS 20031, Westminster WST 14051, and with the Royal Philharmonic on RCA Victor GL 32533, now Menuet/TIS CD 160 016-2.) See discussion of this issue in Montgomery, "Franz Schubert's Music in Performance."

Tempo, Time, and Character 253

Finally, in terms of metrical modulation, the third movement of the C-major String Quintet D956 shows a relationship between the main body of the movement and the trio that yields a quantifiable tempo for the main body (see Table VI: Part II, below).

Other apparent relationships are more problematic. In the D-major Symphony D82 Schubert already had begun the kind of referentialism described directly above concerning the C-major Symphony D944. In the recapitulation of the *Allegro vivace* (first movement), he quotes from the slow introduction, doubling the values to a 1:2 relationship, and again we might presume that this quote gives us the key to the beginning *Adagio* at a 1:2 relationship with that *Allegro vivace:*

EXAMPLE 6.29a/b
a1.

As confirmed by the initial thematic material of the two sections, however, the only possible metrical / speed relationship between them is not 1:2, but 1:4:

b.

The literal solution to this problem (and we find that taking Schubert literally is usually the best policy) is to perform the opening as written at 1:4 and let the later quotation run twice as fast as the material from which it was taken. However, if we believe in a metrical relationship here (and it seems clear that Schubert was thinking along these lines, somehow, for there would be no point in a quotation that was twice the speed of the original), we have several other choices: 1) perform the *Allegro vivace* at a 2:1 relationship with the *Adagio,* i.e. at half of the expected speed, an unacceptable solution, for it would allow the tail, so to speak, to wag the dog! or 2) double the speed of the *Adagio* (actually to combine every two measures into one, regarding the correct meter sign as ¢¢, as in the G♭ Impromptu). The latter solution does far less violence to the work, but is it correct?

To begin with, we can see a context for this problem. The four-hand Fantasie D48 has an *adagio* introduction in ¢ that also bears a 1:4 relationship with the following *Allegro agitato*. We can say the same for the C-major String Quartet D46 and the Overture to *Der Spiegelritter* D11. Likewise, a half-year later Schubert was still in the throes of the problem, for the C-minor String Quartet movement D103 shows exactly the same 1:4 relationship (*Grave* in C – *Allegro* in ¢), as does the Second Symphony D125, the Third Symphony D200 and the B♭ Overture D470. The first such Schubert work to bear a 1:2 relationship is the D-major Overture D556 (*Allegro maestoso* in C – *Allegro* in ¢).[34] From this point (May 1817) forward, and without exception, all of his works with duple-meter introductions leading to duple-meter *allegro* first movements exhibit a 1:2 relationship: the symphonic fragments D615, the E-major symphonic sketch D729, the Overture to *Alfonso und Estrella* D732 (we must disregard the spurious metronome markings) and, of course, the *Great* C-major Symphony D944. In this light, then, we would be forced to double the tempo of all of Schubert's early 1:4 openings in order to correct a single relationship in D82, and this seems like a rather radical solution (in terms of our colloquial metaphor, the same little tail wagging an even larger dog). It appears, then, that our theorist's desire for tidy metrical relationships in early Schubert must go unsatisfied. We cannot agree completely with the conclusion drawn by René Leibowitz, who also sought to remain faithful to Schubert's notation, but as well to rationalize the difference between the cases of the First and "Ninth" Symphonies on motivic grounds.[35] In light of the context demonstrated above, we believe instead that until 1817 Schubert was simply working through the problem. Once it was solved, it remained solved.

The following table represents Schubert's tempo hierarchy, divided according to rubric and metronome markings and ordered within in the context of the following generic categories: *Presto / Allegro / Allegretto / Andantino / Andante / Adagio*

TABLE VI:

Presto
I. *Prestissimo.*
No quantified models.
Tempos: as fast as possible.

---

[34] Even at this point Schubert's musical language had not evolved completely, for in the same month he wrote the A♭—E♭ Sonata D557, which begins in one key and ends in another.
[35] "Tempo et caractère dans les symphonies de Schubert" in *Le compositeur et son double. Essais sur l'interprétation musicale* (Paris: Editions Gallimard, 1971): 147/8.

II. *Presto*
Even, Type B: 270–360. Odd: 204–270.

Commentary: Schubert left no direct models, but we are able to interpolate tempos for this category, based on a metrical modulation in the C-major Quintet D956. Here the dotted half note of the *scherzo*: *Presto* (3/4) equals one basic beat of the *Andante sostenuto* (𝄵) that follows. Because the basic beat of the *Andante sostenuto* can be derived from the bottom of an already quantified range (MM 60–72, see *Andante*, below), we can calculate a tempo of 120 to the dotted half, or quarter = 360 for the *scherzo*. Practicality tells us that this is about the maximum speed it might be taken, especially if we believe in a *prestissimo* category beyond it.

Note that in contrast to the slower categories, the tempo ranges in this category begin only at the point where the B types in *Allegro* left off. This is because at the extreme tempos of *Presto* and *Prestissimo*, we find only B types. These points of reference (MM 270, where *Allegro molto* leaves off, and MM 360, where *Presto* finds its natural limit) then provide us with a theoretical tempo range for the other 3/4 *scherzos* in this group, and, by extension, for the entire *Presto* group. Readers should take note, however, that the basic beat of the Quintet's *Andante sostenuto* should not be considered the quarter, as traditionally marked in scores, but in most likelihood the half note. Unfortunately, the autograph is lost, but this is almost certainly one of those meters in that group along with the opening of the *Great* C-major Symphony or the middle movement of Beethoven's *Emperor* Concerto, whose *alla breve* signs were altered to 𝄵 by irresponsible nineteenth-century editors to suit slower tempo concepts of a later age. Neither Schubert nor Beethoven wrote whole movements of *Andante* in 𝄵, especially not past their formative years. Readers will note that in Table VI, which includes all of Schubert's piano sonatas, symphonies and major chamber works, we find not one such movement in the Andante category.[36] Other strong arguments for changing this sign to 2/2, in effect, for doubling the tempo, are the movement's motivic structure (strongly related to the opening of the first movement) and the bowing marks, which can be effected only in the faster tempo.

Allegro
III. *Allegro molto, Allegro vivace*
Even, Type A: MM 160–204. Even, Type B: MM 212–270. Odd: Type A: MM 120–152, Type B: MM 160–204.

IV. *Allegro.*
Even, Type A: MM 144–160. Even, Type B: 190–212. Odd: 108–120.

𝄴: *Erlkönig* D328 (*Schnell* ♩ = 152)

2/4: *Rastlose Liebe* D138 (*Schnell, mit Leidenschaft* ♩ = 152)

6/8: *Der Flug der Zeit* D515 (*Etwas geschwind,* ♩. = 112)

V. *Allegro moderato, Allegro ma non troppo*
Even, Type A: MM 100–144. Even, Type B: 132–190. Odd: 76–108.

9/8: *Drang in die Ferne* D770 (*Etwas geschwind,* ♩. = 76)

---

[36] The introductory 4/4 *Grave* of the String Quartet [fragment] in C minor D 103 must be taken in some *andante* tempo if it is to modulate metrically into the *Allegro* at a 1:4 relationship, but it is not so marked. In any case, Schubert had not yet worked out his concept of such modulations, nor his terminology. See Montgomery "For Once: Beethoven in the light of Schubert" for elaboration.

Allegretto

VI. *Allegretto*
Even, Type A: MM 90–100. Even, Type B: 120–132. Odd: 68–76.

    ¢: *Die abgeblüthe Linde* D514 (*Mäßig*, ♩ = 92) +

+The term "*Mäßig*" does not seem to fit the character of *Allegretto* as much as it might fit that of *Andante*, but we are constructing this table foremost according to what we believe to be authentic metronome markings and categories.

    6/8: *Gretchen am Spinnrade* D118 (*Nicht zu geschwind*, ♩. = 72)

Andantino / Larghetto / Andante con moto, Andante, Andante molto
VII. *Andantino / Larghetto / Andante con moto*
No models available: Projected tempo averages: Even, Type A: [72–90]. Odd: [54–68]. No B types.

VIII. *Andante*
Even: 60–72. Odd: 45–54. No B types.

    ¢ : *Morgenlied* D685 (*Ziemlich langsam*, ♩ = 63)

    2/4: *Der König in Thule* D367 (*Etwas langsam*, ♩ = 66)

    2/4: *Der Fischer* D225 (*Mäßig*, ♩ = 60)

    2/4: *Heidenröslein* D257 (*Lieblich*, ♩ = 64)

    ¢: Messe D872, *Zum Eingang* (*Mäßig*, ♩ = 60)

    ¢: Messe D872, *Zum Gloria* (*Mit Majestät*, ♩ = 69)

    3/4: Messe D872, *Schlußgesang* (*Nicht zu langsam*, ♩ = 63)

    12/8: *Nähe des Geliebten* D162 (*Langsam, feierlich mit Anmut*, ♩. = 50)

Commentary: In D872 "Zum Gloria", the instruction "*Mit Majestät*" would seem mismatched with MM 69, the highest of the *Andante* markings. Here, however, we merely have another case of Schubert's unhelpful omission of a main tempo category. This one might better have read "*Mässig, mit Majestät*" or even "*Nicht zu langsam, mit Majestät*". *Nähe des Geliebten* D162, exhibits the slowest instruction (*Langsam, feierlich*) in this group.

IX. *Andante molto*
Even: 52–60. Odd: 40–45. No B types.

    ¢ : *Der Tod und das Mädchen* D531 (*Mäßig*, ♩ = 54)

    ¢: *Antigone und Oedip* D542 (*Langsam*, ♩ = 54)

    ¢: *Erster Verlust* D226 (*Sehr langsam, wehmütig*, ♩ = 54)

    ¢: Messe D872, *Nach der Wandlung* (*Sehr langsam*, ♩ = 56)

    3/4: Messe D872, *Zum Sanctus* (*Sehr langsam*, ♩ = 56)

    6/8: *Schäfers Klagelied* D121 (*Mässig*, ♩. = 40)

Commentary: According to context, apparently, *Langsam* can be slower than *Sehr langsam* (cf: D542 / D872). Again we see evidence of "thinking down, thinking up".

Adagio-Largo
X. *Adagio, Grave, Langsam, Sehr langsam*
Even: MM 36–52. Odd: MM 26–40. No B types.

    ¢: *Wandrers Nachtlied* I, D224 (*Langsam, mit Ausdruck*, ♩ = 50)

    3/4: *Am Grabe Anselmos* D504 (*Langsam*, ♩ = 50)

    3/4: Messe D872, *Zum Offertorium: Sehr langsam*, ♩ = 50

    6/8: Messe D872, Zum Agnus Dei (*Mäßig*, ♩. = 26.7)

    6/8: Messe D872, Anhang: *Das Gebet des Herrn* (*Mäßig*, ♩. = 26.7)

    6/8: Messe D872, *Zum Evangelium und Credo* (*Nicht zu langsam*, ♩. = 26.7)

Commentary: Schubert has marked *Sehr langsam* for movements which belong in three different tempo categories, ranging from *Andante molto* to *Adagio molto*. In such cases, we must look to the character of a given movement (motivic quality, harmonic movement, etc.), and then to its metronome mark, to determine its place in the hierarchy.

XI. *Adagio molto / Largo / Lento / Sehr langsam*
Even: to MM 38. No distinction between A and B types. Odd: to MM 26.

    ¢ : *Meeres Stille* D216 (*Sehr langsam, ängstlich*, ♩ = 36)

    ¢ : *Der Wanderer* D489 (*Sehr langsam*, ♩ = 31.5)

    ¢ : *Memnon* D541 (*Sehr langsam, schwärmerisch*, ♩ = 25)

    2/4: *Jägers Abendlied* D368 (*Sehr langsam, leise*, ♩ = 31.5)

Commentary: *Nicht zu langsam* and *Mäßig* in these three odd-meter movements would indicate that Schubert was thinking up from an even slower conception. Thus we must adjust down to 24, at least, and possibly further for the average slowest beat.

To the headings in Table VI we now add the major works (apart from the operas and choral works), the instrumental works grouped by their Italian markings, the songs according to German equivalents. We have included *Die schöne Müllerin, Winterreise,* and *Schwanengesang,* plus the complete symphonies, piano sonatas, violin sonatas, piano trios and string quartets, the *Trout* Quintet, the *Wanderer* Fantasy, the C-major Fantasy for Violin and Piano, the C-major String Quintet, several overtures, and his three most important four-hand works: the *Grand Duo* Sonata, the F-minor Fantasy and the *Lebensstürme Allegro*. It might be objected, not unjustly, that many of these works were written some years later than the early songs. Still, Schubert's professional career spanned only about fifteen years, and his sense of tempo would not have changed so radically as to render our procedure useless.

    One of the most important functions of such a chart is to view an entire group of similar movements, comparing the essential characteristics that call for similar tempos.

Space does not permit us to comment on each of the interesting discoveries to be made through such comparison, but we might offer an example.

In the *Andante* group, under 2/4: Type A, we find five movements of the *Andante con moto / Allegretto quasi andantino* type:

    D173/2 String Quartet in G minor, *Andantino*

    D537/2 Piano Sonata in A minor, *Allegretto quasi andantino*

    D929/2 Piano Trio in E♭, *Andante con moto*

    D944/2 Symphony in C major, *Andante con moto*

    D951 Rondo in A major for Piano four hands, *Allegretto quasi andantino*

Two of these movements, D929/2 and D944/2, are strikingly similar in their basic features: to begin with, both of them are second movements, both are marked *Andante con moto*, both are in 2/4, both are in minor keys and were written about the same time. Furthermore, both movements are driven by repetitive staccato eighth-note chords in their accompaniments, which support articulated melody lines:

EXAMPLE 6.30a/b
a. D944, *Andante con moto* in 2/4

b. D929, *Andante con moto* in 2/4

Despite these fundamental similarities, however, nothing could be more dissimilar than the two traditional approaches to these movements. Where the *Andante con moto* of the Symphony is usually taken in a reasonable two-to-the-measure, with a truly articulated melody befitting its marking, the E♭ Trio melody is approached most often as a dolorous prayer at four-to-the measure. Cellists not only revel in this melody, but appear highly offended at any suggestion of "con moto in two" or the corresponding melodic articulation and ornamental accentuation (discussion, Ch. V). This tradition arose, apparently, in the late nineteenth century and later was captured on disc by a number of early twentieth-century piano trios. Now, sadly, it appears to be sealed in wax forever.

Table VI, above, was constructed according to what we can regard as authentic metronome indications, regardless of the uncertainties of Schubert's German instructions (what is "*Nicht zu geschwind*", or "*Ziemlich langsam?*"). Table VII, on the other hand, has been constructed according to the linguistic groupings, both Italian and German (all "*Allegretto*" movements together, all "*Geschwind*" movements, etc.). With two provocative exceptions (for which we have no explanation at present), Schubert's tempo, meter, and character instructions fall into remarkably consistent and practical groups within the following table. Readers should not forget that we have offered a range of tempos for each group. Even so, we come across movements or songs (particularly songs) which traditionally have been performed at speeds slower or faster than those set out for the groups in which they fall. Examples might include *Abschied* D957/7, which has often been taken beyond the limit of MM quarter=144 suggested for its group here, or *Die Stadt* D957/11, which traditionally is taken slower than the slowest tempo suggested for its group, quarter=MM 100. In the face of such problems, the professional musician's first impulse is to reject the structured theory in favor of what we know as tradition, or what may be more "comfortable" for us. But we might find it interesting first to reexamine the work in question before reverting to that great quagmire of common practice. It could well be that Schubert had something more interesting in mind. If, after true contextual analysis, we still disagree with the findings, we will at least have provided ourselves with the best possible basis for true artistic decision-making.

Table VII

Prestissimo, Presto

I. *Prestissimo.*
Tempos: as fast as possible. No A types.

    3/4: Type B

        D87/2 String Quartet in E♭ major, Scherzo: *Prestissimo*

II. *Presto*
Even, Type B: 270–360. Odd: 204–270. No A types.

    2/4: Type B

        D94/4 String Quartet in D major, Finale: *Presto*
        D125/4 Symphony in B♭ major, Finale: *Presto vivace*

3/4: Type B
> D18/1 String Quartet in G minor / B♭ major: *Presto vivace*
> D18/4 String Quartet in G minor / B♭ major, Finale: *Presto*
> D112/4 String Quartet in B♭ major, Finale: *Presto*
> D760/3 Fantasy in C major for Piano, Scherzo: *Presto*
> D574/2 Sonata in A major for Violin and Piano, Scherzo: *Presto*
> D589/3 Symphony in C major, Scherzo: *Presto*
> D667/3 Piano Quintet in A major, *Presto*
> D956/3 String Quintet in C major, Scherzo: *Presto*

6/8: Type B
> D32/1 String Quartet in C major, *Presto*
> D200/4 Symphony in D major, Finale: *Presto vivace*
> D810/4 String Quartet in D minor, Finale: *Presto*

Allegro molto, Allegro vivace, Allegro con moto, Allegro, Allegro moderato, Allegro ma non troppo

III. *Allegro molto, Allegro vivace, Rasch, Sehr Schnell*
Even, Type A: MM 160–204. Even, Type B: MM 212–270. Odd: Type A: MM 120–152, Type B: MM 160–204.

¢ : Type A
> D384/1 Sonata in D major for Violin and Piano, *Allegro molto*
> D850/1 Piano Sonata in D major, *Allegro vivace* +
> D934/3 Fantasy in C major for Violin and Piano, *Allegro vivace* +

+ The two movements directly above would be wildly fast in ¢, leading us to ask if they should have been marked in C. The sonata was published during Schubert's lifetime (see Montgomery, "Schubert and *alle breve*" in *Die Brille* 29). The Fantasy was published long after Schubert's death, and only a first draft exists.

> D82/4 Symphony in D major, *Allegro vivace*
> D173/1 String Quartet in G minor, *Allegro con brio*

2/4: Type A
> D353/4 String Quartet in E major, Finale: *Allegro vivace*
> D485/4 Symphony in B♭ major, Finale: *Allegro vivace*
> D812/4 Sonata in C for Piano four hands, Finale: *Allegro vivace*

2/4: Type B
> D845/4 Piano Sonata in A minor, Finale: *Allegro vivace*
> D898/4 Piano Trio in B♭ major, Finale: *Allegro vivace*
> D944/4 Symphony in C major, Finale: *Allegro vivace*
> D946/1 *Klavierstück, Allegro assai*

3/4: Type A
> D125/3 Symphony in B♭ major, Menuetto: *Allegro vivace*
> D173/3 String Quartet in G minor, Menuetto: *Allegro vivace*
> D200/3 Symphony in D major, Menuetto: *Vivace*
> D279/3 Piano Sonata in C major, Menuetto: *Allegro vivace*
> D353/3 String Quartet in E major, Menuetto: *Allegro vivace*
> D784/3 Piano Sonata in A minor, Finale: *Allegro vivace*

    D850/3 Piano Sonata in D major, Scherzo: *Allegro vivace*
 3/4: Type B
    D32/4 String Quartet in C major, Finale: *Allegro con spirito*
    D157/3 Piano Sonata in E major, Menuetto: *Allegro vivace*
    D417/3 Symphony in C minor, Menuetto: *Allegro vivace*
    D485/3 Symphony in B♭ major, Menuetto: *Allegro molto*
    D566/3 Piano Sonata in E minor, Scherzo: *Allegro vivace*
    D574/4 Sonata in A major for Violin and Piano, Finale: *Allegro vivace*
    D810/3 String Quartet in D minor, Scherzo: *Allegro molto*
    D812/3 Sonata in C for Piano four hands, Scherzo: *Allegro vivace*
    D845/3 Piano Sonata in A minor, Scherzo: *Allegro vivace*
    D887/3 String Quartet in G major, Scherzo: *Allegro vivace*
    D940/3 Fantasy in F minor for Piano four hands, "Scherzo" : *Allegro vivace*
    D944/3 Symphony in C major, Scherzo: *Allegro vivace*
    D959/3 Piano Sonata in A major, Scherzo: *Allegro vivace*
    D960/3 Piano Sonata in B♭ major, Scherzo: *Allegro vivace*
 3/8: Type B
    D537/3 Piano Sonata in A minor, Finale: *Allegro vivace*
    D575/4 Piano Sonata in B major, Finale: *Allegro giusto*
 ₵:
    D2B/1 Symphony in D major, *Allegro con moto*
    D46/1 String Quartet in C major, *Allegro con moto*
    D353/1 String Quartet in E major, *Allegro con fuoco*
    D667/1 Piano Quintet in A major, *Allegro vivace*
    D760/1 Fantasy in C major for Piano, *Allegro con fuoco ma non troppo*
 6/8: Type B
    D384/3 Sonata in D major for Violin and Piano, Finale: *Allegro vivace*
    D703/1 String Quartet in C minor, *Allegro assai*
    D887/4 String Quartet in G major, Finale: *Allegro assai*

IV. *Allegro, Geschwind, Schnell*
Even, Type A: MM 144–160. Even, Type B: 190–212. Odd, Type A:108–120. Odd, Type B: 144–160.
 ₵:
    D46/4 String Quartet in C major, *Allegro*
    D94/1 String Quartet in D major, *Allegro*
    D417/4 Symphony in C minor, *Allegro*
    D485/1 Symphony in B♭ major, *Allegro*
    D556 Overture in D major, *Allegro*
    D589/1 Symphony in C major, *Allegro*
 2/4: Type A
    D173/4 String Quartet in G minor, *Allegro*
    D667/4 Piano Quintet in A major, *Allegro giusto*
    D840/4 Piano Sonata in C major, *Allegro*
    D946/3 *Klavierstück, Allegro*

    D795/15 *Eifersuch und Stolz, Geschwind*

        D957/3 *Frühlingssehnsucht, Geschwind*

2/4: Type B

        D68/2 String Quartet in B♭ major, *Allegro*

        D87/4 String Quartet in E♭ major, *Allegro*

        D385/4 Sonata in A minor for Violin and Piano, *Allegro*

3/4: Type A

        D74/3 String Quartet in D major, Menuetto: *Allegro*

        D112/3 String Quartet in B♭ major, Menuetto: *Allegro*

        D408/1 Sonata in G minor for Violin and Piano, *Allegro giusto*

        D958/1 Piano Sonata in C minor, *Allegro*

3/4: Special *étude* type quasi in three

        D899/2 Impromptu (*étude* type), *Allegro*

3/4: Type B

        D32/3 String Quartet in C major, Menuetto: *Allegro*

        D36/3 String Quartet in B♭ major, Menuetto: *Allegro*

        D46/3 String Quartet in C major, Menuetto: *Allegro*

        D385/3 Sonata in A minor for Violin and Piano, Menuetto: *Allegro*

        D459/2 Piano Sonata in E major, *Allegro*

        D898   Piano Trio in B♭ major, Scherzo: *Allegro*

        D929/1 Piano Trio in E♭, *Allegro*

        D958/3 Piano Sonata in C minor, Menuetto: *Allegro*

3/8: Type B

        D935/4 Impromptu, *Allegro scherzando*

₵:

        D2A Overture in D major, *Allegro*

        D36/1 String Quartet in B♭ major, *Allegro*

        D68/1 String Quartet in B♭ major, *Allegro maestoso*

        D74/4 String Quartet in D major, *Allegro*

        D556 Overture in D major, *Allegro maestoso*

        D760/4 Fantasy in C major for Piano, *Allegro*

        D784/1 Piano Sonata in A minor, *Allegro giusto*

        D810/1 String Quartet in D minor, *Allegro*

        D959/1 Piano Sonata in A major, *Allegro*

6/8: Type A

        D795/14 *Der Jäger, Geschwind*

6/8: Type B

        D958/4 Piano Sonata in C minor, *Allegro*

V. *Allegro moderato, Allegro ma non troppo, Ziemlich geschwind, Etwas geschwind, Mäßig geschwind*
Even, Type A: MM 100–144. Even, Type B: 132–190. Odd: 76–108.

    ₵ :   D74/1 String Quartet in D major, *Allegro moderato*

            D157/1 Piano Sonata in E, *Allegro ma non troppo*

            D605A Grazer Fantasie, *Moderato con espressione*

            D812/1 Sonata in C for Piano four hands, *Allegro moderato*

    D840/1 Piano Sonata in C major, *Moderato*
    D845/1 Piano Sonata in A minor, *Moderato*
    D944/1 Symphony in C major, *Allegro ma non troppo*
    D947 Allegro in A minor for Piano four hands, *Allegro ma non troppo*

    D795/11 *Mein!, Mäßig geschwind*

2/4: (Type A)
    D408/4 Sonata in G minor for Violin and Piano, *Allegro moderato*
    D589/4 Symphony in C major, *Allegro moderato*
    D804/4 String Quartet in A minor, *Allegro moderato*
    D911/4 *Erstarrung, Ziemlich schnell*
    D960/4 Piano Sonata in B♭ major, *Allegro ma non troppo*

    D795/1 *Das Wandern, Mäßig geschwind*
    D795/17 *Die böse Farbe, Ziemlich geschwind*
    D911/22 *Mut* (2nd version), *Ziemlich geschwind, kräftig*

3/4: Type A
    D557/1 Piano Sonata in A♭ major, *Allegro moderato*
    D567/1 Piano Sonata in D♭ / E♭ major, *Allegro moderato*
    D759/1 Symphony in B minor, *Allegro moderato*
    D887/1 String Quartet in G major, *Allegro molto moderato*
    D894/3 Piano Sonata in G major, Menuetto: *Allegro moderato*
    D929/3 Piano Trio in E♭, Scherzando: *Allegro moderato*

    D795/7 *Ungeduld, Etwas geschwind*
    D957/8 *Der Atlas, Etwas geschwind*
    D957/11 *Die Stadt, Mäßig geschwind*

C: Type A
    D850/4 Piano Sonata in D major, Rondo: *Allegro moderato*
    D87/1 String Quartet in E♭ major, *Allegro più moderato*
    D112/1 String Quartet in B♭ major, *Allegro ma non troppo*
    D279/1 Piano Sonata in C major, *Allegro moderato*
    D385/1 Sonata in A minor for Violin and Piano, *Allegro moderato*
    D459/1 Piano Sonata in E major, *Allegro moderato*
    D566/1 Piano Sonata in E minor, *Moderato*
    D574/1 Sonata in A major for Violin and Piano, *Allegro moderato*
    D664/1 Piano Sonata in A major, *Allegro moderato*
    D804/1 String Quartet in A minor, *Allegro ma non troppo*
    D898/1 Piano Trio in B♭ major, *Allegro moderato*
    D899/1 Impromptu in C minor, *Allegro molto moderato*
    D935/1 Impromptu in F minor, *Allegro moderato*
    D940/1 Fantasy in F minor for Piano four hands, *Allegro molto moderato*
    D956/1 String Quintet in C major, *Allegro ma non troppo*
    D960/1 Piano Sonata in B♭ major, [*Allegro*] *molto moderato*

    D957/7 *Abschied, Mäßig geschwind*

D795/12 *Pause, Ziemlich geschwind*
D911/18 *Der stürmische Morgen, Ziemlich geschwind, doch kräftig*

6/8:

D537/1 Piano Sonata in A minor, *Allegro ma non troppo*
D557/3 Piano Sonata in A♭ major, *Allegro*
D664/3 Piano Sonata in A major, *Allegro*
D929/4 Piano Trio in E♭ major, *Allegro moderato*

D957/10 *Das Fischermädchen, Etwas geschwind*
D795/5 *Am Feierabend, Ziemlich geschwind*
D911/2 *Die Wetterfahne, Ziemlich geschwind*
D911/13 *Die Post, Etwas geschwind*
D911/19 *Täuschung, Etwas geschwind*

12/8:

D894/1 Piano Sonata in G major, [Allegro] *molto moderato e cantabile*

Allegretto

VI. *Allegretto, Nicht zu geschwind, Nicht zu geschwind. Etwas bewegt*
Even, Type A: MM 90–100. Even, Type B: 120–132. Odd: 68–76.

₵ :

D894/4 Piano Sonata in G major, Finale: *Allegretto*
D956/4 String Quintet in C major, Finale: *Allegretto*
D959/4 Piano Sonata in A major, [Finale] Rondo: *Allegretto*

2/4: (Type A)

D36/4 String Quartet in B♭ major, *Allegretto*
D200/2 Symphony in D major, *Allegretto*
D506 Rondo in E major for Piano, *Allegretto*
D566/2 Piano Sonata in E minor [Finale]: *Allegretto*
D934/1 Fantasy in C major for Violin and Piano, *Allegretto*

D957/5 *Aufenthalt, Nicht zu geschwind*

3/4: Type A

D911/8 *Rückblick, Nicht zu geschwind*
D911/16 *Letze Hoffnung, Nicht zu geschwind*

3/4: Type B

D82/3 Symphony in D major, Menuetto: *Allegretto*
D94/3 String Quartet in D major, Menuetto: *Allegretto*
D840/3 Piano Sonata in C major, Menuetto: *Allegretto*
D804/3 String Quartet in A minor, Menuetto: *Allegretto*
D899/4 Impromptu (étude type): *Allegretto*
D575/3 Piano Sonata in B major, Scherzo: *Allegretto*
D887/3 String Quartet in G major, Scherzo trio: *Allegretto*
D935/2 Impromptu, *Allegretto*

6/8:

D567/3 Piano Sonata in D♭ / E♭ major, *Allegretto*
D946/2 *Klavierstück, Allegretto*

Tempo, Time, and Character

　　　　　　D795/3 *Halt!, Nicht zu geschwind*
　　　　　　D911/11 *Frühlingstraum, Etwas bewegt*

Andantino / Larghetto / *Andante con moto, Andante, Andante molto*

VII. *Andantino, Larghetto, Andante con moto, Nicht zu langsam*
Even, Type A: [72–90]. Odd: [54–68]. No B types.

　　₵ :
　　　　　　D810/2 String Quartet in D minor, *Andante con moto*
　　　　　　D94/2 String Quartet in D major, *Andante con moto*
　　　　　　D887/2 String Quartet in G major, *Andante un poco mosso*

　　　　　　D911/3 *Gefrorne Tränen, Nicht zu langsam*
　2/4: Type A
　　　　　　D173/2 String Quartet in G minor, *Andantino*
　　　　　　D537/2 Piano Sonata in A minor, *Allegretto quasi andantino*
　　　　　　D667/4 Piano Quintet in A major, *Andantino*
　　　　　　D929/2 Piano Trio in E♭ major, *Andante con moto*
　　　　　　D944/2 Symphony in C major, *Andante con moto*
　　　　　　D951　Rondo in A major for Piano four hands, *Allegretto quasi andantino*
　3/4: Type A
　　　　　　D46/2 String Quartet in C major, *Andante con moto*
　　　　　　D850/2 Piano Sonata in D major, [*Andante*] *con moto*
　　　　　　D934/2 Fantasy in C major for Violin and Piano, *Andantino*

　　　　　　D957/2　*Kriegers Ahnung, Nicht zu langsam*
　　　　　　D911/23 Die *Nebensonnen* (2nd version), *Nicht zu langsam*
　3/8: Type A
　　　　　　D574/3 Sonata in A major for Violin and Piano, *Andantino*
　　　　　　D759/2 Symphony in B minor, *Andante con moto*
　　　　　　D845/2 Piano Sonata in A minor, *Andante, poco mosso*
　　　　　　D959/2 Piano Sonata in A major, *Andantino*

VIII. *Andante. Mäßig*
Even: 60–72. Odd: 45–54. No B types.

　　₵₵ : Type A
　　　　　　D899/3 Impromptu in G♭, *Andante*
　₵ : Type A
　　　　　　D784/2 Piano Sonata in A minor, *Andante*
　　　　　　D946/1 *Klavierstück, Andante*
　　　　　　D804/2 String Quartet in A minor, *Andante*
　　　　　　D935/3 Impromptu, *Andante*
　　　　　　[D956/3 String Quintet in C major, *Andante sostenuto*] +

+See discussion under Table V, *Presto*.

D795/20 *Des Baches Wiegenlied, Mäßig*

IX.   *Andante molto, Ziemlich langsam*
Even: 52–60. Odd: 40–45. No B types.

    2/4: Type A
        D567/2 Piano Sonata in D♭ major, *Andante molto*

        D795/18 *Trockne Blumen, Ziemlich langsam*
    6/8: Type A
        D934/1 Fantasy in C major for Violin and Piano, *Andante molto*

        D795/10 Tränenregen, *Ziemlich langsam*

Adagio, Adagio molto, Grave, Largo, Lento

X.   *Adagio, Grave, Langsam.*
Even: MM 36–52. Odd: MM 26–40. No B types.

    ¢ : Type A
        D82/1 Symphony in D major, *Adagio**

*Under "fast tempos" above, note the relationship of this *Adagio* to the *Allegro vivace* D82/1, at almost exactly 1:4.

        D760/2 Fantasy in C major for Piano, *Wanderer, Adagio*
        D897 Piano Trio in E♭, Notturno, *Adagio*
        D957/9 *Ihr Bild, Langsam*
    2/4: Type A
        D958/2 Piano Sonata in C minor, *Adagio*

        D911/7 *Auf dem Flusse, Langsam*
        D911/12 *Einsamkeit, Langsam*
        D795/6 *Der Neugierige, Langsam*
    3/4: Type A
        D589/1 Symphony in C major, *Adagio*
        D2B/1 Symphony in D major, *Adagio*
        D505 [Klavierstück] in D♭ major for Piano, *Adagio*

        D911/6 *Wasserflut, Langsam*
    3/8: Type A
        D911/9 *Irrlicht, Langsam*

    C: Type A
        D46/1 String Quartet in C major, *Adagio*
    6/8: Type A
        D87/3 String Quartet in E♭ major, *Adagio*
    12/8: Type A
        D956/2 String Quintet in C major, *Adagio*

XI. *Adagio molto, Largo, Lento, Sehr langsam*
Even: to MM 38. Odd: to MM 26. No B types.

    ¢ : Type A
        D957/12 *Am Meer, Sehr langsam*

    C: Type A
        D940/2 Fantasy in F minor for Piano four hands, *Largo*

        ―――――
        D911/21 *Das Wirtshaus, Sehr langsam*

    3/4: Type A
        D957/13 *Der Doppelgänger, Sehr langsam*

    C: Type A
        D407/1A Terzett [*Adagio*] *sostenuto*

An overview of Tables VI and VII shows us that, with the two exceptions mentioned in Part III (D850/1 and D943/3), Schubert used Italian tempo terms with far more precision than he used German ones. Despite occasional unclear instructions arising from his habit of "thinking up, thinking down" ("…. *molto moderato*"), which he took over from the way he gave German instructions ("*Nicht zu geschwind*"), his Italian terminology can be organized into a relatively clear typology. Perhaps the explanation for the discrepancy between his two terminology systems can be explained through his ambitions, divulged in the famous "Kupelwieser" statement (see Ornamentation and Embellishment, Ch. V) wherein he expressed his hopes to "pave the way to the Grand Symphony." The pieces he wrote with German texts and instructions were songs, which he wrote mostly for his friends, or at the very most, for a larger Viennese audience. Psychologically, he probably imagined that he would always be present when they were performed. But the chamber works and, especially, the symphonies: these he wrote with an eye toward a place in the larger scheme of things. These were for a much wider public, and clearly for all times, when surely he would no longer be present to hear them or to watch over them. They were for the world; they belonged to genres that the world understood, and thus they needed tempo and character instructions in the world's official musical language. Perhaps also, because these works fell more easily into a typology than did the songs, Schubert assumed that Italian instructions would be clear enough without the addition of metronome markings which, even to the end of his career, remained a kind of novelty.

According to the metronome markings we have been able to derive for Schubert's instrumental works, the range of his tempos appears to be wider even than that of Beethoven's. On the fast end, his markings challenge players in the same exciting and technically daunting ways as do Beethoven's, and on the slow end performers must summon up the same mastery of the profound coupled with the lyrical as they must in the music of the older master. The next great composer in the larger Austro-German line, Felix Mendelssohn, was already professionally active during Schubert's last years. Upon examination of his tempos, we would find that, for all of Wagner's objections to Mendelssohn as a "classical speed demon," the latter's metronome markings do not match Schubert's on the fast end. Schumann, too, called for slower tempos in general. By the time of Brahms, those breakneck *Presto* and *Allegro molto* markings were largely a thing of the past. The classical stance that Brahms shared with Schubert was one of structure, phrasing, and architectural balance, but it was not one of tempo and meter. Gone, too, was much of the ideological struggle and brilliance that had coupled early musical romanticism to the wider artistic world of its time, and which pervaded Schubert's works. He was truly the last master of an entire line of thought and expression in sound.

In Conclusion

If I were asked to identify the single most interesting aspect of Franz Schubert's music in performance, I would not know where to begin. All of it fascinates me. But if I were asked to identify the single most problematic aspect of his music in performance, I would say without hesitation that it was the recognition of the existence of problems in the first place. Most of this book, then, has been devoted to such recognition, particularly in the areas of performance traditions and textual inaccuracies.

Throughout these chapters, readers may have noticed the absence of that warm and fuzzy verbiage that is so often used in discussions of the life and music of Franz Schubert, and, indeed, I plead guilty of withholding it. But if, in the reader's mind, I have helped in some way to nudge Schubert up alongside Bach, Beethoven, Brahms, and others whose notated legacy is discussed with the utmost critical seriousness and respect, then I have been doing my job. And if, in the course of it, I have been a bit hard on a number of players and scholars, I can assure you that my own earlier approaches to Schubert's music in performance would not have stood up to the kinds of examination I have offered here. The way in which most of us have been taught to perform classical music, and to think about it—essentially as a wonderful vehicle for the performer's own interpretive powers and talent—is not really consistent with the images of mastery and genius that we actually cherish for our great composers. Perhaps one of the most telling marks of this conflict lies in the marketing of classical recordings, the covers of which more often bear images of performers than of composers.

Although I have given only minimal space for practical solutions to the problems raised in this book, I would offer two bits of advice for performers who take these things seriously. The first is never to listen to a recording of Schubert's music without following it critically with the score. Passive musical thinking (or non-thinking) is for audiences, not for performers. The second suggestion is to use the score while playing at all times, even in performances. The habit of memorizing concert music arose in the middle of the nineteenth century, well after Schubert's death. While it may contribute to a performer's confidence and leave him or her free to concentrate on the necessary technical polish, it also contributes heavily—for the same reason—to the obscuring of notated detail. Obviously, in order to carry out these two suggestions, one is obliged to find reasonably accurate scores, and in some cases, that search will prove frustrating. Here, a good marking pen and a large supply of white-out are surely worth a thousand *urtexts*. The trick is to know where to use them.

David Montgomery
San Francisco, 2002

Appendix IA

Tempo rubato: a short overview

Other names: temps dérobé, temps troublé, contre-temps, tempo disperato, tempo disturbato,tempo perduto,contra-tempo, imbroglio, confundere, confusione, strascino, Tonverziehung, Setzverbindung, Rückung, Verrückung, Verwirrung, Verwicklung, Vermengen, Wirrwarr, Zusammentreffen, Zusammenfliessen, syncopation, dragging, dragged notes, stolen time.

Although the first documented use of the term *"tempo rubato"* in the critical literature of music was by Pier Francesco Tosi in his singing treatise of 1723, the concept itself may be at least a century older. Some musicologists claim that it goes back to the late Italian Renaissance / early Baroque. Frederick Niecks and others after him believed that in the preface to *Nuove musiche* (1601) Caccini was describing *tempo rubato* when he wrote about a "noble manner of singing that does not subject itself to a regulated measure, often lessening the value of the notes by half in accordance with the sense of the words, whence arises the manner of singing, which I call *sprezzatura*." [Trans. Friedrich Niecks in "Tempo rubato" in *Monthly Musical Record* XLIII/506 (1 February 1913):30.] But Caccini's description seems concerned more with declamation or recitative than with anything resembling the eighteenth- and nineteenth-century *tempo rubato* in the context of a regular meter. Furthermore, none of the rest of Caccini's preface bears out such an interpretation. R.D. Cerone's treatise of 1613, however, had come much closer to the mark:

> The singer is obliged to adorn the work according to its character. For this he should know that specified notes are to be accompanied by accents, which are shaped by a hesitation and holding back of the voice [part]. This is done in such a way that one takes away something from one note and gives it to another. [Trans. from Boris Bruck, "Wandlungen des Begriffes Tempo rubato," Inaugural Dissertation, Friedrich-Alexander Universität Erlangen (Berlin: Paul Funk, 1929):2.] The Spanish original reads: "El cantor es tenido adornarlos segu propriedad de la letra. Por esso ha de saber que las dichas Notas, se acompañan con unos acentos causados de algunas tandanças y sostamiendos de voz, que se haze con quitar una parte de una Figura y darla à otra." : Libro octavo, Cap. primero, p. 541f.]

In our discussion of the *"tenuto-agogic"* delivery in Schubert, we have pointed out the association of accents with "holding back" (cf. Swoboda and Starke on the "kleine Anschwellungszeichen," Ch. IV). Although Cerone's description seems reasonably complete and modern (including "taking away" and "giving back"), it was Tosi, apparently,

Appendix IA

who actually introduced the term "larceny" (*rubato*), with which we associate this technique today:

> He who does not know how to drag the notes can certainly not compose nor accompany; and he remains bereft of the best taste and the most beautiful insight. The dragging of the notes in the style of pathos is a particularly glorious larceny, which helps to make one person sing better than another, provided that he has the foresight and wit to make a lovely restitution. [*Opinioni de' cantori antichi e moderni o sieno osservatzioni sopra il canto figurato* (Bologna, 1723):99.]

Some modern writers read similar concepts into period descriptions of music-making by Frescobaldi and Froberger, as well as into extant performance instructions by these musicians. Unfortunately the available corroborating evidence, either for or against the practice of *rubato*, is too slim to support anything but speculation about these two great keyboard players. The trouble with *tempo rubato* as a device of the early Baroque lies in the difference in musical styles between that era and the middle-late Baroque of Tosi's time, one century later. Apropos "stolen time," the most important difference lies, as one might expect, in the nature of the bass and its relative function as a timekeeper—especially in vocal music.

Bruck also points out that German writers had described *tempo rubato* well before Tosi's manual was printed: for example, Johann Crüger (1660) and M.H. Fuhrmann (1706), both of whom treat accentuation in terms of expression and/or syncopation. Germans clearly practiced a form of *tempo rubato* by the middle of the eighteenth century. Perhaps their use of it was indigenous, but it may have been inspired as well by Italian musicians working in the country. Johann Joachim Quantz wrote in his autobiography that he remembered hearing Santa Stella Lotti, wife of the composer Antonio Lotti, employ *tempo rubato* in her singing at Dresden. ["Herrn Johann Joachim Quanzens Lebenslauf, von ihm selbst entworfen" in *Kritische Beiträge* I:III:197–250, ed. F.W. Marpurg (Berlin): 214.] This would have been before the Lottis left Dresden to return to Italy in 1719. Later in the same document Quantz described the style of the great Venetian singer Faustina Bordoni (the wife of the composer Hasse) who sang in Dresden:

> She sung [sic] adagio, with great passion and expression, but was not equally successful, if such deep sorrow were to be impressed on the hearer, as might require dragging, sliding, or notes of syncopation, and tempo rubato. [Trans. Charles Burney in *The Present State of Music in Germany* (London, 1775), ed. Percy Scholes as *An Eighteenth-Century Musical Tour* (London: Oxford, 1959):I:192/3. Bordoni was in residence in Dresden from 1731–1763.]

Among the late Baroque/early *galant* German sources concerning *tempo rubato* were Johann Friedrich Agricola's gloss of Tosi's manual, published as the *Anleitung zur Singkunst* in Berlin (1757) and Friedrich Wilhelm Marpurg's *Anleitung zur Musik überhaupt, und zur Singkunst besonders* (Berlin: Arnold Weber, 1763).

Tosi's concept of *tempo rubato* as opposed to contemporaneous German practices is not entirely clear to us today. To begin with, he discusses it in at least two different places in his treatise. The first mention of it includes the famous characterizations of "stealing" and "returning" the stolen time, and those two terms have pervaded subsequent definitions into the twentieth century. This kind of *tempo rubato* seems to have been a bit less structured than the later German type, which was metrically strict and was generated through syncopation, accent displacement, and hemiola. Tosi's second description of *tempo rubato*, or "dragging"—at least if we are to believe the notated example offered by his first English translator, Galliard (1742)—was a wildly expressive device that included a great scalar sweep from high to low, with sobbing rhythmical effects in between, similar, in fact, to certain ornaments in Monteverdi and other early seventeenth-century composers. [See examples provided by Monteverdi in his own music (for example, the alternative vocal reading in Orfeo's aria "Possente spirto") or more theoretical models in, say, Antonio Brunelli's *Varii essercitii* (Florence, 1714), one of which is reproduced in *Musikalische Interpretation,* op. cit: 231/2.] Galliard does not show the basic original versions that such ornaments might have graced (if indeed these are models for improvisation), and so it is difficult to know exactly how these examples of "dragg" derived from Tosi's "stolen time".

We may assume that all eighteenth-century types of *tempo rubato* featured some form of melodic displacement against a steady bass. Mozart's famous letter describing his own use of *tempo rubato*, has usually been interpreted within the context of the Italian school—i.e. Tosi's first type—although considering Mozart's phrase about playing strictly in tempo, it could also be understood as a German type:

Letter to Leopold Mozart 24 October 1777

That I always play strictly in tempo [within the meter, "im Tact"] gives them all cause for wonder. They simply cannot fathom how, in the tempo rubato of an adagio, I keep the left hand from knowing what the right hand is doing.

Unfortunately, we have unearthed relatively few Italian descriptions of *tempo rubato*—that is, other than those based on Tosi's first type. It is conceivable, although not yet demonstrable through research, that the Italian and German types were not really so different. Regardless of the variety of names by which one characterized *tempo rubato*, the most widely used alternate term for it was internationally consistent. In Italian it was "*strascino*," i.e. "holding back" or "drag." Likewise the main German term, "*Verziehung*," the Dutch word, "*sleep*," and the contemporaneous English term, "*dragg*," all meant the same thing. Like Tosi, Joseph Martin Kraus (1770) and C.P.E. Bach (1787) confined their descriptions of *tempo rubato* to the dragging concept. J.A.P. Schulz (in Sulzer, *Allgemeine Theorie der schönen Künste,* 1771-74) described the dragging of notes as well as the anticipation of other notes (*retardatio* and *anticipatio*)— as did Marpurg and Türk. The Germans also gave these two techniques a new umbrella term, namely, *Rückung* or "displacement." *Rückung*, then, consisted of 1) tying a note over into the following note (dragging); or 2) halving a note in order to rush into the following note (anticipating). The Germans also defined *tempo rubato* in terms of displaced accentuation, hemiola, and sesquialtera.

One of the basic problems in comparing *rubato* types is the relative imparity of detail supplied by different authors. Tosi, for example, was cryptic at best - whereas Marpurg was typological and detailed. One might speculate that the many notated examples of syncopation and accent displacement in German sources were meant only as approximations of more subtle rhythmic manipulations; or, on the other hand, that Tosi was actually

Appendix IA

talking about a more structured technique and simply failed to elaborate it as such. Another problem in comparing *rubato* types lies in the pedagogical object of a given source. Regardless of common cultural ties and similar descriptions, *tempo rubato* for singers (say, Marpurg, Hiller, or Petri - all German sources) may still be a different animal than *tempo rubato* for, say, pianists (say, C.P.E. Bach, Löhlein, Wolf, or Türk - also all German sources). One can easily appreciate a singer's ability to soar more freely above a measured accompaniment (indeed, one often cannot escape it), as opposed to the problems of coordination and manual independence required of the pianist who might wish to achieve the same effect.

Tosi describes *tempo rubato* clearly as a performance art. Likewise, Marpurg (1763), C.P.E. Bach (1787) and Türk (1789) imply that the techniques of syncopation and hemiola —under the rubric of "*tempo rubato*"—were matters for performers. We can make this assumption anyway, if for no other reason than that their books are directed at performers. By 1808, however, Koch could state unequivocally that techniques of "displacement" (syncopation and hemiola) had once been part of the performer's improvisatory art, but were now taken over into notation itself. [Surprisingly, displacement *rubato* is described by Oscar Paul as late as 1873 (*Handlexikon der Tonkunst*, p. 500), cribbed by Friedrich Bremer in *Handlexikon der Musik* (1882, p. 708). As a performance technique, however, this outmoded concept is refuted in Sir George Grove's *Dictionary of Music and Musicians* (1878) and in Hugo Riemann's *Musiklexikon* (1882, p. 787)— both of which identify techniques of displacement as part of the composer's art.]

Tempo rubato is not mentioned as such in eighteenth-century French sources. Many French authors mention syncopation in their treatises, but only as a compositional technique and never as an expressive performance device. Some nineteenth-century French authors describe a form of *tempo rubato*, or "*temps dérobé*," but not with the consistency of German authors, nor even always mindful of the same essence of rhythmical conflict that characterizes the technique in both German and Italian sources. For example, Pierre Baillot (1834) shows "*tempo rubato*" in the form of what we might call "divisions," and Manuel Garcia (1847) demonstrates his conception of "*tempo rubbato*," [sic] or "*temps dérobé*" almost as an extended, ornamented ossia to the singer's passagework.

In the mid-nineteenth century *tempo rubato* was particularly associated with the great virtuoso pianists who lived in Paris. Chopin's use of the device was perpetuated in the memory of his pupils and others who heard him play, although the reader will find that the descriptions of his playing do not all concur. Liszt, too, was a great proponent of *rubato*. And because some of his pupils lived into the early recording era, we often attempt to reconstruct his rhythmic ideas through their legacy. But by this time "*rubato*" had evolved into a universally acknowledged expressive device—universal in the idea of its freedom, that is, but extremely personal in actual delivery. Unfortunately, we cannot hope truly to reconcile the diversity of performance styles that characterized early twentieth century pianism in an attempt to trace the specific practices of the great nineteenth-century masters. We find it noteworthy—but perhaps coincidental —that the two pianists with whom modern agogical *rubato* is first associated, Chopin and Liszt, both grew up in slavic cultures and took an active interest in the rhythms and dances of their native Slavic lands.

In Sulzer's *Allgemeine Theorie* J.A.P. Schulz explained that in writing about *tempo rubato* (in the article by that name) his choice of terms "delay" and "anticipation" was carefully considered so as not to give the impression of "ritard" or "acceleration." These last two terms he would reserve for just that—the slowing down or speeding up of the general tempo—but not for *tempo rubato*. Schulz wished to preserve the idea of a steady bass accompanying a syncopated or even free melody above. Nevertheless, the very mention of the newer interpretation hints at the possibility that the classical concept of *tempo rubato* had already been endangered. And indeed, sometime in the nineteenth century the practice of "*rubato*"—by then no longer called "*tempo rubato*"—came to rely on overall tempo flexibility as its main identifying technique. Ignaz Paderewski, who was otherwise famous for "agogic" delays on specific notes, frankly admitted that *rubato* was often best seen as a general change of tempo. In his view the concept of a free right hand over a stricter left hand perhaps had been appropriate for Mozart. But as he put it, "to play [Chopin and Liszt] with a metronomic left hand is to commit murder in the first degree. Nor should any pianist heed the ridiculous but oft repeated assertion that if you increase the speed for a few bars you must slow up for a few bars subsequently, so that the whole piece will last just as many seconds as if you had made no change in the pace." [Quoted in Henry Finck, *Success in Music and How it is Won* (New York: Scribner's Sons, 1909):429.]

One final and important point is that almost all the sources concerning *tempo rubato* emphasize the great care with which this technique must be used. Tosi sets the tone by admonishing singers to return what they have stolen. The Germans insist that *tempo rubato* must be used only by musicians who have a solid grounding in harmony, and they also delimit the extent of the technique—some even say specifically that it should not last longer than half or, at most, one full measure. Almost all writers warn that *tempo rubato* must be used with "taste". But as we noted above, the "taste" to which these writers refer does not represent an innate capability on the part of the modern musician. It is a matter of historical understanding to be gained partially through analysis of the information contained in the existing pedagogical sources.

APPENDIX IB

Ludwig van Beethoven

66. So oder so

Text von Karl Lappe

WoO 148

Ziemlich lebhaft und entschlossen

Nord o-der Süd! Wenn nur im war-men Bu - sen ein Hei-lig-tum der Schön-heit und der Mu - sen, ein göt-ter-rei-cher Him - mel blüht! Nur Gei-stes-ar-mut kann der Win-ter mor - den, Kraft fügt zu Kraft und Glanz zu Glanz der Nor-den.

2. Stadt oder Land! Nur nicht zu eng die Räume,
  Ein wenig Himmel, etwas Grün der Bäume
  Zum Schatten vor dem Sonnenbrand!
  Nicht an das Wo ward Seligkeit gebunden.
  Wer hat das Glück schon außer sich gefunden?
    Stadt oder Land!
    Die Außenwelt ist Tand.

[3. Knecht oder Herr! Auch Könige sind Knechte.
  Wir dienen gern der Wahrheit und dem Rechte.
  Gebeut uns nur, bist du verständiger.
  Doch soll kein Hochmut unsern Dienst verhöhnen.
  Nur Sklavensinn kann fremder Laune fröhnen.
    Knecht oder Herr!
    Nur keines Menschen Narr!]

4. Arm oder reich! Sei's Pfirsich oder Pflaume!
  Wir pflücken ungleich von dem Lebensbaume.
  Dir zollt der Ast, mir nur der Zweig.
  Mein leichtes Mahl wiegt darum nicht geringe.
  Lust am Genuß bestimmt den Wert der Dinge.
    Arm oder reich!
    Die Glücklichen sind gleich.

5. Blaß oder rot! Nur auf den bleichen Wangen
  Sehnsucht und Liebe, Zürnen und Erbangen,
  Gefühl und Trost für fremde Not!
  Es strahlt der Geist nicht aus des Blutes Welle.
  Ein andrer Spiegel brennt in Sonnenhelle.
    Blaß oder rot!
    Nur nicht das Auge tot!

6. Jung oder alt! Was kümmern uns die Jahre!
  Der Geist ist frisch, doch Schelme sind die Haare.
  Auch mir ergraut das Haupt zu bald.
  Doch eilt nur, Locken, glänzend euch zu färben,
  Es ist nicht Schade, Silber zu erwerben.
    (Etwas verzögernd) Jung oder alt!
    (Erstes Zeitmaß) Doch erst am Grabe kalt!

7. Schlaf oder Tod! Willkommen, Zwillingsbrüder!
  Der Tag ist hin; ihr zieht die Wimper nieder.
  (Etwas verzögernd bis zum ersten Zeitmaß)
  Traum ist der Erde Glück und Not.
  Zu kurzer Tag! Zu schnell verrauschtes Leben!
  Warum so schön und doch so rasch verschweben?
    Schlaf oder Tod!
    (Erstes Zeitmaß) Hell strahlt das Morgenrot.

Appendix IIA

The Pedagogical Sources: Methods and Tutors

The following list represents pedagogical works relevant to the study of Viennese music from about the middle of Wolfgang Mozart's career to well beyond the time of Schubert's death. Perhaps, in the context of the present book, we should say "represents as best it can," for it must bridge a few notable gaps. Chief among them are the lack of specific references to Franz Schubert and his style, as well as several lost or never-completed tutors. Whereas Johann Nepomuk Breitschädel's hard-to-find piano tutor of 1818 would have appeared too early to include Schubert, Max Leidesdorf's *Neue Wiener Clavierschule* (advertised but not published) might have discussed his works. Certainly Johann Michael Vogl's unfinished and now-lost notes for a singing tutor would have done so. We also know of a lost pedagogical work by Schubert's teacher Antonio Salieri, the *Libro di partimento di varia specie per profitto della gioventù tedesca*, although its title would promise far less about performance practice than the others mentioned above.

Viennese tutors for voice, piano, strings, harp and some winds are plentiful, but we have not found one for every instrument. Late eighteenth-century bassoonists, for example, may have had to seek out foreign tutors not distributed in Vienna for written instruction: French tutors by Abraham (1780) and Ozi (1787), or perhaps the German tutor by Almenraeder (1795) and various updates as the instruments developed; likewise trumpet players might have consulted Altenburg (1795) [see other works mentioned in this book, below].

The list below includes foreign works with documentable relevance, and / or possible Viennese commercial currency. We know, for example, that the house of Traeg represented Breitkopf & Härtel in Vienna from 1798–1818, and although they may not have carried all of B&H's items their catalogue identifies several important ones: cf. Emanuel Aloys Förster, *Anleitung zum Generalbass*, 1805. In any case, one surely was able to order from this catalogue, if the item were not on hand. Other major foriegn firms also must have had representation in Vienna: not just the German companies (Simrock, Schott, André, Peters, Schlesinger, Hoffmeister, etc.), but the Italian firm of Ricordi (Milan and Lucca) and certain Parisian publishers as well. Apropos the latter, the numerous "Paris Conservatory" tutors by Cherubini and others seem to have reached Vienna and other cultural centers fairly quickly, particularly because that institution served as a model for other nineteenth-century conservatories.

Items in large print in the list below were published in Vienna. Foreign items in small print were undoubtedly known in Vienna (Türk, Cramer, etc.), but probably had to be ordered. Some of the small-print items may have been stocked or even printed in Vienna as well, despite our inability to establish this fact at the present state of research. The second list below gives items for which no date has been established. Here we have trod upon uncertain ground, for several of the small-print items could not be checked even for their appropriateness to the period. Still, we included them, in the desire not to overlook possible sources relevant to study. Finally, we include a short list of items mentioned in this book, but which do not belong in the two main bibliographies.

Legend: 'b'=before/ 'a'=after. For example: "b.1800"= "before 1800;" 'a.1800' = "after 1800." The sign "?" is used to represent an exact year if the author's research is correct, whereas 'c' is used only where an approximate year can be determined. As mentioned in the list of abbreviations at the beginning of this book, "*GMF, RC*," or simply "*RC*" refers to the manuscript list of music books acquired by the Archduke Rudolph and catalogued by him or his personal librarian. His considerable collection is now part of the Gesellschaft der Musikfreunde.

1774 Giambattista Mancini (1716-1800), *Pensieri, e rifflessioni sopra il canto figurato* (Vienna). 2nd ed. 1777 as *Rifflessioni sopra il canto figorato*. Becker [see App. IIB] lists 1777 as the year of the 3rd ed. Fr. ed. as *L'art du chant figuré* (Paris: Duport, 1796). Mancini was the court singing master in Vienna.

1779 Franz Xaver Paul Riegler [Rigler](c.1747-1796), *Anleitung zum Clavier für musikialische Lehrstunden* (Vienna: Joseph Edlen von Kurzbäck). 2nd ed.(Vienna:1791, with 24 cadenzas/6 works). Also ed. (Ofen:Universitätsbuchdruckerei, 1798).

1781 Johann P. Kirnberger (1721-1783), *Grundsätze des Generalbasses als erste Linien zur Composition* (Berlin and Wien: Hoffmeister)

1784? A. Lolli, *L'Ecole du violon en quatuor* (Berlin and Amsterdam: Hummel/Offenbach:André).

1785 Leopold Mozart (1719-1787), *Violinschule. . . .*3rd ed. (Vienna: Volcke). Original published as *Versuch einer gründlichen Violinschule* (Augsburg: Lotter, 1756). New ed.[Neukomm, ed.] as *Violinschule, oder Answeisung die Violine zu spielen...*(Leipzig: Kühnel, 1804). 4th ed. 1791. Further ed.: Joseph Pirlinger, ed. as *Neue vollständige theoretische und praktische Violinschule* (Vienna: Wallihauser/ also Vienna: Hoffmeister, 1799) and under the same title by Schiedemayer (Vienna: Haslinger). Another Viennese ed. by Cappi. Many other editions throughout Europe.

1785 Ignaz Schweigl (c. 1735-1803), *Grundlehre der Violin* (Vienna: Author). 2nd ed. as *Verbesserter Grundlehre der Violin, zur Erleichterung der Lehre und zum Vorteil der Schüler gründliche Unterricht, die Violin zu spielen* (Prague: Widtmann? Pt I., 1794; Pt.II, 1795).

Appendix IIA *279*

1785 Johann Georg Tromlitz, "Neuerfundene Vortheile zur besseren Einrichtung der Flöte," in *Miscellaneen artistichen Inhaltes* (Erfurt). Also: *Kurze Abhandlung vom Flötenspielen* (Leipzig: B&H).

1787 Ferdinand Kauer (1751-1831), *Kurzegefaßte Klavierschule [für Anfänger]* (Vienna: Artaria, pl.no.100). Also: *Neue Clarinettschule* (Vienna: Bermann).

1787 Ferdinand Kauer, *Violinschule für Anfänger* (Vienna: Artaria, pl. no. 107).

1787 Johann Anton Kobrich, *Praktisches Geig-Fundament, das sich mehr in Zeichen und Noten, als in vielen ausgesinnten Erklärungen für schwächere Lehrlinge leicht auszeichnet. Worin das Violin, Alt-Viola, Bassetto, und Violon in sechserlei Verstimmungen mit 3,4 und 5 Saiten auf die leichteste und kürzeste Art zu erlernen ist* (Augsburg: Matthäus Riegers sel. Söhnen).

1787 Étienne Ozi (1754–1813), *Méthode nouvelle et raisonnée pour le basson* (Paris: Boyer / Le Menu). 2nd ed. as *Nouvelle méthode de basson adoptée pour le conservatoire* (Paris: Conservatoire). See extended discussion in Becker: 356.

1787 Daniel Gottlob Türk, *Von den wichtigsten Pflichten eines Organisten ...* (Halle) rev. 1838, F. Naue. 240 pp.

1788 Ferdinand Kauer, *Kurzgefaßte Anweisung, die Flöte zu spielen* (Vienna: Artaria, pl. no. 169).

1788 Ferdinand Kauer, *Kurzgefaßte Anweisung, das Violoncell zu spielen* (Speyer: Bossler). A later ed. (Vienna: Artaria, pl. no.184, 1789).

1788 Franz Anton Schlegel, *Gründliche Anleitung, die Flöte zu spielen nach Quanzens Anweisung* (Graz: F.G. Weingrand & Fr. Gerstl). See commentary by Warner, p. 40.

1789 *Singschule von verschiedenen Componisten* (Vienna: Artaria).

1789 Daniel Gottlob Türk, *Klavierschule, oder Anweisung zum Klavierspielen für Lehrer und Lernende* (Leipzig and Halle). New ed. 1800.

1790 Johann Georg Albrechtsberger, *Gründliche Anweisung zur Composition ... mit einem Anhange von der Beschaffenheit und Anwendung aller ...musikalischen Instrumente* (Leipzig). Socratic style. Includes a glossary. Enl. 3rd ed. 1821.

1790? Bartolomeo Campagnoli, *L'Art d'inventer à [l']improviste des fantaisies et cadences pour le violon* (Leipzig: B&H).

1791 Johann Georg Albrechtsberger (1736–1809), *Kurzgefaßte Methode, den Generalbass zu erlernen* (Vienna: Artaria). Enl. 2nd ed. 1792. English and French translations, 1815. Also: n.d., "Generalbass- und Harmonielehre" (ms, GMF). Also Fr. ed.

1791 *Die Singschule, oder Solmisation, desgleichen noch keine zum Vorscheine gekommen, worinnen die nothwendigsten Regeln und eine Menge musikalische und fugirte Stücke u.s.w. enthalten sind, mittelst welchen ein Schüler in kurzer Zeit zur Vollkommenheit gelangen kann. Componiert von 8 berühmten Kapellmeistern aus Europa* (Vienna: Hohenleitner). Appears to be a German edition of (actually 68 pages of excerpts from) the *Nouvelle Edition des solfèges d'Italie composés par Hasse, Durante,*

Scarlatti, Porpora, Mazoni, Caffaro, Gravé par Michot (Paris: Pleyel, n.d.); which is 286 pages, including an introduction to music and singing. Cf. *Singschule* (Vienna: 1789).

1791 Johann Georg Tromlitz, *Ausführlicher und gründlicher Unterricht die Flöte zu spielen* (Leipzig: Adam Friedrich Böhme).

1792 François Devienne (1760–1803), *Nouvelle méthode théorique et pratique pour la flûte* (Paris: Imbault). First edition listed in *New Grove* as 1794. Subsequent editions (Paris: Naderman, 1795), (Hamburg: August, 1800), (Offenbach: André, 1805), (Paris: Pollet, c1810), (Vienna: Chemische Druckerei, 1810), (Paris: Benoit, 1815), (Paris: Janet et Cotelle, 1815), (Paris: Joly, 1820), (Paris: Dufaut et Dubois, 1822), (Paris: Joly, 1825), (Paris: Aulagnier 1825), (Paris: Petit, 1825), (Paris: J. Meissonnier, 1830), (Paris: Colombier, 1860), [L. Doninx], *Méthode pour la flûte d'après celle de Devienne* (Paris: H. Lemoine, 1860), [Françoise Devienne], *Méthode de flûte, système ordinaire et Boëhm* (Paris: Beuscher, 1950).

1792–98 Justin Heinrich Knecht, *Gemeinnütziges Elementarwerk der Harmonie und des Generalbasses*, 4 parts (Augsburg). Also: *Theoretisch-praktische Generalbass Schule*, (n.d.). Cf. the *Gemeinnütziges Elementarwerk*.

1793 Johann Friedrich Hugo von Dal[h]berg (1760–1812), *Kurzgefaßte Methode den Generalbass zu erlernen* (Vienna: Artaria).

1794 Ferdinand Kauer, *Singschule nach dem neuesten System der Tonkunst* (Vienna: Artaria, pl. no. 510). Some sources list the original date of publication at 1790.

1794? Johann Gottfried Vierling, *Versuch einer Anleitung zum Präludiren für Ungeübtere mit Beispielen ...*, new ed.? (Leipzig: B&H).

1795 François Devienne, *Méthode de flûte théorique et pratique, contenant tous les principes, des petits airs, duos et sonates faciles, prédédée d'un prélude à la tête de chaque morceau* (Paris: Imbault). Ger. as *Neue theoretische und praktische Flötenschule, oder Anweisung in den Anfangsgründen der Musik, in den Grundregeln des Flötenspiels, in der Art, die Flöte zu halten, anzusetzen, in Zungenschlägen, Bindungen u.s.w.* (Leipzig: Kühnel / Augsburg: Gombart / Vienna: Bermann / Vienna: Haslinger, Vienna: Hoffmeister, 1803, pl.no. 321: also Steiner and Chemische Druckerey). New Ger. ed. as *Neue vollständige theoretisch-praktische Flöten-Schule* (Cappi). The Devienne method has been updated and reprinted many times, well into the middle of the twentieth century. Also: *Abrégé de la Méthode de flûte* (Paris: Langlois / Vienna: Haslinger, n.d.).

1795–98 Justin Heinrich Knecht, *Vollständige Orgelschule für Anfänger und Geübter*e, 3 vols. (Leipzig: B&H). Becker gives the date as 1796. Also ed. Munich, 1814.

1796 Matthieu-Frédéric Blasius, *Nouvelle méthode de clarinette et raisonnement des instruments, principes et théorie de musique dédiés aux élèves du Conservatoire* (Paris).

Appendix IIA 281

1796   Jan Ladislaw Dussek, *Instructions on the Art of Playing the Piano Forte or Harpsichord* (London). Also: French trans. as *Méthode pour le piano forte* (Paris, 1796); Ger. trans. as *Pianoforte-Schule* (Leipzig:1802) 4th ed. 1815, and many other editions. Also see Pleyel and Dussek, 1796.

1796   August Eberhard Müller, *Anweisung zum genauen Vortrage der Mozartschen Clavierconcerti hauptsächlich in Absicht richtiger Applicatur* (Leipzig: B&H / Schmidt & Rau). Also: *Wegweiser für den Unterricht im Klavierspiel* ... (Author, n.d.). A much later edition listed for 1876.

1796   I.J. Pleyel and J.L. Dussek, *Méthode pour le piano forte* (Paris) Ger. trans. as *Vollständige Anweisung das Pfte. zu spielen* (Braunschweig: Spehr). Ed. 1800. Also: I.J. Pleyel, *Méthode de pfte.* (Paris: Pleyel, n.d.). Cf. Dussek's own method by the same name published in Paris 1796. Also see: I.J. Pleyel, *Vollständige Klavierschule nebst 24 Übungsstücken* (n.d., 4th Aufl. 1800?). Also: *Grosse Klavierschule, nebst 27 Uebungstücken* (Vienna: Cappie et C. 1815?) and *Klavierschule, nebst 30 Uebungsstücke* ... (Leipzig: Peters, n.d.). Also: I.J. Pleyel, *Kleine Klavierschule* (Brauns: Spehr, n.d.) (Vienna: Haslinger). Ignaz Joseph Pleyel's activities as an author and co-author (in conjunction with Dussek and others) of pedagogical works is sometimes difficult to distinguish from his activities as a publisher. See J. Zsako, "Bibliographic Sandtraps: The "Klavierschule', Pleyel or Dussek?" in *CM* 12 (1971). Also see Rita Benton, *Ignace Pleyel: A thematic Catalogue of his Works* (NY: Pendragon, 1977): 355-360.

b.1797   Bartolomeo Campagnoli, *Metodo per violino*. Also ed. 1797 (Milan: Lucca). Eng. trans. John Bishop as *A New and Progressive Method* (London: 1856). Fr. trans. as *Nouvelle méthode de la mécanique progressive du jeu de violon ... distribuée en 132 leçons progressives pour deux violons, et 118 études pour un violon seul*, op. 21 (Leipzig: 1791). 2nd ed. 1803. Ed. 1824. Another ed. (Milan: Ricordi, 1827).

1797   Joseph Franz Schwanenberg, *Vollständiges theoretisch-praktisches Lehrbuch zur Davids- und Pedalharfe, mit vielen in Kupfer gestochen Figuren, Notenbeispielen, und einem Anhange von Tonstücken, mit Bezeichn;luung der Fingersetzung* (Vienna: Author).

1798   Louis Adam and L.W. Lachnith, *Méthode ou principe général du doigté p. le pfte, adopté dans le Conservatoire de Musique*, in 4 parts (Paris: Sieber). 2nd ed. 1814. The method was printed in Ger. / Fr. by Simrock in Bonn and Haslinger in Vienna. It was also translated as L. Adams *Pianoforteschule des Conservatoriums zu Paris (*Leipzig: B&H). It. trans. as *Sistema per imparare il pianoforte* (Florence: Lorenzi). Also a Spanish translation for Schott in Mainz.

1798   F.-J. Garnier l'aîné, *Méthode raisonnée pour le haut-bois* (Paris). Also ed. 1800 (Offenbach: André), in Ger. / Fr., and another ed. 1802. Also: *Extrait de la Méthode* (Offenbach: André, n.d.). Or is the *Extrait* the ed. of 1802?

1798   Franz Xaver Paul Riegler [Rigler], *Anleitung zum Gesange, und dem Klavier, oder Orgel zu spielen* (Budapest/ Ofen: Königl. hungar. Universitätsbuchdruckerei). Riegler's main work.

1798/99 Joseph Agus, Charles-Simon Catel, Marie Luigi Cherubini and François-Joseph Gossec, *Principes élémentaires de musique arrêtes par les membres du Conservatoire, suivis de* solfèges (Paris).

1799 Carl Kreith (c1746–1807?, *NG* 2001 lists his death at 1803), *Anweisung, wie alle Töne auf der Flöte traversiere richtig zu nehmen sind nebst ihren gehörigen Benennungen* (Vienna: Artaria). Also: *Scala für den Czakan* (Vienna: Bermann, n.d.).

1799 Johann Georg Tromlitz, "Abhandlung über den schönen Ton auf der Flöte, und dessen wahre und ächte Behandlung ...," in *AmZ*:II:301/316.

1800 Louis Adam, *Méthode de piano du conservatoire* (Paris). Also (Bonn: Simrock: 1814 or 1815). Eds. 1803 / 4 / 5 / 10. Ger. trans. Carl Czerny as *Pianoforte-Schule des Conservatoriums in Paris* (Vienna: Haslinger, 1826 (Becker, 1828) / Leipzig: B&H). Cf. Adam, Méthode, 1802.

1800 Johann Georg Albrechtsberger, *Klavierschule für Anfänger* (Vienna: Artaria) Also ed. 1808. Original title in ms, "Anfangsgründe zur Klavierkunste".

1800 Marie Luigi Cherubini (1760–1842), Pierre Garat (1762–1823), François Joseph Gossec (1734–1829), Louis-Joseph Guilchard, Etienne-Nicolas Méhul (1763–1817), Pierre Louis Ginguené (1748–1816), Honoré François Marie Langlé (1741–1807), B. Mengozzi (1758–1800), Charles Henri Plantade (1764–1839), [ ] Richer, et al, *Méthode de chant du Conservatoire de musique*. Another edition (Paris: 1802 / 3). Ger. as *Singschule des Conservatoriums der Musik in Paris* (Vienna: Cappi, n.d.). It. as *Metodo di canto del conservatorio di Parigi adottato dall' ... conservatorio di Milano* (Milan: Carulli, 1825).

1800 Philipp Dornaus, "Einige Bemerkungen über den zweckmässigen Gebrauch des Waldhorns" (Leipzig: *AmZ*:III:308).

1800 *Gesanglehre des Conservatoriums der Musik in Paris* ... (Leipzig). Cf. Cherubini, 1800.

1800 Franz Xaver Glöggl, *Allgemeine Anfangsgründe der Tonkunst* (Linz / Offenbach).

1800 Ferdinand Kauer, *Kurzgefaßte Generalbass-Schule für Anfänger* (Vienna: Artaria). Another edition (Cappi, 1802, pl. no. 904).

1800? L. Kiechle, *Anleitung zum Violinspielen ...* (Augsburg). Eds. through 1883.

c1800 Carl Kreith, *Kurzgefaßte Anweisung die Flöte zu spielen* (Vienna: Cappi / Braunschweig: Spehr). See commentary by Warner, p. 56.

c1800 Carl Kreith, *Schule für die Flöte, jedem Spieler dieses Instruments sehr nützlich, sowohl für Finger, als auch Zunge in 115 Lectionen* (Vienna: Bermann).

1800 [ ] Lefils. *Méthode très-facile pour jouer au violon les sons harmoniques dans tous les tons majeurs et mineurs* (Vienna: Artaria). See Whistling: 166, also Gerber and Lichtenthal. Can this author have anything to do with

Appendix IIA   283

> Joseph-Barnabé Saint-Sévin, an earlier author on violin playing who also was known as L'Abbé le fils?

1800   Anton Reicha, *Études ou théories pour le pianoforte, dirigées d'une manière nouvelle*, op.30.

1800? Johann Friedrich Schubert, *Neue Singe-Schule* ... , in 3 pts. (Leipzig: B&H). 146 pages, to be recommended. Becker gives the date as 1804, but with 252 pages. This must be a second edition.

1800   Johann Georg Tromlitz, *Ueber die Flöten mit mehrern Klappen*. Part II of the *Unterricht,* see 1791 (Leipzig: Adam Friedrich Böhme).

a1800 Luigi Tonelli, *Metodo completo per il violino* (Milan: Ricordi). Includes a section on "basso d'accompagnamento". Another ed. 1823.

1800–02 Justin Heinrich Knecht, *Kleine theoretische Klavierschule* (Munich: Falter). 2nd ed. (Part II?) as *Bewährtes Methodenbuch beim ersten Klavierunterricht* (Freiburg: Herder, 1825).

1800–20 Danzi, F[ranz]: *Singübungen für eine Bass-Stimme*, opp. 24 / 32 / 50 (Leipzig: B&H).

1801   Joseph [or Johann] Alexander, *Anleitung zum Violoncellspiel* (Leipzig: B&H) Also ed. 1854.

1801? Johann Georg Heinrich Backofen (1768–1839), *Anleitung zum Harfenspiel* (B&H), based on a method by Ernst Johann Benedikt Lang (1749–85). Probably distributed by Traeg in Vienna.

1801   Muzio Clementi, *Introduction to the Art of Playing on the Piano Forte* (London). Rev. 1826. Ger. trans. as *Einleitung in die Kunst das Pfte zu spielen ...* (Leipzig: Peters / Hoffmeister & Kühnel. Vienna: Cappi et C. / Mollo. Gera: Menzel, 1810). Fr. trans. as *Introduction à l'art de toucher le Pfte ...* (Paris: Pleyel) (Leipzig: Peters). Cf. Clementi, *Gradus ad Parnassum,* 1817–26. Emil Breslauer cites the date of the original London publication as 1797 (*Der Klavier-Lehrer* IX / VI:105, 1 May 1883). The reader is advised to consult Sandra Rosenblum's listing of all editions in the Da Capo reprint of this work (NY, 1974), as well as Alan Tyson's thematic catalogue of Clementi's works.

1801   Charles Doisy-[L'Intant], *Principes généraux de la guitare* (Paris: Author). 2nd ed. as: *Principes généraux et raisonée de la guitarre, ornés et augmentés d'un supplement* (Paris:Nadermann, 1802). Dedicated to Madame Bonaparte. Ger. trans. as *Allgemeine Grundsätze für die Guitarre, diese leicht und vollkommen spielen zu lernen* (Leipzig: B&H). Also: *Petite Méthode de guitarre extraite des principes généraux, suivie d'airs faciles etc.* (Paris, Nadermann).

1801   Ferdinand Kauer, *Violinschule* (Vienna: Bermann, pl. no. 149). Also: *Neuverfaßte Violinschule nebst Tonstücke zur Übung (*Vienna: Bermann, n.d.) – possibly the same tutor.

1801   Ferdinand Kauer, *Scuola pratica overo 40 Fantasien und 40 Fermaten samt einem Arpeggio* [violin] (Vienna: Bermann, pl.no. 149).

1801/02 Johann Andreas Steiner, *Kurze Bemerkungen über das Spielen, Stimmen und Erhalten der Stein'schen Fortepiano in Wien; nur für deren Besitzer* (Vienna: Steiner). This booklet is also attributed to Johann Andreas

Streicher, Stein's son-in-law, but in this case the title omits the word "Stein'schen:" *Kurze Bermerkungen über das Spielen, Stimmen und Erhalten des Forte-Piano* (Vienna, 1801 or 02)

1802   Louis Adam, *Méthode nouvelle pour le piano* (Paris). 5 eds. 2nd ed. 1805. Sp. trans. as *Metodo de Pf.* (Mainz: Schott). Cf. Adam / Lachnith 1798 and Adam 1802.

1802   Johann Georg Albrechtsberger, *Ausweichungen von C Dur und c moll in die übrigen dur und moll Töne* (Vienna: Traeg, pl.no. 168).

1802   Johann Georg Heinrich Backofen, *Anleitung zum Harfenspiel* (Leipzig). Also ed. 1807.

1802   Frédéric Duvernoy, *Méthode pour le cor* (Paris: Conservatoire de musique). Ed. 1810.

b.1802   G. Gatayes, *Méthode de guitarre* (Paris: Janet). Also: *Nouvelle Méthode de guitarre ou lyre (*Paris: Leduc, 1802). Ger. / Fr. edition (Offenbach: André, n.d.). Also: *Petite Méthode de guitarre* (Paris: Janet).

1802   Ferdinand Kauer, *XXIV piccole Cadenze per il violino* (Vienna: Bermann, pl.no. 213).

1802   Xavier le Fèvre (Lefèvre, Lefebre,1763–1829), *Méthode de clarinette* (Paris: Conservatoire de musique).

1803   Johann Georg Heinrich Backofen, *Anweisung zur Klarinette nebst einer kurzen Abhandlung über das Basset-Horn* (Vienna: Capppi / Leipzig: B&H). Also: *Clarinettschule* (Vienna: Haslinger).

1803   Pierre Marie François de Sales Baillot, ed., *Méthode de violon par Baillot, [Pierre] Rode et [Rudolph] Kreutzer (Paris: Successors to Ozi)* / Paris: Schlesinger / Brussels: Weissenbruch). A German-French edition (Leipzig: Kühnel / Leipzig: Breitkopf & Härtel / Berlin: Lischke / Berlin: Schlesinger / Vienna: Haslinger). It. ed. (Turin: Reycend). This method was adopted by the Paris Conservatory.

1803   Ferdinand Kauer, *Neuverfaßte Klavierschule mit 12 Bruchstücken und 2 Kadenzen samt einer Anweisung, das Pfte. Gut zu stimmen* (Vienna: Bermann, pl.no. 275).

1803   Justin Heinrich Knecht, *Allgemeiner musikalischer Katechismus* (Biberach). Becker lists an "angeführte" musikalischer Katechismus, a new, improved edition, and notes that it appeared in Vienna (Steiner, 1822) as well as in Germany. It was translated in Czech by Norbert Waniek (Prague, 1834).

1803   Alessandro Rolla (1757–1841), *Etude en dix Leçons* (2 violins), op. 4 (Vienna: Traeg, pl.no. 201).

1804   [anon.], *Vollständige Guitarrenschule oder Anleitung zu einem fasslichen Unterricht auf der Guitarre nebst Handstücken* (Vienna: Hofmeister).

Appendix IIA

1804 [Pierre Baillot, Jean Henri Levasseur, Charles-Simon Catel and Charles-Nicolas Baudiot], *Méthode de violoncelle et de basse d'accompagnement, rédigée par Mssrs. Baillot, Levasseur, Catel et Baudiot.* Eng. trans. c1850.

1804 Johann Baptist Cramer, *[42] Studio per il pianoforte.* Another set of 42 in 1810. Kullak says that these studies were known before the end of the 18th century, but no evidence bears him out. Beethoven annotated 21 of these studies for his nephew Karl's use. The annotations are possibly in Schindler's handwriting, but if so they were probably taken either from another copy in Beethoven's possession, or from verbal instructions from Beethoven. The annotations would not have been written before 1816, when Beethoven became Karl's legal guardian, and probably date from a year or two afterwards. Karl would have been 10 in 1816 and possibly not yet proficient enough to have tackled the Cramer études. In a handwritten note on the edition Schindler mentions an article about metronome marks in the *AMZ*:37 (1817). Perhaps, then, 1817 or 1818 might be the most accurate period in which to place these annotations. See *21 Etüden für Klavier: nach dem Handexemplar Beethovens aus dem Besitz Anton Schindlers,* ed. Hans Kann (Vienna: Universal Edition, 1974).

1804 Antoine Hugot et [actually, completed by] Johann Georg Wunderlich, *Méthode de flûte du conservatoire* (Paris: Conservatoire). (Leipzig: Kühnel). Also: *Méthode abrégée de flûte* (Mainz: Schott). In Ger. and Fr. Also a Ger. ed. as: *Kleine Flötenschule* (Berlin: Lischke / Schlesinger) (Hamburg: Böhme / Cranz). Also: (Wunderlich), *Principes élémentaires pour la flûte* ... (Paris: Benoit).

1804 Johann Heinrich Liebeskind, "Über die Doppelzunge [for flute]," in *AmZ*:XII:665.

1804 August Eberhard Müller, *[Grosse] Klavier- und Fortepiano-Schule* (Jena). This is actually the 6th ed. of Löhlein's method, as revised by Müller and again as the 8th ed. by Czerny in 1825. See Löhlein, 1865.

1804 *Vollständige Guitarrenschule oder Anleitung zu einem faßlichen Unterricht auf der Guitarre nebst Handstücken* (Vienna: Hoffmeister).

1804 [Johann Wanhal?], *Flötenschule* (lost). Some sources list a publication of 1813, but it has not been located.

1804 Paul Wranizky' (1756–1808), *Violinfundament, oder Kurzgefaßte Violin-Schule* (Vienna: Cappi), new edition. Wranizky' was a violinist and director of the court theater. Wrote a text to *Oberon*? (see Thayer). *New Grove 2001* mistakenly attributes this work to his brother Anton, who wrote a separate method (see 1828).

b.1805 Joseph Wölfl (Woefl, Wölffl, 1773–1812), *Méthode de piano* ... op. 56 (Offenbach: André). Wölfl was Beethoven's most important keyboard rival in the last few years of the 18th century, and gained his respect as a musician.

1805 Johann Anton André (1775–1842), *Anleitung zum Violinspiel, stufenweise geordnet* ... op. 30 [Vienna: Artaria?]. Republished as late as 1853.

1805 Emanuel Aloys Förster (1748–1823), *Anleitung zum Generalbass* (Leipzig). Enl. ed. 1823. Also: *Praktische Beyspiele ... als Fortsetzung zu seiner Anleitung,* i–iii (1818); *30 Praeludien ... als Fortsetzung der praktischen Beispiele (1830); 4 Fugen ... als Fortsetzung der praktischen Beispiele (1830), 50 Präludien* (Prague).

1805 Alexis de Garaudé, *Méthode de chant*, op. 25. 2nd ed. rev. as *Méthode complète de chant*, op. 40. (Paris: 1809?), rev. 1811 as *Nouvelle Méthode de chant..* 3rd ed. 1854. It. trans. as *Metodo completo di canto* (Milan: Lucca). Also: (Herz?) *Méthode complète de piano* (n.d.) and *Petit Méthode* (n.d.). Also: Alexis Garaudé, L. Jadin, J. Herz et L. Levasseur *Méthode complète de pfte*. op. 100, 2 pts. (Paris: Vaillant, n.d.). Cf. Adolphe Garaudé, n.d. The title of the last work would lead us to ask if these two authors were one person.

1805 Friedrich Guthmann, "Einige Worte über die Applikatur beym Choralspiel auf der Orgel und auf dem Pianoforte," *AMZ*:VIII (24 July 1805): 693–95. Also: *Pianoforteschule, nach einer neuen Methode* ... (Leipzig: Hofmeister, n.d., but clearly after ca. 1830). Contains an appendix with piano works by Czerny, Haslinger, Hummel, Kalkbrenner, Moscheles, Müller, Ries and Winneberger. Also a new edition for Hofmeister.

1805 Pierre François Olivier Aubert (1763–c1830), *Méthode ... pour le violoncelle [Méthode de violoncelle]*, op. 11 (Paris: Janet / Bonn: Simrock).. Also eds. Imbault (n.d.) and ed. 1813. Ger. trans. as *Kurze Anweisung zum Violoncellspiel* (Vienna: Träg, pl. no. 260, repr. Artaria, 1818). Also: *Nouvelle Méthode pour la lyre ou guitarre à cinq et six cordes* ... (Paris: Janet et Cotelle, n.d.).

1805 Daniel Steibelt, *Méthode de pianoforte* (Paris: Janet et. C.). Whistling cites: Fr. and Ger. edition (Offenbach: André); Fr. and Ger. edition (Leipzig: B&H). Sp. trans. as *Metodo para apprender el Pf.* (Mainz: Schott).

1805 Johann Gottlob Werner, *Kurze Anweisung für angehende und ungeübte Orgelspieler Choräle ... zu begleiten* (Penig). Also: *Preludierschule* (Augsburg, n.d.). Also: *Theoretisch-praktische Pianoforteschule nach dem Standpunkte unserer Zeit*, ed. J. Knorr (Leipzig: Hofmeister, n.d.). Went into at least five editions.

1805 Johann Gottlob Werner, *Musikalisches A-B-C oder Leitfaden beim ersten Unterricht im Klavierspielen nebst Anmerkungen für den Lehrer etc.* (Penig: F. Dienemann) (Mainz: Schott). Many reissues. [ ] Werner, *Klavierschule oder Lehrbuch für den ersten Unterricht im Klavierspielen* ... (Leipzig: Hofmeister, 1870) is probably a reissue.

1806 J.T. Lehmann, *Neue Guitarren-Schule* (Dresden: Arnoldische Buchhandlung). Eds. 1809 and 1820 (Leipzig: Hoffmeister). Also: *Kleine Guitarrenschule oder Anweisung die Guitarre in kurzer Zeit spielen zu lernen* (Leipzig: Hoffmeister, n.d.). Also: *Ansicht der Guitarre in natürlicher Grösse, mit richtig bezeichneter Mensur, nebst Darstellung der auf jeder Seite liegenden Töne* (Leipzig: Hoffmeister). Also: *Méthode pour la guitarre, ou règles les plus simples pour apprendre à pincer cet instrument sans maître* (Leipzig: Hoffmeister, n.d.). Could be a translation of one of the German works above.

1806 Pietro Lichtenthal, *Harmonik für Damen* (Vienna). Is this the same as his *Harmonik, oder vom Generalbass* (ms, RC, GMF)?

1806 Simon Molitor (1766–1848), *Preface, Grosse Sonate für die Guitare allein, als Probe einer besseren Behandlung dieses Instruments, mit beigefügten Anmerkungen für den Spielenden. Gesetzt und Herrn Fr. Tandler [Tendler] gewidmet von S. Molitor. Mit einer Vorrede des Verfassers, enthaltend eine historische Darstellung der Hauptperioden der Cyther und ihrer Abstämmlinge von den ältesten bis auf unsere Zeiten, nebst Gedanken über die Guitarre und deren Behandlung,* Op. 7 (Vienna: Artaria, pl. no. 1856). Fétis (VI:162 / 3 citing Schilling IV: 730) appears

Appendix IIA

to confuse him with a Sebastian Molitor (no dates available), ostensibly born in Liége and active in Vienna at the same time as Simon. Fétis then claims that "Simon Molitor" was a pen name used by Raphael Georg Kiesewetter when attacking Fétis! Molitor was the most important representative of the guitar in Vienna before Giuliani (see a1806).

1806   Johann Baptist Wanhal (1739–1813), *36 Cadenzen, oder übungen für die Orgel, oder Forte-Piano wo allmögliche Intervallen vorkommen* (Vienna: Cappi, 1806?). See also Steiner: pl. no. 1528 (1810), *36 Übungen* ...

a1806–b1813   Mauro Giuliani, *Studio, per la Chitarra*, op. 1 (Vienna: Artaria). Italian, French and German. Giuliani was also a virtuoso cellist, and played the lyre-guitar (arpeggione).

1807   Johann Anton André, *Instruktive Variationen über 5 Töne* [for piano], op. 31.

1807   J.H.C. Bornhardt, *Guitarrenschule* (Leipzig: B&H). 5th ed. 1836. Also: *Kurze Anweisung die Gitarre zu spielen, nebst einigen Übungen, leichten Liedern und einer Anweisung die Gitarre bequem zu stimmen:* nd. New ed. (Hamburg: Cranz). Cf. Bornhardt, 1850. Becker gives it as: *Gründliche Anweisung die Guitarre leicht spielen zu lernen, mit 9 leicht arr. Opernarien u.s.w. von A.L. Weiss* (Berlin: Struve). Also: *Ansicht der Guitarre* (Braunschweig: Spehr). At leasts 3 eds.

1807   A. [Heinrich] Domnich, *Méthode de premier et second cors* (Paris: Conservatoire de musique). Subsequent eds.

1807   August Friedrich Christoph Kollmann, *A Second Practical Guide to Thorough-Bass*. Ger. ed. 1808 as *Anleitung zum General-Bass* (Offenbach: André).

1807   [Abbé Georg Joseph Vogler], *Vogler's Anleitung zum [ ] vierstimmig [ ] Saiteninstrument [ ]* (ms, *GMF, RC*).

1807?   Johann Baptist Wanhal, *Anfangsgründe des Generalbasses* (Vienna: Steiner). Also ed. 1817?

1808   Karl Christian Friedrich Krause, *Vollständige Anleitung allen Fingern beider Hände in kurzer Zeit gleiche Stärke u. Gewandtheit zu verschaffen, etc. Ein ergänzender Beitrag zu jeder Klavierschule* (Dresden: Arnold). Also ed. 1820, under a slightly different name in *GMF, RC*, p. 3.

1808   *Über das Violoncell* (Leipzig: AmZ:XI:593).

1808   Johann Wenzel, *Pedal- und Hackenharfen-Schule nach Lang, Krumpholz, Bierfreund und Backoven* (Vienna: Cappi). Wenzel was the son of the Czech pianist Johann Wenzel, who published and also transcribed some of Mozart's works in Prague. The harp tutor is based on the teachings of Wenzel's own instructor, [ ] Bierfreund (no dates available), plus Wenzel Krumpholz's (attr:) *Principes pour la harpe* (Paris, 1800), Johann Georg Heinrich Backoven's *Anleitung zum Harfenspiel* (B&H, 1802), and a method by Ernst Johann Benedikt Lang (1749–85), upon which Backoven is based. Wenzel's tutor is of interest mostly to harpists, but it also contains a clear statement concerning dots, wedges and dots under slurs, an unsolved issue of some importance for this period.

1809 Bonifazio Asioli, *Primi elementi di canto* (Milan).

1809 Bonifazio Asioli, *Transunto dei principi elementari di musica, e breve metodo per flagioletto, pianoforte e fagotto* (Milan: Bertuzzi). Includes exercises and "divertimenti". Also ed. 1811. Trans. Eng. and Fr. Ger. trans. Büttinger as *Lehrbuch der Anfangsgründe der Musik* (Mainz: B. Schott Söhne, 1823).

1809 Xavier Desargus, *Traité général sur l'art de jouer la harpe* (Paris: Nadermann). Also: C*ours complet de harpe, rédigé sur la méthode de pianoforte à l'sage du conservatoire* (Paris: Author). Also: *Traité complet et raisonné composé pour l'enseignement des harpes à simple et à double mouvement* (Paris: A. Petit).

1810 Johann Baptist Cramer, *Instructions for the Pianoforte* (London). Fr. ed. as *Instructions p. le Pfte.* (Paris: Erard / Bonn: Simrock / Mainz: Schott). Ger. ed. as *Anweisung, das Pfte zu spielen* (Mainz: Schott / Bonn: Simrock / Leipzig: Peters, 1812 / 20).

1810 [ ] Maier, *Versuch einer elementarischen Gesanglehre für Volksschulen [& 20 Singstücke zur Rotweilschen Gesanglehre]* (*RC, GMF*, with title as "20 Versuche ...", ms. 1811). Becker lists it as published.

1810? Pleyel, Clementi and Dussek, *Kleine Theoretisch-praktische Pfte-Schule, nebst Anweisung zum Stimmen* (Vienna: Diabelli and Cappi) (Augsburg: 1810). A later edition as *Kleine theoretisch-practische Pianoforte-Schule. Neueste, nach den jetzigen Bedürfnissen ganz umgearbeitete und vermehrte Ausgabe* (Vienna: A.Diabelli & Co.). See *WZ*: 30 November 1841. Also: I.J. Pleyel, *Klavierschule nach Clementi, Cramer etc.* (n.d.). New ed. Drechsler, 2 pts. (Vienna: Artaria). Also: I.J. Pleyel and Wanhal, *Kleine Pfte-Schule* (Hamburg: Cranz). Cf. Pleyel, 1815.

1810–11 Franz Joseph Froehlich [Fröhlich], *Vollständige theoretisch-praktische Musikschule für alle beym Orchester gebräuchlichen wichtigeren Instrumente* ... 4 pts and many individual vols., divided: *General and Singing School / Woodwinds (including serpent) / Brass / Strings*. A *5th pt.* advertised for *Timpani and Piano* (Bonn: Simrock). The first complete set of methods by a single author, and one of the most important sources for this period. Eds. 1813, 1825. Also: *Singschule* (Bonn / Cologne: Simrock, n.d.).

1811 Anton Gräffer (1786–1852, according to unpublished research from St. Michael's Parish records by Michael Lorenz), *Systematische Gitarren-Schule,* 2 pts. (Vienna: Strauß). Eds. 1812 / 22. Gräffer also authored a strange little interdisciplinary volume entitled *Über Tonkunst, Sprache und Schrift* (Vienna, 1830).

1811 Joseph Preindl (1753–1823), *Gesang-Lehre*, op. 33 (Vienna: Steiner). 2nd ed. 1833. Hand lettered. Examples by Salieri, all in operatic, 18th-century manner with figured basses. Also a section on *Choralgesang*. In this tutor we already find trills beginning on main notes. Preindl was Kapellmeister in the Haupt- und Metropolitan- Kirche zu St. Stephan. Becker cites another ed. brought out by Haslinger, n.d.

1812 Joseph von Blumenthal (1782–1850), *Theoretisch-praktische Violinschule* (Vienna: Haslinger). Blumenthal was the choirmaster of the Piaristenkirche in Vienna.

Appendix IIA

1812 Johann Baptist Cramer, *Instructions for the Forte Piano* (London: Chappell). Fr. as *Instructions pour le pianoforte* (Paris: Erard). Ger. as *Anweisung, das Pianoforte zu spielen* (Bonn: Simrock / Mainz:Schott). Another ed. 1820. *AmZ* (1816) reviews a new German edition, saying that the *Instructions* have been known as long as Cramer's *Grand Études*.

1812 Ambrogio Minoja, *Lettera sopra il canto* (Milan: Luigi Mussi). Ger. trans. as *Minoja, über den Gesang, ein Sendschreiben an B. Asioli* (Leipzig: B&H, 1815). "B. Asioli" was Bonifazio Asioli, see 1809 (2 entries) and 1813.

1812 Simon Molitor and R. Klinger, *Versuch einer vollständigen methodischen Anleitung zum Guitare-Spielen nebst einem Anhange, welcher das Nothwendigste von der Harmonielehre nach einem vereinfachten Systeme darstellt.* Book I. (Vienna: Steiner, pl. no. 1880), 2 vols. Fr. trans. as *Nouvelle Methode de Guitarre* (Vienna: Steiner, pl. no. 1881).

1812 Francesco Pollini, *Metodo pel fortepiano* (Milan: Ricordi). 84 pages. Another edition 1834.

1812 Johann Baptist Wanhal, *Cadenzen um von C-Dur in die gewöhnlichsten übrigen Tonarten modulieren zu können* (Vienna: Traeg, pl.no. 551).

1812 Johann Baptist Wanhal, *Skalen sowohl für die rechte als linke Hand nebst Cadenzen durch alle 24 Tonarten* (Vienna: Traeg, pl.no. 552).

1812 Friedrich Wilke, *Leitfaden zum praktischen Gesangsunterricht, besonders auf dem Lande, nebst einer Abbildung des Octochords* (Berlin: Maurer). 68 pages. Also: *Leitfaden zum praktischen Gesangsunterricht.* Excerpted in *AmZ:*XIV:339–345. This must have been a preview, because it would have come out in 1811.

b.1813 Johann Baptist Wanhal, *Kurzgefaßte Anfangsgründe für das Pianoforte* (Vienna: Steiner). Announced but may not have been printed. Wanhal died in 1813.

1813 Bonifazio Asioli, *Trattato d'armonia e d'accompagnamento* (Milan).

1813 J.C. Wöltzel [Wötzel] (?–1836), *Grundriß einer pragmatischen Geschichte der Declamation und Musik, nach Schoeher's Ideen* (Vienna: von Hirschfeld). *RC* p. 5, col. 3 lists the date at 1815.

a1813 [ ] Schacky, *Gründliche, auf praktische Erfahrung sich stützende Anleitung die Guitarre spielen zu lernen, zum Selbstunterricht, nach Giuliani's Methode und Fingersatz* (Munich: Falter). See Giuliani, a1808–b1813.

1814 Bonifazio Asioli, *Corso di modulazioni classificate a4 e più parti* (Milan).

1814 Antonio Peregrino Benelli, *Regole per il canto figurato, o siano precetti ragionati per apprendere i principj di musica, con esercizj, lezioni, ed in fine solfeggi per imparare a cantare,* oder: *Gesanglehre, und gründlicher Unterricht zur Erlernung des Gesanges mit Beispielen, Lectionen und Solfeggien* (Dresden: Arnold). 2nd ed. 1819. Published in Italian and German. Also: *Metodo per il canto, con ritratto* (Milan: Ricordi, n.d.).

1815 Johann Baptist Cramer, *Grosse Praktische Pianoforte Schule,* 5 pts. (London). Also in Lischke, Magazin f. Musik (Berlin). New ed. as *Theoretisch-praktische Pianoforteschule* ... , (Hanover: Nagel / Bonn: Simrock / Braunschweig: Meyer / Leipzig: B&H, Hofmeister, Kistner, and Peters). Fr. ed. as *Méthode de Pf.,* with trans. in Eng. and Ger. (Offenbach: André, n.d.). Many eds., copies, borrowings, etc.

1815   August Eberhard Müller, *Elementarbuch für Flötenspieler* (Leipzig: C.F. Peters). Possibly a further edition of the *Kleine Flötenschule, verbesserte und vermehrte Auflage* (Altona: Kranz, b1800), itself a new edition.

1816   [August Eberhard] Müller, *Instructive Uebungsstücke für Pianoforte, für die ersten Anfänger, [als] erstes (zweytes) Suppl. zum kleinen Elementarbuch* [1807]. See *WZ*: 18 December 1816.

1815   [Johann Michael?] Nicolai, "Das Spiel auf dem Kontrabass" (Leipzig: *AmZ* XVIII: 257).

1815   I.J. Pleyel (1757–1831), *Grosse Klavierschule, nebst 27 Übungstücken* (Vienna: Cappi, 1815?) and *Klavierschule, nebst 30 Übungsstücken...* (Leipzig: Peters, n.d.). Cf: I.J. Pleyel, *Vollständige Klavierschule nebst 24 Übungsstücken* (n.d., but 4th printing 1800?) and I.J. Pleyel / J.L. Dussek, *Méthode pour le piano forte* (Paris: 1797) Ger. trans. as *Vollständige Anweisung das Pfte. zu spielen* (Braunschweig: Spehr) Also: I.J. Pleyel, *Méthode de pfte.* (Paris: Pleyel, n.d.) [Cf. Dussek's own method by the same name (Paris/London1796)]. Also: [anon.],*Klavierschule, kurzgefasste, nach Kirnberger, Pleyel, Clementi u. Dussek* (Mainz: Schott / Vienna: Cappi, n.d.), I.J. Pleyel, *Kleine Klavierschule* (Brauns: Spehr / Vienna: Haslinger, n.d.). Also: *I.J. Pleyel, Klavierschule nach Clementi, Cramer etc.* (n.d., but a.1812, the publication year of Cramer's *Instructions for the Piano Forte [*London: Chappell]), new ed. Drechsler, 2 pts. (Vienna: Artaria), although "nach ... Cramer" could also refer to the latter's *Grosse Praktische Pianoforte-Schule* of 1815. Pleyel's activities as an author and co-author of pedagogical works are sometimes difficult to distinguish from his activities as a publisher.

1815   Friedrich Wilke, *"Ueber das Registrieren der Organisten"* (Leipzig: *AmZ*:XVIII: 801–823).

1816   Bonifazio Asioli, [ ] *I. Scali e salti per il solfeggio. II. Preparazione al canto ed ariette* (Milan).

1816   Ludwig van Beethoven, *Bestimmung des musikalischen Zeitmasses nach Mälzel's Metronom* (First and Second Installments: Vienna: Steiner, 1817).

1816?   Antonio Bartolomeo Bruni, *Méthode pour l'alto-viola contenant les principes de cet instrument suivis de 25 études* (Paris and Milan / Ricordi). Also ed. 1825 (London / Brussels: Schott). German eds through 1890 as *Bratschen-Schule* (Braunschweig: Litolff). Also: *Nouvelle Méthode de violon très-claire et facile, précéde des principes de musique, extrait de l'Alphabet de Mad. Duhan* (Paris: Dufaut).

1816   Joseph Drechsler (1782–1852), *Fortschreitende Generalbassübungen, nebst Anleitung und Beispielen zum Präludiren auf der Orgel* (Wien: Diabelli [et Cappi]). A later ed. as *Generalbass-Übungen mit Zifferbezeichnung, nebst einer Anleitung mit Beispielen zum [richtigen] Präludiren* (Vienna: Lithographisches Institut, 1824). Even later: *Fortschreitende Generalbass-Übungen, nebst einer Anleitung sammt Beispielen zum richtigen präludiren* (Vienna: Diabelli, 1838, see WZ: 17 January 1839). Also: *Praktische Übungen.*(Vienna: André?, n.d.). Drechsler was a professor of harmony at St. Anna and kapellmeister to the court.

Appendix IIA

1816? Joseph Drechsler, *Harmonie- und Generalbasslehre* (Vienna: Steiner). 2nd ed. as *Harmonie- und Generalbasslehre; nebst einem Anhange vom Contrapuncte...* (Vienna: Haslinger, 1828 / ann. *WZ*: 1 December 1827).

1816 Antonio Salieri, *Scuolo di canto, in versi e i versi in musica* (ms, *GMF*). Also: *Libro di partimenti di varia specie per profitto della gioventù tedesca* (lost).

1816 Johann Schenk, *Grundsätze des Generalbasses in Beispielen* (ms, *GMF*).

1816–18 Carl Scholl, see 1823.

1817? [Ludwig van Beethoven], Annotations to J.B. Cramer's *Studio per il pianoforte*. Modern editions available.

1817 Louis Kindscher, *Anleitung zum Selbstunterricht im Klavier- und Orgelspielen etc.* (Leipzig: Hofmeister). Also ed. 1830.

1817–26 Muzio Clementi, *Gradus ad Parnassum, or The Art of Playing on the Piano Forte* (London, Leipzig, and Paris). Fr. as *Méthode de pfte. en 2 parties?* (Paris: Carli). Also: Dual language version in French and German (Offenbach: André).

1818 [J.N.] Breitschädel, *Versuch einer theoretisch-praktischen Klavierschule mit Uebungsstücken zum Selbstunterricht,* 2 pts. (Vienna: Mechetti). 2nd ed. 1826 or 1827.

1818 Ferdinand Kauer, *Neue Clarinettschule* (Vienna: Bermann, pl.no. 409). Implies the existence of a previous clarinet method, n.d.

1818 Franz Schubert, *Sing-Übungen* D619. Probably written for the Countesses Maria and Karoline Esterházy, to be sung with their father, Count Johann Carl Esterházy.

1819 Luigi Marescalchi, *Scale semplici e doppie per forte-piano in tutti i dodici tuoni maggiori e minori secondo il metodo antico ...* (Milan: Ricordi).

1818–21 J.Ch. H. Rinck [Rink], *Praktische Orgelschule,* op. 55, 6 pts. (Bonn: Simrock). Also: *Studium f. angeh. Componisten, Organisten u. Klavierspieler,* op. 99 (Mainz: Schott, n.d.).

1819 Bonifazio Asioli, *L'allievo al clavicembalo* (Milan), 3 pts.

1819 Carl Bärmann, *Über die Natur und Eigenthümlichkeit des Fagotts, über seinen Gebrauch als Solo- und Orchesterinstrument* (Leipzig: *AmZ:*XXII:601). Also: 1864–75, *Vollständige Clarinett-Schule* (Munich) – clearly a much later edition of a clarinet method from around the same time as the bassoon treatise.

1819 [W.A. Mozart, attr.], [*Klavierschule*], ed. A.M.Cramer (Prague: Enders).

1819–21 Friedrich Starke (1774–1835), *Wiener Piano-Forte Schule in III Abtheilungen mit Verbindung einer leichten Anweisung das Pianoforte rein zu stimmen, nebst Modulations-Regeln, und einer kurzen Sing-Methode zum Gebrauch für Lehrer und Lernende mit Benutzung der besten bisher erschienenen Anweisungen systematishe bearbeitet,* op. 108. (Pt. 1, Vienna: Author; Pt. 2, Vienna: D. Sprenger; Pt. 3, Vienna: Author / also J. Bermann, formerly Eder).. See *WZ*: 12 June 1820.

1820? Carl Almenraeder, *Abhandlung über die Verbesserung des Fagotts* (Mainz:). Fr. ed. 1822 / 3 as *Traité sur la perfectionnement du basson avec deux tableaux.* See *Cäcilia*:II:123–140).

1820?   Theobald Boehm, *Griff- und Triller-Tabelle zu den von Grevé ... in München verfertigten Flöten gewöhnlicher Construction* (Munich). Ed. 1871 (Munich). Also: *Die Flöte und das Flötenspiel ...* (Munich). Ed. 1871 ed. Ludwig Boehm (Munich: Aibl), Eng. trans. Dayton Miller Cleveland, 1908.

1820   Wilhelm Klingenbrunner, *Neue theoretische und praktische Csakan-Schule nebst vierzig zweckmässigen Übungsstücken,* op. 40 (Vienna: Chem. Druck. Steiner). 2nd ed. (Vienna: Haslinger). Czakan [Hungarian] = cane-flute. Also: *Neue theoretische und praktische Flöten-Schule* (Vienna: Steiner, n.d.).

1820   August Friedrich Christoph Kollmann, *Bemerkungen über Hrn. J.B. Logiers sogenanntes Neues System des Musikunterrichts, AMZ* xxiii. Eng. trans. as *Remarks on what Mr. Logier calls his "New System of Musical Education"* (London: 1824, and enl. 1824).

1820   Jacques Féréal Mazas, *Méthode de violon, suivie d'un traité des sons harmoniques ... d'après le système de Paganini* (Paris: Frey). Eds. 1830 (Bonn: Simrock), 1861. Eng. trans. W.J. Westbrook (Mainz: Schott, 1885).

1820?   *Natürliche Scala für die Flöte mit einer Klappe* (Munich).

1820?   Jean-Joseph-Benoît Pollet, *Méthode de harpe* (Offenbach: André). In a dual language edition, French and German.

c.1820   Friedrich Starke, *Kurzgefaßte Gesang-Methode* (Vienna: Anton Strauß). This is the *"kurze Sing-Methode"* mentioned in the title of Starke's *Piano-Forte-Schule.* But although today we find it bound together with the latter, it was clearly a separate work and was probably released as such.

1820   Karl August Stieler, *Lärobok i de första grunderna for Musik och Sang ving ungdomens underwisning:* Scolor och Gymnasier, af etc. (Stockholm, also Leipzig: B&H).

1820?   *Tablature de serpent accompagnée des notices ... sur la manière de jouer ...* (Offenbach).

1820   Peter von Winter, *Vollständige Singschule* (Mainz). Eds. 1824 or 25 / 1874.

1821   *Bemerkungen über das Flötenspiel*, in *AmZ*:XXIV:115.

1821   [ ] Mizius, *Praktische Anleitung zum Gesangsunterricht für Schulen*, in 2 vols. (Mainz: Schott).

1822   Benedetto Negri, *Supplemento ai Metodi di pianoforte, composto e dedicato alle sue allieve* (Milan:Ferd. Artaria). 21 pages. A supplement, which implies a previous publication (or, in the case of this title, publications).

b.1822   Anton Teyber (Deiber, Taiber, Tauber, etc. 1756–1822), "Fondamento per l'accompagnamento" (ms: ÖNB). Teyber was a Viennese pianist and cellist who had studied with Padre Martini in Italy; his pupils included the Archbishop Rudolph, who also studied with Beethoven. Teyber was the first Viennese court composer after Mozart.

c.1822   Georg Bayr, *Chromatische Tabelle für den ganzen Umfang der [...] G Flüte* (Vienna: Mollo). RC, GMF, .p. 8, col. 1.

1822   Wilhelm Braun, *Bemerkungen über die richtige Behandlung und Blasart der Oboe (AmZ:*XXV:165ff).

1822   Carl Czerny, *Die Kunst des Fingersatzes ... in einer Sammlung classischer Compositionen* (Vienna: Cappi & Diabelli). See: *WZ*: 9 September

Appendix IIA 293

1822). See continuations: 1827 and 1830. Also: *Praktische Pianoforteschule zu 4 Händen, 4 pts.* (Leipzig: Hofmeister, n.d.).

1822 August Ferdinand Häser, *Versuch einer systematischen Übersicht der Gesanglehre* (Leipzig: B&H). First came out in the *AmZ:* 14/15 (1811/12). Becker gives the date of the book as 1834.

1822 Joseph Hoerger, *Kurze und faßliche Sing-Anleitung* (Augsburg: Boehm).

1822 Ernst Krähmer (1795–1837), *Neueste theoretisch-praktische Czakan-Schule, nebst 30 fortschreitenden Uebungsstücken, und einer Triller-Tabelle für alle Töne, und der des Trillers verwandten Stellen,* op. 1 (Vienna: Cappi & Diabelli). See *WZ:* 14 January 1822. Also see *RC, GMF.* p. 8, col 1. New edition as *Neueste theoretisch-practische Csakan-Schule, nebst 40 fortschreitendnen Uebungsstücken und Tabellen aller ausführbaren Trille auf dem einfachen und complicirten Csakan* (A. Diabelli & Co., 1830, see *WZ:* 28 April 1830). See Krähmer 1833 for Pts. II/III. Also: *Tonleiter für die [Wiener?] u. [ ] [ ] Czakan* (Vienna: Diabelli). *RC,* p. 13, col.1. Possibly published by Cappi & Diabelli, which would place it between 1818–24. Cf. Krähmer, 1833. Cf. Krähmer 1830.

1822 Ernst Krähmer, *Zwölf Veränderungen in fortschreitender Manier zur Uebung der Finger, des Notenlesens und der verschiedenartigsten Eintheilung,* op. 2 (Vienna: Cappi & Diabelli). See *WZ* 14.1.1822.

1822 Adolph Müller, *Das wichstigste über die Einrichtung und Beschaffenheit der Orgel* (Meissen: F.W. Gödsche). 4th ed. 1860. See RC, p. 9, col. 3. 822 Also as: *Die Orgel, ihre Einrichtung und Beshaffenheit sowohl, als das zweckmässige Spiel derselben* (printed by the author). 2nd ed. 1823; 3rd ed: (Meissen: F.W. Gödsche, 1830). Müller was an opera singer, cantor, teacher, kapellmeister and vocal composer who came to Vienna in 1823.

1823 Bonifazio Asioli, *Elementi per il contrabasso, con una nuova maniera di digitare* (Milan: Ricordi).

1823 Franz Bathioli (–1830), *Gemeinnützige Guitarre-Schule, oder: gründlicher und vollständiger Unterricht in die Kunst, die Guitarre auf eine leichte und angenehme Art gut und ganz nach Regeln spielen zu erlernen, nebst einer Kurzen Einleitung im Singen in zwei Lehrcursen, wo von jeder in zwei Theile zerfällt, in den theoretischen und praktischen. Der erste Lehrcurs handelt von dem harmonischen, der zweite von dem melodischen Theile der Guitarre und der Singkunst* (Vienna: Author). Diabelli catalogue (Weinmann) also lists this work, but possibly a later edition. He may have taken it over when Bathioli moved to Vienna in 1825. Also: *Guitarre-Flageolet-Schule mit Bemerkungen über den Guitarrenbau* (Vienna: Diabelli). Also: *Neueste wiener-Guitarrenschule. Deutsch, französisch und Italienisch* (Vienna: Diabelli)

c.1823 Georg Bayr, *Praktische Flötenschule,* Pt. I (Vienna: Mollo). *RC, GMF.*, p. 8, col. 1. Pt. II (Vienna: Mollo, 1831, pl. no. 1987).

1823 Johann Christian Gottlieb Junghanns, *Theoretisch-praktische Pianoforte-Schule* (Vienna: Cappi & Diabelli). See *WZ:* 28 March 1823. Copies are rare, but one can be seen in *SBB.* One of the more important and inclusive piano methods, with examples based on the music of serious masters.

1823 Carl Scholl (1778–?), *Neueste Tabelle für den ganzen Umfang der Flöte mit G Fuß [von der Erfindung des Herrn Stephan Koch]* (Vienna: Diabelli [et Cappi]?). *RC, GMF*, p. 8, col. 1. Cf. Bayr, *Chromatisch Tabelle*, n.d. Also: *Neueste Tabelle für die Flöte nach der neuesten Art, mit G-Fuss und allen Klappen zum Selbstunterricht* (Vienna: Cappi). If the publisher were really "Cappi," the first version of this work must have appeared between 1816–1818.

1824 [Max Joseph Leidesdorf, *Neueste wiener Clavierschule*]. This tutor was announced, but apparently never printed in Vienna. Leidesdorf later worked in Tuscany, and his tutor might have been printed there. Not in *GMF* or *CSF*. May exist only in ms.

1824 Johann Christian Markwort, *Erster Unterricht in der Tonkenntnis. In Musikalischer Hausfreund* III:13–22 (Mainz: Schott). Also: *Elementar-Unterricht für das Pianoforte ...* (Frankfurt:Fischer).

c.1824 Joseph von Blumenthal, *Abhandlung über die Eigenthümlichkeit des Flageolet (sons harmoniques oder sons flûtés) als Einleitung zur praktischen Ausübung desselben auf der Violine,* op. 43 (Vienna: Anton Diabelli).

b.1825 Ambros Rieder (1771–1857), *Anleitung zum Fugiren auf der Orgel* (Vienna: Diabelli et Cappi.). (The firm Cappi & Diabelli was dissolved in 1824 and then became Diabelli & Co. for subsequent publications.) Becker lists the title as "*Anleitung zum Fugieren auf der Orgel oder dem Piano forte*" as Rieder's op. 84 (Diabelli & Co.), but he probably meant the *Anleitung zum Präludieren*, op. 84. *WZ* (14 August 1828) lists an *Anleitung zum Fugieren* as Rieder's op. 95, published by Diabelli & Co.

b.1825 Anton Wranizky´ (1761–1820), *Kurzgefaßte Violin-Schule, worin die ersten Grundsätze dieses Instruments klar und faßlich vorgetragen werden* (Vienna: Cappi & Diabelli). This *Violin-Schule* is listed in some sources as 1828, but not only was the firm Cappi & Diabelli dissolved by then, but the author had died eight years before.

1825 Franz Bathioli, *Gemeinnützige Guitarre-Schule in deutscher, französischer und italienischer Sprache[n], nebst einer kurzen Anleitung in Singen* (Vienna: Diabelli und Comp.). See *WZ* 10 March 1825.

1825 Ferdinando Carulli, *L'harmonie appliquée à la guitare* (Paris). Also: *Méthode complète de guitare ou lyre* (Paris: Carli, n.d.). Ger. trans. as *Vollständige Anweisung um ... die Guitarre spielen zu lernen*, 5th ed. (Leipzig: 1829). Also *Vollständige Guitarrenschule* (Munich: 1830). Appeared in Leipzig, Munich and Bonn with the title: *Vollständige Anweisung, um auf die leichteste und einfachste Weise die Guitarre spielen zu lernen ...*, op. 241 (Leipzig: Kistner). Also: *Tablature de guitarre / Das Griffbrett und die Lagen auf der Guitarre* (Bonn: Simrock). Ital. trans. as *Studio del manico della chitarra* (Milan: Ricordi).

1825 Joseph Czerny (1785–1831), *Der wiener Clavierlehrer, oder theoretisch-practische Anweisung, das Pianoforte nach einer neuen erleichterten*

Methode in kurzer Zeit richtig, gewandt und schön zu lernen, op. 51 (Vienna: Anton Strauß, but Becker cites Haslinger). *RC* (p. 15, col. 1) lists the publication year as 1826. The work is divided into two parts, an instructional section and a collection of exercises and practice pieces. It was published in Italian in 1830 (Becker). For American colleagues, a French edition can be seen in *NL*. From Pt. II Czerny published separately: *48 Passagen-Übungen f.d. Pianoforte mit Bezeichnung des Fingersatzes* (Haslinger, pl. no. 5861); *24 Aufgaben f.d. pianoforte zur Ausbildung im gebundenen und gesangvollen Spiele*, op. 66 (Haslinger, pl. no. 5862); and *12 Studien f.d. Pianoforte zur eigentlichen Vervollkommung schon geübter Spieler* (Haslinger, pl. no. 5863). In addition to his activities as a publisher, Czerny was a respected piano teacher, whose best pupil was Josephine Blahetka (1810 – ?), one of Vienna's most talented young pianists. She participated in the first public concert where Schubert's works were played. Also: Joseph Czerny, *Praktische Lehrgang des Violinspiels* (n.d.)

c.1825 Vincenz Schuster, *Anleitung zur Erlernung des von Georg Staufer neuerfundene Guitarre-Violoncells, mit einer genauen Abbildung dieses Instruments* (Vienna: Diabelli, pl. no. 2052). *RC, GMF*. p. 14, col. 1. This is the tutor for the arpeggione. See *WZ*: 14 September 1825.

1825 Josef Sellner, *Theoretisch-praktische Oboeschule* (Vienna: Sauer & Leidesdorf). Came out in three separate parts: Pts. II / III (Vienna: Leidesdorf) 2nd edition 1837. See review by Ignaz von Seyfried in *Cä 4*, pp. 215–225, and Wilhelm Braun (principal oboist, Berlin and Ludwigslust) in *AMZ* 27, p. 786. Italian trans. 1827. New edition 1901. Also: *Méthode courte et facile pour le hautbois* (Paris: Richault). Sellner was a professor at the Vienna Conservatory. Sellner established the basic form of the modern Viennese-German oboe.

1825–26 Ignaz Moscheles, *24 Studien*, op. 70.

c.1826 Conrad Berg, "Ideen zu einer rationellen Lehrmethode für Musiklehrer überhaupt, mit besonderer Anwendung auf das Klavierspiel," foreword by G. Weber, 4 pts. in *Cäcilia* (Mainz: Schott). Includes a section on tuning. Another ed. 1835.

1826 Carl Czerny, *Neue praktische-methodisch geordnete Clavier-Schule für die Jugend* (Vienna: Haslinger, n.d.). Is this the *Mnemosyne musicale pour la jeunesse, ou choix des Compositions faciles, brillantes et instructives pour le Pianoforte avec et sans accompagnement* (A. Diabelli & Co.)? See: *WZ*: 29 July 1826.

1826 A.B. Fürstenau, *Flöten-Schule*, op. 42 (Leipzig: B&H). Reviewed in *AmZ*:XXX (1827):568.

1826 Johann Christian Markwort, *Umriss einer Gesammt-Tonwissenschaft; wie auch einer sprach- und Tonsatzlehre und einer Gesang- Ton- und Rede-Vortragslehre insbesonders* (Darmstadt: Leske / Mainz: Schotts).

1826 Adolph Bernhard Marx, *Die Kunst des Gesanges* (Berlin: Adolph Martin Schlesinger).

1826 Ambros Rieder, *Kurze Anleitung zum Präludiren auf der Orgel oder dem Pf.*, op. 81 (Vienna: Diabelli). Variant: *Anleitung zum Präludieren auf der Orgel oder dem Pianoforte*, op. 84 (Vienna: Diabelli, pl. no. 2653).

1826 August Swoboda, *Allgemeine Theorie der Tonkunst* (Vienna: Strauß). Also: *Gesanglehre*, n.d. (possibly 1828) and a *Harmonielehre*. See *WZ*: 30 April 1828. Swoboda taught at the Conservatory and St. Anna.

1826–28 Charles-Nicolas Baudiot, *Méthode complète du violoncelle*, op. 25 (Paris: Pleyel). Also: *Méthode de violoncelle* (Berlin). Cf. Méthode, 1804.

c.1826–28 Ambros Rieder, *Der Generalbass in Beispielen zur Selbstübung für angehende Organisten*, op. 106 (Vienna: Diabelli & Comp.). Becker cites it as op. 103. Later ed. 1833.

1827 Franz Bathioli, *Kleine gemeinnützige Guitarre-Schule in deutscher, französischer und italienischer Sprache[n]* (Vienna: Diabelli und Comp.). After Giuliani. See *WZ* 23.February 1827

1827 Carl Czerny, *Fortsetzung des periodischen Werkes: Die Kunst des Fingersatzes*. Book 21:. *Große Triller-Uebung in Form eines brillanten Rondos*. Op. 151. Book 22 : *Große Uebung des vollkommenen und des Septimen-Accords in zerbrochenen Figuren durch alle 24 Tonarten*. Op. 152. (Vienna: A. Diabelli & Co.). See: *WZ* 17.12.1827. Ref: Czerny, 1822.

1827? Louis Drouet (1792–1883), *Méthode pour la flûte* (Paris). Probably the same as: *Méthode pour la flûte, ou traité complet et raissonné pour apprendre à jouer cet instrument* (Antwerp: A. Schott). It. trans. 1828 (Milan / Florence: Ricordi) Also: *Cent études pour la flûte*. This is a large and important volume of studies and other works for the flute.

1827 Andr. Nemetz, *Neueste Posaune-Schule*, op. 16 (Vienna: A. Diabelli & Co.). *WZ*: 24 September 1827. Nemetz was a trombonist at the Kärntnertortheater.

1827 Andr. Nemetz, *Allgemeine Trompeten-Schule*, op. 17 (Vienna: A. Diabelli & Co.). *WZ*: 24 September 1827.

1827 Joseph Preindl, *Wiener-Tonschule, oder Anweisung zum Generalbasse, zur Harmonie, zum Contrapuncte und der Fugen-Lehre* (ed. posthumously, Ignaz Ritter von Seyfried), a book mostly on harmony and composition, but containing some information relating to performance practice. 2nd ed. (Vienna: Haslinger, 1832).

1827 Ambros Rieder, *Anleitung zum Präludieren*, op. 84 (Vienna: A Diabelli & Co.). See *WZ*: 14 July 1827.

1828 Franz Thaddäus Blatt, *Méthode de clarinette,* 3 pts. (Mainz: Schott). Dual language ed. in Fr./ Ger.

1828 Joseph von Blumenthal, *Neueste theoretisch-practische Violinschule. Ein zweckmäßiger Auszug aus der großen Violinschule von Rode, Kreutzer und Baillot, nebst einem Anhange von drey leichten Duetten* (Vienna: A.Diabelli & Co.). See *WZ*: 18 October 1828).

1828 Don Nicolo Eustachio Cataneo, *Grammatica della musica, ossia Elementi teorici di questa*

Appendix IIA 297

bell'arte compilati da ... (Milan: Gerrario). The work is Socratic in form (questions and answers). 2nd ed. 1832 (Milan: Ricordi).

1828 Guido Cimoso, *Principii elementari di musica seguendo il metodo di Bonifazio Asioli* (Vicenza: Picutti). A comprehensive tutor of 212 pages, plus illustrations and tables.

1828 Carl Czerny, *Aneiferung zur musikalischen Bildung der Jugend. ... als unmittelbare Fortsetzung jeder Clavierschule.* Op. 163 (Vienna: A. Diabelli & Co.). See: *WZ* 16 August 1828.

1828 Carl Czerny, *Systematische Anweisung zum Fantasieren auf dem Pianoforte*, op. 200 (Cassel: Loeber / Vienna: Diabelli / London: Boosey / Paris: Schlesinger). See *WZ*: 30 April 1829. Part II as *Die Kunst des Präludirens [auf dem] Pfte.*, op. 300 (Vienna: Diabelli).

c1828 Alexander von Dömény, *Anweisung, das Pianoforte richtig zu spielen ...* (Pesth: Miller). Influenced by Türk (1789) and Berg (1826).

1828 Jacques-François Gallay, *Trente Études pour le cor* (Milan).

1828 Wilhelm Häser, "Andeutungen über Gesang und Gesanglehre," in *Cäcilia* VII–IX. Treats breathing, *portamento*, enunciation, carrying the voice, registers, *messa di voce*, "Glockenton" (*nota sostenuta*), solmisation, "Mutation", recitative, trills; postscript by Gottfried Weber.

1828 Johann Nepomuk Hummel (1778–1837), *Ausführliche theoretisch-praktische Anweisung zum Pianoforte-spiel* (Vienna, Haslinger). It. trans. as *Metodo compiuto teorico-pratico per il pianoforte, dai primi elementi sino al più alto grado di perfezione* (Vienna: Haslinger). Whistling lists: J.N. Hummel, *Anweisung zum Pftespiele vom ersten Unterricht an bis zur vollkommensten Ausbildung,* new ed. (Vienna: Haslinger, n.d.). Hummel's method was actually written several years before 1828, and was held up by the censors for a time.

1828 Joseph Keßler, *Étüden für das Pianoforte* (Vienna). Keßler was a contemporary of Franz Schubert.

1828 Ignaz [von] Mosel, *Abhandlung über die Eigenthümlichkeit des Flageolet (son harmonique ou sons flûtes), als Anleitung zur practischen Ausübung desselben auf der Violine* (Vienna: A. Diabelli & Co.). See *WZ*: 18 October 1828.

1828 Rieder, see b1825.

1828 Johann Baptist Schiedermayer [Schiedermayr], *Theoretisch-praktische Chorallehre zum Gebrauch beim katolischen Kirchenritus* (Linz: Cajetan Haslinger).

1828 Simon Sechter, *Wichtiger Beitrag zur Fingersetzung bei dem Pianofortespiel ...* op. 42 (Vienna: Trentsensky). Also c1828: *Practische Generalbass-Schule in 120 progressiven und mehrfach ausgeführten Übungen im Generalbasse, mit besonderer Rücksicht für jene, welche sich im Orgel-Spiele vervollkommen,* op. 49, Part I (Vienna: Czerny). New ed. 1835. Also: *Unterricht im Clavierspielen,* n.d. (ms, *GMF*).

1828 August Swoboda, *Guitarre-Schule für Damen* (Vienna: Anton von Haykul). 2nd enl. ed. (Vienna, 1836).

1828 Friedrich Dionys Weber, *Allgemeine theoretisch-praktische Vorschule der Musik.*

1828 Anton Wranizky´ (1761–1820), *Kurzgefaßte Violin-Schule, worin die ersten Grundsätze dieses Instruments klar und fasslich vorgetragen werden* (Vienna: Cappi & Diabelli), new edition.

1829 Johann Anton André, *Instruktive Variationen* [for 2 flutes], op. 53.

1829 Franz Thaddäus Blatt, *Kurzgefaßte theoretisch-praktische Gesang-Schule, mit besonderer Rücksicht auf Jene, welche sich diese Kunst zu ihrem Vergnügen auch ohne Meister eigen machen wollen* (Prague: Jos. Rudl). 55 pages.

1829? Carl W.F. Guhr, *Über Paganinis Kunst die Violine zu spielen* (Mainz: B. Schotts Söhne). 69 pages and a portrait of Paganini. It. trans. (Milan: Ricordi, 1834). Guhr was the Director and the Kapellmeister of the Frankfurt Theater.

1829 W. Hause, *Méthode complète de contrebasse, approuvé et adoptée par la direction du Conservatoire de Musique à Prague ...*, in 2 pts. (Mainz / Paris / Antwerp). Also: *Kontrabassschule* (Dresden: Hilscher, n.d.).

1829 Carl Gottlob Horstig, "Die Elemente des Gesanges," in *Cäcilia,* Vol 10:209–224.

1829 Andr. Nemetz, *Horn-Schule für das einfach, Maschin- und Signal-Horn,* op. 18 (Vienna: A. Diabelli & Co.). *WZ*: 1 May 1829.

1829 *Über den musikalischen Vortrag* [Author unsigned] (Pesth). Contains a section on the metronome.

1830 Franz Blatt, *Kurzgefaßte theoretisch-praktische Gesangschule* (Prague).

1830 C. Chaulieu, *L'indispensabile esercizio giornaliero per piano-forte* (Milano: Lucca). Treats chords, scales, octaves, fingering, etc., the metronome, etc. 2nd ed. 1832.

1830? Carl Czerny, *Briefe über den Unterricht auf dem Pianoforte vom Anfange bis zur Ausbildung als Anhang zu jeder Clavierschule* (Vienna: Diabelli). Also ed. 1837–41. Trans. J.A. Hamilton as *Letters to a Young Lady, on the Art of Playing the Pianoforte* (NY: Hewitt & Jacques, 1837–41?). Rus. trans. (St. Petersburg: 1842). At least 2 other Eng. trans., ca 1846. Also: Part II as *Letters on thorough-bass ...* , trans. J.A. Hamilton (London: Cocks, n.d.) and (Vienna: 1840?).

1830 Carl Czerny, *Fortsetzung des periodischen Werkes: Die Kunst des Fingersatzes auf dem Pianoforte, mit Bezeichnung der zweckmäßigsten Applicatur,* 21–24. Heft. (Vienna: A. Diabelli & Co.). See: *WZ* 23.10.1830. Ref: Czerny, 1822.

1830 Joseph Fahrbach, *Theoretisch-practische Flötentriller-Schule,* op.3. (A.Diabelli & Co.). See *WZ*: 28? April 1830. Also: *Grifftabelle für die Flöte bis tief H, sammt Triller-Tabelle* (Vienna: Diabelli, n.d.).

c1830 Gottfried Wilhelm Fink, *"Über das Pianofortespiel"* (Leipzig: *AmZ*:XXXIII:821–824).

1830 Friedrich Wilhelm Michael Kalkbrenner, *Méthode pour apprendre le piano-forte à l'aide du guide-*

Appendix IIA

mains, op. 108 (Paris). 3rd. ed. 1837. Eng. trans. 1866. Ger. ed. as *Anweisung, das Pfte. mit Hülfe des Handleiters spielen zu lernen* (Leipzig: Kistner, 1815 / 32).

1830 Ernst Krähmer, *Tonleiter und Trillertabelle für den einfachen und complicirten Csakan* (Vienna: A. Diabelli & Co.). See *WZ*: 28 April 1830. Cf. *RC* entry, listed under Krähmer, 1822.

1830? Friedrich August Kummer, *Violoncell-Schule für den ersten Unterricht Nebst einhundert und ein zweckmässigen Uebungsstücken mit Bezeichnung des Fingersatzes*, op. 60 (Leipzig: Hoffmeister). Also ed. 1839.

1830 Franz Pfeifer, *Praktische Guitarre-Schule, enhaltend: leichte und fortschreitende Original-Sätze für eine Guitarre* (Vienna: Josef Czerny).

1830 Fernando Sor, *Méthode pour la guitarre ...* (Paris). Ger. trans. as *Guitarrenschule ...* (Bonn: Simrock).

1831 Georg Bayr, *Schule für Doppeltöne auf der Flöte,* Pt. I (Vienna: for author by F.R. Ascher).

1831 Joseph Drechsler (1782–1852), *Kleine Orgelschule zum Gebrauche bei den öffentlichen Vorlesungen bei St. Anna* (Wien: Haslinger / Steiner). See *WZ*: 19 October 1830.

1831 Christian Friedrich Georgi, *Gesangschule zunächst für Militair - und andere Männergesang-Vereine bearbeitet ...* (Leipzig: B&H).

1832 Franz Bathioli, *Guitare-Flageolet-Schule mit Bemerkungen über den Guitarebau* (Vienna: A. Diabelli & Co.). See *WZ* 25 May 1832)

1832 Johann Justus Friedrich Dotzauer, *Violoncell-Flageolett-Schule.*

1832 Johann Justus Friedrich Dotzauer, *Violoncell-Schule* (Mainz: Schott). Another ed. (Vienna: 1836). Also as *Große praktische Violoncellschule*, op. 155 (Leipzig: J. Schubert and Co, n.d.). Lichtenthal lists the first edition as having appeared in 1825.

1832 Joseph Gartner, *Kurze Belehrung über die innere Einrichtung der Orgeln, und die Art, selbe in gutem Zustande zu erhalten, wie auch kleine Ausbesserungen derselben in Ermangelung eines Orgelbauers selbst vorzunehmen. Für angehende Orgelspieler..* (Prague).

1832 Martin Kichler, *Vollständiges theoretisch-practisches Lehrbuch im Pianofortespiele,* op. 42 (Vienna: Haslinger). Fétis lists this as op. 12.

1832 Anton Reicha *Vollständiges Lehrbuch der Harmonielehre* (Vienna: A. Diabelli & Co.). Ann. *WZ* 6.4.1832, with a contents list of Pt. 10. Translated from the French and with commentary by Carl Czerny. It is a three-year course, and appeared originally in 30 books, one after the other. The 10th book came out on 14 January 1833, the 12th on 14 March 1833, the 14th on 14 May, the 17th on 14 August, etc.

1832 Anton Roesner, *Leitfaden einer Gesanglehre für Schüler, nebst zwei praktischen Beilagen* (Vienna: Strauss). Table of Contents and 48 pages. Roesner was a professor of singing at the Vienna Conservatory.

1832 Louis Spohr, *Violinschule mit erläuternden Kupfertafeln* (Vienna: Haslinger). Eng. trans. C. Rudolphus as *Louis Spohr's Grand Violin School* (London:

Wessel & Co., 1843). American ed. trans. U.C. Hill (Boston: 1852). Fr. trans. Heller, as *École ou méthode pour le violon, à l'aide du teneur de violon, traduit de l'allemand par Heller* (Paris: Richault, 1835).

1832 August Swoboda, *Instrumentirungslehre (Partitursetzkunst), nebst Anleitung zum zweckmässigsten und nützlichen Gebrauche aller Instrumente* (Vienna: Author). 30 pages and 5 musical pieces in score.

1832 Nicola Vaccai, *Metodo pratico di canto italiano per camera divisio in 15 lezioni, ossiano solfeggi progressivi elementari spora parole di Metastasio* (Milan: Ricordi) Also London. 2nd ed. 1837. Many editions and reissues, extending far into the 20th century.

1832/33 Georg Kopprasch, *[Sixty etudes for cor alto (premier cor)]*, op. 5 (Leipzig: B&H). Also: *[Sixty etudes for cor basse (second cor)*, op. 6]. Based on the etudes of Domnich (see 1807) and Dauprat (see 1824). Together these books of studies constitute one of the pedagogical foundations of modern horn playing.

1833 Michael Haydn, *Partitur Fundament* (Salzburg: Verlag der Oberersehen lithographischen Anstalt).

1833 Friedrich Hünten, *Méthode pour pfte*, op. 60 (Mainz: Schott). Eng. trans. (Mainz: Schott). Also *Méthode nouvelle pour le piano*.

1833 Ernst Krähmer, *100 Übungsstücke für den Czakan in allen Dur- und Moll-Tonarten, mit deren Scalen, nebst 20 Vorübungen zur leichtern Besiegung der grössten Schwierigkeiten, einer Abhandlung über die Doppelzunge, vielen Beispielen, Anmerkungen und Bezeichnung des Fingersatzes, als zweiter und dritter Theil der Csakan-Schule*, op. 31 (Vienna: Haslinger). See Krähmer, 1822.

1833 Gottfried Rieger, *Theoretisch-praktische Anleitung die Generalbass und Harmonielehre in 6 Monaten gründlich und leicht zu erlernen* (Vienna). Cf. J.G. Rieger, n.d.

1833 Karl Wicek, *Erörterte und erläuterte Geheimnisse der Violin zum Behufe der lernenden als geübteren Violinspieler und Liebhaber dieses Instruments* (Prague: Fürstbischöfl. Buchdruckerei).

1833 Therese Emilie Henriette aus dem Winkel, "Einige Worte über die Harfe mit doppelter Bewegung." in the *AmZ*: XXXVI:65–71.

1833/34 Hans Georg Nägeli, "Gesangbildungswesen in der Schweiz ... " in *AmZ*:36/37, with examples.

1834 Peter Friedrich Julius André, *Anleitung zum Selbstunterricht im Pedalspiel* (Offenbach). See also 1845.

1834 Pierre Baillot, *L'Art du violon: nouvelle méthode* (Paris).

1834 Carl Czerny, *Die Schule des Legato und Staccato,* op. 335. (Vienna: A. Diabelli & Co.). See: *WZ* 4. Juli 1834.

1834 Joseph Drechsler, *Theoretish-praktische Leitfaden, ohne Kenntnis des Contrapunctes phantasiren oder präludiren zu können. Als Anleitung zu den öfftentlichen Vorlesungen in der Harmonienlehre und dem Orgel-*

Appendix IIA

spiele bei St. Anna (Vienna: Tendler). A further edition c.1840?

1834 Joseph Fahrbach, N*eueste Wiener Flötenschule* (Vienna: Diabelli). See: *WZ* 18 July 1835.

1834 Joseph Fischhof, *Anleitung zum Gebrauch des Handleiters, ein nothwendiger Beytrag zu jeder Klavierschule* (mit 130 Beyspielen), op. 35 (Vienna: Haslinger, pl. no. 6552). Fischhof was a professor of piano at the Vienna Conservatory – not the present establishment, but the forerunner of today's Hochschule für Musik. He also published a history of piano-making, *Versuch einer Geschichte des Klavierbaus* (Vienna, 1853).

1834 Julius Knorr, *[Neue] Pianoforteschule ..., oder Materialen für den Unterricht und das Selbststudium* (Leipzig: Friese). Also: *Classische Unterrichtsstücke für Anfänger auf dem Pianoforte* (Leipzig: C.F. Kahnt; Dresden: Hermann Otto, n.d.). Also: *Wegweiser f.d. Klavierschüler im ersten Studium* (Leipzig: B&H, n.d.).

1834 Wilhelm Adolf Müller [Schmid], *Accordion-Schule, oder: vollständige Anleitung, das Accordion in kurzer Zeit richtig spielen zu erlernen ...* (Vienna: Diabelli).

1834 Gustav Nauenburg, Orthoepik. "Ein Beitrag zur Gesanglehre ..." in *Cäcilia,* vol 16:1–16. Also: *Kritische Bemerkungen über Methodik des Gesangunterrichts.* Becker says that this was first published in the *"Leipziger musikalische Zeitung"* XXXI:813–819, 836–839. Probably the *AmZ,* which would have made the year 1828.

1834 Simon Sechter, *Musikalischer Rathgeber,* op. 57 (Vienna). Another ed. 1845? See *WZ*: 6 December 1834.

1835 Julius Knorr, *Ausführliche Klaviermethode*: Part I, Methode. Part II, *Schule der Mechanik*. Also ed. 1859 / 60.

1835? Carl Georg Lickl (1801–1877), *Theoretisch-praktische Anleitung zur Kenntniß und Behandlung der Physharmonika, mit erläuternden Beyspielen ... ,* op. 50 (Vienna: Diabelli). See *WZ*: 13 April 1835.

1835 Anton Reicha, *Vollständiges Lehrbuch der musikalischen Composition* (Vienna; A. Diabelli & Co.). See *WZ*: 18 February 1835. Trans. from the French by Carl Czerny.

1836 Victor Cornette, *[Methode for ophicleide],* and further methods for this instrument in 1854 and 1861. Cornette knew many instruments intimately, but was principally a trombonist. Thus, his most important tutor is probably the *Méthode de trombonne; contenant les principes de cet instrument, des gammes, des exercices, de leçons avec bass ou trombonne,* 4 duos conc. 2 trios et 6 gr. Etudes (Paris: Richault, n.d.). Dual language ed. in Fr. / Ger., Pt. I (Mainz: Schott, n.d.). Also: methods for viola, harp, oboe, trumpet, organ, in addition to the dated methods listed further.

1837 Johann Georg Albrechtsberger, *Sämmtliche Schriften* (Vienna: Haslinger). This little "Gesamtausgabe" encompasses most of the writings above.

1838 M. Carcassi, *Vollständige Guitarreschule in 3 Abtheilungen,* op. 59 (Mainz: Schott). German and French. Pt. 3 contains 50 pieces.

1838 Carl Czerny, *Die Schule der Geläufigkeit,* op. 229. (Vienna: A. Diabelli & Co.). See: *WZ* 17.9.1838.

1838   L. de la Hye, *Méthode théorique et pratique pour l'orgue expressif* ... (Paris: Aulagnier / Leipzig: Hofmeister). De la Hye was a professor of harmony at the Paris Conservatory.

1838   Joseph Drechsler, *Harmonie und Generalbasslehre* (Vienna).

1838   Joseph Fahrbach, *Modulationen, oder: Uebergänge*, op. 11 (Vienna: A. Diabelli & Co.). See *WZ*: 8 August 1838.

1839   Carl Czerny, *Vollständige theoretisch-praktische Pianoforte-Schule von dem ersten Anfange bis zur höchsten Ausbildung fortschreitend, und mit allen nöthigen, zu diesem Zwecke eigends componirten zahlreichen Beispielen, in 3 Theilen,* op. 500 (Wolfenbüttel, Hollesche Buch-Kunst- & Musikalien-Handlung, pl. no. 494). See: *WZ* 23 March 1829. Pt. IV: *Die Kunst des Vortrags der älteren und neueren Klavierkompositionen* (Vienna: Diabelli). English version as *Complete Theoretical and Practical Pianoforte School*, op. 500 (London). The treatise applies to music from the classical era, addressing many issues now in dispute.

1840   Carl Czerny, "Briefe über den Generalbasses", see 1830, Pt. II.

1840   Carl Czerny, *Die Schule des Vortrags und der Verzierungen*, op. 575 (Haslinger: pl. no. 7781).

1840   François Fétis and Ignaz Moscheles, *Méthode des méthodes de piano* (Paris: Schlesinger). Also: Ignaz Moscheles, *Studien für das Pianoforte*, op. 70 (n.d.).

1840?   Francesco Florimo, *Metodo di canto.* 2nd ed. 1841–3. 3rd ed. (Milan: Ricordi, 1861). Also *Breve metodo di canto.*

1840   Manuel Garcia, *Traité complet de l'art du chant,* Part I. 2nd ed. 1847. Part II (Paris: Author). 3rd. ed. 1851. Enl. Eng. trans. R.[A.?] Garcia as *Hints on Singing* by Manuel Garcia (London: Ascherberg, 1894). It. trans. as *Trattato completo dell'arte del scuola di Garcia* (Milan: Ricordi).

1840   Laurenz Weiss, *Gesangschule für das Conservatorium der Musik in Wien,* 2 pts. (Vienna). Also, *Nachtrag zur Wiener Conservatoriums-Gesangschule* (Vienna: Diabelli, n.d.).

1840–50 Louis Lablache, *Méthode complète de chant* ... (Mainz: Schott). It. trans. as *Metodo completo di canto* (Milan: Ricordi).

1841   Johann August Dürnberger, *Elementar-Lehrbuch der Harmonie-und Generalbass-Lehre* (Linz).

1841   Joseph Fahrbach, *Neueste Wiener Clarinetten-Schule*, op. 16 (Vienna: A. Diabelli & Co.). See *WZ*: 15 March 1841.

1842   Carl Czerny, *"Erinnerungen aus meinem Leben" (ms).* Eng. trans. *MQ* XLII (1956):302ff.

1842   Joseph Lanz, *Das System der Musik-Schlüssel* (Vienna: A. Diabelli & Co.). See *WZ*: 12 February 1842.

1842   Ignaz Moscheles, *Tägliche Studien über die harmonisierten Skalen,* op. 107 [4 hands].

1842   Anton Reicha, *Die Kunst der dramatischen Komposition,* in 6 bks. (Vienna: A.Diabelli & Co.). See *WZ*: 25 February 1842.

1844   Wilhelm Adolf Müller, *Grosse Gesangschule in vier Abteilungen*, op. 55 (Haslinger: Vienna, pl. no. 9600). No evidence of voluntary ornamentation. Melodious examples. *Coloratura* table for operatic style, and 203 excellent examples of cadences.

WORKS WITH NO ESTABLISHED PUBLICATION DATES

Bayer, Anton : *Tonleiter für die Flöte* (Prague: Berra). Not to be confused withViennese flutist Georg Bayr . *Beschreibung und Tonleiter der Gottfried Weber'schen Doppelposaune, mit 4 Tabellen* (Mainz: Schott).

Bierfreund, [ ]   :   [*harp method*, see Wenzel, 1808]. Possibly Viennese.

Blüher, C.G.A. : *Kurzer Elementar-Unterricht im Gesange* (Leipzig: B&H).

Blum, Carl : *Neue vollständige Guitarrenschule, nebst Solo- und Gesangstücken ...* (Berlin: Schlesinger). In 2 parts, theoretical and practical.

Bona, P. : *Metodo per il canto / Breve metodo per canto* (Milan: Ricordi).

Bortolazzi, Bartolomeo (1773–1833) : *Neue theoretische und praktische Guitarr[e]-Schule, oder gründlicher und vollständiger Unterricht, die Guitarre auf eine leichte und faßliche Weise gut und richtig spielen zu lernen / Nuova ed esatta scala per la chitarra, ridotta ad un metodo il più semplice, ed il più chiaro* (Vienna: Chem. Druck. Steiner, pl. no. 128, in German and Italian). 8 editions until 1833. Also: *Anweisung die Mandoline von selbst zu erlernen, nebst Übungsstücken* (Leipzig: B&H, n.d.). Fétis lists a Fr. ed. as *Méthode pour apprendre sans maitre à jouer de la mandoline,*giving B&H as the publisher, thus it is not clear if a native French edition existed. Probably distributed by Traeg.

Bucher, [ ] : *Anleitung, den Pianoforte unterricht mit dem Gesang und der Harmonielehre zu verbinden* (Augsburg: Böhme). Early 19th c.

Burgmüller, Johann August Franz : *Praktische Anweisung für die ersten Anfänger im Klavierspiel* (Bonn: Simrock). Early 19th c.

Celli, [ ] : *Neue gründliche theoretisch-praktische Guitarrenschule, nebst allen möglich Cadenzen, Accorden und Arpeggien durch alle Tonarten deutsch und italienisch* (Vienna: Cappi). Also: *Guitarre-Griffbret* (Vienna).

Czakanschule, nebst Tonleiter und Uebungsstücken (Mainz: Schott).

Diabelli, Anton (1781–1858): *Ansicht der Guitarre nach Legnanischer Form, sammt dem Griffbrett derselben im ganzen Umfange, und leichten Cadenzen in den üblichsten Tonarten* (Vienna). This work could have been written anytime after 1819, when Legnani made his first appearance in Vienna, but most likely c1830, when Legnani's guitar designs became widely popular.

Dominik, Franz : *Neue theoretisch-praktische Violinschule* (Augsburg: Böhm). In 2 pts.

Elementi di musica e principj per flauto, con varj exercizj ed alcuni pezzi di progressiva difficultà (Milan: Ricordi).

Ellenrieder, [ ] : *Unterricht für die Bass-, Tenor- und Altposaune nebst Uebungen* (Augsburg: Böhm).

Francia, Ferdinando : *Metodo teorico-pratico ... [per chitarra]* (Milan: Ricordi).

François, [ ] and Allemand, [ ] : *Tablature de serpent* (Offenbach: André).

Frantz, C.W. : *Anweisung zu moduliren, für angehende Organisten u. Dilettanten der Musik in Beispielen dargestellt* (Leipzig: B&H).

Gossec, François Joseph : *Exposition des principes de la musique.* Cf. Agus, 1798 / 9. May be joint authorship. In any case would be written c.1800.

Gründliche Unterricht das Accordion in kurzer Zeit ohne musikalische Vorkenntnisse spielen zu lernen ... (Vienna: Berka).

Hasel, Johann Emerich : *Tabellarische Übersicht des theoretischen Unterrichts im Klavierspielen* (Vienna).

Hermann, Friedrich : *Violin-Schule*, 2 pts. (Leipzig: Peters).

Hermann, [ ] : *Anweisung ... aus Hermann ...* (Leipzig) (*GMF, RC*)

Herz, Henri [Heinrich] : *Praktische Pianoforte-Schule* (Berlin: Schlesinger). At least 5 eds. Cf. Garaudé, 1805, *Méthode complète de piano*.

Kauer, Ferdinand : *Neuverfaßte Violinschule nebst Tonstücke zur Übung* (Vienna: Bermann).

Keinersdorfer, [ ] : *Vorbereitung für Klavierspieler zum Generalbass* (Linz: Haslinger).

Klavierschule, kurzgefaßte, nach Kirnberger, Pleyel, Clementi u. Dussek (Mainz: Schott) (Vienna: Cappi et C.).

Kníze, Frantisek Max. : *Vollständige Guitarrenschule, oder leicht faßlicher Unterricht, dieses Instrument gründlich spielen zu lernen ...* , 2 pts. (Prague: Kronberger & Weber). b1840.

Matiegka, Wenzel Thomas (1773–1830) : *Kurzgefaßte Czakanschule* (Vienna: Cappi). Possibly published in conjunction with Kreith (see 1799 and 1800). *RC*, p. 8, col. 1. In any case before 1824.

Méthode de serpent adopté pour le Conservatoire de Musique (Paris: Ozi / Berlin: Schlesinger).

Mozart, [W.A.] [attr.], [*General-Bass-Schule*] (Vienna: Steiner).

Niemelschek, [ ] : *20 Grundregeln allgemeine mit besondere Hinsicht auf das Clavier* (ms, *GMF, RC*).

Piccolo metodo per piano-forte, ossia Raccolta di pezzi facili estratti dalle opere di simil genere de' migliori compositori, ed ordinati seondo le regole della buona scuola (Milan: Ricordi).

Plachy, Wenzel : *Der praktische Klavierlehrer, oder Anfangsgründe, Tonleitern, Uebungen, Passagen und kleine Handstücke in fortschreitender Ordnung mit Bezeichnung des Fingersatzes, zur Erleichterung des Unterrichts am Pianoforte* (Vienna: Josef Czerny).

Righini, Vincenzo (1756–1812), *Übungen um sich in der Kunst des Gesanges zu vervollkommen,* op. 60? (NG 2001 lists it as op. 10, which probably would date it in the Vienna period 1777–1877). Fr. ed. as *Exercises pour se perfectionner dans l'art du chant* (Paris: n.d.). Righini was head of the Italian opera in Vienna 1780–87 and a popular singing teacher.

Rotondi d'Arailza, [ ] : *Neue grundliche Anweisung zur Erlernung der Guitarre* (Vienna: Bermann).

Savinelli, [ ] : *Avviamento all'arte del canto. Metodo completo,* 3 pts. (Milan / Lucca: Ricordi).

Appendix IIA 305

Schiedermaier [Schiedermayr], Johann Baptist (1779–1840), *Neue theoretisch-praktische Violin-Schule* (Haslinger?). Essentially a remake of Leopold Mozart's *Violinschule*, and includes excerpts from the music of W.A. Mozart.

Schuster, Vincenz, *Anleitung zur Erlernung des von Georg Staufer neuerfundene Guitarre-Violoncells, mit einer genauen Abbildung dieses Instruments* (Vienna: Diabelli, pl. no. 2052). *RC, GMF.* p. 14, col. 1. This is the tutor for the arpeggione. c1825.

Schiedler, J.F. : *Nouvelle Méthode pour apprendre la guitarre ou la lyre* (Bonn / Cologne: Simrock).

Senes, Guiseppe : *Nuovo metodo per chitarra* (Milan: Ricordi).

Spina, A. : *Primi elementi per la chitarra, con testo in italiano e tedesco* (Vienna: Artaria). Dual language publication.

Stählin, J.J. : *Kurzgefaßte Guitarrschule, nebst Uebungsstücken und Gesängen* (Offenbach: André). Also: *Anleitung zum Guitarrenspiel* (Offenbach: André).

Stiastny [Stasny], Johann [Jan Frantísek] : *Méthode de violoncelle* (Paris). Also (Mainz: Schott) in a dual language ed., Fr. / Ger. Early 19th c.

Studio del manico della chitarra (Milan: Ricordi).

Tabulature du serpent accompagnée des notions élémentaires sur la manière de jouer de cet instrument (Offenbach: André). Dual language ed., Fr. / Ger.

Tabulature pour la guitarre (Offenbach: André). In French, German and English.

Tonleiter und Erklärung für die Clarinette nach der neuesten Erfindung mit vermehrten Klappen (Mainz: Schott).

Traeg, Andreas (1748 – ?) : *Guitarre-Schule, nebst Handstücken* (Vienna: Traeg).

Über meine Violine (Vienna: Kurzbeck) *GMF, RC.*

Violinschule des Pariser Conservatoriums (Mainz: Schott).

Wälder, G. : *Neue theoretisch-praktische Orgelschule* ... (Augsburg: Böhm).

Walter, A[nton?] : *Elementarwerk für Pfte-Spieler* ... (Bamberg: Author). Early 19th c. If this is Anton Walter, the pianomaker, then the work is of particular interest.

Zenker, Fr. : *Praktische Anweisung des Fingersatzes bei Abhandlung der Doppelscalen in allen Dur-und Molltonarten* ... (Prague: Berra). Early 19th c.

OTHER HISTORICAL SOURCES MENTIONED IN THIS BOOK

1686   W.M. Mylius (Möller), *Rudimenta musices, das ist: Eine kurtze und gründliche Anweisung zur Singe Kunst* (Gotha).

1752   Johann Joachim Quantz (1697–1773), *Versuch einer Anweisung die Flöte traversiere zu spielen* (Berlin).

1753   C.P.E. Bach (1714–1788), *Versuch über die Wahre Art das Klavier zu spielen* (Pt. I: Berlin. Pt. II, Berlin: 1762)

175-?   Giuseppe Tartini (1692–1770), *Regole per arrivare a saper ben suonar il violino.*

1774 Johann Adam Hiller (1728–1804), *Anweisung zum musikalisch-richtigen Gesange* (Leipzig: Johann Friedrich Junius).

1780 [ ] Abraham, *Méthode du basson* (Paris: Frêre).

1803 Johann Ernst Altenburg (1734–1801), *Anleitung zur heroisch-musikalischen Trompeter-und Paukerkunst* (Halle). It is not known who brought this method out after Altenburg's death.

b.1800 Anna Pellegrini-Celoni, *Grammatica, o siano regole de ben cantare* (Rome)

1840 Manuel Garcia, *Traité complet de l'art du chant*, Pt. I (Paris).

1844 C. G. Nehlich, *Gesang-Schule* (Berlin).

1884 Julius Stockhausen (1826–1906), *Gesangmethode* (Leipzig: Peters).

APPENDIX IIB

Selected Period and Modern Literature
(not including methods and tutors)

Adorno, Theodor. *Einleitung in die Musiksoziologie* (Frankfurt, 1968).

Anon. "Metronome" in *AmZ,* cited in *WamZ* for 1813: 388.

Bachmann, J.H. *Die Schule des Musiknoten-Satzes* (Leipzig, 1865).

Badura-Skoda, Eva and Branscombe, Peter, eds. *Schubert Studies* (Cambridge, 1982).

Badura-Skoda, Paul. "Triolenangleichung bei Schubert – ein noch immer ungelöstes Problem?" in *UeM* 4 (1992).

——. Preface to the *Wiener Urtext* edition of Schubert's Impromptus.

Bauer, W.A. and Deutsch, O.E., eds, *W.A. Mozart: Briefe und Aufzeichnungen* 4 (Kassel / Basel, 1963).

Bayly, Anselm. *The Alliance of Music, Poetry and Oratory (London: printed for Stockdale,* 1788 / reprinted Hildesheim, 1989).

Becker, Carl. *Systematisch-chronologische Darstellung der Musikliteratur von der frühsten bis auf die neueste Zeit* (Leipzig: 1836–39).

Beethoven, Ludwig van. *See* Brandenburg.

Bestimmung des musikalischen Zeitmasses nach Mälzel's Metronom [two installments] (Vienna: Steiner, 1817).

Biba, Otto. *"Franz Schubert und seine Zeit": Ausstellung im Archiv der Gesellschaft der Musikfreunde 1978:* Katalog (Vienna, 1978).

Bilson, Malcolm. See Montgomery, "Triplet Assimilation".

Boime, Albert. *Art in an Age of Bonapartism* 1800-1815 (Chicago, 1990).

Brandenburg, Sieghard, ed. *Ludwig van Beethoven. Briefwechsel Gesamtausgabe* (Munich, 1996).

Branscombe, Peter. See Badura-Skoda, Eva.

Bremer, Friedrich. *Handlexikon der Musik* (1882).

Brown, A. Peter. "Performance Tradition, Steady and Proportional Tempos, and the First Movements of Schubert's Symphonies" in *JMus* 5 (1987): 296–307.

—. "Schubert's Tempo Conventions" in *Schubert Studies,* ed. Brian Newbould (Aldershot, 1998): 1–15.

Brown, Clive. *Classical and Romantic Performing Practice, 1750-1900* (Oxford, 1999).

Brown H.M., and Sadie, S., eds. *Performance Practice: Music after 1600* (New York, 1989).

Brown, Maurice. *Essays on Schubert* (London, 1966).

Bruck, Boris. *Wandlungen des Begriffes Tempo rubato,* Inaugural Dissertation, Friedrich-Alexander Universität Erlangen (Berlin, 1929).

Budde, Elmar. "Bemerkungen zur Problematik praktischer Ausgaben" in *Schubert-Kongress Wien 1978*: Bericht, ed. Otto Brusatti (Graz, 1979).

—. "Akzent, Nachdruck und Sforzato" in *Mu* 34/4 (1980): 366/7.

Budde, Elmar and Fischer-Dieskau, Dietrich. Preface to *Winterreise* (Frankfurt, 1975).

Burney, Charles. *The Present State of Music in Germany* (London, 1775), ed. Percy Scholes as *An Eighteenth-Century Musical Tour* (London, 1959).

Casella, F. *Compendio dell'opera sulle teorie per l'arte del canto* (Rome, 1848).

CCS, see Gibbs.

Chusid, Martin. "Schubert's Overture for String Quintet and Cherubini's Overture to Faniska" in *JAMS* XV (1962):78–84.

—. Foreword to Vol. VI/2 of the *NSA*.

Cone, Edward. *The Composer's Voice* (Berkeley, 1974).

—. *Musical Form and Musical Performance* (New York, 1968).

Czerny, Carl. "Erinnerungen aus meinem Leben" ed. Walter Kolneder in *Collection d'études musicologiques,* vol. 46 (Strasbourg / Baden-Baden, 1968).

—. "Recollections From My Life," trans. Ernest Sanders (*MQ* 42, 1956) from "Erinnerungen aus meinem Leben" (ms, *GMF*).

—. *A Systematic Introduction to Improvisation on the Pianoforte,* trans. Alice Mitchell (New York, 1983) from *Systematische Anleitung zum Fantasieren auf dem Pianoforte,* op. 200 (Kassel, 1828?).

Dale, Kathleen. "Schubert's Indebtedness to Haydn" in *ML* 21 (1940).

Danuser, Hermann, ed. *Musikalische Interpretation* (Wiesbaden, 1992).

Dehn, Siegfried. Review of Karl Adam Bader and Felix Mendelssohn in *BamZ* (5 December 1827). Reprinted in *AmZ* (16 January 1828).

Deutsch, Otto Erich, ed. *Schubert: Die Dokumente seines Lebens* (Kassel, 1964).

—. *Franz Schubert: Thematisches Verzeichnis seiner Werke in chronologischer Folge,* Schubert, Franz. Neue Ausgabe sämtlicher Werke. Series VIII: Supplement, Band IV (Kassel, 1978).

—.*Schubert: Die Erinnerungen seiner Freunde* (Leipzig, 1957)

—.also see Bauer, W.A.

Dolinszky, Miklós. "Die schöne Müllerin – eine authentische Fälschung? Neue Dokumente zur Vorgeschichte der Diabelli-Ausgabe" in *MF* 52/3 (1999).

Donington, Robert. *Baroque Music: Style and Performance* (NY, 1982).

Dressler, Ernst Christoph. *Theaterschule für die Deutschen, den ernsthafte Singe-Schauspiel betreffend* (Hannover / Kassel, 1777).

Dürr, Walther, ed. *Franz Schuberts Werke in Abschriften: Liederalben und Sammlungen, NSA* VIII: 8, Quellen II (Kassel, 1975).

—. Reply to Montgomery in *EM* 26/3 (1998): 534.

Dürr, Walther and Krause, Andreas. *Schubert Handbuch* (Kassel, 1997).

Eibner, Franz. "The Dotted-Quaver-and-Semiquaver Figure with Triplet Accompaniment in the Works of Schubert", trans. Maurice Brown in *MR* 23 (1962)

Erickson, Raymond, ed. *Schubert's Vienna* (New Haven, 1997).

Finck, Henry. *Success in Music and How it is Won* (New York, 1909).

Fink, Christian Gottfried Wilhelm. *Musikalische Dynamik,* cf. Schilling.

Fischer-Dieskau, Dietrich. See Budde.

Fischhof, Joseph. *Versuch einer Geschichte des Klavierbaus* (Vienna, 1853).

Fiske, Roger. Preface to the C-major Symphony D944 (Eulenburg No. 410, print 6742).

Forbes, Elliott, ed. [Alexander Wheelock] *Thayer's Life of Beethoven.* German edition: Deiters, H. / rev. Riemann, H. (Leipzig 1907 / 1917).

Forkel, Johann. *Allgemeine Literatur der Musik* (Leipzig, 1792).

Friedrich, C.D. See Hinz.

Georgiades, Thrasybulos. *Schubert: Musik und Lyrik* (Göttingen, 1967).

Gibbs, Christopher, ed. *The Cambridge Companion to Schubert,* hereafter *CCS* (Cambridge, 1997).

Gibbs, Christopher. " 'Poor Schubert' : Images and legends of the composer" in *CCS:* 36–55.

Godel, Arthur. *Schuberts letzte drei Klaviersonaten* (Baden-Baden, 1985).

Grasberger, Franz. "Schubert und Bruckner" in the report of the *Schubert-Kongress Wien 1978* (Graz, 1979): 215–228.

Griffel, L. Michael. "Schubert's orchestral music: 'strivings after the highest in art' " in *CCS:*193–206.

Grove, George, ed. *Sir George Grove's Dictionary of Music and Musicians* (London, 1878). (cf. Stanley Sadie).

Hanson, Alice. *Musical Life in Biedermeier Vienna* (Cambridge, 1985). A newer version of this book appeared in German as *Die zensurierte Muse: Musikleben im Wiener Biedermeier* (Vienna, 1987).

Hardenberg, Fr. von., see Mähl.

Harding, Rosamond. *The Metronome and its Precursors* (1938, repr. Henley-on-Thames, 1983).

Hauschild, Peter. Preface to the C-major Symphony D944 (Breitkopf, 1998).

Hilmar, Ernst. "Datierungsprobleme im Werk Schuberts" in *Schubert–Kongress Wien 1978:* Bericht, ed. Otto Brusatti (Graz, 1979).

—. *Franz Schubert in His Time,* trans. Reinhard Pauly (Portland, 1985).

—. *Verzeichnis der Schubert-Handschriften in der Musiksammlung der Wiener Stadt- und Landesbibliothek.* Catalogus Musicus VIII (Kassel, 1978).

Hilmar, Ernst and Jestremski, Margret. *Schubert Lexikon* (Graz, 1997).

Hinrichsen, Hans-Joachim. *Sonatenform in der Instrumentalmusik Franz Schuberts* (Tutzing, 1994).

Hinz, Sigrid, ed. *Caspar David Friedrich in Briefen und Bekenntnissen* (Berlin, 1968).

Hoeckner, Berhold. "Schumann and Romantic Distance" in *JAMS* 50/1 (1997).

Hofmeister. See Whistling.

Jestremski, Margret. See Hilmar.

Kagan, Susan. "Schuberts Lieder für das Pianoforte" in *Die Brille:* Mitteilungen 15.

—. "Downes" (Kuriosa) in *Die Brille:* Mitteilungen 27.

Kamienski, Lucian. "Zum 'tempo rubato'" in *AMW* I (1918/19):108–126.

Keller, Hermann. *Phrasierung und Artikulation* (Kassel, 1955).

Kleist, Heinrich von. "Empfindungen vor Friedrichs Seelandschaft", *BA* (October 13, 1810).

Koch, Heinrich Christoph. *Kurzgefasstes Handwörterbuch der Musik* (Leipzig: Johann Friedrich Hartknoch, 1807).

—. *Musikalisches Lexikon, welches die theoretische und praktische Tonkunst, encyclopädisch bearbeitet, alle alten und neuen Kunstwörter erklärt, und die alten und neuen Instrumente beschieben, enthält* (Frankfurt a. M., 1802).

Költsch, Hans. *Franz Schubert in seinen Klaviersonaten* (Leipzig, 1927).

Kolisch, Rudolf. "Tempo and Character in Beethoven's Music" in *MQ* 29 (1943): 165–187 / 291–312.

—. "Zur Theorie der Aufführung", in conversation with Berthold Türcke in *Musik-Konzepte* 29/30, ed. Heinz-Klaus Metzger and Reiner Riehn (Munich, 1983): 21–28.

Komma, Michael. "Franz Schuberts Klaviersonate a-moll op. posth. 64 (D537)" in *ZMT* 3 (1972).

Kravitt, Edward . "The Influence of Theatrical Declamation on Composers of the Late Romantic Lied" in *AM* 34 (1962).

Krause, Andreas. See Dürr.

Kreißle von Hellborn, H. *Franz Schubert* (Vienna: 1865).

Kullak, Adolph. "Kritik und geschichtlicher Überblick der Klavierschulen und Schriften über Klavierspiel" in *Ästhetik des Klavierspiels,* 10th ed., W. Niemann (Leipzig, 1922).

Kullak, Franz. *Beethoven's Piano-Playing,* trans. Th. Baker (New York, 1901).

Kuzniar, Alice. *Delayed Endings : Nonclosure in Novalis and Hölderlin* (Athens, 1987).

Leibowitz, René. "Tempo et caractère dans les symphonies de Schubert" in *Le compositeur et son double. Essais sur l'interprétation musicale* (Paris, 1971).

Lichtenthal, Pietro. *Dizionario e bibliografia della musica* (Milan, 1826).

Liess, Andreas. *Johann Michael Vogl: Hofoperist und Schubertsänger* (Graz / Köln, 1954).

Mähl, Hans-Joachim and Samuel, Richard, eds., *Novalis : Werke, Tagebücher, und Briefe* (Munich, 1978).

Mailer, Franz, ed. *Johann Strauss (Sohn): Leben und Werk in Briefen* (Tutzing, 1998).

McKay, Elizabeth Norman. *Franz Schubert: A Biography* (Oxford, 1996).

Moens-Haenen, Greta. *Das Vibrato in der Musik des Barock* (Graz, 1988).

Montgomery, David. "Exchanging Schubert for Schillings" in *EM* 26/3 (1998): 534.

—. "For Once: Beethoven in the light of Schubert: Realizing the implications of meter and tempo proportions between slow introduction and allegro sections" in *Die Brille* 25 (2000): 75–102.

—. "Franz Schubert's music in performance: a brief history of people, events, and issues" in *CCS:* 270–283.

—. "Franz Schubert's Scores: Meticulous Documents or Informal Springboards for Improvisation?" in *Die Brille* 23: 75–102.

—. "Modern Schubert Interpretation in the light of the pedagogical sources of his day" in *EM* 25/1 (1997):101–118.

—. *Musical Tutors, Methods and Related Sources* (Huntingdon, 1996).

—. "Notation and Performance in Schubert: A Discussion and Review of the Relevant Sections from Clive Brown's Classical and Romantic Performing Practice 1750–1900" in *Die Brille* 27 (2001).

—. "Performance concerns and criteria for Franz Schubert's Symphony in C major D944" in *Die Brille* 24:95–126.

—. "Schubert and *alla breve*" in *Die Brille* 29: 15-28.

—. "The Tenuto 'Hairpin': Evidence for a Third Interpretation in the 'Accent vs Decrescendo' Issue" in *Die Brille* 24:89–94.

—. "Triplet Assimilation in the Music of Schubert: Challenging the Ideal" in *HP* 6/2 (1993) and the ensuing exchange with Malcolm Bilson in *HP* 7/1: 27–31.

Morrow, Mary Sue. *Concert Life in Haydn's Vienna: Aspects of a Developing Musical and Social Institution* (Stuyvesant,NY. 1989).

Mosel, Ignaz von. "Die Tonkunst in Wien während der letzen fünf Decennien" in *WamZ* 3 (1843).

Mozart, W.A. see Bauer.

Nettl, Paul. "Schubert's Czech Predecessors" in *ML* 23 (1942).

Neubacher, Jürgen. "Zur Interpretationsgeschichte der Andante Einleitung aus Schuberts großer C Dur Sinfonie (D944)" in *NZM* 150 (1989).

"Neue Erfindungen: Malzels [sic] Chronometer" in *WamZ* 41 (13 October 1813): 623–631.

Neumann, Frederick. *Essays in Performance Practice* (Ann Arbor, 1982).

Newbould, Brian. *Schubert and the Symphony: A New Perspective.* (London, 1992).

—. *Schubert: The Music and the Man* (Berkeley, 1997).

Newman, William. "Freedom of Tempo in Schubert's Instrumental Music" in *MQ* 61 (1975): 544.

Niecks, Friedrich. *Frédéric Chopin as a Man and Musician,* 2 vols. (London / NY, 1888).

—. "Tempo rubato" in *MMR* XLIII/506 (1913).

Novalis, see Mähl.

Parker, Mary Ann, ed. *Eighteenth-Century Music in Theory and Practice: Essays in Honor of Alfred Mann* (Stuyvesant, NY. 1994).

Partsch, E.W., ed, *Franz Schubert – Der Fortschrittliche?: Analysen – Perspektiven – Fakten* (Gen. ed. Ernst Hilmar, International Franz Schubert Institute series vol. IV).

Paul, Oscar. *Handlexikon der Tonkunst* (1873)

Quantz, Johann Joachim. "Herrn Johann Joachim Quanzens Lebenslauf, von ihm selbst entworfen" in *Kritische Beiträge* I:III:197–250, ed. F.W. Marpurg (Berlin).

Recensionen und Mittheilungen über Theater und Musik, cited in the preface to *Die schöne Müllerin: Reprint der Diabelli-Ausgabe von 1830,* ed. W. Dürr, trans. J. Bradford Robinson (Kassel, 1996).

Reed, John. *Schubert: The Final Years* (London, 1972).

—. *The Schubert Song Companion* (New York, 1985).

Rellstab, J.C.F. *Versuch über die Vereinigung der musikalischen und oratorischen Declamation, hauptsächlich für Musiker und Componisten mit erläuternden Beyspielen* (Berlin, 1786).

Riemann, Hugo. *Musiklexikon* (1882).

—. *System der musikalischen Rhythmik und Metrik* (Leipzig, 1903).

Ries, Ferdinand. See Wegeler, Franz.

Rosen, Charles. "Schubert's inflection of classical forms" in *CCS*: 72–98.

Rosenblum, Sandra. *Performance Practices in Classic Piano Music* (Bloomington, 1988).

—. "The Uses of Rubato in Music, Eighteenth to Twentieth Centuries" in *PPR* 7/ (1994).

Rousseau, JJ. *Dictionnaire de Musique* (1764, pub. 1768).

Salzer, Felix. *Die Sonatenform bei Schubert.* Dissertation, University of Vienna (1926).

Samuel, Richard. See Mähl.

Schiller, Friedrich. "Über naive und sentimentalische Dichtung" (1795).

Schilling, Gustav. *Musikalische Dynamik*. (Stuttgart, 1843)

—. *Universal Lexikon*

Schubert, Franz. See Deutsch.

Schulz-Storck, Ruth. *Tempobezeichnungen in Franz Schuberts Liedern* (Tübingen, 1985).

Schwarmath, Erdmute. *Musikalischer Bau und Sprachvertonung in Schuberts Liedern* (Tutzing, 1969).

Schwarz, Vera, ed. *Zur Aufführungspraxis der Werke Franz Schuberts* (Munich / Salzburg, 1981).

Shawe-Taylor, Desmond. "Schubert as written and as played" in *LST* (30 June 1963) and subsequent forum in *MT* (September 1963).

Sonnleithner, Leopold. "Über den Vortrag des Liedes, mit besonderer Beziehung auf Franz Schubert", in *Bemerkungen zur Gesangskunst* IV (7 November 1860) in *WZK*, "Rezensionen und Mitteilungen über Theater und Musik".

Stowell, Robin. "Leopold Mozart revised: articulation in violin playing during the second half of the eighteenth century" in *Cambridge Studies in Performance Practice* 1, ed. L. Todd / P. Williams (Cambridge, 1991):126–157.

— ed. Performing Beethoven. *Cambridge Studies in Performance Practice* 4 (Cambridge, 1994).

Strauß, Adele, ed. *Johann Strauß schreibt Briefe* (Berlin, 1926).

Strauß, J., see Mailer.

Sulzer, Johann Georg. *Allgemeine Theorie der schönen Kunste* (Leipzig: 1771–74): musical articles by J.A.P. Schulz and J.P. Kirnberger.

Tassel, Eric van " 'Something utterly new': listening to Schubert lieder" in *EM* 25/4 (1997): 707.

Thayer, see. Forbes.

Vaughan, William. *German Romantic Painting* (New Haven, 1980).

Waidelich, Till Gerrit. *Franz Schubert: Alfonso und Estrella: Eine frühe durchkomponierte deutsche Oper* (Tutzing, 1991).

Wagner, Richard. *Gesamte Werke*, vol. 9 (Leipzig, 192?): 290/1.

Walker, Ernest. "The Appoggiatura [in Schubert]" in *ML* 5: 132–144.

Wegeler, Franz and Ries, Ferdinand. *Biographisches Notizen über Ludwig van Beethoven,* (Koblenz, 1838): 106/7.

Weinmann, Alexander. *Beiträge zur Geschichte des Alt-Wiener Musikverlages*. ca. 30 volumes printed by various publishers from 1948ff.

Wiora, Walter. *Das deutsche Lied* (Wolfenbüttel, 1971).

Youens, Susan, ed./ann. *Franz Schubert: Winterreise: The Autograph Score in the Pierpont Morgan Music Manuscript Reprint Series* (New York: Dover, 1989).

Whistling, Carl Friedrich. *Handbuch der musikalischen Literatur* (published anonymously, Leipzig: 1817). From 1819, supplements published by Friedrich Hofmeister.

Warner, Thomas E. *An Annotated Bibliography of Woodwind Instruction Books, 1600–1830* (Detroit: Detroit Studies in Bibliography 11: 1967).

Wöltzel, J.C. *Grundriss einer pragmatischen Geschichte der Declamation und Musik, nach Schoeher's Ideen* (Vienna, 1813).

Wolf, G.F. *Kurzgefaßtes Musikalisches Lexikon* (1806).

Ziffer, Agnes. *Kleinmeister zur Zeit der Wiener Klassik* (Tutzing, 1984).

APPENDIX IIC

Recordings Mentioned in this Book

Ludwig van Beethoven
Instrumental

Symphony No. 6 in F major, Pastorale:
> Hermann Scherchen, cond.; Vienna State Opera Orchestra (MCF / Millenium)
> Hermann Scherchen, cond.; RTSI Orchestra Lugano (LP) ABT ERZ 6001

Carl Loewe
Instrumental

Grand Duo Sonata
> David Montgomery and Camelia Sima, pianists (Klavier KCD 11094).

Lieder

Frauenliebe und Leben / other songs
> Brigitte Fassbaender, mezzo-soprano, and Cord Garben, piano (Deutsche Grammophon 445 575 - 2)

Franz Schubert
Instrumental

Symphony in C major D944:
> Wilhelm Furtwängler, cond. (Berlin Phil): Deutsche Grammophon 447 439 - 2).
> René Leibowitz, cond. (Royal Philharmonic): RCA (GL 32533). Menuet/TIS 0.
> René Leibowitz, cond. (Vienna State Opera Orch.): Whitehall WHS 20031 (Westminster WST 14051)
> Charles Mackerras, cond. (Orch. of the Age of Enlightenment): Virgin (555 561 245 2).
> Roger Norrington, conductor (London Classical Players): EMI (567-749 949-2).

Grand Duo Sonata in C major D812:
> Andreas Groethuysen and Yaara Tal, pianists (Sony Classical CD 68 240)
> David Montgomery and Camelia Sima, pianists (Klavier KCD 11094).

Octet D803:
: Atlantis Ensemble (Virgin Classics 791120-2)

Piano Sonatas in A minor D537 and D major D850:
: Robert Levin, pianist (Vivarte SK 53364)

Piano Trio in B♭ major D898:
: Isaac Stern, Leonard Rose and Eugene Istomin (SM2K 64515 in *A Life in Music*, Box III: Sony SX12K 67195).

Lieder

"Complete" Lieder:
: Dietrich Fischer-Dieskau, baritone (Deutsche Gramophon FOOG 29097/118 in 22 CDs)

Lieder:
: Brigitte Fassbaender, mezzo-soprano, and Cord Garben, piano (Sony SK 53104)

Lieder nach Gedichten von Johann Wolfgang von Goethe:
: Christoph Prégardien, tenor, and Andreas Staier, fortepiano (Deutsche Harmonia Mundi 05472 77342 2)

Lieder nach Gedichten von Friedrich Schiller
: Christoph Prégardien, tenor, and Andreas Staier, fortepiano (Deutsche Harmonia Mundi 05472 77296 2)

Die schöne Müllerin D795
: Lotte Lehmann, soprano, and Paul Ulanowsky, piano (LYS 821 66 07)

Winterreise D911
: Brigitte Fassbaender, mezzo-soprano, and Cord Garben, piano (EMI 574 99 46)
: Lotte Lehmann, soprano, and Paul Ulanowsky, piano (VA 821 12 20)
: Roman Trekel, baritone, and Ulrich Eisenlohr, piano (Naxos 8 554471 in co-production with SFB, Berlin).

Am Meer D957/12:
: Gustav Walter, tenor (G & T 042097, 1904, reissued in EMI's collection, *Schubert Lieder On Record* 1898-1952, RLS 766)

Robert Schumann

Dichterliebe, op. 48
: Lotte Lehmann, soprano, and Bruno Walter, piano (Sony MPK 44840)

Index

Index of Franz Schubert's works mentioned in this text, except those listed in Table VII (beginning on p. 259), where readers will find the song cycles, many of the important single songs, and all of the major instrumental works, in systematic order by tempo.

Deutsch No.	Work	Page
5	*Hagars Klage*	11, 11fn
8	Overture in C minor	11
10	*Der Vatermörder*	217
11	*Der Spiegelritter*:Overture	254
18	String Quartet [g/B♭]	36
46	String Quartet in C major	254
48	Fantasy (duo)	254
50	*Die Schatten*	214
52	*Sehnsucht*	215
74	String Quartet in D major	51, 136
82	Symphony in D major	253-254
87	String Quartet in E♭ major	136
97	*Trost an Elisa*	74–75
100	*Geisternähe*	75–76, 77
103	String Quartet in C minor	254, 255fn
104	*Der Befreier Europas*	217
105	Mass in F minor	17
113	*An Emma*	61, 78–80, 195
118	*Gretchen am Spinnrade*	17, 20, 24, 28, 29fn, 35, 47, 48–50, 220, 245–247, 256
119	*Nachtgesang*	60, 62
120	*Trost in Tränen*	60, 62
121	*Schäfers Klagelied*	220, 256
125	Symphony in B♭ major	254
138	*Rastlose Liebe*	24, 30, 220, 255
142	*Geistes-Gruß*	86
162	*Nähe des Geliebten*	220, 256
167/6	Mass in G	217
171	*Gebet während der Schlacht*	195
173	String Quartet in G minor	258
190	*Der vierjährige Posten*	216
196	*An die Nachtigall*	235fn
197	*An die Apfelbäume*	63fn
200	Symphony in D major	254
216	*Meeres Stille*	221, 229, 257
217	*Kolmas Klage*	63fn
218	*Grablied*	63fn
219	*Das Finden*	63fn
220/3	*Fernando*: Romanza	105–106
224	*Wandrers Nachtlied*	155-156, 221, 257
225	*Der Fischer*	195, 221, 229, 256
226	*Erster Verlust*	221, 256
233	*Geist der Liebe*	25
250	*Das Geheimnis*	33
255	*Der Rattenfänger*	62
257	*Heidenröslein*	30, 221, 256
259	*An den Mond*	60, 62
263	*Cora an die Sonne*	63fn
279	Piano Sonata in C major	144, 152
280	*Das Rosenband*	63fn
286	*Selma und Selmar*	61
290	*Die frühen Gräber*	63fn
310	*Sehnsucht* (1st version)	156
321	*Mignon*	63fn
328	*Erlkönig*	16fn, 17, 20, 21fn, 23, 24, 25, 26, 27–28, 29, 202, 221, 228, 237fn, 248fn, 255
367	*Der König in Thule*	221, 256
368	*Jägers Abendlied* (2nd version)	195, 221, 236, 257
383/1	*Stabat mater*: chorus	217
403/1	*Ins stille Land*	62
417	Symphony in C minor	53–54, 100–101, 137, 185, 240
432	*Der Leidende*	63fn

434	*Erntelied* 63fn	720	*Suleika* 5fn

434 *Erntelied* 63fn
459A/2 *Klavierstück* 80-81
459A/3 *Klavierstück* 92
470 Overture in B♭, major 254
478 *Wer sich der Einsamkeit* 6fn, 195
485 Symphony in B♭ major 141
489 *Der Wanderer* 212, 221, 257
492 *Zum Punsche* 62
504 *Am Grabe Anselmos* 221, 257
508 *Lebenslied* 63fn
514 *Die abgeblühte Linde* 221, 256
515 *Der Flug der Zeit* 221, 255
524 *Der Alpenjäger* 234
528 *La pastorella al prato* 217
530 *An eine Quelle* 62
531 *Der Tod und das Mädchen* 24, 33-34, 180, 211, 221, 256
537 Piano Sonata in A minor 38, 42fn, 43fn, 45–46, 47fn, 101–102, 145, 170, 233, 258
541 *Memnon* 221, 257
542 *Antigone und Oedip* 195, 221, 256
550 *Die Forelle* 61, 109, 212, 234
554 *Ganymed* 16fn
556 Overture in D major 254
557 Piano Sonata [A♭/E♭] 36, 38, 81–82, 254fn
564 *Gretchen im Zwinger* 62
567 Piano Sonata in D♭ major 92
568 Piano Sonata in E♭ major 145–146
574 Sonata in A major (vln/pn) 233
589 Symphony in C major 3fn
590 Italian Overture in D major 3fn
591 Italian Overture in C major 3fn
593 2 Scherzos [B♭, D♭] 38
602 3 *Marches Héroiques* (duo) 203fn
615 symphonic fragments 254
617 Sonata in B♭ major (duo) 203fn
623 *Das Marienbild* 62
624 Variations in E minor (duo) 203fn
626 *Blondel zu Marien* 195
632 *Vom Mitleiden Mariä* 63fn
644 Overture: *Zauberharfe* 101
647/6 *Die Zwillingsbrüder*: aria 216
659–662 *Hymnen an die Nacht* 62–63
659 Hymne I 63
660 Hymne II 63
661 Hymne III 63
662 Hymne IV 63
664 Piano Sonata in A major 38, 231
667 "Trout" Quintet 116fn, 212, 257
672 *Nachtstück* 6–7, 15, 169
685 *Morgenlied* 221, 256
689 *Lazarus* 217
689 *Lazarus*: opening 153–154
706 Psalm 23 17
711 *Lob der Thränen* 177
719 *Geheimnes* 246, 247

720 *Suleika* 5fn
723 *Das Zauberglöckchen* 18fn
729 symphonic sketch in E major 254
732 *Alfonso und Estrella* 198, 211, 211fn, 221–225 (MM markings), 225fn, 226
732 *Alfonso und Estrella*: Overture 107, 149–151, 234, 254
732/1 *Alfonso und Estrella*: chorus 175
732/4 *Alfonso und Estrella*: duet 103-104
732/5 *Alfonso und Estrella*: aria 215
732/6 *Alfonso und Estrella*: duet 235fn
732/21 *Alfonso und Estrella*: aria 215–216
732/25 *Alfonso und Estrella*: duet 183
732/27 *Alfonso und Estrella*: duet 102-103, 183
732/30 *Alfonso und Estrella*: ensemble 103
740 *Frühlingsgesang* 154
741 *Sei mir gegrüßt* 211–212
759 Symphony in B minor *xiii*, 21fn, 41fn, 53, 54-55, 162–163, 165, 208, 233, 240, 248
760 *Wanderer* Fantasy 11, 21fn, 36, 41fn, 45, 46, 77, 82, 140–141, 203fn, 204, 212, 236, 236fn, 257
764 *Der Musensohn* 28fn, 234
770 *Drang in die Ferne* 221, 255
780 *Moments musicaux* 107, 203fn
780/4 *Moments musicaux*/C♯ minor 107–108
780/5 *Moments musicaux*/F minor 107–108
784 Piano Sonata in A minor 12, 121–123, 169, 226–227
795 *Die schöne Müllerin* 16fn, 18, 21fn, 22, 22fn, 23fn, 30, 31, 32, 70, 94, 195, 195fn, 197-198, 200fn, 201, 257
795/3 *Halt!* 30, 176–177
795/4 *Danksagung an den Bach* 30
795/7 *Ungeduld* 20, 30, 94-95, 233
795/8 *Morgengruß* 30
795/9 *Des Müllers Blumen* 30-31
795/11 *Mein!* 198–200
795/16 *Die liebe Farbe* 30-31
795/17 *Die böse Farbe* 30-31
795/18 *Trockne Blumen* 23, 30
796 *Fierabras* 180, 181
797 *Rosamunde* 18fn
797/1 *Rosamunde*: Entre-Acte I 161
797/5 *Rosamunde*: Entre-Acte III 212
800 *Der Einsame* 23, 195
803 Octet 104, 147fn, 205fn
804 String Quartet in A minor 41, 51–52, 140, 165, 166–167, 168, 212, 230
810 String Quartet in D minor *x*, 13, 110–111, 114-116, 163–164, 182, 186, 187, 189, 211, 232
812 "Grand Duo" in C major 39, 39fn, 42, 42fn, 160, 203fn, 230–231, 232, 257
813 Variations in A♭ major (duo) 203fn
818 *Divertisssement à l'hongroise* 230
819 6 Grandes Marches (duo) 203fn

Index

823/1–3 Divertissement (duo) 204
827 *Nacht und Träume* 28
829 *Abschied von der Erde* 24, 26
834 *Im Walde* 196-197
845 Sonata in A minor 40, 143, 203fn, 226-227, 230–231, 244
847 *Trinklied* 62
850 Piano Sonata in D major 42fn, 119–120, 123, 203, 232, 235
872 Deutsche Messe 211, 223, 226, 236, 237, 256, 257
875 *Mondenschein* 62
880 *Im Freien* 15
887 String Quartet in G major 10, 50, 53, 70, 136-137, 145, 165, 240–241
894 Piano Sonata in G major 110, 140, 244
895 *Rondeau brillant* 204
898 Piano Trio in B♭ major 87, 87fn, 147–148, 203fn
899 Impromptus 29, 203fn
899/1 Impromptu in C minor 98–99, 228fn
899/3 Impromptu in G♭ major 86, 228, 228fn, 254
902 *Drei Gesänge* 34
902/1 *L'incanto degli occhi* 34
902/2 *Il traditor deluso* 34
902/3 *Il modo di prender moglie* 34
911 *Winterreise* x, 16fn, 30, 97, 98, 257
911/1 *Gute Nacht* 244-245
911/4 *Erstarrung* 99
911/6 *Wasserfluth* 86fn, 95fn, 97–98, 99
911/24 *Der Leiermann* 24, 34, 48, 51, 109fn
912 *Schlachtlied* 62
932 *Der Kreuzzug* 20
934 Fantasy in C major (vln/pn) 148, 212, 257

929 Piano Trio in E♭ major 145–146, 188, 203fn, 206fn, 206–207, 252–253, 258–259
935 Impromptus 29, 93, 203fn
935/1 Impromptu in F minor 65–73, 82–83, 144, 147
935/3 Impromptu in B♭ major 93–94, 212
935/4 Impromptu in F minor 161-162, 167
940 Fantasy in F minor (duo) 41, 172, 203fn, 217, 257
944 Symphony in C major *xiii*, *xiv*, 14, 40, 41, 41fn, 112–114, 114fn, 141–143, 151, 161, 162, 163fn, 165, 167, 226, 242fn, 242–243, 251, 252, 254, 255, 258–259
946/1 *Klavierstück* (Impromptu) 95–96
946/3 *Klavierstück* (Impromptu) 157–158
947 *Lebensstürme Allegro* (duo) 12–13, 257
951 Rondo in A major (duo) 258
956 String Quintet in C major 3fn, 8, 72, 125, 138, 147, 165, 240–242, 253, 255, 257
957 *Schwanengesang* 30, 257
957/1 *Liebesbotschaft* 50
957/7 *Abschied* 259
957/8 *Der Atlas* 24
957/11 *Die Stadt* 86, 259
957/12 *Am Meer* 28, 52, 135
957/13 *Der Doppelgänger* 51
958 Piano Sonata in C minor 90, 154-155, 232
959 Piano Sonata in A major 9–10, 46, 50, 144, 151, 175, 244
960 Piano Sonata in B♭ major 8, 37, 37fn, 165, 170–171, 235
968B/1 *Marche caractéristique* 139
968B/2 *Marches caractéristiques* 203fn